"Senator Davenport, out there—in the bars and bistros, in the streets of London, Tel Aviv, Capetown, and this country—are superbly trained men and women. Trained for a mission that's been aborted because of their governments' cowardice. They're angry, frustrated, disillusioned, and probably broke. Your countercult force, Mr. Davenport. It's out there."

Courtney Davenport walked over to the head of his Cape buffalo and rubbed the horns. "These . . . these people. Do you know where they are?"

"I anticipated that question when we received your invitation two weeks ago," Portumo answered, shaking a piece of paper. "Here is a list of eighty people I can contact, starting tomorrow. Is it go, Senator, or do we sit on our collective asses and do nothing?"

Courtney Davenport smiled, rubbed his chin, and let out a nervous sigh. "It's go, Nick. Do your thing."

THE
CULT

Look for all these Soldier of Fortune books from Tor

THE CULT CRUSHERS
DOORGUNNER
MISSING BY CHOICE

SOLDIER OF FORTUNE
MAGAZINE PRESENTS:

THE CULT CRUSHERS

CARL H. YAEGER

TOR
A TOM DOHERTY ASSOCIATES BOOK

This is a work of fiction. All the characters and events portrayed in this book are fictional, and any resemblance to real people or incidents is purely coincidental.

THE CULT CRUSHERS

First printing: May 1987

A TOR Book

Published by Tom Doherty Associates, Inc.
49 West 24 Street
New York, N.Y. 10010

ISBN: 0-812-51204-9
CAN. ED.: 0-812-51205-7

Printed in the United States of America

0 9 8 7 6 5 4 3 2 1

Power corrupts men,
and absolute power
corrupts men
absolutely.

THE CULT CRUSHERS

I.

When Courtney Davenport spoke to his God, it was usually in the language of high finance—six figures or more.

Courtney's God was a demanding God—financially demanding. It was rumored that Courtney consecrated half of his profits from the DAVROCK Development Corporation to his various religious enterprises. The Kingdom of God, Courtney Davenport's portion of it at least, was a very tangible kingdom. His stewardship included an extensive hospital and missionary system in West Africa; road-building projects and leper colonies in India; and several converted hospital ships which carried their healing arts to the underdeveloped nations of the world. And then, there was the network of Davenport-Rockland Christian schools, supported and coordinated by Davenport-Rockland University of Tulsa, Oklahoma, whose 250-acre campus was dominated by the 800-foot Tower of Power in the center.

The Tower of Power was the voice of Courtney's God in the year 1989. It was a voice of warning and hope, which was beamed worldwide to a planet that was decaying and crumbling in moral degeneracy; a planet falling prey to the twin evils of communism and the galloping inroads of religious cultism.

The Tower of Power—KDRM: the voice of Davenport-Rockland Ministries; the beacon of hope in the darkness that was 1989; 150,000 clear-channel watts of Christian electronic power which was dedicated to informing an erring world that Courtney Davenport's God was alive and well . . . in Tulsa, Oklahoma.

Courtney stood by his floor-to-ceiling window on the twenty-fifth floor of the Davenport Building, world headquarters for DAVROCK Development. He rubbed the deep cleft in his massive jutting chin. His blue-gray eyes looked out over his beloved Tulsa. Tulsa! How he loved her—oil equipment capital of the world and the last bastion of Christian conservatism in the United States. There were more churches in Tulsa per thousand people than any other place in the country. The last census had proven that. Indeed, Tulsa was becoming a refugee center for those who wanted to live and raise their families in a decent, wholesome environment.

Courtney Davenport had been instrumental in creating that environment and in orchestrating the machinery of government on the local and state levels, and—as Senator Courtney Davenport—even in the Congress of the United States. Some say that he had been the Lord's chosen instrument for cleansing the city of moral lepers, of porno shops, of X- and R-rated movie houses, and of gay bars.

It was rumored that if the laws of the land ran counter to the wishes of Courtney's God, then Courtney Davenport would use more "direct" methods—but only after fasting and prayer. Whenever he circumvented the laws of the land, however wrong they might be, he wanted to be sure the Almighty approved. He always did.

The rash of unexplained fires in the evil places were clearly the work of Courtney's God. The near hit-and-runs, the near-fatal accidents, the constant threats: Those who perpetrated the devil's program in Tulsa quickly got the message.

The local laws, the judges, the juries involved in litigation against the evil ones—all reflected the will of Courtney's God. Yes, Tulsa was being purged and cleansed. The refugees were pouring in and the evil ones were departing. Like Noah's Ark, Tulsa was a righteous vessel adrift in a sea of degeneracy.

• • •

Whenever Gypsy Joe Rockland spoke to his God, it was usually to second a motion initiated by Courtney. The two were inseparable—a business/religious team. With Davenport's business acumen and Gypsy Joe's evangelical skills, they had developed a formidable portion of the kingdom.

Rockland stood fifty feet away from the huge crane that was lifting the final glass panel into place. He took off his hard hat and scratched his head where the vinyl headband had matted down his straight blue-black hair. He adjusted his photo-gray aviator-style sunglasses and squinted at the sunlight reflecting off the twenty thousand tempered glass panels of his creation: the Cathedral of Light. It was a monument to the God who directed the affairs of Davenport-Rockland Ministries and DAVROCK Development. The Cathedral of Light was a fulfillment of a promise that Joe Rockland had made to his God that cold February day near the Chosen Reservoir in Korea in 1951.

It seemed so long ago when Joe Rockland, a twenty-year-old punk kid, lay bleeding from multiple wounds in a snow-covered ditch. He was a young recruit then, barely out of basic training in those early, desperate months of the Korean War. His unit was overwhelmed and decimated by the first of the millions of Chinese soldiers who would soon pour into Korea.

The glass panel hung in midair—suspended—as the crane operator lined it up with the last open square in the glass edifice. It rotated slowly, throwing off shimmers of sunlight. Its near-hypnotic effect triggered off a rush of memories in Gypsy Joe.

It was in a prison camp on the outskirts of Mukden, Manchuria, that Joseph Rockland dedicated his life to his God. While his fellow prisoners made their peace with their communist captors and collaborated in various degrees, he resisted. His decision to resist was inspired by the execution death of a fellow prisoner—a young, blond Mormon boy from Utah, with gentle blue eyes. His crime? He bore his testimony of a living God after a particularly brutal and intense "reeducation" session in the camp compound. The enraged camp commandant forced the young soldier to kneel on the muddy, rock-strewn ground as he shot him in the nape of the neck. The emaciated young soldier shouted "God lives" before the 9mm bullet ended his life.

At the moment, Joe Rockland began to live. The alcoholic, ex-convict son of a Negro father and Cherokee mother—the outcast of both the Cherokee reservation of western Oklahoma and the black ghetto of Oklahoma City—realized that his mission in life was to bring this living God to the people. As he stared numbly at the life's blood of the executed prisoner reddening the Manchurian snow, he felt a warm, almost numbing sense of peace, and thought surely that this young soldier would go to a just reward . . . to his God.

Simultaneously, as he looked at the sneering Korean commandant, who stood over the shattered body of the American—smoking pistol in his hand—he felt no hatred. Instead, he felt a curious kinship. He, too, was a victim of a society which denied him an opportunity to find his God. He was to be pitied, not hated. The commandant, like millions of others behind the Iron Curtain and the developing nations of the world—the new nations of the people of color—had to find the God that that young soldier had found. It was then that young Rockland dedicated his life to helping others find the light that he had found that bleak winter morning in Manchuria.

The workers inside the huge glass and aluminum beam structure pulled the glass panel into place and bolted the frame into position. A cheer went up from the spectators, mostly students from the university, as the project was completed. Joe Rockland's promise to the Almighty was fulfilled. His Cathedral of Light was a huge, 10,000-seat evangelical center on the Davenport-Rockland University campus, where the word of the Lord was to be preached daily. The great experiences of the spirit in the Cathedral were to be shared with the world via the 800-foot Tower of Power nearby.

How far the Lord had taken Gypsy Joe Rockland: from his itinerant preaching in backwater country towns, where he performed healings in his multipatched, old circus tents, to the Cathedral of Light. Surely the Good Lord chooses unique and wonderful instruments to accomplish His purposes. The

Lord's chief instrument in this calling, His most unusual instrument in the life of Joe Rockland, stepped out of his Mercedes-Benz, walked up to the preacher, and stood by his side, staring up at the shimmering angles of glass.

"Joseph, my friend . . . we did it! We finally did it!" exclaimed an enthusiastic Courtney Davenport. "I just wish that Dora and Elsie were here to see it."

The black-haired evangelist continued to stare—almost hypnotized by the reflection of the morning's sun on the many angles which jutted heavenward from the Cathedral. His dark olive skin, stretched tightly over his high, prominent cheekbones and hawklike nose, was slightly flushed with excitement. A lump accompanied by a general ache in his throat formed when he thought of Elsie and Dora—their wives—who were killed in a tragic small-plane crash in 1976, as they were on their way to a revival in Little Rock. Perhaps if their daughters had their mothers, they . . . but that was another story—out of his control. Joe Rockland felt nothing but profound love and respect for Courtney Davenport, the instrument the Lord had sent him to help him fulfill the promises he had made during those bleak days in Korea and Manchuria.

It didn't seem that long ago, but it was—the summer of 1952. A disheveled, defeated, alcoholic Courtney Davenport stumbled into Rockland's little tent during a revival in Shreevesport. He could remember the desperate eyes of that man who had taken a seat in the back row—eyes that pleaded for answers: how to save his failing business, restore his ailing health, salvage his marriage, and regain his self-respect. Their eyes connected, and the Cherokee-black evangelist ignored his prepared sermon and spoke by the spirit, giving Courtney Davenport the answers he so desperately needed. Courtney answered the altar call and stood trembling before the traveling faith healer. As Gypsy Joe Rockland placed his hands on the massive head, he blessed him and pronounced him whole. From that day, Davenport-Rockland Ministries, Inc., was born.

II.

''A submarine service in the Paraguayan Navy? You gotta be kidding!'' exclaimed the young American military adviser incredulously.

''As a matter of fact, I'm not,'' replied a smiling Steve Lancaster, U.S. commercial attaché to the Republic of Paraguay. ''They got three French 'D' class subs, 1968 vintage, moored up at Fuerte Olimpo—upriver about 350 miles north of here. That's as far as the Paraguay River is navigable for shallow-draft vessels . . . and these subs can make it if they sail on the surface.''

The adviser shook his head as he swirled the ice cubes in his rum and coke. ''This country's a joke. They're mad! The annual per capita income is $420 a year, and fifty percent of the national budget goes to national defense.''

''And half of *that* probably goes for uniforms,'' said the BBC correspondent, joining in. ''Look at those chaps walking in.'' He winked, jerking his thumb at three splendidly uniformed officers of the Paraguayan Navy, whose chests were encrusted with ribbons and medals awarded for nonexistent exploits.

The three continued their idle chatter as they looked out the huge curved window of the elaborate Club Circular Militar, the $10-million officers club perched on the bank of the jut of land where the Paraguay and Pilcomayo rivers met.

Below the huge edifice, which was located in the exclusive

Lucpue suburb of Asunción, Paraguay's capital, the sparkling white beach sand—imported by barge from Uruguay's Atlantic coast—sloped to the river where it halted in abrupt contrast to the muddy waters of the Pilcomayo. A hundred feet from shore, three high-speed powerboats of the Paraguayan Navy plowed back and forth. Their sole mission was to create a small artificial surf so the children of the Officers' Corps could ride the swells in their little plastic air mattresses.

"Are they going to use those subs to sweep the river clear of piranhas so they don't nibble the balls off those fat colonels down there?" asked the adviser as he watched a bevy of corpulent field-grade officers frolic with their children in the muddy water.

"That would be a national tragedy, old chap," replied the British correspondent. "There aren't too many balls to go around in this country."

"What do you mean?" asked the adviser.

"Damn, Captain. Didn't State give you an orientation briefing before they sent you here?"

"I was assigned by MAC-P . . ."

"MAC-P?" asked the Briton.

"Military Assistance Command–Paraguay. I'm to act as an adviser to the new Escuela para Comando up at Mariscal Estigarribia in the Chaco."

"Oh, ho . . . you'll love it up there." Lancaster chuckled. "If you did your homework on this crazy little country . . ."

"Hey, wait a minute," interrupted Captain Angel Caro of the U.S. Army Special Forces. "So far this tour has been great. The women, especially, are the most friendly, forward, and best-looking I've seen in Latin America—and they're all over the place."

Lancaster and the Briton smirked at each other slyly, as if sharing a superior secret. Captain Caro leaned back in his chair and squinted at the pair.

"I think . . ." he drawled deliberately in a slight Puerto Rican accent, "I'm beginning to catch on. This country is supposed to be—according to all the reports sent back to Washington—the worst duty in the U.S. Army Latin American Command. And yet, everybody stationed here keeps on extending their tours. You want to keep all this for yourselves . . . don't you?"

"Oh, ho! He's wising up," the Briton said, chuckling.

"Just a little history on this crazy little country, Captain—and don't spread the word, or USALAC is going to get flooded with requests for transfers to MAC-P. Paraguay fought the combined might of Argentina, Brazil, and Uruguay in the 1860s and came close to whipping all three, but was overwhelmed. The male population was reduced to under twelve thousand—*twelve thousand,* Captain," said Lancaster. "Add to that the Chaco War in the 1930s, which was fought over *rumors* of huge oil reserves in the Chaco, which some say is still there—billions of barrels of oil. Standard Oil backed Paraguay and Shell backed Bolivia, and the Third Reich sent military advisers to both sides. Paraguay beat the hell out of Bolivia, but her male population was reduced again. Add to that the exiles from the Febrista party, the soldiers killed in guerrilla skirmishes, and you can see why Paraguay can't afford to lose any more balls. The ratio is seven to one, Caro . . . our favor."

The white Arabian stallion galloped at breakneck speed over the undulating grasslands, broken only by little clumps of quebracho trees. The rider skirted the dense scrub, urged his panting, frothing horse up a small hill, and reined to a slow walk upon reaching the top.

Carlos Von Reinach sat his mount proudly and impressively. His dark, straight brown hair contrasted sharply with his pale, almost electric-blue eyes. His barrel-shaped chest sloped down to a slim waist and muscular thighs—the thighs and legs of a cavalryman, of one who had spent hours in the saddle. He reined to a halt and picked out several burrs from the white stallion's mane as he scanned the low-lying, subtropical plain of Paraguay's Gran Chaco below him.

Carlos Von Reinach, son of Hermann Von Reinach, who was the German military adviser to the Paraguayan Army in 1937, was immensely proud of his heritage. His father, sent by the Third Reich in 1936 to advise the Paraguayan Army during the bloody Chaco war against Bolivia, became the chief strategist of Lieutenant Colonel José Félix Estigarribia, Paraguay's national hero. Under Von Reinach's tutelage, Estigarribia created a war of maneuver. Later historians referred to him as an early Latin American Rommel, as he might have been. Von Reinach had studied tactics under Erwin Rommel at the Potsdam Military Academy.

As a reward for his services, a grateful and victorious Paraguay granted Hermann Von Reinach over 250,000 acres of land in the Gran Chaco—land full of valuable stands of quebracho lumber, with the faint promise of oil—and the hand of María Ynsfran, the beautiful daughter of the Guaraní war hero, Colonel Félix Ynsfràn.

Von Reinach received an additional assignment from Heinrich Himmler, head of the dreaded S.S., to establish himself commercially and politically in Paraguay. In order to create an extension of the Greater Third Reich in Latin America, he was to create a secure base of Germanic interest that would encourage immigration of German colonists to his lands in the Gran Chaco. Another assignment, which was implied but never written, was to create a haven for the men and families of the S.S.—a refuge in the event that the war being planned by the Führer did not succeed.

Carlos Von Reinach heard the clatter of hoofbeats on the old logging road. He spun his Arabian around, then smiled broadly as he recognized the ascetic-looking, ramrod-straight old *patrón* trotting to meet him.

"*Hola,* Uncle Francisco!" shouted Carlos.

The old man reined in his dainty black Paso Fino mare to a halt and shook his nephew's hand. The grip was firm—surprisingly firm for his eighty-three years. His full head of white hair and neatly trimmed beard contrasted sharply with his reddish-brown skin. His ascetic countenance gave him the look of a prophet, which—in a way—Francisco López Estigarribia was to thousands in Paraguay. Carlos Von Reinach's Uncle Francisco was the Hermano Mayor; the Chief of Chiefs; the Great Brother of the Sacred Garduna, the Holy Warriors of Paraguay.

"Good morning, nephew," Francisco smiled. "And how

are things progressing in this corner of the Kingdom of God?''

''Very well, Uncle Francisco. We are expecting a pack train, within the hour, of 180 donkeys loaded with the finest of Santa Cruz raw cocaine for the refinery. It is truly an act of the Almighty that the United Nations has imposed its economic embargo upon us. Since that time the demand has been astronomical.''

They trotted casually down the old quebracho logging road, then urged their horses up a small incline and halted. Below them was a scene incongruent for this part of the world, which was almost a thousand miles from the sea. A submarine—a small French ''D'' class submarine, vintage 1968—was warping its way to the pier of the Parachaco Development Corporation at Fuerte Olimpo.

A Toyota Land Cruiser with four uniformed armed men approached the two horsemen as they sat their mounts, overlooking the scene below. The Land Cruiser lurched to a stop and the front seat passenger stepped down—the Heckler & Koch automatic rifle held at the ready—and walked toward Von Reinach and his uncle. Recognizing them, he slung the weapon over his shoulder and saluted smartly.

''Señor Von Reinach . . . Hermano Mayor! Forgive us for disturbing your peace.''

Francisco smiled a beneficent smile. ''Think nothing of it, my son. It pleases us to see you carrying out your duties with such dispatch.''

Carlos Von Reinach hauled himself gracefully down from his Arabian and walked over to the Land Cruiser. He picked up the microphone of the vehicle's two-way radio. He manipulated the dials until the crackling static was clear and the voice of the submarine commander came in loud and clear.

''Good morning, O Conqueror of the Deep. How was your voyage?''

''Long and boring,'' replied the commander in a thick German accent. ''We had some maintenance problems and had to lay over for repairs at Puerto Concepción in the Dominican Republic, but we reached Parramore Island on time. There was very little shipping in American coastal waters, so we were able to run on the surface most of the way. We can thank OPEC for that."

"But you were able to pick up the shipment?"

"Oh, yes," replied the commander, "and some new meat for your stockyard."

Both Von Reinach and the old man winced at the irreverent reference to the new novitiates for Colonia Gardún, but they had to put up with it. Submarine commanders, along with their crews, were difficult to find outside the major navies of the world.

Carlos hung the mike back on the dashboard and walked over to the bluff overlooking the small river port. He took his Zeiss binoculars out of the cowhide case, adjusted the insta-focus, and observed the activity on the wharf.

The sub was secured and the cargo was being unloaded. The modified cargo hatch on the submarine's forward deck swung open and the portable crane lifted out the precious wooden crates for which Von Reinach waited, and which held the newest, most sensitive geophysical and seismic electronic equipment for oil exploration available in the world. And more important, diamond-tipped drilling bits of unusual durability.

The crates were hurriedly forklifted into the corrugated steel warehouse and stacked carefully onto pallets. A crew of trusted Gardún members painted out the stenciled letters denoting the origin of the equipment: DAVROCK DEVELOPMENT CORP., TULSA, OKLA., USA.

The braying of donkeys could be heard above the rumble of the unloading activities. Burlap bags were unloaded by husky Guaraní Indians and stacked on pallets. The forklifts rumbled down the wharf to the refinery and picked up the 150 bags which were purchased clandestinely by the Parachaco Development Corporation from the cocaine processors at El Roboré in the Santa Cruz department of eastern Bolivia, for a little over $80,000. With a second-stage refining at Fuerte Olimpo, the estimated street value would be over $6 million in the United States.

The other cargo walked off the submarine—their eyes glazed and blinking as they felt the hot, early-morning January sun.

These were the *chivatos*—"little goats"—the new recruits for the Holy Order. They would soon be leaving for the new Gardunian commune at Colonia Gardún.

Von Reinach focused the binoculars again, this time on the seventeen young women and five young men walking with halting steps down the gangplank. He smiled in anticipation as he noticed the blond, blue-eyed Caucasoid features of the female *chivatos*. Suddenly he frowned as his binoculars locked into focus upon a young woman—not more than eighteen—with long blue-black hair, brown eyes, and full, sensual lips. He walked briskly to the Land Cruiser and picked up the microphone. He spoke sharply, demanding to speak to the head of the *guapos,* who were the overseers for this particular voyage.

"José! . . . the girl . . . the dark one. Why is she here? How does she fit into our plans? You know the requirements!"

The radio crackled in reply. "Señor Von Reinach, the girl was inseparable from her companion. One would not come without the other, and her friend meets all of the requirements for . . . the project."

"That is unfortunate," sighed Von Reinach. "We will have to dispose of the dark one, and that will create problems at the colony."

"Perhaps you might reconsider, *patrón*. The girl is—or claims to be—a full-blooded Cherokee Indian from the American state of Oklahoma. They are, perhaps, the most advanced and civilized of the North American aboriginal people. They have become immensely wealthy because of their participation in the American petroleum industry."

"Petroleum . . . Oklahoma?" Carlos' eyes lit up.

"Yes, I believe that this little female *chivato* will meet the requirements of the Order, *patrón*."

Von Reinach agreed, hung up the microphone, and rejoined his uncle on the bank overlooking the port.

Below on the pier perched over the muddy, piranha-infested waters of the upper Paraguay River, the new *chivatos* were motioned by the *guapo* mayor to board the Mercedes minibus.

After storing their baggage, Olivia Davenport and Susan Rockland boarded the Mercedes for the trip to Colonia Gardún in the Gran Chaco.

III.

The wide-bodied DC-10 taxied with a high whine of its jet engines to the United Airlines terminal of Washington's National Airport. Courtney Davenport, Oklahoma's junior senator, pawed the floor with the heel of his boot as he waited for the aircraft to maneuver to the passenger off-ramp, which was now telescoping outward to meet the plane.

How he hated airports! Especially Washington National! Here is where they all congregated—like filthy beggars in the teeming train stations of Oriental cities. Cultists! Dozens of them. Since he had parked his car and walked to the terminal lobby he had been accosted by—or propositioned by—at least ten of them: shaven-headed Hare Krishnas in their saffron robes selling holy books and flowers; Moonies collecting money for a "peace commune" on the West Coast. He had passed a booth where Scientologists were hawking electronic gadgets to stimulate one's magnetic flow or chart their Emmgrams. And then there were the lesser-known cults—the ones who used their young female members to hustle their bodies in order to finance their gurus. Their bodies were all that they had left—their minds were gone. In most cases, scrambled by the ever-accessible supplies of cocaine—the main drug of choice among cultists.

The passengers started to trickle into the lobby, and the trickle became a flood. The senator scrutinized each passenger as he or she entered the lobby. His steel-gray eyes locked upon a young couple as they sauntered off the loading ramp. He walked over to meet them.

"Mr. Portumo? Miss Macranskia?"

They nodded.

"I'm Senator Davenport. I'm so happy to meet you. Welcome to Washington . . . cult capital of the world."

He sized up Nicholas Portumo and liked what he saw—a muscular young man with the lithe body of a natural athlete. His medium brown hair, sharp green-gray eyes, and slightly olive complexion gave him the look of anything but a candidate for a Ph.D. in clinical psychology at the University of British Columbia.

He shook the hand of Andrea Macranskia and was, quite frankly, overwhelmed. Her honey-blond hair, wide and deep green eyes, and shapely athletic body seemed to complement her articulate English, which she spoke with a pronounced Hungarian accent. Courtney figured that both were in their late twenties.

"Mr. Davenport," the Hungarian woman spoke softly. "I am so glad I could make it and even happier that your Senate subcommittee has seen fit to have us present our data. It seems like it has taken your government so long to move in this critical area."

"This is just a pinprick Miss Mack-ran-ka—how do you say it?"

She laughed a low, throaty laugh and grabbed the senator's elbow.

"Please, Senator, call me Andrea. I'm afraid that Hungarian surnames are a little beyond the English tongue."

The young man with a face full of acute acne watched the two leave the United lobby and walk casually to the baggage terminal. He took out two small white capsules and pitter-pattered to a drinking fountain, his orange saffron robe making a swishing sound as he walked.

He downed the pills, and within seconds felt the euphoric rush as the Bolivian cocaine entered his bloodstream. He walked more rapidly, palms sweating, beads of water forming on his shaven head. His sandals flipped in a clip-clop on the carpeted floor of the ramp. His slightly glazed eyes focused with difficulty on his target—the blond Hungarian woman between the older and the younger man. He moved faster as he closed the gap between himself and the target. His hand reached inside his orange robe and clutched the carved handle of the razor-sharp Oriental ceremonial hatchet.

Nick Portumo tensed slightly as he heard the slip-slap of the sandled feet get closer. His years of training as a commando in Britain's elite Special Air Service had attuned his senses to potential threats. Even though the accelerated steps behind him might reveal a hurrying passenger trying to catch a plane, he somehow felt they signaled danger.

The acne-faced young cultist yanked out the hatchet and closed the few remaining yards to Andrea with a run. He raised his weapon, focusing on the full head of honey-blond hair, and with a scream, in some Asian tongue, started to swing downward.

Nick Portumo uncoiled like a cobra, spinning around and pushing Andrea to the floor. She dropped automatically when she felt Nick's push. The senator watched shocked and speechless at the lightning-quick moves of the SAS man as he disabled the shaven-headed would-be assassin. The weapon dropped to the carpeted floor with a thud, and the orange-robed cultist crumpled unconsciously beside it.

"Good Lord!" bellowed Davenport. "That fellow meant to *kill* you, Andrea!"

She nodded her head slowly. Portumo ordered an airport security officer to find a policeman. Within minutes, two District officers were on the scene, interviewing the principals and the witnesses.

The cultist began to stir. Nick knelt down, yanked him into a sitting position, and said softly, "All right, my bald-headed friend, who put you up to this?"

The cultist stared at him uncomprehendingly.

Portumo shook him. "Who put you up to this?" he demanded.

"Just a minute, fella. He doesn't have to say anything unless he has legal counsel," piped a high-pitched voice from the crowd.

The three looked up to see an effeminate-looking young

man with long dirty-blond hair elbow his way through the circle of spectators to the saffron-robed young man.

"He doesn't have to say anything unless he has legal representation—in other words, a lawyer," the long-haired young man sneered.

"And that's you?" asked Portumo.

"That's right." He yanked out several business cards and passed them around. They read: "Rodney Crampton, Attorney-at-Law, American Civil Rights Association."

Senator Davenport read his card and felt the anger, which rose from the nape of his neck, make the back of his scalp tingle.

"The ACRA . . . friend of cults and cultists. You creeps must hang around airports just waiting for an incident, so you can protect these people."

"That's right," the young lawyer smiled slyly. "We believe that the First Amendment of the Constitution applies to everybody."

"Miss Macranskia, give me an address where you can be reached. I suppose you'll want to prefer charges," said the officer.

"You have the right to remain silent. Have they read you your rights?" whined the ACRA attorney.

Portumo tensed and untensed his muscles as he stifled the urge to throttle the ACRA representative.

"Yes . . . to be sure," replied the Hungarian. "Will he be interrogated?"

"Yes," replied the officer.

"Good. I want to find out if the attempt to kill me was just a drug-crazed urge or if somebody else programmed him to kill me."

"Do you suspect that somebody is behind this, Andrea?" asked the senator.

Andrea nodded as she and Nicholas exchanged a knowing glance.

Dr. Martin Weishaupt kept out of sight behind the Avis car rental booth as he watched the police lead the cultist away. He silently cursed the muscular young man who had foiled the attempt. He breathed deeply with relief, however, as he remembered that he did not inform his superiors of this attempt. After all, KGB Central doesn't have to know everything. But Andrea Macranskia must die . . . and soon. This former intern psychologist of the Sverdlosk Institute must be made an example of to others who would defect to the West.

Martin Weishaupt watched through narrowed eyes, which were magnified by the thick horn-rimmed glasses that seemed too big for his head. His brow was wreathed in a wrinkled frown that seemed to extend to the crown of his bald head. He watched his elusive target walk to the glass exit doors to the parking lot . . . to her rendezvous with the Senate Subcommittee on Cults and Alternative Societies of which Senator Courtney Davenport was the chairman.

The high-ceilinged, richly wood-paneled committee room of the Senate Office Building was almost filled to capacity when the doors were closed. Nick Portumo felt a twinge of anxiety as he took his seat on the raised platform in front of the crowd of about 250. Other members of the Senate Subcommittee on Cults and Alternative Societies took their places at the long, polished walnut table facing the audience. Senator Davenport raised his hand for quiet and began.

"Ladies and gentlemen . . . respected members of the press. Let's begin. Smoke if you wish. Loosen your ties, your shoelaces, and relax. We may be here in session for some time. I would appreciate it if you didn't leave until each speaker has completed his presentation.

"Our first speaker," the senator continued, "is a remarkable young woman, Dr. Andrea Macranskia, currently a research fellow at the University of British Columbia." The honey-blond Hungarian psychologist smiled slightly and nodded.

"Just a little background on Andrea," Courtney Davenport drawled. "She is a native of Hungary . . . a pampered product of the communist society in that country. She was born in Budapest just a year after the first anticommunist uprising in 1956. She went through the Hungarian public school system and participated in all of the Communist party youth organizations, even holding national office in some. Her trusted credentials enabled her to receive a full scholarship to the University of Budapest, from her freshman year to the completion of her Ph.D., where she majored in clinical psychology, specializing in behavior modification."

A slight murmur of excitement and anticipation rippled through the audience.

"Dr. Macranskia was awarded a prestigious internship upon the completion of her doctorate—to a mental health facility in the Soviet Union, the Sverdlosk Institute. She spent a year at the institute and returned to Budapest a changed person . . . changed so much after witnessing the destruction of human minds at the Sverdlosk Institute that she became one of the freedom fighters in the second Hungarian uprising of 1988. She escaped deportation to Siberia and death—the fate of tens of thousands of other Hungarians—by a daring escape to Austria. Because of her detailed knowledge of what went on—and is still going on—at the institute, she has been selected for disposal by the KGB. In fact, she narrowly escaped an attempt on her life at the airport this morning."

The audience waited impatiently for Courtney to finish his lengthy introduction. Finally, Andrea spoke.

"Thank you, Senator Davenport," she said, smiling. "As the senator told you, a shaven-headed young man, not more than twenty-three years of age, tried to do a little number on me with an Oriental type of hatchet. According to the data I had received from the District police a little while ago, this young man is a stereotype of our subject today . . . the young cult member. His name is John; I can't give you his last name. He is a native of your state of Massachusetts and had been an excellent student from preparatory school through his studies at Yale University, where he received a bachelor's degree. He was a religious boy, but certainly not a zealot. He held strong moral convictions, had lots of friends, and had been accepted into a fine graduate school on the West Coast. John seemed to have everything going for him. What would cause such a young man to try to split the head open of a perfect stranger with the full assurance that he would be caught?''

The beautiful Hungarian psychologist had the rapt attention of the audience. Many in the session room were the parents of children who had run away and joined religious cults; Courtney Davenport among them.

''To many young people like John, the world is seen as a hostile, often unjust world. American society—with the divorce rate now seventy percent, and violent crime out of control, and the paralysis of our, pardon me, *your* government to curb it—has become threatening and illogical. Sensitive young people, like John, have tried to find answers through traditional, mainline religious denominations. Unfortunately, these churches seem to have a collective death wish, and have embarked upon a course of social gospel actions, such as providing funds to aid terrorists. This policy has spiritually disemboweled them.''

There was a shuffling of feet and some embarrassed coughing from some of the clergymen in the audience.

Dr. Macranskia outlined the social and spiritual sickness which described the United States in 1989: the paralysis of will of governmental, religious, and private institutions to deal with the breakdown of society or with the aggressive advocate actions of many individuals and organizations in defending the actions of cults.

''Before the police even arrived on the scene,'' she continued, ''there was a representative of the American Civil Rights Association by this young cultist's side, advising him of his rights. This ACRA volunteer evidently hangs around the Washington National Airport to ensure that cult members are free to do their thing, whether it's selling flowers or offering their bodies for sale.''

The old Regulator clock on the paneled wall chimed eleven o'clock, but the audience didn't notice. The Hungarian continued:

''John, like the typical cult recruit, was uncertain and unsettled when he came into contact with his group. He had reached a point in his life when many young people are vulnerable to cult indoctrination. He is typical of those well-educated, religiously oriented, white middle-class young people with wealthy parents. They are approached by seemingly concerned, loving, and accepting individuals who appear to have answers to many of the titanic "life" questions that they are struggling with. At the time of their greatest susceptibility, they are taken to an isolated retreat as novices, and literally bombarded with love and attention. Who can withstand such a thing? Teams of hard-core members are assigned to them in relays, talking incessantly, never giving the novice a chance to ask or answer questions. They are psychologically and physically worn down until they are brought under complete mind control. They then fall into an autohypnotic state where their wills are no longer their own—often resembling zombies. They belong to the cult leader."

The audience appeared thoughtful and reflective as the attractive blond psychologist outlined several case studies of cult members who had been successfully deprogrammed by herself and others. She concluded with a request for questions from the audience. Many hands went up from the sea of people in the now-crowded room. She answered them all.

"One more question," commented the senator, "before we go on to our next speaker."

A journalist raised his hand quickly.

"Dr. Macranskia, you never mentioned just *why* the young man wanted to kill you. Did he have some foreknowledge that you were going to testify before this committee and wanted to prevent you?"

The silver-haired senator rose again and spoke.

"I believe that our next speaker can answer that. Let me say a few words about Dr. Nicholas Portumo, presently a doctoral student in clinical psychology at the University of British Columbia.

"Mr. Portumo has a most fascinating background," Courtney Davenport continued. "He was born on the island of Cyprus in 1956. His father was Spanish—a Basque—who performed as a British agent during the Spanish Civil War. Barely escaping the clutches of Franco's secret police, he swam to the British outpost of Gibraltar. He was given British citizenship for his services, and a commission in the Royal Marines.

He later married an English girl. So . . . Nick Portumo was brought up as a product of British military life."

The senator rubbed his chin and continued. "He was well educated in Britain and the outposts of the Empire . . . the few that Britain has left. He received an appointment to Sandhurst, Britain's West Point, and graduated from there in 1977. He has had a variety of assignments, but for the past five years, he has been associated with his country's elite Special Air Service Regiment, the SAS."

The audience showed a heightened interest when the SAS was mentioned. In a world in which the Western democracies were consistently humiliated by terrorist organizations, where embassies were routinely taken over in Third World nations—hostages held for ransom or political blackmail—it was organizations like the SAS which gave the man in the street a feeling that something could be done if governments had the will to act.

Every time the SAS, America's Blue Lights, West Germany's GSG-9, or their counterparts in the Western nations pulled off a spectacular mission, there was a feeling of collective pride in the West. Indeed, if there were any heroes left in the world of 1989, it was the men and women of these elite antiterrorist organizations.

Nick Portumo launched into his subject with vigor. He was articulate and had a firm grasp of the psychological concepts underlying the appeal of cults to young people. But of more interest to Courtney Davenport were the descriptions of the SAS in penetrating and neutralizing armed cultists during those instances in Britain when cults had taken hostages. Indeed, much of Portumo's work in the SAS had been directed against violence-prone, paramilitary cults in Britain and elsewhere, which had undertaken the kidnaping of hostages. He concluded with some remarks about the murder attempt on his colleague.

"The programming techniques of many cults have changed dramatically over the past two years. These changes have been concurrent with the politicalization of cults—usually in conformity with the foreign policy objectives of left-wing or communist regimes. We have also witnessed a militarization of these cults, starting back with the Jonestown tragedy in 1978, and the paranoid efforts of such cults to organize into paramilitary communes. Indeed, there is a consensus among many scholars and experts in this field that the current trends are creating a gigantic, communist-oriented fifth column—via cults—in the Western democracies."

There was an uneasy shuffling in the room and then silence, as the audience anxiously waited for Portumo's explanation.

"I believe—and Dr. Macranskia concurs—that there is an organized intelligence orchestrating the worldwide organizational and operational changes in cults. For example, the programming techniques of many cults within the last two years follow the same format used by the Sverdlosk Institute in the Soviet Union to change the behavior and personality of political dissenters in that country. This is not surprising when you consider that the same department of the KGB which administers the Sverdlosk Institute, and dozens like it in the communist bloc nations, was given the additional duties two years ago of infiltrating and controlling religious organizations in the West. I believe that the young man at the airport was programmed by the KGB—via his cult—to kill Dr. Macranskia because of her detailed knowledge of the Sverdlosk Institute and its operational techniques."

Courtney Davenport listened, stroking the cleft in his massive chin with his index finger. His gray-blue eyes bored into Portumo, lost in thought as he spun a fantasy—a fantasy which soon crystallized into logic: With Portumo's military skills and Andrea Macranskia's deprogramming skills, an organization working outside of government interference—accountable to no political entity or other interest—just might be able to. . . . He broke off his thoughts abruptly and turned to a trusted aide and whispered, "Get me a complete background report on Portumo and Macranskia—everything they've done or been involved in for the past ten years. Have it for me within a week."

IV.

Legend has it that when the *viento del norte,* the north wind, blows its hot and humid wind into Paraguay during the summer months of December, January, and February, tempers are the shortest and the country's dictators are the cruelest.

Olivia Davenport caught the blast of the *viento del norte* before she yanked up the window of the Mercedes minibus. The wind was hot, humid, and laden with insects picked up from its sweep across Brazil's Mato Grosso jungles. The temperature was over one hundred degrees.

She rubbed the insects out of her eyes and glanced over at Susan, who was sleeping fitfully as the bus crunched over the gravel road. She turned toward the scenery outside. It was pleasant enough. Small adobe huts with palm-thatched roofs clustered together to form tiny villages. The country several miles west of Fuerte Olimpo was scenic. Mango trees heavily laden with fruit grew in back of peasant huts. Shawled Guaraní Indian women tended small plots of corn, cabbage, and mandioca.

The land was a bright kelly green this time of the year. It had been a wet spring and the lapacho trees still had their purple, white, and yellow flowers. As the bus swerved to avoid the numerous chuckholes, Susan Rockland stirred to wakefulness.

"Livvy? Wh . . . where are we?" She yawned.

"About forty-five minutes out of Fuerte Olimpo, that little town we came in at."

Susan shook her long blue-black hair and smoothed the few stray strands from her forehead. Her wide dark brown eyes peered out the open window at the rolling countryside. She frowned in surprise as she noticed the preponderance of strange crooked trees—the *palos borrachos,* or drunken sticks, as the natives called them, with their spiny trunk and dark pink flowers shaped like Easter lilies.

She glanced at Olivia and noticed how confident and self-assured she appeared. The gnawing feelings of doubt about the future and their past actions stirred within Susan. Her mind wandered back to the secure haven that was Bryson Academy, located ten miles out of Charlottesville in the Virginia countryside. Bryson Academy was not only geographically distant but a million light-years away from their destination—Colonia Gardún in Paraguay's Gran Chaco.

The two girls had always been rebellious. They never fit into the molds that their fathers had tried to pour them into. The other children in their families did. Why didn't they?

Perhaps it was the birth order, Susan mused. Both were the third child in each family. Perhaps it was timing. Both Olivia and Susan were born in 1971. The years following their birth were frenzied years and tragic. It was a time when their fathers were feverishly building up their corner of the Kingdom of God, and a time when their mothers were killed.

Somehow the corporate approach to things spiritual did not take root in the girls. The structured environment of private schools, which their parents had locked them into to shield them from the influences of Babylon, had created a spiritual vacuum. For years, as preadolescents and as teenagers, they had lived a counterfeit existence. Outwardly they conformed to the expectations that their fathers and the closed society of Davenport-Rockland Ministries, Inc., had of them. They were "good girls." They said all of the things and did all of the things which led all who observed them to believe that they were saved, sanctified, and ready to ascend.

Susan could remember her father's revivals, which were held in auditoriums, conference centers, and circus tents throughout the country. How she hated them! Especially when, as a child, she had to stand in front of vast throngs and conduct them in singing "Amazing Grace" or "Just the Way I Am." Both girls were expected to be not only examples but performers. Olivia was the more articulate of the two and at ten was billed by her father as a "child evangelist." At that age, she gave sermons and theological discourses to congregations at Gypsy Joe Rockland's revivals.

Troubles in Tulsa, such as experimenting with marijuana; joyriding with boys in a stolen car one night; Olivia's involvement, at sixteen, with a drummer in a rock band; and other incidences of what their fathers considered "un-Christian behavior" led them to the conclusion that Bryson Christian Academy for Girls, deep in rural Virginia, was the place that both Olivia and Susan had to go to develop "Christian" character.

Bryson Academy was a beautiful place. Red brick colonial buildings with white trim; spacious lawns; gigantic, majestic elms and maples lent themselves to an air of tranquillity—of spiritual calm in a sea of unrest. But Bryson Academy was far from a tranquil little island. It was an institution, part of the chain of Davenport Christian Schools which specialized in the rebellious—those children from religious homes whose very salvation was in question because of their behavior. The curriculum was rigid, the discipline severe, and the faculty well screened and selected to accomplish the school's motto: "Making bad girls good, and good girls better."

Susan smiled to herself as she thought of the school's motto. She glanced out the window. The countryside was rapidly changing, becoming flatter, less attractive. The level grasslands, with occasional stands of quebracho trees, were more typical of the Chaco than the country near Fuerte Olimpo.

Closing her eyes again, Susan continued her thoughts about Bryson. No matter how carefully a school screens its faculty, one like Randy Spivak occasionally slips in.

Randy Spivak was hired as a teacher of English and art at Bryson. He was an emergency replacement for Miss Grayson, who took a sudden and extended sick leave. The word got around quickly among the "bad girls to be made good" that Randy Spivak was different. He was not a member of the "Establishment" at Bryson. He had some things going on the outside which could prove exciting to those seeking excitement—and who wasn't at Bryson?

One of the things that Randy Spivak had going for him was cocaine—the best and the purest Bolivian cocaine. Another thing which made Spivak "different" was his involvement in the Garden Children, and the Garden Children had all of the ingredients which appealed to Susan Rockland and Olivia Davenport.

When Randy introduced the girls to the Garden Children, they were ready for commitment. The Children, mostly teenagers and young adults, surrounded them with enthusiastic attention and what appeared to be unconditional love. At first, the meetings were held in the Garden Coffee House in nearby Charlottesville. How warm and accepting the Children were! How unlike their own families.

Randy Spivak was more than a teacher and friend; he was a disciple of Julio Barrajas, the Chicano evangelist who broke from the Jesuit Order when he was a priest. Barrajas was the charismatic leader—the latter-day prophet—of the Garden Children. His converts, mostly white Anglo-Saxon youth, upper-middle class to wealthy, well educated, and suffering from spiritual emptiness, were ready and willing to surrender their will to the Prophet Barrajas.

The message was simplistic and appealing. The Western world was hopelessly corrupt and degenerate. The only hope for saving the world was for an "elect" youth, such as the Garden Children, to remove themselves physically and spiritually from their polluted environment. Communal life, or colonies, was the answer. The Children preached a spiritual revolution against the system—the Establishment—and demanded a total commitment of their members to the Garden Children.

The colonies grew like splitting blobs of amoeba. Colony "shepherds" monitored every phase of a new convert's existence, constantly hammering in the theology of alienation: alienation from parents, former friends, former religious affiliations, education, and society in general. The shepherds proceeded in a calculated, systematic manner to change the established behavior patterns of the convert.

The Prophet and the shepherds of the Garden colonies preached the "end of time" theology: The end of the age is upon us; humanity has become just about as full of wickedness as it can get; every agency of civilization and all of the creations of man are in rebellion against God. In one of his sermons the Prophet Barrajas thundered:

"God's rod is pointed for the blow, and His judgments are about to fall. The White powers of the Western world are about to collapse under the rising tide of color! The White man's doom is impending. The only salvation for God's people is to get themselves hither to a promised land—a land set apart for his children—a land that was the original Garden of Eden."

Susan smiled a cynical little smile as she gazed at the parched dryness. Who would have thought that the land set apart—the "original Garden of Eden"—was the Gran Chaco of Paraguay, she mused.

The Prophet Barrajas promised the converts that they would be among the remnants of God's people who would be saved—part of the 144,000 who would flee to the Garden during the period of the Great Tribulation—that era of titanic struggles between the people of the Lord and the Antichrist.

For one to prepare for the love and fellowship which would prevail in the Garden, one had to partake of the rituals and sacramental emblems which would aid in the process of translation—translation from the mundane and ungodly to the sublime and holy.

The sacramental emblem, a mannalike substance provided by a benevolent God to aid his chosen children in the process of overcoming the world and of blending the new convert's individual spirit with the "Supreme Oversoul," was cocaine. The purest, the best available Santa Cruz cocaine, grown in the foothills of the Andes, where the borders of Bolivia, Paraguay, and Brazil meet. The new Golden Triangle. Cocaine was the drug of choice among most cults in 1989.

Susan Rockland and Olivia Davenport had committed the

ultimate act of rebellion against the structured, corporate religion of their fathers. The act that was designed to hurt the most was their dropping out of their world and boarding the strange submarine which was moored off Parramore Island, Virginia, last month.

"Your parents are the true rebels against God! Your natural family is evil, wicked, and bad! To be born again, you must reject your natural parents and accept no other authority but me—the Prophet Barrajas—and my shepherds."

Susan wasn't so sure, but Olivia was. At the time, the message was so convincing. Susan stared at the flat marshes, now dry and lifeless. The bus was entering the dry zone of the Chaco. The corpses of cattle which had died of thirst littered the ground. Tens of thousands of white and yellow butterflies covered the corpses in quivering masses, trying to suck out what little moisture was left from the bloated carcasses.

Olivia was sleeping. Susan reached over and brushed several insects from her forehead. She wondered if she would be here if it wasn't for the enthusiastic arguments of Olivia—arguments which were quoted verbatim, like scripture, from the sermons of Barrajas.

The minibus slowed down as it approached a barbed-wire gate and a guard post. Outside were young Guaraní soldiers in camouflaged fatigues and black berets. Waved through, the bus rolled into the main compound of the Escuela para Comando at Mariscal Estigarribia.

V.

Nicholas and Andrea noticed the difference as soon as they stepped off the loading ramp into the Air Canada lobby at Tulsa's International Airport. There were no shaven-headed, saffron-robed cultists thrusting holy books and flowers into their hands. No Moon or Sun children soliciting funds for various "peace and unification" projects. The only sign of any religious activity was two clean-cut young people handing out pamphlets entitled "Jews for Jesus" and the ubiquitous Christian Science literature racks.

"Greetings, my good friends," boomed Courtney Davenport as he walked briskly to meet them. Andrea smiled slightly as she noticed how different the senator appeared on his home turf. His massive six-foot three-inch muscular frame was encased in a pair of tight-fitting, western-cut tan slacks, a plaid cowboy shirt, and hand-carved belt. The buckle was silver with the symbol of an oil derrick inlaid in gold. From his tan custom Stetson to his sea-turtle-skin boots, Courtney Davenport was every inch the successful Western businessman.

"Good morning, Senator," replied Andrea as her eyes fastened upon the gold derrick. "I get a distinct feeling—just from the vibrations here at the airport—that things are somewhat more to your liking here in mid-America," she said, laughing.

Courtney's eyes twinkled humorously. "We . . . I mean, *we,* the citizens of Tulsa, try to maintain a *few* standards,

Andrea. Sometimes we have to resort to a few unorthodox methods to enforce these, but they seem to be effective.'' He winked.

''And that's why we've been invited to spend the weekend with you at your expense—right, Senator? To discuss some unorthodox methods to deal with cults?'' asked Portumo matter-of-factly.

Davenport was taken by surprise, but pleased with the SAS captain's directness.

''Why, yes, Nick, that's why you're both here; to discuss unorthodox methods in dealing with those vipers.'' He draped a massive arm around Portumo's shoulder and walked toward the revolving baggage unloader.

The young blonde handed her ''Jews for Jesus'' pamphlets to her partner and walked to the phone booth. From her vantage point she could watch Courtney Davenport and his guests as they waited for the Air Canada baggage to roll off the conveyor to the revolving drum. She put a quarter in the phone and dialed a long-distance, toll-free number.

''Hello? . . . This is Faith. Yes, I'm with Hope. Let me talk to Charity.'' There was a faint buzzing on the other end of the line. It stopped. A cultured voice with a slight German accent answered.

''Charity here. What can you tell me, Faith?''

''Our friends have arrived. They are with the senator now. Shall we attempt to make contact?''

''No! No, not yet. Follow them. Try to find out what they are up to and why they are in Tulsa. Let's put off the termination of our Hungarian friend for the time being. Get all of the data you can on what is transpiring, and do not attempt any termination procedures until I give you permission.''

The blonde hung up and joined her partner. After waiting a few minutes, they followed their quarry out to the parking lot.

Two thousand miles away in New York City, Dr. Martin Weishaupt, code name Charity, placed the phone in the cradle. He reached over on the file cabinet and retrieved a manila file folder entitled "Davenport-Rockland Ministries, Inc."

It was a two-hour drive from the airport to the Davenport ranch in eastern Oklahoma's Boston Mountains near the Arkansas border. The bright blue sky and unseasonably warm weather for mid-March gave the promise of an early spring. The rolling, forested countryside gave way rapidly to a shallow valley encircled by low and well-worn mountains. Cradled snugly in the small valley was the ranch, a large, single-story, rambling home surrounded by gleaming white barns and stables. A freshly painted white fence enclosed Courtney Davenport's passion—his addiction—thoroughbred Paso Fino horses, imported from Puerto Rico, which he was attempting to breed for export.

As Davenport's Mercedes approached the main gate, the senator pushed a button on the dashboard. Automatically the gate swung open and they roared through toward the house. The Mercedes lurched to a stop, and two young, attractive Cherokee Indians in their early twenties walked out to meet them.

"Aha! Frank . . . Brian. How are you? How are things here at the ranch?"

"No change, Mr. Davenport." The taller Indian smiled. "It's been quiet . . . except that the mare in stall number three foaled—a little beauty."

"Mother and child doing okay?"

"Yes, sir," replied the other Indian. "An easy birth. The little filly is healthy and strong."

"Good! . . . Good!" boomed an excited Courtney Davenport. "Take the bags of our guests to their rooms. Andrea . . . Nick, after you get settled, meet me in my study. It's the paneled room off the living room. You'll find it."

An hour later, Davenport's guests joined him in his study. It was a large room for a study, actually more of a combination library and trophy room. The shelves were lined with volumes specializing in religious subjects and military history. The stuffed heads of big-game animals, from Cape buffalo, which were shot in Tanzania, to a Kodiak bear, stared down from the walls. Hunting rifles and shotguns of various calibers and gauges hung on wall racks and in lined walnut cabinets. Certificates of breeding and awards for his Paso Finos dotted the walls. Among them were the framed certificates and diplomas of various military schools. Portumo walked over to one and read aloud: "U.S. Army War College."

"Are you still in the military in some capacity, Senator Davenport?"

Davenport laughed. "Oh, I'm a professional weekend warrior—a two-week commando. I keep my hand in military affairs as much as I can. I'm a colonel in the reserves. You might say it's a hobby."

Nick suddenly felt a kinship with the tall senator. He sat in one of the large leather chairs and opened his briefcase on his lap. He shuffled through some papers, took them out, and put the case on the floor. He waited for the senator to begin.

"Nick . . . Andrea," the senator began haltingly. "From the data presented at the hearing at which you spoke, you know how insidious, how threatening the growth of the cults has been. Nobody knows better than you two of the tremendous damage these cults have done to the very moral fiber of our society. There have been attempts by parent groups, religious and citizen groups to curb their activities; but they received no help or encouragement from government or legal sources. One would almost believe that the government is in league with cult leaders."

"It's almost approaching that, Senator Davenport," commented Andrea. "In the past two years, five representatives elected to your Congress are active in one cult or another, although there are no senators yet."

"Thank God for that!" exclaimed Courtney.

"No senators . . . yet," continued the Hungarian. "But there are senators who are apologists for—and even advocates for—some of the larger cults, particularly if they represent places like Southern California, the Miami area, or the population core from Boston to Norfolk. The political, economic, and social pressures exerted by the leadership of the cults has become enormous. They have injected themselves and their organizations into every political issue, from abolishing nuclear energy to the latest proposal to declare San Francisco an all-gay city and off limits to straights."

Davenport sighed. "Yes, I know all that." His steel-gray eyes bore into the couple as he spoke. "I'll come right to the point. I believe that the only way to handle this problem is to . . . er, ah . . ."

"Through extralegal action, Senator?" Portumo said, smiling slightly.

"Why, yes, dammit!" Courtney exclaimed, pounding the tan leather chair.

Andrea laughed, shaking her heavy blond hair. "Well, gentlemen, it's out in the open. Do we agree that extralegal action is the only approach to solving the problem? Have we, and others concerned, exhausted every other possibility?"

There was silence. Then the senator spoke slowly and deliberately, weighing every word carefully and painfully.

"Nick . . . Andrea. About four months ago my daughter, Olivia, became involved with a cult back East called the Garden Children. Olivia's best friend, who is the daughter of my best friend—my partner—joined with her."

Davenport hung his massive head, shaking it slightly as he folded and unfolded his hands. "God knows, I haven't been the most sensitive, attentive father in the world to Livvy. It seems like since she was born eighteen years ago my partner, Joe Rockland, and I have been so busy trying to accomplish the Lord's work. Trying to make up for lost time, you might say. Both girls were always headstrong and rebellious, and now they've inflicted the ultimate punishment upon us. They've joined the very forces we've committed ourselves to fight."

The senator's voice grew louder as he stood and paced the floor. "These young girls, our daughters, were approached by . . . by this damned cult while they were in school. One of *my* schools in Virginia, mind you! They were systematically programmed and alienated from every value and tradition they've been instilled with. They've been introduced to cocaine, and God knows what other drugs. And now they've disappeared! Just disappeared! I've had detectives infiltrate the communes—they call them colonies—of the Garden

Children, and nothing! It's like they've vanished into thin air."

"Your situation is so similar to thousands of other parents," Andrea said.

"But the irony of it is, Andrea, that I've committed myself and my resources, upon the altar of the Almighty, to fight these cults, the very forces that are thwarting His holy purpose. Why me and my daughter? Is . . . is God putting me through some kind of a test? If he is, I'm flunking it."

"I suppose that you could always draw some comfort from the story of Job, Senator," Andrea responded thoughtfully.

Portumo leafed through some papers. "I'm more impressed with the example of Joshua, the one who fought the battle of Jericho. I believe that his modus operandi is more applicable to Mr. Davenport's situation than just passive suffering."

Courtney Davenport walked to the door, looked in the other room, then outside. The two young Cherokees were in the hills mending fences.

"Nick, Andrea, I've given this a great deal of thought, so hear me out. I believe that the only way to fight is to fight fire with fire—to use the devil's own tools and methods against him. I'm not sure how I would put all this together; but we must create a . . . a counterforce, a countercult movement to destroy . . . yes, I'm talking about the physical destruction of cult leaders, their installations, communes, and those who support them."

"Like ACRA?" asked Andrea.

"Yes, like ACRA—like the whole damned infrastructure of cultism."

"What you're advocating, Senator, is highly dangerous . . . illegal . . . and, if feasible, costly."

"Nick, I can commit five million dollars, up-front money, right now. I can promise the very best in salaries, equipment, and legal representation to anybody who gets caught."

"And . . . and what about those young people who are in the cults which are paramilitary in nature? Some of the colonies and communes are like armed and guarded concentration camps," the Hungarian psychologist added.

"Like my daughter and Joe's, perhaps? They must be extricated and deprogrammed forcefully. I can see no other way."

There was silence except for the scribbling of Portumo's ballpoint pen on notepaper. The tall senator looked at the couple and waited for a reply.

Nick spoke. "What we're looking at is a force, structured for combat, to neutralize cult personnel—the leadership, I presume—and destroy their assets and resources. A second element, working in conjunction with it—but not a physical part of it—is a deprogramming center, an isolated, secret location where cult members like Olivia and Susan can be brought and deprogrammed in a totally controlled environment."

Nick Portumo stood and walked to the window, parted the blinds, and looked outside. It was quiet except for the neighing of two Paso Fino mares.

"So, Mr. Davenport, we are talking about a mercenary force . . ."

"What? Mercenary? Soldier of fortune? I don't really think . . ."

"Senator Davenport!" Portumo barked. "Just *what* in the hell did you expect to use for this project, sophomores from your university? We're talking about creating a force of some eighty to a hundred men—and some women—who are going to undertake dangerous missions to crush these cults. In the crushing we're not talking about some abstract principle of struggle—as between good and evil. We're talking about finding qualified people with the skills, background, and attitudes necessary to kill other human beings. Yes, Mr. Davenport—killing! In various degrees and methods. This is a central part of the scenario. What kind of people do you think will do this?"

Davenport furrowed his brow and rubbed the cleft in his chin. He pursed his lips, deep in thought. "And . . . and such men can be found, Nick?"

"Yes, such men can be found."

"And such women, too," added Andrea.

"Where?"

"Okay. Let me present a little data. If you remember, the

nations of Israel, West Germany, Britain, South Africa, and the United States had rather large antiterrorist forces in being. Their effectiveness in attacking and neutralizing terrorists, and their willingness and ability to cross national borders to rescue hostages, created an outcry in the United Nations, since that organization is now controlled by the communist bloc and their third-world client states."

"Commies and cannibals!" snorted the senator.

"The success of these elite units was their undoing," continued Portumo. "Through a combination of U.N. pressure and domestic left-wing lobbying, these organizations were axed to death by governmental budget cuts and personnel cutbacks. These organizations are, perhaps, forty percent of the strength and potency they were a year ago. The gutless policies of their nations have severely curtailed their activities, and terrorism and hostage-taking have grown apace. OPEC, too, has added its weight to eliminating these groups. As it stands now, Senator, some cults have become terrorist groups, and vice versa. There are no effective means to stop them."

"What's your status with the Special Air Service, Nick?"

"Tenuous at best. I'm still an active unit member, but on extended leave. My so-called career path, which is getting a doctorate in clinical psychology, is indicative of my government's chicken-shit policies toward terrorism—using the SAS to negotiate a crisis rather than combat it. It's a no-win situation."

Andrea put a soft hand on the senator's arm. Her green eyes probed into his.

"Senator Davenport, out there—in the bars and bistros, in the streets of London, Tel Aviv, Capetown, and this country—are superbly trained men and women. Trained for a mission that's been aborted because of their governments' cowardice. They're angry, frustrated, disillusioned, and probably broke. Your countercult force, Mr. Davenport. It's out there."

Courtney Davenport walked over to the head of his Cape buffalo and rubbed the horns. "These . . . these people. Do you know where they are?"

"I anticipated that question when we received your invitation two weeks ago,'' Portumo answered, shaking a piece of paper. ''Here is a list of eighty people I can contact, starting tomorrow. Is it go, Senator, or do we sit on our collective asses and do nothing?''

Courtney Davenport smiled, rubbed his chin, and let out a nervous sigh. ''It's go, Nick. Do your thing.''

VI.

The Guaraní commando students measured up to the expectations of Captain Angel Caro—even beyond. Unlike most other Latin American soldiers he had trained, the Guaraní thrived on hardship, sacrifice, and discipline.

Caro stood on the small rise of the Escuela para Comando complex observing and taking notes. The sweating, grunting, camouflage-fatigued soldiers were put through their paces, as they learned the various arts of special warfare.

Caro had been fascinated by the Guaraní and the unique history of Paraguay. It was the warlike Guaraní which kept the armies of the Incas from conquering the lands beyond the eastern foothills of the Andes. It was the Guaraní who refused to submit to the Spanish conquistadores. The Incans, Mayans, and Aztecs may have been overwhelmed by their horses, steel swords, gunpowder, and tales of returning white gods—but not the Guaraní.

There was the fascinating period of history, in the seventeenth and eighteenth centuries, when the Jesuit Order achieved what the Spanish and Portuguese military could never do. They induced the warlike Guaraní to accept Christianity and settle in reductions, or *reducciones,* as they called them. These plots of land were expanded into a huge Jesuit-Guaraní, socialistic, utopian empire.

The several hundred thousand Guaraní converts were disciplined for modern warfare and trained in the use of firearms and military tactics by militant priests of the Society of Jesus. The 10,000-man Guaraní Army not only protected the *reducciones*, but prevented Spanish and Portuguese slavers from ravishing the Guaraní people.

The American captain, adviser to the new Paraguayan Army school for commandos, squinted at the hot yellow fireball as it sank slowly over the treeless plains of the Chaco Boreal at Mariscal Estigarribia. A slight smile flickered over his face as he remembered, in his reading of Paraguayan history, something about the Guaraní belief that this vast, lonely land, which was full of insects, jaguars, monkeys, and peccaries, was once a "Garden of Eden" and would again "blossom as a rose."

Indeed, the Jesuits accomplished exactly that in the eastern part of the country. A remarkable socialistic society was created and protected by a formidable military force. The Guaraní were quick to learn. Quicker, perhaps, than other indigenous people in Latin America, since their culture and traditions were not firmly rooted in a stable and ancient agricultural society.

Angel Caro could understand why the Jesuits invested so much of their resources and talents into the Guaraní. They were a joy to work with. The early Jesuit military advisers, no doubt, felt the same degree of affection for these remarkable Indians as he did. Isolated and xenophobic, proud of their warlike heritage, these dusky, stocky, self-contained people were good-natured, intelligent, physically strong, and fearless. Also passionately in love with their country.

"José . . . Rueben! Get your asses down before they get shot off!" the captain yelled in Spanish through the electronic megaphone.

The two sweating Guaraní troopers lowered their profiles as they crawled through the maze of barbed wire, which was part of the school's obstacle course. Overhead, inches from their quivering buttocks, live rounds of a .30-caliber machine gun snapped and cracked.

Caro felt a sense of accomplishment. His students were mastering the complex art of counterguerrilla warfare. Not every foreigner among the Guaraní was as well accepted as he was.

Compared to the rest of Hispanic or Luso America, Paraguay was unique. The treeless vastness of the Chaco had created a special mentality. One historian called Paraguay "the Russia of Latin America." Another developed a more appropriate title: *país sin suerte* (the luckless land).

"I wonder what this country would have been like if the Jesuit experiment had succeeded," Caro pondered as he watched the last of his commandos wiggle under the barbed wire and complete the obstacle course.

The failure of the Jesuits was due to their success. Their Guaraní students learned too well. By the 1750s Paraguay had become immensely productive. The Guaraní-Jesuit *reducciones* exported surplus farm products in competition with the Spanish and Portuguese plantations in Argentina and Brazil.

Ripples of discontent became a flood of complaints to the Spanish and Portuguese kings. In 1767 Charles III of Spain, with the Pope's blessings, banished the Jesuits from Paraguay. To ensure that they were rooted out completely, the action arm of the Inquisition, known as the Garduna—the Holy Warriors of Spain—was imported by the Spanish king to cleanse Paraguay of the Jesuit heresy.

The Jesuits were exiled, and the Guaraní departed into the jungles of the east and the vastness of the Chaco. But the Garduna remained, becoming absorbed into the xenophobic isolation that was Paraguay in the nineteenth century.

Caro sauntered over to the middle of the compound. His starched camouflage fatigues fit snugly, showing the ripples of his thigh muscles when he walked. He adjusted his pistol belt, picked some loose grass off his boot, and rubbed the toe on the back of his calf, to increase the shine. He felt that a sharp trooper, one who had pride in his appearance, was an effective soldier; and effectiveness was what his mission was all about.

His attention became riveted on a commotion near the main gate. He moved in quick, catlike motions to the edge of a small crowd of commandos for a better look. A dust-covered Mercedes minibus, gears grinding, drove slowly through the gate and headed for the camp headquarters building. It crunched to a halt. Caro watched, wiping the insect-laden sweat from his tan brow. His dark eyes widened in surprise as he saw the young men and women, who were clearly American by their looks and clothing, descend from the bus, blinking in the bright sunshine.

"Who are they?" he asked in a whisper to a smiling Paraguayan officer of European extraction.

"Aha . . . Captain Caro. These are the new *chivatos*."

"Little goats?"

"Sí . . . the *chivatos* . . . the new entrants for the Holy Order."

Caro rubbed the side of his nose, a nose that was slightly pug and seemed too small for his face. New converts for a Holy Order? Funny, he thought, I didn't recall any mention of a monastery or nunnery near Mariscal Estigarribia—or anywhere else in the Chaco.

"Everybody pick up your baggage and report to the building to the right of the one we'll check into . . . over there," barked the *guapo* who had herded the small group off the submarine at Fuerte Olimpo. "You are to keep to yourselves and talk to no one . . . no one! Is that understood? We will spend the night here and have breakfast at six in the morning before we leave for Colonia Gardun. All right! Pick up your baggage and get moving."

Susan Rockland stood out clearly from the others. Her long blue-black hair, olive skin, and full lips contrasted sharply with the Caucasoid, almost uniform Northern European features of the others. She glanced in the American captain's direction. Her heart pounded when she noticed the U.S. Army patch on his left fatigue pocket. Her eyes locked into his, trying to get his attention.

Caro couldn't help but notice her. Her tight-fitting blue jeans looked like she was poured into them. Her loose blouse, tightened by a slight breeze, clung to her firm but ample breasts. But it was her eyes—light brown eyes under heavy, naturally arched eyebrows. She was so different from the rest of the *chivatos*. Clearly, here was one who was not enthusiastic about being locked up in a nunnery.

The captain stared, and a look of understanding passed between them. He smiled slightly and nodded. He jerked his hand slightly toward the small makeshift chapel a few meters from the outdoor latrine. Susan frowned and then smiled in acknowledgment. If possible, she would meet him after dark.

Olivia went to sleep immediately. Susan waited until she was sure that her friend was completely out before she made her move. The *chivatos* were housed for the night in a one-story army barracks with cement floors, stucco walls, and an outside latrine; standard for the enlisted men of the Paraguayan Army. The lumpy mattress sack was stuffed with fresh straw, giving the barracks the smell of a stable.

She slipped on her jeans and tiptoed to the door. It was unlocked. Susan slipped quietly out the door and stalked to the latrine. It was quiet except for the chirping, humming, and squeaking of the millions of insects which provide the nighttime music of the Chaco. It was light out, lighter than she was used to for 11:30 at night. The stars of the Chaco shone with a brilliance unlike the stars over Virginia or Oklahoma.

She trotted the thirty feet from the latrine to the small adobe chapel and flattened herself against the wall and listened. Just the insects. Then . . .

"Pssst! Hey! You here?" whispered a voice in English.

Her heart pounded. She waited.

"Pssst! Hey! It's me . . . the American! Is that you?"

"Yes!" answered Susan as she slid against the chapel wall. She rounded the corner and saw Angel Caro. "Hi," she said, feeling rather stupid for her trite greeting after all of the dramatics leading up to their meeting. "Are . . . are we safe here?" she stammered.

They sat against the rear wall of the old adobe structure, both struggling for the next thing to say.

"I'm Susan Rockland . . . from Tulsa, Oklahoma."

"I'm Angel Caro, U.S. Army Special Forces. I'm an adviser to the Paraguayan Army. Now that you know why

I'm here . . . why are you here? You don't look like a prospective nun."

"Nun?"

"Yeah. Aren't you and your group novitiates for a Holy Order somewhere out in the Chaco?"

The brilliant stars of the Chaco night gave Susan enough light to study the face of the Puerto Rican captain. His black, tight, curly hair and sensitive brown eyes—spaced a little too far apart for his small nose—gave him a boyish look. In contrast, his muscular thighs and arms could be seen clearly through his tailored uniform.

"Do . . . do they have guards roaming around here, Captain Caro?" she asked, avoiding his question.

"Not in this sector, so we have all the time in the world. Tell me, Susan, how did a nice girl from Tulsa, Oklahoma, get involved in a Holy Order in Paraguay?"

She turned toward Caro, leaned her shoulder against the adobe wall, and pulled her knee up. She took a deep breath and sighed softly.

He reached over and took her slim hand in his. He patted it gently, almost as a father would pat a daughter who was about to confess a misdeed. "Susan, what do you want to tell me? You didn't get me out here just to talk about the weather."

She was flooded by feelings of trust toward the captain. "Captain Caro . . ." she began.

"Knock off the "captain" bit. Call me Angel . . . okay?"

"Okay . . . Angel." Susan managed an embarrassed smile. The smile soon disappeared. "This Holy Order that I'm going to . . . it's not a nunnery or anything like it. It's a colony, a religious colony called Colonia Gardún."

Caro frowned, rubbing the side of his pug nose. He had heard about the colony from his Guaraní troopers, although they spoke of it in hushed voices and abruptly changed the subject whenever he showed an interest in it.

The Chaco experienced several religious and ethnic colonies which started off with a lot of fanfare and high hopes, but then died. There was Colonia Menonita, Caro remembered. It was a Mennonite colony which started in the early 1950s, flourished briefly in the 1960s, only to die a whimpering death in the 1970s. There was Colonia Palestina, a short-lived experiment when Palestinian refugees tried their hand at communal farming. It, too, failed—more from internal bickering among rival factions than for economic reasons. And then there was Colonia Alemán, the German colony, started in the late 1930s, immediately after the Chaco War. According to rumor, Colonia Alemán still existed and provided a haven for hunted Nazis—especially for members of the S.S. and their families.

"Okay, Susan, tell me how you wound up in this God-forsaken part of the world, headed for a commune run by some religious cult."

The word "cult" released a torrent of emotions in Susan Rockland. She felt the desire to unload the entire story of her odyssey . . . from her childhood evangelist days, to her "incarceration" at Bryson Academy, to her involvement with the Garden Children, and her submarine voyage from Parramore Island to Fuerte Olimpo.

Her story, which she whispered in short, fragmented sentences, took almost an hour. The Puerto Rican listened—fascinated—still holding her hand. "Why are you telling me all this, Susan? If you chose a life in Colonia Gardún you must be a true believer; aren't you?"

Susan lowered her head. The tears came slowly, but they came—silently dripping on the parched earth. The captain pulled her to him. She responded, merging her body with his.

It was so long since he had held a woman like Susan Rockland. Soft, yielding, vulnerable. The women of Paraguay were different—like coils of barbed wire. Tough, aggressive, and numerous. They had to compete for the few men available, and every man—foreign military advisers included—was fair game.

The strong aggressive Guaraní women were referred to by the early Spanish settlers as a *bella mezcla de diosa y pantera*. Yes, a beautiful blend of goddess and panther; however, Angel Caro experienced more of the panther and little of the goddess in Paraguay's women.

"Angel," choked Susan. "I . . . I really screwed things up." She suddenly felt stupid for what seemed to be an inappropriate remark. "I . . . mean . . . I let myself be talked into getting involved with the Garden Children and coming here with Olivia."

"Your friend—right?"

"Yes, I've always been the follower. Olivia's been able to talk me into anything, and then I have to use my cool to get us out. I'm afraid we're in a situation we're going to have to ride out for a while."

Caro held her shoulders and looked into her light brown eyes . . . his nose less than an inch from hers.

"Susan, what do you want me to do?"

"Somehow let our parents know where we are and that you've seen us, and that we're all right."

The captain leaned forward and kissed her lightly, but fully, on the lips. She didn't move, but her lips responded.

"Thanks," she flushed. "I needed that."

He kissed her again. She put her arms around his back and held him. Suddenly she pulled away.

"What's the matter?" asked Caro.

"I . . . I'd better get back to the barracks. They might pull a bed check."

"Hey . . . your parents. Who are they?"

"Contact the Reverend Joseph Rockland, Davenport-Rockland University in Tulsa. He's my dad. Get word to Olivia's dad, too . . . Mr. Courtney Davenport. Same address."

"Okay. I got it. Before I let you go, Susan, I want to tell you that I'm going to check out Colonia Gardún. I don't know what you and your friend are getting into, but I think it has wider implications than just a religious colony . . . much wider."

"What do you mean?" asked Susan.

"I can't put my finger on it, but I know a little about the Garduna, the organization which runs the colony. It's sort of a religious-political movement. It started in Spain centuries ago as a guerrilla movement to fight the Moors. It was sent to Paraguay in the 1700s to help root out the Jesuit Order of the Church. After that, the Garduna became involved in Paraguay's politics: establishing dictators, overthrowing governments, and supporting wars of expansion. There's also evidence that they've been smuggling Nazi war criminals from Spain to Paraguay—not to mention having a big part in the cocaine trade. Those are the rumors I've heard anyway."

"But how do the Garden Children fit into all this?" asked Susan, her smooth brow knitted into a puzzled frown. "Unless . . . hey, the Prophet Barrajas was a defrocked Jesuit priest and traveled all over South America. Angel, do you suppose the Garden Children are sort of a feeder organization for this colony?"

Caro ran his fingers through his curly black hair and stared straight ahead. Susan slipped her arms around his hard waist, hooking her thumb into his pants' pocket. She put her head on his shoulder, leaned back, and stared at the brightness of the Chaco night.

Angel Caro felt stirrings for this runaway cult member—feelings he usually suppressed. Suddenly he wanted to protect her and care for her, to see her again, no matter what the risk. He had grim feelings of foreboding about her future in Colonia Gardun.

"Susan . . ." He turned to her, putting his hand on her knee. "If . . . if this colony turns out to be what I think it might be . . ."

"And what's that?" Her eyes were wide with apprehension.

"I'm not sure . . . yet. But I'm going to do my homework and *somehow* I'm going to get out there. It's only about a hundred miles from here. I've got to know if you are okay."

Her eyes smiled into his. "Do you care what happens to me, Angel?"

"Yeah . . . I care," he whispered hoarsely.

"Why should you?"

He kissed her on the forehead, then the tip of her nose, and then her lips. Her face was tilted upward, lips half parted.

She pulled his head to hers and kissed him. It was a long, passionate kiss, and their kisses became more frequent, more heated. Suddenly she stood up, brushed the dried grass from her jeans, and looked at her watch.

"Holy mackerel!" she exclaimed. "It's three-thirty in the morning. I've got to get back. We've been out here for four hours!"

"It seemed like four minutes," Caro replied.

They stood . . . bodies pressed closely together, arms locked around each other's waist. They kissed again.

"Susan, I've got to see you again."

"And I've got to see you, Angel . . . but be careful. Please come for me and . . . let my father know."

"I'll get to you, I promise."

She kissed him quickly on the cheek and darted into the darkness and back to the barracks where the *chivatos* were sleeping.

VII.

Mike "Puerter" Detlefs couldn't believe it, or perhaps it was becoming too believable lately. It seemed like every time he read the paper or turned on the television, the news confirmed that the guts were being ripped out of his country.

His pale blue eyes stared angrily at the TV screen above the neatly stacked bottles of liquor and kegs of beer in the Wild Boer pub on Pretoria's Pienaar Stratte. He worked the muscles in his jaw, trying to control his rage as the newscaster commented: "The United Nations has demanded that the Republic of South Africa cede all territory twenty kilometers below the enclave of Walvis Bay to the combined United Nations peacekeeping forces and Southwest African People's Organization Liberation Army. Units of the Soviet South Atlantic Fleet will be based in Walvis Bay to ensure compliance with U.N. SWAPO directives."

It was only a few months ago that the tall, rangy South African read in a Capetown paper: "U.N./OPEC nations pressure South Africa to disband elite antiterrorist military forces. Noncompliance will result in a U.N./OPEC boycott of the Republic of South Africa."

The patrons at the bar swirled their dark lager beer quietly and passively. They were getting used to such news. The little country of South Africa, the last white toehold on a continent seething with black nationalism and revolutionary expansion, was being disemboweled by internal left-wing forces and spineless politicians. It was being stripped of its defenses and its pride by U.N. decrees, Western apathy, and OPEC demands.

Puerter Detlefs, also known as "Bigfoot," was a former sergeant of the recently disbanded elite antiterrorist strike force, the South African Reconnaissance Commandos. He placed his size twelve on the polished brass railing that ran the length of the mahogany bar. He gazed absentmindedly at the slightly built young man, with horn-rimmed glasses, who just entered. The young man whispered something to the bartender, who then pointed to Puerter. The big Afrikaaner leaned his back against the bar and swilled the last of his dark lager.

"Mr. Detlefs? Michael Detlefs?"

"Aye . . . you're looking at him," he replied. His pale blue eyes sized up the stranger.

"Could we talk? Privately?"

The ex-commando motioned to a booth in the back of the pub.

"May I order lunch for you, Mr. Detlefs?"

"Well, that would be nice, my friend. It's been a long time since I had something in my belly," the Afrikaaner replied warily.

"Yes, I know," the man said. "A man with your specialized training might find it hard to find employment in the civilian sector."

Detlefs looked up quickly in surprise. His eyes glinted with suspicion.

"Would you be interested in a job . . . in your . . . ah . . . professional area of expertise, Mr. Detlefs?"

The Afrikaaner's expression turned from suspicion to interest. "Tell me more, my friend."

"I can't right now, not here. But you'll hear from me later. I have your address and phone number," the stranger replied, as he got up to leave. "Enjoy your meal. I'll let you order." He slipped an American fifty-dollar bill under Detlefs' cigarette case.

"Oh . . . my card. I wrote my Pretoria hotel and phone

number on the back. The slightly built American walked out the swinging doors of the old pub.

Detlefs looked at the card: Mr. Paul W. Lancaster, Sales Representative, DAVROCK Development Corporation, Tulsa, Oklahoma, U.S.A.

Eli Shem Revvim surfaced near the red and white buoy. It swayed in the slight swell of the Gulf of 'Aqaba. A mile in the distance he could see the gleaming whiteness of Elat, Israel's only port city in the south. The harbor was cluttered with freighters and empty tankers, ships which had been stranded since the OPEC nations and the Soviet Navy had blockaded the entrance to the Red Sea, at the Gulf of Aden, three months ago.

He pulled his face mask up on his dark lined forehead. Water dripped from his black curly hair. He heaved his stocky, muscular body up on the buoy, took off his air tanks, and leaned back to enjoy the harbor scene.

Eli was enjoying his "enforced" vacation. The tension of the last four years was being drained through an endless round of scuba diving, sailing, swimming, and helping his parents manage their small beachfront hotel. At times the inactivity got to him. The last four years were years of furtive activity as a team chief of Israel's elite Mossad Alayah Beth, Israeli intelligence's antiterrorist assassination team. Perhaps the "enforced" retirement was timely, he mused. The personnel turnover rate in the Alayah Beth was abnormally high, due to death, wounds, or emotional burnout.

The Mossad Alayah Beth was one of the most successful, if not *the* most successful, of the Western democracies' antiterrorist organizations. That was its problem. It was too successful. Its operations ranged worldwide, crossing national boundaries at will, penetrating Palestinian terrorist organizations at the highest levels and wasting their key personnel. So effective was the Mossad Alayah Beth that there was no effective protection against it except through economic and political pressure through international organizations. The weak and vacillating policies of the United States led to a vote in the United Nations to impose economic sanctions against

Israel. The U.S. delegate abstained, naturally. An OPEC campaign against the West followed: Either Israel comply or they'll shut off the oil tap. The Soviet Union offered its Indian Ocean fleet to the U.N./OPEC forces to enforce the blockade. Israel complied and dismantled its antiterrorist organization. The blockade of the Red Sea remained in force.

A slight gurgling noise caused Eli to yank his knife from his utility belt. The water bubbled near the side of the buoy and a crown of heavy honey-blond hair appeared. Two slim, tanned arms reached for the steel uprights on the red and white buoy as Eli watched open-mouthed. As he sheathed his dagger, a shapely bikini-clad body heaved itself gingerly up on the swaying buoy. Heavy, wet blond hair fell in long strands around her face mask. Her body, it seemed to Eli, was tanned all over, even under her bra. Here is one who must tan in the nude, he thought, as he watched his intruder push the rubber face mask to her forehead, revealing deep green eyes and full sensual lips, which were enhanced by little dimples in her cheeks when she smiled. Her smile broke into a husky laugh.

"Aha, Mr. Revvim. Did I break into a session of deep meditation?"

Eli blinked, searching for an appropriate comeback. "A visit by a mermaid—or is it a sea-goddess?—is always welcome."

He glanced over her slim, muscular body, partly in approval and partly to determine if a weapon could be hidden in her scanty swimwear. There was no way.

"I'm . . . I'm sorry," he stammered. "You have the advantage. What is your name?"

"Andrea . . . Andrea Macranskia."

"Hungarian . . . right?"

"Correct."

"And what can I do for you, Miss Macranskia, way out . . ."

"Andrea, please, Eli," she interrupted.

"All right . . . Andrea. What can I do for you?"

"What makes you think you can do anything for me?" she replied coyly.

"If you went to the trouble to find out my name and where I go to 'meditate,' you must want something besides my company on a harbor buoy."

"Perhaps I am concerned about your psychological well-being, not to mention your financial well-being."

He stared at her with narrowed eyes. "Continue, please." It was a demand.

Andrea breathed deeply, trying not to show the anxiety she felt as she anticipated the reaction her next statement would bring. She met his stare.

"Since your release from the Mossad Alayah Beth two months ago, Eli . . ."

His hand shot out, grabbing her wrist in a viselike grip.

"Who are you?" he demanded, his voice hissing menacingly. "Who do you represent?"

She expected this reaction. Without flinching, her emerald-green eyes probed into his. Her calm reaction had a disarming effect. "If you want me to tell you, release me; if you think I'm a Palestinian assassin, then kill me and feed me to the sharks."

Embarrassed, his grip lessened, and he tried to smooth out the indentations on her wrist.

"Eli," she started, "you're unemployed. You're bored, angry, and frustrated."

His dark eyes flickered acknowledgment.

"And you have skills—extraordinary skills and experience—which your own government, or any other Western government, would not touch right now. Correct?"

Eli nodded, amazed at the trust he was forming for the strange Hungarian woman.

"I represent an organization from the private sector in America which is interested in employing your skills for a period of from six months to over a year—maybe two. Salary and benefits are superb. Interested?"

Eli nodded, but was still suspicious.

The view from the watchtower toward the east was deceptively beautiful. The tall stands of evergreens, sprinkled with maples and elms, gave a furry softness to the rounded hills that passed for mountains in eastern Bavaria's Bohemian Forest on the Czechoslovakian border.

Paul Redecker adjusted his binoculars on the little valley between the forested hills. The stretch of plowed earth sown with mine fields and covered by multiple watchtowers with machine guns was enclosed by three barbed-wire fences.

As a sergeant in West Germany's Grenzschutzgruppe, the border patrol, this was Redecker's little kingdom—his domain. It was the stretch of border from Mittenteich in the north to Deggendorf in the south. It was a large area to patrol, but a relatively inactive stretch of border. His small squad of the recently disbanded Grenzschutzgruppe 9, or GSG-9, West Germany's famed antiterrorist unit of Mogadishu fame in 1977, was transferred to the regular border patrol. If this small but superbly trained unit couldn't control this quiet forested sector, who could?

Redecker heard the low whine of the BMW utility vehicle as it labored up the steep incline to the tower. He turned, his steel-gray eyes peering through his Zeiss binoculars, focusing on the vehicle as it approached. He brushed back his closely cropped blond hair before putting on his service cap. His full, wide mouth broke into a grin as he recognized the driver.

Paul raced down the tower, heavy boots clanging on the metal steps. He reached bottom as the dust-covered BMW lurched to a stop.

"Nicholas! Nicholas Portumo!" boomed Redecker. He embraced the SAS captain almost before he emerged from the vehicle. Redecker, a gigantic bear of a man, engulfed Portumo with his thick, muscular arms, almost crushing him in his enthusiasm.

"Hello, Paul." Portumo smiled, slightly embarrassed and ruffled from Redecker's greeting. "It's been a long time. Too long."

"Yes . . . yes," exclaimed the large German. "Since our combined training in Wales at your SAS country club at Hereford."

"Which has turned into a fairly inactive consulting service, by the way," said Portumo.

"At least your people are still intact. You still in, Nicholas?"

"Sort of."

"Sort of?"

"I'm on sabbatical leave. I'm getting an advanced degree in clinical psychology."

"Clinical psychology?" laughed the German.

"Oh, yes, my friend," sighed the SAS captain, brushing his dark brown hair back from his forehead. "That's the name of the game now. Negotiate with terrorists. Don't use violence—use psychology. We can't afford to offend the United Nations, OPEC, or the World Federation of Churches."

The huge German didn't notice the second man as he emerged from the passenger side of the BMW. He was a slight but wiry man in his early thirties, with coal-black hair, piercing, hawklike eyes, and a slight mustache—all of which contrasted with his almost too white skin.

"Oh, forgive me, Paul. Let me introduce you. This is Former Lieutenant Jean Trucdeau, formerly of Le Deuxieme Régiment Etrangère de Parachutistes."

Redecker recognized the unit, and his tone became respectful as he held out his hand and took the French lieutenant's.

"Any member of the Foreign Legion Parachute Regiment, especially the Second, is welcome in my neck of the woods—if you'll pardon the expression."

They all laughed.

"I understand that your unit has been disbanded," said the German.

"It is true, Monsieur Redecker. I am, how you say, temporarily unemployed."

"I almost envy you, Lieutenant Trucdeau. I can't call this job employment. You fellows worked yourself out of a job. Probably wasted all of the terrorists in France."

"Not quite, monsieur. The abolishment of our unit was a political decision emanating from forces and influences beyond our borders."

Nicholas Portumo put an arm on both of their shoulders as they walked toward the tower.

"Paul, let's go upstairs. I think I've got a proposition which might interest you."

• • •

For a horse ranch, it was large by Puerto Rican standards. Indeed, owning 150 acres of anything, even hilly grassland, near the provincial city of Caguas in the eastern-central part of the small island, made one a land baron.

Raúl Caro watched the attendant put the dainty little Paso Fino mare through its paces. Its gait was nearly perfect. No doubt the mare would please the buyer, who would be arriving shortly.

A silver-haired *patrón* in an embroidered blue Spanish wedding shirt and wearing a large Panama hat urged his mount up to Raúl, dismounted, and joined his son.

"Hello, son. Is the little one ready for showing?"

"Sí, Papa, as ready as she'll ever be," Raúl replied without enthusiasm.

The senior Caro rubbed the annoying age spots on the back of his hand, which were a constant reminder of his sixty-two years. He studied his son: his dark, brooding eyes; his restless energy; his inability to immerse himself into the family ranch.

"Perhaps he should have stayed in the army like his brother did," mused the *patrón*.

But Raúl's army was unlike most other armies. His was special. As a former member of the U.S. Army's special antiterrorist unit, the Blue Lights–Delta Team at Fort Bragg, his army was constantly at war at a time which passed for peace. After the disastrous rescue attempt which was aborted in the Iranian desert in 1980, the Blue Lights went through an excruciating self-assessment. They corrected their shortcomings and emerged one of the most effective antiterrorist forces in the free world.

The Blue Lights were only as effective as a weak-kneed administration and Congress would let them be. Indeed, their most successful mission—the rescue of the U.S. Secretary of Energy from a Libyan prison in downtown Tripoli—brought down upon the United States the howls of protest from the Arab world, the United Nations, and the OPEC bloc. The nation paid for this spectacular success . . . literally. OPEC raises in the price of crude oil increased the price of gasoline to $3.15 a gallon at the pump—a price which would increase rapidly, OPEC threatened, unless America showed its good faith by dismantling the Blue Lights.

The outcome was predictable. Pressure groups and congressmen, writhing in moral agony over America's use of force to deal with global terrorism, pressured a vacillating administration to abolish the elite antiterrorist group.

The Blue Lights were deactivated and the price of gasoline fell to $2.75 a gallon. Like Pavlov's experiment, OPEC rang the bell and U.S. policies were formulated.

"Restless, son?" The *patrón* slapped his son's blue-jeaned thigh.

Raúl nodded as he lit his third cigarette since his father's arrival. "Just thinking, Dad. If I'd stayed in the army, I could have wound up with an assignment like Angel's."

"But you're not like your brother, Raúl. Angel is more flexible. He kept his options open. You put all of your career eggs in one basket when you volunteered for the Blue Lights."

"Yeah . . . and now, ex-Blue Lights are shit in the regular army. If your 201 file shows any involvement, your career is screwed. No promotions, shitty details. We're pariahs, Dad—military lepers. All that specialized training and time-consuming exercises for nothing!

"Yeah, if I stayed straight Special Forces, I might be in Paraguay with Angel right now—trying to teach a bunch of dumb Indians to be commandos."

The two men turned toward the gate as they heard a heavy automobile crunch up the crushed-gravel driveway. The rented Continental glided to a stop and a tall, well-built man emerged. A golden oil derrick emblem shone from his wide, silver belt buckle.

"Aha! Señor Davenport," the older Caro exclaimed as he pumped the senator's hand with both of his. "So good to see you again."

"And it's good to see you, Señor Caro."

"Oh . . . Señor Davenport. This is my son, Raúl."

Courtney Davenport's gray-blue eyes ranged over the young Puerto Rican as if he were judging horseflesh. He liked what he saw.

"Yes, Raúl. How do you do?" He shook his hand with an

iron grip. "And how are you adjusting to the life of a horse rancher?"

"Just hanging loose, Senator," replied Raúl, wondering how the tall Oklahoman knew that he was "adjusting" to anything. "I'm relearning the trade, and trying to shape up these little mares."

"Ah, yes, these little mares," sighed Davenport. "I'm afraid that Paso Finos are my little addiction in life. I'm getting to the point where I'll pay almost anything for them."

"The addiction's spreading, Mr. Davenport," said Raúl. "A gentleman rancher from Paraguay, Francisco Estigarribia, wanted this little beauty so badly that I was afraid he'd have a stroke when I told him she was sold."

"And—she's yours, Señor Davenport," the *patrón* smiled. "Her papers and the contract are inside the house. If you'll come with me . . ."

"Er . . . ah, in a minute, Señor Caro. Would you get them ready for signing? I'd like to spend a few moments talking to your son. I'll join you later, if I may."

Davenport watched as the *patrón* disappeared into the hacienda. The ex-Blue Light perched on the white rail fence, arched his eyebrow, and said, "Business . . . Senator Davenport?"

"Yes, Raúl . . . business."

Each contact was able to make numerous other contacts on his own. Puerter Detlefs recruited not only ten of his former Reconnaissance commandos in South Africa but also fourteen unemployed ex-members of the elite forces of Rhodesia, or what was once the white-dominated nation of Rhodesia. Some were Grey's Scouts, which was a horse-mounted antiguerrilla group. Others were members of the PATU—Police Anti-Terrorist Unit—a group which could operate in the jungles for weeks at a time.

Recruiting was no problem for Eli Shem Revvim. Israel was a small country and every member of the once potent Mossad Alayah Beth was in the country, either taking their extended leave time or reemployed in the tedious tasks in the grip of the dull-gray routine of government bureaucracy. He discovered his assistant team chief sorting mail in a Haifa post office. Eli recruited nine men.

Paul Redecker had an understanding with the Bonn government, as did all of the ex-members of the disbanded GSG-9. They could leave government service for up to three years and pursue academic, vocational, or personal pursuits—no questions asked—and return to service without forfeiting pay or privileges. Before Nick Portumo left the watchtower, Redecker had convinced his entire squad of twelve to join the new venture.

Jean Trucdeau had no trouble finding members of the disbanded Foreign Legion Parachute Regiment. They could be found in the bars of Marseilles and in the unemployment offices of Paris. The recently transferred 13ème Demi-Brigade de la Légion Etrangère had its antiterrorist component, too, though now defunct. Trucdeau picked up seven men there.

Raúl Caro had the easiest time of all. The vast majority of Blue Lights had told the army to "shove it" when they were offered new positions in the transportation, quartermaster, or other noncombat branches of the service. Infantry, armor, and artillery wouldn't touch them; too specialized. So they drifted, having lived on adrenaline for so long that they failed to adjust to a passive, civilian society which was hostile to the military. They were easy to find: in bars, in jails, in federal rehabilitation centers. Caro found them—sixteen in all—and offered them a new opportunity for self-respect and to employ their rusting but still lethal skills.

Nicholas Portumo's task was broader—of a worldwide scope. After the GSG-9 mission, he contacted members of the Special Air Service in Britain, and SAS groups in Australia and New Zealand. Although they were in separate countries, they were one military fraternity—a series of very private armies bound together by similar missions and a similar motto: Who Dares, Wins.

The enforced inactivity of SAS units worldwide gave him twenty-two recruits, which were more than enough. Portumo ran the figures through his head as the Pan Am 747 made the final approach to Dulles International. Eighty-four. Eighty-four members for the combat elements of the countercul organization. And twelve deprogrammers, clinical psych types, which Andrea picked up in Europe and North America.

Portumo checked through customs, picked up his baggage, and went to the DAVROCK Corporation's private parking area. He hopped in the new Ford company sedan and drove along the airport industrial road to the far end of Dulles International—toward the corporate hangars. At the far end of the road, separate from the other hangars, were the large blue and white hangars of the DAVROCK Corporation.

Nick parked the car in front of hangar number one and heard the raucous laughter of eighty-four men and a few females engaged in a reunion. Men who had trained together in their own units, or cross-trained with antiterrorist units of other countries, knew at least several other people. Nobody was a stranger. Welding them together into a cohesive organization would not be that difficult.

Portumo slipped in the side door of the hangar and joined Andrea and Courtney Davenport. Outside the building, patrolling the chain link fence with the triple strands of barbed wire on top, were DAVROCK company guards. The area was secure. There were brief whispers among Portumo and others, and then the three ascended the three feet of stairs to the makeshift platform. The chattering ceased. All eyes were riveted on the three figures on the platform. Nicholas held the mike up to his mouth and with the other hand motioned for silence.

"Gentlemen . . . and ladies. Let me tell you why you are *really* here."

VIII.

The Mercedes minibus slipped into second gear and, engine whining under the strain of the incline and the one-hundred-degree heat, climbed the few remaining yards until the gravel road became level. It slowed to a crawl and then stopped.

"Everybody out!" the *guapo* barked. "You can get a look at your new home from up here."

The *chivatos* tumbled from the bus, blinking in the bright sunshine. They were herded to the edge of a barren, treeless bluff. Below them was a scene which looked like the Garden of Eden, especially after their ride through the dryness of the Gran Chaco.

Colonia Gardún was larger than any of them expected. To most of the young American cult members a commune was a small collection of believers who shared a few rooms in an inner-city tenement, or a rural temple/agricultural complex of not more than three hundred members. Even Jonestown, the ill-fated cult colony of ten years before, wasn't as big as the sprawling complex below them.

Colonia Gardún was more than a colony. It was a command center. A factory . . . and a breeding station.

Lying in a shallow valley, with red sandstone bluffs rimming it, was a collection of eighty-five buildings, which ranged in size from the Parachaco oil derrick assembly sheds to the individual homes of the Gardún leaders. The streets were lined with large flowering jacaranda trees, and were neatly cobbled. The buildings were sturdy white cement block. Some had red-tiled roofs. The lesser buildings were thatched with palm fronds. A small river, one of the few in the Chaco, meandered through the valley, spilling its life-giving liquid into myriad irrigation ditches which fed the green fields stretching in all directions from the colony.

"Imagine . . . way out here . . . a new society being built!" Olivia beamed. "A society being built on the principles of peace and brotherhood, with everybody involved in the building. Susan . . . that's it! Down there! One of the last chances to build a new order of things!"

Susan Rockland's mind was over a hundred miles away—in the arms of a young American army captain at Mariscal Estigarribia. Her mind snapped back to the present.

"Yeah, a new order," she replied dryly. No sooner had she said that when she noticed the collection of buildings on the eastern edge of the colony complex. They looked like army barracks—similar to the ones they stayed overnight in at Mariscal Estigarribia. They were positioned oddly, joining each other at right angles and forming a peculiar pattern. By the size of the large quebracho and jacaranda trees planted in their vicinity, the one-story white cement barracks must have been the early core of the colony—the first buildings built.

Susan squinted against the bright sunlight as she traced the pattern of the buildings with her finger. Her eyes widened in surprise as the pattern came together as a recognizable symbol. There was no mistake, nor was the pattern of building an accident of planning. The core buildings were in the shape of a swastika.

On the southern edge of Colonia Gardún, squatting along the bank of the muddy river, were the stockyards and slaughter sheds. They were so positioned that the prevailing winds would carry the stench away from the colony. One small building stood apart from the slaughter sheds, although its mission, too, was of slaughter: not of cattle or sheep, but of dissident colony members. The method of disposal was unique—a blend of the old and the new. It was a devilish invention of the neo-Nazi/Gardún ideology which guided the theology of the colony. It was a method as effective as any garbage disposal in a modern North American kitchen. After all, those selected for disposal *were* garbage, either racial garbage or disobedient garbage.

Carlos Von Reinach and his uncle, Francisco López Estigarribia, sat behind a small table, leafing through a stack of paper. Standing in front of them were a young couple in their early twenties—typically American. They stood naked, their hands tied behind their backs. The rawhide thongs cut into their wrists, drawing blood. Their backs, buttocks, and lower legs were slashed and striped from the lash of the *ceputo,* which was a uniquely Paraguayan cat-o'-nine-tails, utilizing the poisonous spines of the ceputo cactus.

The young couple had just undergone the *cepo paraguna.* Again, a uniquely Paraguayan form of torture, in which the victim sat on the ground, knees up and legs tied together, hands tied behind the back, palms outward. Wide sheets of rawhide were wrapped around the victim and soaked with water. The shrinking of the rawhide contracted the body into a little ball and the effect was similar to being placed inside a trash compactor. In the case of the young couple standing before the Hermano Mayor and his nephew, the thongs were cut before they passed out from pain.

"The charges brought before you are most grievous, my children." The Hermano Mayor smiled in a beneficent manner, his gold-capped teeth gleaming in the little shaft of sunlight that came from the small window near the ceiling.

"It is bad enough that you have defied the genetic commandments and had sexual relations, but you have attempted to flee to Bolivia and tell our enemies of our activities here."

"Hermano Mayor . . . please!" the girl bleated. "We're in love. All we wanted to be was . . ."

"Silence!" barked Von Reinach. "Your petty bourgeois notions of romantic love do not interest us. They have no place here! When you arrived you were examined, genetically determined and coded. You were assigned mates. If romantic love did not occur within that relationship, then it is your fault, not ours."

"Look . . . we've paid, all right?" sobbed the boy. "Okay,

we've made a mistake. Let us go back to our assigned mates."

The old *patrón* looked steadily into the boy's eyes—eyes that stared back in unrelieved panic. The Hermano Mayor pressed the tips of his fingers together, elbows resting on the small wooden table. He bowed his head as if in prayer and suddenly stood up.

"It is to be done. Feed our little friends," he said rapidly in Guaraní to the two Indians standing expectantly nearby. "The girl first."

The Indians leaped joyfully to their task. They spun her around and fastened steel cuffs to her wrist. By the use of a screwlike device, they tightened the cuffs until the blood streamed freely. A sliding chain hoist was cranked directly over the girl, who was now screaming hysterically. The end of the chain was fastened to the cuffs. Slowly the chain was tightened, pulling her arms up in back of her.

The screaming became unearthly, animal-like, as her arms were winched backward—up toward the hoist. The tearing of muscle and cartilage could be heard as her arms became horizontal to her body. She tried to bend with the chain to relieve the pain and pressure on her arms, but her body weight worked against her.

Finally, her shoulders and sockets were dislocated completely—in a jarring wrench—as her arms were pulled straight up. The young cultist passed out from pain.

"Revive her . . . quickly!" bellowed Von Reinach, a glint of anticipation in his eyes. "She must savor every stage of her punishment."

One of the Guaraní took a gleaming chrome hypodermic needle out of a plastic case and filled it with an amber liquid. He injected it directly between the breasts of the female *chivato*, punching it under the breastbone and into the heart. Within minutes she revived, screaming and mumbling incoherently.

The Indians then cranked her upward until she was three feet off the floor. The blood from her wrists and whip lacerations formed dark red pools on the gray cement floor. Another crank moved the hoist along a monorail overhead and stopped. She was positioned over a well-like opening five feet in diameter. Her blood now streamed freely down her body in little rivulets into the muddy water in the bottom of the well, which was ten feet below the cement lip.

As the blood spread over the water, several bubbles appeared—bubbles which soon became a frenzy of frothy water.

"Let me!" smirked Von Reinach as he relieved the Indian on the crank. "This must be done artistically—with style."

He lowered the screaming girl slowly into the opening, watching the chain as it slipped through the pulley overhead. Every foot of chain had a marker, a red link that enabled the executioner to know exactly how far his victim was from—or into—the water. To Von Reinach, punishment was a creative endeavor designed to purge the victim and satisfy his desire to inflict pain. After all, pain was what life was all about. The history of Paraguay and of Nazi Germany, his ideological homeland, was founded on pain and suffering—the kind of pain which ultimately, if endured well, purifies and refines the race and the soul of a nation.

Her feet were less than five inches from the muddy, bloody water when the first of the piranhas leaped out, its vicious jaws locking onto her heel, ripping and tearing a large piece of flesh. Quickly, Von Reinach hoisted her until her hands almost touched the pulley. Three piranhas were fastened on her heel and toes.

The girl looked down at her feet, uncomprehending, as the vicious little fish fell back into the frothing water with their bloody morsels of meat.

Von Reinach cranked her into the well as her hysterical sobs echoed through the shed. Her legs up to her knees were immersed for a full thirty seconds—just long enough for the little fish to strip away the flesh and muscle to the bone. Again, she was hoisted to the pulley. The flesh had been gnawed off neatly to her knees by hundreds of razor-sharp little teeth. Her well-formed thighs ended abruptly, giving way to the gleaming whiteness of calf and shin bones. The cartilage was neatly cleaned from the small bones of the feet.

Von Reinach marveled at how artfully the piranha could

enter the smallest dimensions, orifices, and cavities of a human body and reduce it to bone. Surely his little friends in the well were the most artful executioners of all.

The girl's sobbing ceased as she went into shock. She looked uncomprehendingly at her lover, her knees buckling, her chin falling on her chest.

Von Reinach sighed and lowered her completely into the water, the well becoming a frenzy of thrashing, frenzied activity as her hands disappeared into the muddy darkness.

Five minutes passed. Francisco Estigarribia, the Prophet of Paraguay, nodded. His nephew cranked the chain upward. The lightness of the load at the end of the steel cuffs told Von Reinach that the job was completed. At least eighty pounds had been removed from the end of the chain—distributed into the hundreds of bellies of the voracious little piranhas. The dangling skeleton of the female *chivato* was dancing grotesquely, completely devoid of flesh, muscle, or cartilage. The smaller fish were able to gnaw through the soft tissue of the eyes into the cranial cavity and clean out the brain tissue. The tail of one small, determined piranha still flicked through an eye socket as it continued to gorge.

The skeleton was moved on the gleaming monorail to the far end of the shed to rest over a large funnel. One of the Guaraní reached over from a catwalk and undid the cuffs. The girl's remains clattered into a sheet-metal hopper. The sweating Guaraní emptied a large bin of cattle bones into the hopper on top of the skeleton. Von Reinach pushed a red button on the bone-crushing machinery. It roared into life and ground its human and animal cargo into a coarse powder, which emerged from the bottom of the crusher, filling a double-reinforced paper sack.

"At least now she will be useful." The Hermano Mayor smiled, his teeth shining in the sparse sunlight. "She will fertilize the fields of the colony."

He turned to the boy, who was now traumatized into insensibility by the fate which awaited him, and snapped his fingers. "The boy next."

• • •

The Mercedes minibus entered the main gate of the far north side of Colonia Gardún. The white cement gate was arched and flanked by huge, flowering jacaranda trees, which heralded the entrance to a neatly cobbled street, lined with clean, low, red-tiled buildings. Overhead in the wideness of the concrete arch was painted the motto of the colony: "The Will of God Is Obedience."

IX.

"Dammit, Courtney! You . . . you organized all this and funded it without consulting me?" sputtered an irate Joe Rockland. It was hard to tell if his swarthy skin was flushed or not, but Courtney Davenport had seldom seen his partner so angry.

"Ah, Joseph—Joseph, my good friend," cooed Davenport, slapping a large rawboned hand on his partner's shoulder. "I meant to tell you, but you were out of town and I was back in Washington. C'mon Joseph, you know we've talked about this; and now that our daughters are missing . . ."

Rockland grew sullen, his dark eyes half hidden behind purplish-blue lids. He gazed out the window of Courtney's office—out over the cleanness of Tulsa.

"Courtney, I've often had a hard time justifying, at least in my own mind, what you were doing here in Tulsa. God knows, it's contrary to what I preach from the pulpit."

Davenport sighed wearily. "Joseph, we're churning up old ground. The *real* world, my friend, the one out *there*"—he jabbed a massive finger toward the window—"is not a world that can be dealt with with love and scripture reading! Joseph, the devil's not only on the loose, he's winning because he's a realist. He's using every force, every organization, and every stratagem he can to win!"

The senator continued, the rage building. When he became like this, Joe Rockland acquiesced and listened. "Joseph, this—this devil that you preach against . . . Dammit, he's not an abstract *thing,* he's real! You know where the term devil comes from!"

Rockland sighed and sat down, shaking his head.

"It's a Greek term, Joe. It's *diabolos*: derived from a verb that means 'to throw into confusion . . . to set at odds . . . to put asunder.' He's a real and cosmic power. Our Lord Jesus knew that. He had a testimony of the existence of demons and of the reality of Satan!"

Joe Rockland smiled slightly and leaned back in the big leather chair in an attitude of surrender. "I think, Courtney, that our roles are reversed. You should have been the evangelist."

Davenport continued without responding to his partner's comment. He flipped through a New Testament.

"Right here, Joseph . . . in the sixth chapter of the Epistle to the Ephesians, the Apostle Paul describes the kind of adversary with which we have to contend in these cults. Listen . . ."

"Courtney, I know that scripture. You don't have to . . ."

" 'For our fight is not against any physical enemy: it is against organizations and powers that are spiritual. We are up against the unseen power that controls this dark world, and spiritual agents from the very headquarters of evil.' "

Joe Rockland's brow furrowed under his thick black hair. "If an enemy is not physical, as the scripture says, why did you hire a force of mercenaries to combat it!"

"Because, Joseph," Davenport thundered, "the physical part consists of the *agents*—the human dupes, willing and unwilling. They are the physical components of the devil's ultimate goal, which is to foster a demonic conspiracy to subvert the true Gospel of Jesus Christ through human agents whose minds have been blinded by the evil one."

Rockland sunk further into the leather chair as if he were trying to burrow away from the strange logic of his partner.

"Joseph," said Davenport, "it's as the Lord intended. You've always taken care of the spiritual end of the Kingdom of God—our part of it at least—and I've taken care of the physical. Because of this, we've grown into a mighty force to be reckoned with. We've drawn thousands—tens of thousands—into our cause."

"And yet the cults keep growing in size and influence," Rockland murmured thoughtfully.

"That's because we've fought the battle primarily on a spiritual plane. The Lord wants us to fight it here!" Courtney jabbed his finger toward the window, toward his beloved Tulsa.

"Do you honestly feel, Courtney, that the Lord approves of your actions in sending out teams of mercenaries to destroy these cults?" Joe Rockland had surrendered to the point where he was seeking divine affirmation to a plan already formulated and ready to begin operations.

Davenport walked behind the large chair and put his hands on his partner's shoulders. He turned it around on its swivel to face the open window.

"Joseph, we made a covenant with the Almighty to raise up a righteous force to cleanse our land. Within every generation, every period of crisis, the Lord raises up an elect to fight his battle. He's tossed us the ball, Joseph. We have to run with it, and the laws of the land be damned! As a covenant people, and that's all of us involved in this struggle, we have to put the laws of God before the Mammon-inspired laws of man. Remember, Joseph, the Good Lord commanded the children of Israel to fight his battles and, in some cases, destroy everything—men, women, children, and even animals—of the ungodly."

Courtney Davenport ended with a thoroughly memorized scripture from the old Testament: " 'Now therefore, if ye will obey my voice indeed, and keep my covenant, then ye shall be a peculiar treasure unto me above all people: for all the earth is mine.' "

Paul Lancaster's mission was simple and should prove to be enjoyable. He opened up his slim attaché case on his hotel bed and pressed a small button near the screws holding the handle in place. The faceplate of a small rectangular box, not more than five by two inches, sprung loose, revealing the finely machined mechanism of a spring-propelled weapons system. A thin, hollow tube ran from the box, along the top of the attaché case. It ended with a small hole, barely visible to the naked eye, on the top edge of the case. In a plastic magazine jutting from the box were thirty tiny needles, which were coated with Enthrop Nine, an unusually powerful convulsive poison, which acted ten minutes after injection.

Paul removed the magazine and substituted one of noncoated needles. He closed the attaché case. He stood, case in hand, right index finger on the nearly invisible trigger embedded inside the inner part of the handle. Slowly he walked toward the small white target tacked on the opposite wall. The case lined up with the black circles. When he was ten feet away, he pressed the trigger. His finger movements were barely visible. The small needles hissed silently from the tube, leaving the upper edge of the attaché case with impressive speed and accuracy. When Paul closed to within five feet of the target, all thirty of the tiny needles were within the circle. He smiled as he ejected the empty magazine and inserted the deadly one with the coated needles. He felt good. Fulfilled. He had mastered a unique and difficult weapon. The armorer at Westwind One had created a little jewel in this attaché case weapons system.

He slipped into his raincoat, grabbed his case, and took the elevator to the basement parking lot. He walked briskly to his car, humming a few bars of "Amazing Grace," and nosed into the early morning traffic of Oakland. He darted onto the on-ramp and entered the freeway to the airport.

The first countercult operation of Courtney Davenport's holy crusade was about to commence.

To land at San Francisco's International Airport, retrieve one's baggage, and find one's way to the parking lot or public transportation was usually a bizarre experience for even the most seasoned traveler in 1989.

The homosexual majority of the city, some 87 percent of the total population by last count, had effectively gained control of the machinery of municipal government. Homosexual excesses within the city proper had all but driven out the business and professional classes. The straight middle class had mostly departed across the bay to Oakland, or south to San Jose. The economy was stagnant; and yet the organized homosexual lobby on the state and federal levels ensured an infusion of public welfare funds for the city's gay population.

A homosexual religious cult was the real power in the city. The Lavender Family was a cult with an economic base founded on crime and the drug traffic. Its theology was rooted in the ancient deities of the city-states of Sodom and Gomorrah.

The Family had preyed upon the few remaining straights in San Francisco, and when this source of extortion had dried up, it expanded its operations to neighboring cities and eventually to other states.

The action arm of the Lavender Family was a sadomasochistic core of strong-arm men and some lesbians. Their grisly trademark, which they left on their victims, was various forms of mutilation and the surgical-style removal of the victim's genitals. Victims of their ritualistic murders were found as far away as Washington, D.C., and Miami. Their modus operandi was reflected in their name: the Gay Blades.

Paul Lancaster drove up to the automatic barrier and slipped a dollar bill into the electronic receptor. Nothing. The barrier did not rise.

"Damn!" he muttered. He got out of the car and tried to lift the orange and white pole. It was locked into place. He turned to enter his car and froze. Not more than two inches from his face was a lavender-colored hand, with a red bloodshot eye painted on the palm.

"What the hell!" Paul recoiled backward, falling against the barrier.

The hideous figure in the lavender robe, with shaven head and plucked eyebrows, laughed shrilly. He closed and opened his eyes, revealing a painted eye on each eyelid, which gave the impression of having another set of eyes. A lavender-dyed army web belt with a Gurkha-style curved dagger attached was his badge of authority in San Francisco. A Gay Blade.

"That thing hasn't worked for months, sweetheart," he said softly, yet menacingly. "It will cost you ten dollars if you want to park."

"But the sign says one dollar," insisted Paul.

"That's right, sweetie. One dollar for parking, and a nine-dollar fee for hiring my talents to raise the barrier." The cultist rested his hand on the handle of the curved dagger.

Paul sighed, reached in his wallet, and gave him a ten-dollar bill. The lavender-robed homosexual gave him a grotesque smile and blinked his eyes rapidly, revealing his painted lids. He pressed a small button on the butt of the barrier and lifted it. Paul drove through slowly.

"Stop!" yelled the attendant. "Get out!"

"What now?" moaned Paul, emerging from the car, attaché case in hand.

"Uh . . ." the shaven-headed cultist fumbled for words. "Uh . . . going to catch a plane?"

"Yes . . . as a matter of fact." Paul turned the attaché case toward his lavender target. A slight finger movement sent a tiny needle zipping into the thigh of his opponent, who absently scratched the impacted area, causing the needle to fall to the blacktop.

"Well, I'll be here when you get back. Maybe we can . . . get it together then . . . huh, sweetheart?" He pinched Paul's cheek.

Paul smiled wanly, got back into his car, and minutes later, nosed into a parking place. As he walked to the terminal he glanced toward the gate. There by the orange and white barrier was a clump of lavender, convulsing on the blacktop in a pool of vomit.

Paul felt like a sharp scythe ripping through a field of lavender-colored wheat. "The field is lavender and ready to harvest!" he chuckled to himself as he literally bounced through the massive airport complex, attaché case in hand. In a space of twenty minutes, he had been accosted at least fifteen times by lavender-robed freaks. They were trying either to sell him something or to proposition him. With each encounter, the small hole in his attaché case was aligned with his target. It was amazing how little reaction there was to the needles—not more than one would react if bitten by a mosquito, or if one's underwear fabric caught on his skin.

The magazine was depleted. Thirty needles had been expended. Already he could see clusters of excited people huddled around convulsing clumps of lavender.

Paul entered the public men's room, a mistake one never makes twice in San Francisco. He almost gagged at the scene. The large filth-ridden rest room was almost wall to wall with the lavender-robed ones. Some of them were smoking marijuana—some were openly engaged in homosexual acts, oblivious to the others.

"Hey . . . look what we have here! Prince Charming!" cooed one.

"Yeah! C'mon in, darling. Let's look you over," said another.

"Look . . . I just want to use the bathroom—a stall," said Paul, the panic welling up inside him.

"The coin box on the john charges a quarter, but if you want to leave here with your virginity intact, it'll cost you twenty-five bucks," slurred a grotesquely fat cultist, his sweat staining his robes.

"It's worth it," groaned Paul, slipping two tens and a five to the homosexual. Paul locked the stall door behind him, laid the attaché case on his lap, and changed magazines.

Outside the comparative isolation of the stall, Paul could smell the clouds of marijuana smoke, and hear the raucous laughter and unmistakable sounds of homosexual acts being performed.

He reached in his pocket and removed what appeared to be a small plastic nose-drop bottle. He squeezed the rubber bulb and hastily started for the exit. To his surprise nobody tried to stop him. All of their attention was riveted on a writhing group on the slippery white tile floor. Muffling a gag, Paul dropped the plastic bottle under a sink. Minutes later, the large rest room was enveloped in the deadly vapors of Enthrop Nine.

An hour and a half after parking, Paul drove to the orange and white barrier. His lavender friend was gone. He found the button and raised the gate. As he sped toward the freeway, the corners of his mouth twitched in a smile. He heard the screaming sirens of the few ambulances left in the city speed toward the panic-stricken airport terminal. Frantic appeals were sent to paramedic units and hospitals in neighboring communities. None responded.

To tens of thousands, the corpulent moonfaced Manchurian was God personified; an untouchable deity on earth. His Perfect Holiness, the Spiritual Master, Ha Bai Sun, stood with his staff up by the press box overlooking the vastness of the stadium. Tomorrow night at Soldier Field in Chicago the gigantic rally would take place. His mindless followers, nicknamed Sunspots, had combed the city, selling tickets to the event. They had done their work well. They always did. For a Sunspot to fulfill or overfulfill his quota of items to be sold—whether it was tickets, flowers, incense, or cocaine—meant added blessings and another nudge up the organizational ladder which led ultimately to ecstasy and the sweet annihilation in Sun's personal nirvana. It also meant another upward nudge for the vast commercial empire that Sun and his intimates had created.

Down on the artificially turfed field, the communications technicians were installing the vast complexity of equipment which would carry Sun's message to the stadium audience as well as worldwide.

Mike "Bigfoot" Detlefs glanced up at the bevy of saffron-robed cult leaders near the press box. His sharp eyes focused on Ha Bai Sun, whose corpulent figure caused him to stand out from the rest. Mike smiled grimly as he assembled the microphone—the very one that Sun would be using tomorrow night.

He removed the gleaming microphone head from his tool box, connected the network wires, and screwed it onto the stand. The mike head was slightly larger than standard. It had to be. It contained a miniature claymore-type mine. Implanted in the plastic explosive within the head were hundreds of razor-sharp fleshettes coated with prussic acid.

Detlefs knew Sun's speaking style by heart. He had endured at least a half dozen of his ravings in South Africa and Europe in the hope that he could find some trace of his younger sister, who had joined the cult in Brussels in 1987. This quest was the main reason for the depletion of the

Detlefs family resources. The disappearance of his sister was a contributing factor to his father's fatal heart attack and his mother's chronic depression. Yes . . . Mike Detlefs had a score to settle. Tomorrow night, revenge would be his.

It was a sellout, as the Supreme Master knew it would be. Many came to watch his histrionics and to hear his unique delivery, which featured a voice which could span an incredible band of frequencies. From a deep bass to a desperate high shrill; it was reported to be able to shatter glass.

The variable pitch and rapid-fire pattern of Sun's speaking style had the power to mesmerize and benumb vast throngs. Indeed, Sun himself referred to his voice as being capable of transmitting "divine vibrations" to those whose spiritual molecules would be rearranged and aligned with the teachings of the Supreme Master.

The vast majority came in orange saffron robes to hear the message of alienation; alienation from family, former friends, and country. It reinforced their original motives for joining the Sun Cult.

To the shaven-headed believers, this opportunity to get this close to His Perfect Holiness was a divine opportunity to recharge their spiritual batteries; to realign their spiritual molecules with thc karma of the Unassailable One.

Another member of the huge audience was also interested in the quality and timbre of Sun's voice. Mike Detlefs, who was sitting halfway up the huge stadium with a perfect view of the deadly microphone, surmised that twenty minutes into his sermon Sun would scream shrilly into the mike, grabbing the stand and almost shoving the mike head into his mouth. That was his style—and that should do it! That should activate the tiny frequency-induced activator—the trigger for the explosive charge.

The throngs sat silently in awe as the Sun deity entered the platform. A hymn was sung, in some ancient foreign tongue, by the orange-robed portion of the audience. The hymn was transcended by a chant, which was repeated twenty times.

His Perfect Holiness held up his arms. His pudgy fingers extended as he pronounced a blessing on his followers.

"What a supreme asshole," thought Mike as he reluctantly bowed his head.

Sun wasted no time. He launched into his subject vigorously. Those rational individuals who observed and reported on Sun's movement knew that sooner or later it would come to this . . . but not so soon.

"Yes. . . . Yes, my children," he panted hoarsely into the mike. "It is only too true. There are vast forces of darkness accumulating to obliterate truths—the truths I have taught you." He continued, the pitch of his voice rising.

"There are those in government, in this land and others, who would curb my activities. Those who would limit—yes, liquidate the financial holdings of our movement, which exists only for the welfare of the faithful."

Sun manipulated the masses as a conductor controls a symphony orchestra. He modulated his voice, creating a full spectrum of emotions in the audience. Sun knew them now, and he knew which emotional buttons to push to get the responses he wanted. Even Detlefs, fighting to retain control, felt it. He smiled to himself and relaxed, remembering an experiment conducted at the University of Wisconsin. Some graduate students in psychology played a tape of Sun's speeches for a twenty-four-hour period in a chicken coop. The poor hapless creatures began laying eggs of double and triple yokes, and finally went berserk.

Sun's theatrics now resembled the wild gyrations of a rock singer. He cried; he pleaded; he threatened. The huge rolls of fat quivered under his sweat-soaked orange robe. A voice, on cue, screamed from the audience:

"The sacrament, O Holy One, the sacrament!"

Seemingly from nowhere, saffron-robed Sunspots appeared among the throngs with canvas bars and money changers. The sacrament was passed and sold: two capsules of cut Bolivian cocaine for ten dollars.

"Take it! Take it!" screamed the Holy One. "Feel. Enjoy. Merge with the Supreme Oversoul. Let the purity of nature's gift merge your soul with mine; your will with mine!"

Within minutes the crowds felt the euphoric rush of the cocaine—their sacrament. It was now, Sun surmised. It was the time to announce his new revelation of blood retribution. As was often the case, Sun's revelations were conditioned by the statistical data of certain aspects and trends of American society, which were compiled by the Astral Research Institute, a domestic front for Section VI of the KGB, of which Dr. Martin Weishaupt was the director.

"As the heavy hand of the evil ones smothers us, we bear . . . and we suffer. And we have endured. But I say unto you, we shall endure no longer!"

The agitated throngs roared their approval.

"The blood of our martyrs will be answered with the blood of our oppressors!" Sun thundered, referring to several Sunspots roughed up by a mob of hard hats in St. Louis.

He grabbed the mike and shoved it up and almost into his mouth. He ranted and raved, wildly gyrating on the makeshift stage. His voice reached the high-pitched whine of a jet preparing to take off.

"Take it easy, take it easy, Sunnie boy," Mike murmured. "Don't break those connections."

"Take to the streets. Be free! You can only be free if you cut the connection between yourself and your parents, for only *I* am your true parent!"

On cue, the tens of thousands of Sunspots screamed in a strange tongue and waved razor-sharp Manchurian ceremonial hatchets over their heads.

"I, the Unassailable One, the Supreme Master, command you to cut the ties—and I mean *cut*!"

The thrill timbre of Sun's voice created the appropriate vibrations. The tiny actuator quivered inside the mike as he screamed into it, swinging his hatchet into the podium in a wild arc. The contact between the points was made.

Many thought it was a stunt—another gimmick used by Sun to manipulate the masses. But it wasn't. Mike Detlefs knew that. The microphone exploded with an orange flash which merged with the sweat-stained robe of its target.

When the smoke had cleared, the shredded, unrecognizable face of Ha Bai Sun was visible to the throngs in the east stadium. Mike Detlefs took advantage of the confusion and slipped out the side gate.

The Perfect Master, the Unassailable One, was perfectly dead. On the stand behind him several members of his intimate staff lay screaming and writhing on the blood-soaked planks, as the poisoned fleshettes took effect.

"If you need any additional proof that we're engaged in the work of the Almighty, Joseph, read this."

Courtney Davenport handed his brooding partner a folded newspaper.

"Page two . . . *The Philadelphia Herald* . . . the only newspaper with the guts to tell it like it is."

THE "GOD" THAT DIED

Three days ago we witnessed the assassination of a cult leader and the sudden demise of a movement—a movement which appeared strong and vigorous, but collapsed like a house of cards when its mainspring had sprung.

The "revelations" of Ha Bai Sun's life are now coming to light, and the "God of Light" is beginning to look more like the Prince of Darkness. These facts were known before, but those with the information were afraid to offer it for fear of retaliation.

Born Jang Sic Sun in the little village of Linchiang on the Manchurian side of the Yalu River, Sun affiliated himself early with the Korean Communist party. His primary mission under party leader Kim Il Sung, during his consolidation of power, was to infiltrate and control the major religions of the country.

As Joe Rockland continued to read, his interest peaked. He was jolted and flooded with memories as he saw a picture of Sun—an earlier Sun—taken on the outskirts of Mukden in 1951.

Sun's checkered career revealed a service term in the North Korean People's Army during the Korean conflict. This early photo shows a 31-year-old Sun, a major and commandant of the infamous prison camp, K-8, which incarcerated American POWs, near Mukden, Manchuria.

Rockland could still see that sneering face—the pudgy hand, which held the smoking 9mm Tokerev pistol over the executed young American.

The blast which killed Sun and seven of his top aides effectively ended his cult, which was a cult of personality rather than a cult of theology. His followers had invested all of their emotional eggs in one basket—in one man—who was supreme, perfect, and unassailable. He proved to be none of these.

Oddly, with his death, planned no doubt by a rival cult, his followers did not take to the street and run amok. In fact, the opposite has happened. Within the past few days, Sunspots have reported a sense of liberation—of freedom. Many have offered themselves for deprogramming and psychotherapy.

The healthiest sign of Sun's demise was evidenced by a young cultist who, after throwing her orange robe in the garbage can, ran out, bought a wig and a brand-new wardrobe.

Rockland looked at his partner and smiled his appreciation. He looked back at the obituary photo of the sixty-nine-year-old ex-deity . . . Camp Commandant Jang Sic Sun of K-8.

"Surely, vengeance is mine, saith the Lord," murmured Gypsy Joe.

X.

In March the sun rose over the low red-rock bluffs like a bloody meatball. It flooded the shallow valley with a reddish-purplish hue. The skies were usually cloudless this time of year, and the noise of the insects was silenced by 8:30 in the morning.

The sun seemed to rise into the cobalt-blue sky too rapidly in the Chaco during the late summer. By 10:00 the temperature was nudging one hundred degrees; and by noon the heat was unbearable. Even the insects sought shade and siesta by 2:00 in the afternoon.

Olivia Davenport had lost none of her enthusiasm during her first week at Colonia Gardún. She actually believed what the Prophet Barrajas had told this exiled colony of the Garden Children: that the Gran Chaco of Paraguay was the original site of the Garden of Eden. Adam and Eve were not "cast out" of the Garden as the King James Version of the Bible claims. No . . . they stayed in place, but their sin and the sins of their posterity caused the Lord to curse the land and to dry up the sustenance of the earliest family—hence, the Chaco.

A cursed land, but a promised one, too. Just as converts to the Garden Children are born again, the Garden can be born again. An elect youth, who are clean, purified, and committed, can make the Garden blossom as a rose and restore it to its original glory. When the great Tribulation comes upon the earth, the Children would be safe, and the Lord would visit the Garden and bless the Children for their faithfulness.

Olivia and Susan climbed aboard the old Fiat farm truck with ten of their fellow *chivatos*. They hauled their hoes and shovels up after them.

"This isn't my idea of spiritual fulfillment," Susan whispered sullenly. "All we've done for four days is chop weeds out of irrigation ditches. I feel more like a wetback in Texas than a member of a 'new world.' "

"Ssshhh!" warned Olivia. "Keep your thoughts to yourself, Susan. Where's your faith? Did you expect a week of orientation meetings—like back at Bryson? The shepherds know what they're doing. The spiritual programming will begin soon, I'm sure. In the meantime, we've gotta keep the ditches clear so crops can be watered. Like any other kingdom, the Kingdom of God needs food."

By 11:00 the red meatball blazed down on the young Americans, who were working their way down a series of bone-dry irrigation ditches. They were hunched over their hoes, and shaded by wide, floppy straw hats. They chopped at the resistant weeds locked in the caked rust-colored earth. An unfriendly-looking *guapo,* with a swarthy, pockmarked face, rode his chestnut gelding up and down the ditches, checking on the progress of the *chivatos*. He came upon one of the Garden Children stretched out on his back, resting in a patch of dried weeds.

Susan watched warily from the neighboring ditch as the *guapo* dismounted and walked over to the young man.

"Oh-oh!" she warned. "Mark's gonna get his ass in a wringer. I've told him not to take so many breaks."

"Susan!" Olivia scolded. "That kind of gutter language will stunt your spiritual growth. You've got to watch your mouth."

"Oh, shove it, Livvy!" she shot back, watching the *guapo* overseer approach the sleeping cultist.

The *guapo* stood over the young man, hands on his hips and a disgusted sneer on his face. He nudged him roughly with the toe of his boot. "Come, come little *chivato,*" he said with mock gentleness in very broken English. "The development of the Kingdom is behind schedule. Let's get back on the idiot stick and finish the ditch."

The American stirred and yawned, wiping the sweat from his eyes. "Hey, man, we've been at it for four days without a break. It's hot. We're still getting acclimatized to this . . ."

"Silence, pig!" the *guapo* roared, yanking the young man to his feet. "You were brought here to work—to build for a greater Paraguay!" He slapped his face hard with the back of his hand.

"Susan, don't watch," Olivia mumbled. "Mark has it coming. His attitude has been out of harmony ever since we left Parramore Island."

Mark's reaction was normal for a twenty-two-year-old American, who was a product of the new generation of upper-middle-class affluency. He cocked his arm back and slugged the *guapo* in the jaw, sending him sprawling into the ditch. Blood streamed from the corner of his mouth. The hoeing stopped. A dozen *chivatos* stared at the stocky Guaraní overseer as he wiped the back of his hand across his chin and looked unbelievingly at the blood.

Wordlessly the *guapo* hauled himself out of the dusty ditch and onto his horse. Cursing silently in his native tongue, he spun his mount around and galloped at breakneck speed toward Colonia Gardún.

The Hermano Mayor listened silently, fingertips pressed together as he rested his elbows on the ancient carved quebracho wood table. The assaulted *guapo* continued to blurt out his story as the old man bowed his head and pressed his forehead to his fingers.

"Ah! These are the things I do not like to hear. They must be dealt with."

He arose and clapped his hand on the overseer's shoulder. "You did right, my son, by doing nothing. Such breaches of discipline must be dealt with by me. I am only glad that my nephew is away. He tends to overreact to such things."

"What is to be done with the boy, Hermano Mayor?" asked the *guapo*.

"I think that the time has come," said the Prophet of

Paraguay, the gold caps in his ancient teeth showing as he smiled beneficently, "to introduce our newest *chivatos* to the realities of Colonia Gardún. Go out and bring them in from the fields. Assemble them in the plaza by two o'clock.

"What's going on, Susan?" Olivia asked as the old Fiat lurched to a halt on the cobblestone plaza. "We usually work till five and go directly to the barracks."

Susan Rockland jumped down from the tailgate, slapped absently at the red dust on her well-worn jeans, and brushed her blue-black hair from her eyes. She squinted at Olivia in the bright sunlight and answered, "I'll bet it has something to do with Mark slugging the *guapo*. We're probably gonna get the word."

The *chivatos* were herded up to a raised wooden platform adjacent to the white concrete-block building. The platform itself was connected to the top of the stairs by a wooden ramp. The Hermano Mayor stepped onto the ramp and walked to the edge of the platform, flanked by two burly Guaraní bodyguards. They were accompanied by a slight, balding man with wire-rim glasses. The twelve young Americans stood waiting before the platform.

"Welcome, my children, to Colonia Gardún," said the Hermano Mayor in Spanish. The balding man translated in halting English.

"I am Francisco López Estigarribia, the Hermano Mayor, the Big Brother of the Holy Order of the Sacred Gardúna. I am the one responsible for fulfilling your physical and spiritual needs here at the colony, and I am afraid that I have been somewhat neglectful."

The young cultists relaxed after hearing the conciliatory words of the old man.

"I realize," the old man continued in his high nasal Spanish, "that your voyage here has been long and arduous. It is apparent that it has been a strain and that tempers are short."

Olivia put her hand reassuringly on Mark's elbow.

"It'll be all right, Mark. He understands."

Suddenly the tone in the Hermano Mayor's voice became

harsher, catching the onlookers by surprise at the abrupt change.

"But we must have order here at Colonia Gardún, my children. And, above all, we must have obedience. Those who are placed in trust above you have been appointed through divine inspiration."

"That creep that Mark slugged was divinely appointed?" smirked Susan. "What a farce!"

"*Sssshhhhh!*" whispered Olivia. "Whatever happens will be done in love."

"Oh, bullshit!" muttered Susan, glowering at the bald-headed little man as he translated rapidly.

"Colonia Gardún is like a school classroom," the Prophet Estigarribia said with a smile. "One learns the holy order of things here at the colony, which is in the lap of the Almighty."

"More like his armpit," whispered Susan to herself.

"Your first introduction to the divine rule of the Sacred Order," continued the old man, "was printed on the entrance archway—in English for your convenience: The Glory of God is Obedience. Those who disobey must not only repent but suffer retribution; and, like any classroom, the unruly ones," he hissed, "must be spanked."

At the Hermano Mayor's signal, two stocky Guaraní grabbed Mark from behind.

"Hey, hey, what'ya doing?" he yelled. The young American wrenched an arm free, striking one of the Indians on the side of the face. The other Guaraní dealt a blow to Mark from behind, but he continued to struggle. Two male *chivatos*, the young man's friends, rushed to help.

At that moment five shots rang out, their echoes reverberating throughout the shallow valley. The *chivatos* looked up at the platform and then around the small plaza. Indians armed with automatic rifles ringed the young Americans. The blue smoke from the expended rounds wafted from the platform and plaza.

The two Indians half dragged Mark up to the platform and tied him to an upright post. One ripped the shirt off his back.

"I . . . I don't believe this is happening," stammered Olivia, her hand clutching Susan's arm.

"Just watch, Livvy, and shut up!" warned Susan.

"An eye for an eye and a tooth for a tooth!" barked the Hermano Mayor. "So it is here—so it has always been!" He nodded to the *guapo*.

The *guapo* uncoiled a huge black whip and flipped it backward. The crowd gasped as the lash came cracking down on Mark's back, a huge stripe reddening into an ugly welt.

"Ten lashes," the old man said, "and justice will be satisfied."

The screams of the young American filled the plaza with every crack of the black oxhide whip. The numbing impact of the event—the screams, the heat, the muzzles of the automatic rifles pointed at them—settled over the cultists like a death shroud.

After what seemed to be an eternity, the crash of the lash ceased. Mark sagged on the post sobbing. His back was a series of bloody lacerations. A *guapo* poured a bottle of vinegar into a gallon can and threw it on the young cultist's back. He wrenched violently on the wooden post and let out an animal-like cry, an unearthly scream that could be heard by others working in the fields beyond the plaza.

As the guards cut him down and took him inside the infirmary, the Hermano Mayor spoke to the cowed and silent group of Americans, his words still being translated.

"Do not dwell on this incident, my children, but do not forget it. As in the earlier phases of the Kingdom of God, the chaff must be separated from the wheat and it is sometimes a painful process. If the present discipline of Colonia Gardún seems harsh, remember the glories and blessings which await you if you endure to the end."

A man and woman in white medical coats, stethoscopes dangling from their necks, emerged from the building. They walked out onto the platform and stood flanking the old man. Susan squinted her eyes, which darted over the figures on the wooden planks. The two strangers were not Indians—or even Spanish. They were North American or European.

The Hermano Mayor spoke again. "This is Dr. Heinz Schutzler and his colleague, Dr. Hilda Von Ziegazar. They are a very essential part of our staff here at Colonia Gardún.

As part of your processing you will be given a thorough medical examination."

The two doctors observed the blond, Caucasoid, Aryan-like features of the new *chivatos* and were pleased. However, they looked with displeasure at Susan Rockland and her dark, sensual beauty. They whispered to each other in German.

"Come, come to the infirmary, my children," hissed the Hermano Mayor through gold-capped teeth.

The realities of Colonia Gardún were about to begin.

Carlos Von Reinach undid his seat belt and relaxed when the red light went off. Some of the other passengers started to smoke or order drinks from the attractive stewardesses who prowled the aisle. Below, the bright green of the Venezuelan coastline abruptly gave way to the sparkling blue of the Caribbean. The Paraguair DC-7 clawed for altitude.

This was the first time that he could truly relax since the recruits started coming in from the feeder cults in North America several weeks before. As he often did, Von Reinach took a worn, black, leather-covered book out of his briefcase and pored through it. He started to read as one might read scripture. In a sense, it was scripture. It provided many of the sacred myths, and fed many of the fantasies, which justified the existence of Colonia Gardún. Von Reinach's little black book also provided the body of "scripture" which formed the ideological foundation of Colonia Alemán, the S.S. colony started by his father in 1936.

Alfred Rosenberg's *The Myth of the Twentieth Century* may have long been discredited in the Western world, but to the Sacred Order of the Holy Gardúna it was holy writ. If *Mein Kampf* was considered a form of racial Old Testament to the sacred order, the *Myth* was a racial New Testament. Indeed, the beginning of the introduction clarified the thrust of the book:

> The Myth of the Twentieth Century is the myth of blood, which under the sign of the holy Swastika, unchains the racial world revolution. It is the awakening of the race soul which, after long sleep, victoriously ends the race chaos.

The *Myth* was a racial interpretation of history. Its basic assumption was that God created man not as an individual, nor mankind as a whole, but as individual races of men. The individual man has no soul, nor has humanity by itself—only a race has soul; and no two races have the same soul. Therefore, no two races can understand each other; no two can speak the same moral, aesthetic, or intellectual language. One's personality is the combination of physical heredity and the mystical, nonphysical race soul. Crossbreeding breaks up this divine combination of body and spirit, unless the races crossed possess superior, mutually reinforcing qualities.

And that's what Colonia Gardún is all about, pondered Von Reinach as he looked down at the blobs of verdant green in the sparkling blue water: to re-create the combination of the physical purity of the Guaraní and the racial purity of the Aryan. It was the perfect combination for racial survival in the twenty-first century; and the selective breeding program of the Order of the Sacred Garduna would ensure it.

Von Reinach's fantasies for a new racial order were interrupted by the voice of a stewardess:

"Ladies and gentlemen, we are making our final approach. Please fasten your seat belts."

With a grinding hiss, the flaps were lowered as the DC-7 lost altitude—bumping and yawing from the turbulence caused by the lush, green hills of Puerto Rico. Finally the aircraft broke out over the open sea and circled for the final approach. As the plane banked, Von Reinach looked out the window. He was impressed with the brilliant whiteness of San Juan.

"Aha! Señor Davenport. Isn't she a little beauty?"

Courtney Davenport ran his hands over the cropped mane of the little mare and nodded.

"Yes, Señor Caro, she is. What do you want for her?"

"Oho! This one is not for sale. She is reserved for a special customer from Paraguay. He will be here at any time to look her over, as well as some other breeding stock."

A rented Buick sedan drove through the open gate and braked to a stop. Carlos Von Reinach stepped out.

"Señor Estigarribia?" asked Caro, a puzzled frown on his face.

"No." Von Reinach smiled. "I am his nephew. My uncle had urgent business and could not make it, so he sent me to look over the horses."

"I see." The rancher was pleasant. "Señor . . . I did not catch the name?"

"Von Reinach."

"Oho! Señor Von Reinach. This is Señor Courtney Davenport from Tulsa, Oklahoma. He is also an aficionado of Paso Finos."

The two men approached each other with extended hands, sizing each other up. They were about the same age and build. Both were athletic as well as vigorous for their ages—almost mirror images of each other. Von Reinach was the first to speak.

"This is an honor, indeed. Would you be the Señor Davenport of DAVROCK Development?"

"I am indeed, sir," Davenport said.

"Señor Davenport, I am one of your best and most satisfied customers. I am part owner of the Parachaco Development Corporation."

"In Paraguay! Of course, Mr. Von Reinach. Possibility of massive oil reserves in your Chaco region—right?"

Davenport and Von Reinach walked over the carefully manicured lawns of the Caro ranch examining the stock and exchanging views on a variety of subjects, from the bloodlines of Paso Finos to the moral decay of their respective countries.

"Señor Davenport," Von Reinach explained, "my country is one of the few that have attempted to withstand the inroads of communism and the polluting forces of the Antichrist. Because of the stand we have taken on issues sacred to us, we have been ostracized and condemned by much of the world."

Courtney could identify with Von Reinach's philosophy. Here was another man, in another country, attempting to cleanse and purify—to stem the onrushing tidal wave of evil, in the name of the Almighty. It was heartening to know that such men existed.

"Certainly, Mr. Von Reinach, you can't do this alone. There must be like-minded men and women in your country, as there are in mine, to help you in this struggle."

Von Reinach's electric-blue eyes developed their familiar gleam, the gleam of a true believer. "Surely, Señor Davenport," he answered. "There is an ancient order in our country, established outside of the formal structure of the Church, whose purpose is to preserve and protect our traditions. And"—he smiled slyly—"to contribute our little efforts to the building up of the Kingdom of God, in our little corner of the world, at least."

"An order, Mr. Von Reinach?"

"Sí. Of lay men and women. Not too unlike your own Knights of Columbus."

"What is the name of your order?"

"The Holy Order of the Sacred Garduna: the Holy Warriors of Paraguay."

The senator rubbed his chin as he walked past several neighing mares.

"Evidently, Carlos . . . may I call you Carlos?" he asked, slapping a hand on Von Reinach's shoulder.

"Yes. Please do," beamed Von Reinach.

"Evidently you are doing in your country what I am attempting to do in mine: to combat the forces of the evil one; to prepare our people, our civilization, for the future; and to ensure their survival."

The feelings of kinship grew as the two men walked the grounds.

"Mr. Von Reinach, it's been my distinct pleasure," Davenport drawled, "to have had this opportunity to meet you. I feel that we are brother Christians fighting for the same cause. You can count on me for any help you may need for your projects in Paraguay."

Von Reinach smiled, his eyes gleaming, as he shook Courtney's hand with both of his.

• • •

Three thousand miles away, Olivia Davenport completed her physical exam at the infirmary at Colonia Gardún. The German doctor wrote in a neat Germanic script under the category "racial suitability": "Full Caucasoid. Aryan. North European origins. Suitable for breeding."

XI.

The black metal drilling rig, silhouetted against the purple sky of the Chaco, resembled a prehistoric monster. The diesel engines were silent. The only sounds heard were the screeching of millions of insects and the occasional squawk of a wild parrot in the branches of a quebracho tree. Two mobile trailers which served as drill test laboratories squatted next to the derrick, the early evening sun bouncing dull rays off the aluminum panels.

Scott Rasmussen, head geologist and team chief for the DAVROCK exploration expedition in the Chaco, felt the long black cylindrical core samples which were laid out in neat rows on the wooden tables. They represented 2,500 feet of the same material, which was taken from over a 5,000-acre area.

"Fazzio," said the geologist, "this stuff isn't mineral. What in the hell is it?"

"Quebracho," answered the lab technician.

"Quebracho?"

"Right. We took samples from over two hundred test holes, and ran into a solid stratum of quebracho about seven hundred feet below the surface. We've made some seismic soundings, and from this profile"—the lab assistant held up a computer graphic map—"almost the entire Chaco region sits on top of a layer of ancient quebracho trees—layered like a huge sheet of coal."

"Son of a bitch!" the geologist exclaimed. "This could explain why they never found oil here."

"How's that, Scotty?"

"Quebracho wood, Fazzio, is one of the hardest, most dense organic materials in the world. It's only found in this part of Paraguay. Evidently the Chaco was a vast forest of the stuff millions of years ago. Geological upheavals changed that. Now the quebracho forms a substrata layer like a giant sheet some several hundred feet thick. It's almost as hard as granite, but organic. This would confuse any radiation or radar probe. Organic material that hard, and that dense, would probably emit just enough radiation half-life to confuse the sensors."

"Scotty! The lower fifty feet of the core sample has petroleum absorption—look here!" The lab assistant pointed to several core samples at the end of the table. The geologist took a sample and ran a spectrographic analysis on it. A small mobile computer spit out a long sheet of paper with a confusing jumble of numbers on it.

"Fazzio!" the geologist exclaimed. "This is it! What we're looking at . . ." He waved the findings in front of his assistant. "This is proof that the Chaco has commercially possible fields. This quebracho layer has hidden it! Hell, no wonder they couldn't find oil here back in the 1930s; they didn't have the drills that could punch through that stuff. All of these lower core samples are saturated with petroleum deposits—in other words, old buddy, we're floating on an ocean of oil . . . right here in the Chaco."

The assistant lab technician leaned back in his chair and laughed; "OPEC, your ass has *had* it!"

The old farmhouse in the northern Arkansas Ozarks looked like hundreds of others that dotted the region: a rambling structure of old, weathered clapboard, half hidden in a grove of tall pines and scattered maples. A gravel road led up to it. Inside, however, the decor reflected the purpose and intent of the building. Small rooms—soundproof cubicles, actually—had been constructed in an intensive remodeling effort. Some of the cubicles were lined with stuffed canvas pads. The walls of the padded cells were constructed of reinforced steel studs, and the steel doors of each room contained observation shutters.

Andrea watched Nick lift a heavy piece of paneling and place it over the Sheetrock wall. She wiped small beads of perspiration off her forehead and slapped some white gypsum from her blue jeans. She observed the muscles bulging in interesting little ripples under Nick's T-shirt as he pounded the nails securing the paneling. Her deep green eyes probed over other parts of his body, creating stirrings which she fought to keep under control. Nick turned to her abruptly. Quickly she averted her eyes.

"Andi, the last sheet's up. We can move in the equipment now."

"Oh . . . oh, fine, Nick. The rest of the stuff is out in the van."

An hour later, the sensitive bioelectronic equipment was installed. A small stainless-steel refrigerator was plugged in and the room took on the appearance of a hospital laboratory.

"Well," Andrea said wearily, plopping down in one of the beanbag chairs in the living room, "this place isn't exactly the Sverdlosk Institute, but it's close enough for our purposes."

"What about Units One and Three?"

"The one in Virginia is completed and the one in Nevada is almost done. Do you know anything about the Nevada unit, Nick?" asked Andrea, her eyes twinkling mischievously.

"No."

"It used to be a fly-in brothel."

"A whorehouse?" he asked incredulously.

They laughed and leaned back on the beanbags, knees touching.

"You know, Nick, this is the first time we've been alone—*really* alone like this."

He looked deeply into her eyes, eyes which were alive with expectation. This was his cue, a cue that he had been waiting for since he started working for her as a graduate intern at the University of British Columbia.

"Yes, it is, Andi, and we shouldn't let an opportunity like this escape us."

He leaned over, put his hands on her waist, and kissed her

fully on the lips. Her lips were warm, eager, and full of promise. Her hands gripped his back—massaging, exploring. Their breathing became shorter, more labored, as they pressed their bodies together closer, making slight pelvic movements.

A half an hour later they fell asleep in naked exhaustion in each other's arms, still curled up in the vinyl beanbag chairs.

Outside, the pale Arkansas sun played its waning rays over the old farmhouse which had become, under Andrea Macranskia's direction, a complete deprogramming center . . . the deprogramming center for Countercult Number Two.

"Eli! Eli! Over here!" whispered the dark-clad figure.

Eli Shem Revvim padded over to the edge of the forest clearing. His dark eyes probed the open space below. There it was—in a small valley was the object of the mission: a cluster of shacks and tents surrounding a weather-beaten, old mansion whose faded elegance had seen better days.

He raised his hand and motioned quickly in a sweeping gesture. Ten men dressed in black baggy pants, navy-blue turtleneck sweaters, and black watch caps stole up to Eli. He pointed to the collection of buildings below. Grease-blackened faces scrutinized the target, drinking in the details.

The wind shifted, and the stench from the commune below wafted into the commandos. "Holy shit!" gasped one of the squad.

Eli laughed. "That's *exactly* what it is, my friend, holy shit. The folks down there feel that disposing of human waste is too mundane an activity for them, so they dump it in an open pit along with the garbage. They use it to fertilize their cash crop, and they even bless the fertilizer in a ritual before they distribute it in the fields."

The commandos of Countercult Number One knew their target by heart. A defector from the Church of the Son of the Morning gave them complete details of the commune. The cult, a breakaway group from the original Satanic Temple of Los Angeles, had established itself in Mendocino County, a hundred miles north of San Francisco, in 1986.

The Church of the Son of the Morning was more than a commune devoted to the worship of Satan; it was an economic unit, a plantation devoted to the cultivation and processing of Humboldt Gold—the finest grade of marijuana grown in the United States. Since the complete legalization of marijuana, the annual income of the commune was in the millions. It changed the entire economy of the region. Small farmers, even backyard gardeners, grew Humboldt Gold as a cash crop, and sold their leaves at attractive prices to the cult. The large processing center in the mansion converted the raw material into commercial-grade cigarettes to be sold on the open market. Near the mansion, several warehouses bulged with the raw leaves of the plants, or housed crated cartons of packaged cigarettes. The cult members worked without pay and often without food. Their payment was "spiritual" food—and all of the marijuana they could smoke.

"Take out the pictures and study them once more."

"Again, Eli?" wailed a commando.

"Yes, again, dammit! Burn their faces into your minds. I don't want anybody wasting these people. They've been reserved for deprogramming. Gas 'em and get 'em out of there—back to the vans."

The black-clad commandos passed around a series of photographs of five young people—three girls and two boys in their late teens. From the latest intelligence they had, they were somewhere beyond the maze of filth—in the cluster of huts that surrounded the mansion below them.

"Take care of the dogs first," whispered Eli.

A commando tied a piece of cyanide-laced meat to the front of an arrow and fit it to his bow. With a muffled twang, the arrow arched into the air and thudded into a large pen located some distance from the buildings. Several more arrows, meat dangling from their tips, followed closely. Soon the pen was filled with snarling Doberman pinschers who fought for the morsels of poisoned meat. The snarling was followed by the sounds of whining and whimpering as the dogs convulsed on the ground from the effects of the poison.

Eli Revvim's small squad stalked to the edge of the huts, where the stench from the open pit almost overpowered them. They reached inside of their backpacks and removed gas masks and small canisters of incapacitating gas. After attaching long flexible hoses to the containers, the commandos fanned out in pairs. A commando in each pair slipped the narrow-hosed nozzle through a convenient opening in the huts and pressed a button on the canister. Soon several huts were filled with gas, rendering the inhabitants completely unconscious. The process was repeated until all of the huts were neutralized.

The gas-masked figures slipped in, shining their flashlights on the faces of the sleeping cultists, studying them, looking for their quarry. Four bodies were laid out on the edge of the clearing.

"Who is missing?" asked Eli, clearly agitated.

"The Benson girl," replied a squad member.

"Damn! She's more important than all of the others combined," cursed Eli.

"Why?" asked a commando.

"Her father is the secretary of state, Roger Benson. If we can extricate her and get her head screwed on straight . . . oh, hell! She must be inside the mansion. We'll have to do it the hard way. All right, check your weapons."

The still night air was interrupted by the clicking of bolts and the attaching of silencers as the Uzi submachine guns were made ready. Each commando checked four small packages in his pack—two of plastic explosive and two incendiary devices. Each squad member had committed to memory where the charges would be placed.

"The northwest suite on the second story is where the head cheeses live. Intelligence has it that the cult is having a western regional meeting, and the third floor is acting as a dormitory where they're staying. Okay, got it? Find the Benson girl—first priority. Waste the rest."

Within minutes, Eli's men were positioned near the several entrances to the old mansion. Inside on the first floor they could see the jumble of machines which were used to process the commune's cash crop. Doors and windows were jimmied open and blackened figures padded in, their thick-soled tennis shoes muffling their movements. Timed charges were placed in strategic locations among the machines. Outside, a two-man team laced the warehouses with their destructive charges.

Inside the building, two staircases led to the second floor. Eli's men cautiously mounted the stairs, testing them for creaks. They were solid.

The second story was divided into cubicles which were used for offices and sleeping quarters for the Church's leadership. An old, school Regulator clock chimed 2:00 A.M. From a lighted room down the hall, Eli's men could hear crude language and raucous laughter.

"Aaron . . . Saul . . . check it out," whispered Eli. The two squad members crept down the corridor, weapons on fire and ready. The door was slightly ajar. Inside, five scarlet-robed men, shaved bald with the exception of a tuft of hair sticking out from the crown of each head, were playing some sort of game with dice. Huddled in a corner, her hair matted, face bruised, and her eyes hot blue embers of fear, was a teenage girl in a near-fetal position, sucking her thumb. Nearby was a rumpled bunk bed, the sheets spotted with blood.

"Look closely," whispered Aaron. "It's the Benson girl. Looks like she's in a catatonic trance."

"She should be after those animals got through with her," the other hissed through clenched teeth as he noticed her wretched nakedness. "Let's waste 'em."

The door flew open, and before the scarlet-robed cultists could comprehend what was happening, the silent Uzis were spitting death into their bodies. As they crumpled in bloody heaps, Saul rushed to the girl and clamped a rubber cup, which was attached to a gas canister, over her mouth and nose.

"Saul, take her out! I'll join the rest."

Methodically, two-man teams stalked into each cubicle. In a matter of minutes, dark red pools of blood were seeping under the doors, staining the hallway carpeting. The commandos entered the third-story dormitory from the direction of the two staircases. The large upper room was almost wall-to-wall with sleeping cultists—over a hundred of them.

"By Moses' beard! I think the leadership of the whole bloody cult is here," whispered Saul.

"So much the better, but I didn't expect *this*." Eli pressed a small button on his two-way transceiver. He whispered into the small mike. "Plan B."

Three commandos, gas masks in place, stole among the red-robed bodies. They sprayed a deadly vapor of Enthrop Nine over the sleeping cultists, who convulsed slightly, some vomiting, and shriveled into a death posture.

Their mission accomplished, Eli's Countercult One hauled the five young cultists to the edge of the forest. A hundred yards into the thick pines, two vans roared into life. The commandos carried their human cargo into the trees and hauled them aboard the vehicles. Twenty minutes later, the vans were driven into the belly of a DAVROCK C-130 on an abandoned airstrip. In the distance, beyond the forested ridges of the Mendocino Mountains, a series of explosions rocked the stillness. As the C-130 fought for altitude, ten blackened faces peered out the aircraft window and watched the flames and explosions level and destroy that which was once the resources and personnel of the Church of the Son of the Morning.

"My . . . my name is . . . is . . . is . . . Surbatai . . . Sur . . . ba . . . tai. I am one of Satan's slaves . . . one . . . one of his favorites. I . . . am . . . Surbatai . . . I have no other desire but . . . but to serve Him."

To Elaine Kearney, the pattern was familiar. She bit her lower lip as she felt the mixture of fear and anger churning her stomach. The young blonde stretched out on the hard bunk couldn't have been more than nineteen, Elaine's sister's age when she was deprogrammed.

"How's the Benson girl doing?" asked Bob Talbot, Elaine's assistant at the Countercult One Deprogramming Center.

"She's hanging on to her identity in the cult for dear life," she said thoughtfully. "Right now, it's her only security. We've got to stabilize her physical condition before we can get her involved in therapy. Take a look at her, Bob."

The center director pulled the sheet down to the girl's feet, revealing an emaciated, pasty-white body, which was covered with bruises and small festering sores.

"Good Lord! What in the hell did they do to her?"

"A combination of things over a five-month period: gang rape; humiliation; overwork in the processing plant, no doubt. It was a series of constant abuses to strip her of her identity as Patricia Benson and create Surbatai, an automaton, a slave of the Son of the Morning."

"Satan?"

"That's one of his names. In the Bible, Genesis, I believe, he was referred to as one of the most brilliant of God's creations—the Son of the Morning. He's the same Lucifer who took a third of the host of heaven with him in an act of rebellion against their Father, God." Talbot scratched his head and added, "Hell, parents complain about a few of their kids going astray. God lost a third of His."

Outside in the chill desert air, a coyote howled, emphasizing the loneliness and isolation of the center in the Nevada wilds. It had been exactly three days since the C-130 Hercules landed on the dirt runway and unloaded its unconscious human cargo. The young cultists were barely secured inside the center before the aircraft roared away toward Westwind One.

Elaine adjusted the butterfly valve on the plastic hose between the bottle of sodium pentothal and the needle inserted into Patricia Benson's arm. "I'm going to put her out for a few hours. The best therapy for her right now is lots of sleep. Her body has to mend before we can work on her mind—what's left of it anyway."

As an IV dripped a fluid of high-potency vitamins and other nutrients into the other arm, healing salves and medications were smeared over the girl's open, festering sores.

"Give her three or four days. She'll be ready by then."

"And the others?"

They walked into a larger cubicle. Four bodies were stretched out on identical bunks. Life-enhancing nutrients and sodium pentothal dripped into their veins.

"The same—three or four days."

"Are you going to conduct the deprogramming, Elaine?" asked Talbot.

"No. Dr. Macranskia is. In fact, she's bringing some other

members of the deprogramming staff from Two and Three for observation and training. The Benson girl is going to be our training aid—so to speak."

Inside the smaller cubicle, Patricia Benson—Surbatai—ceased mumbling and twitching, and fell into a deep, numbing sleep.

XII.

"In one month's time . . . in just *one* month!" fumed Martin Weishaupt as he waved a stack of papers in front of his staff.

"Let me read to you: 'In San Francisco . . . the Lavender Family has been decimated by attacks on its people during the airport massacre . . . and selected assassinations later on throughout the city and elsewhere.' "

Weishaupt continued reading aloud, the wrinkles above his thick Coke-bottle lenses to the crown of his bald head reddening in frustration and anger.

"The assassination of Ha Bai Sun was a complete disaster for our department! Sun was one of *ours*! He cannot be replaced. He had been groomed for this specific job for years. The Sun movement in the West is all but dead. It's disintegrating!"

Outside, the chill March wind whistled through the array of antennas on top of the grimy gray buildings of number 22 Normanneustrasse in East Berlin, headquarters for the Hauptverwaltung Aufklärung (HVA), East Germany's junior partner of the Soviet KGB intelligence apparatus.

"I could go on for another hour," wheezed Weishaupt. "The Church of the Son of the Morning was attacked—*attacked*, mind you—by a group of armed men! Five of the members were removed. One of them was the daughter of the American secretary of state. She would have been useful to us later on."

"Perhaps these attacks are the results of rival cults, Herr Doktor?" asked a staff member.

Weishaupt smiled. "Aha! My dear, stupid Günter, that is what they would *like* for us to believe and have the other cults to believe. The other cults have become paranoid and are curtailing their activities. They are isolating their key personnel and losing converts through inactivity. Fear pervades them. Their effectiveness in the West is diminishing. Their advocates are not quite so bold about defending them. No, my friends, there is a central organized intelligence orchestrating these attacks. The modus operandi used is extremely sophisticated and expert."

"The CIA?" offered Emil Günter with a cringing half smile.

"No, you idiot! We give the CIA too much credit. Everything which thwarts us we blame on the CIA. The CIA has been effectively declawed and defanged by the Roberts Committee of the American Senate. No! Not CIA."

"Who, then?" whined a cowed Günter.

Ignoring his aide, Weishaupt whipped a report of several pages, which was enclosed in a red plastic binder. "Let me enlighten all of you as to some of the remarkable events which have happened within the past few months. As you know, the major antiterrorist forces of the nations of the West have been either disbanded or severely curtailed. The personnel released from these organizations have been closely watched and monitored by the KGB."

He continued, his voice rising with a quiver. "We have lost track of ninety-three members of these organizations—ninety-three men, worldwide, from America, South Africa, Israel, and West Germany to name a few places."

"And you believe that these people are being utilized against the cults, Herr Doktor?" asked a staff member.

"If they are, and the CIA is not involved . . . then who?" asked another.

Weishaupt ignored them and continued. "My former assistant, my protégé at the Sverdlosk Institute, is partly responsible," he hissed, his eyes smoldering. "She is in league with forces in the private sector in the United States. With forces which account to no one except Courtney Davenport."

"Courtney Davenport? Who . . . who is he?" asked Günter timidly, fearfully.

"Courtney Davenport, my dear little Emil, of the DAV-ROCK Development Corporation, Davenport-Rockland University, and Christian schools and missions worldwide. Also known as Senator Davenport, chairman of the Senate Subcommittee on Cults and Alternative Societies. Courtney Davenport! A born-again Christian businessman and a leading spokesman against cults and communists. That's what we're all about, eh, Günter?"

His little aide smiled an embarrassed smile.

"Davenport was last seen by my agents in Tulsa, where he has his world headquarters. He was seen with my former intern, Dr. Andrea Macranskia, and a Special Air Service captain, a Nicholas Portumo. Add it up, gentlemen: a born-again multimillionaire, a brilliant psychological deprogrammer, and an effective—a *deadly* effective—counterterrorist. That is a potent combination. We must find a way to neutralize their efforts, or 'Uncle' in Moscow will curtail our independence."

"Herr Doktor . . ." Günter began, almost cringing. "Some information I have. . . . The name Davenport is familiar. I . . . I would . . ."

"Speak up, man!" demanded Weishaupt.

"A cult . . . the Garden Children is in my jurisdictional area. Two new members are Olivia Davenport and Susan Rockland from Tulsa. They are the daughters of Courtney Davenport and his partner, Joseph Rockland, but I had no idea that Senator Davenport was involved in actions against the cults."

"You *know* of this Davenport? You idiot!" Weishaupt smacked his assistant across the top of his head with his glove. "Why didn't you say something?"

"The names, Herr Doktor, didn't match up until now. I . . . I didn't think."

"Didn't think! Didn't think! You are the only people in a People's Republic who are supposed to think! An intelligence organization is supposed to think, you imbecile!"

Günter picked up the director's glove and hesitantly handed it back. Weishaupt snatched it out of his hand.

"All right! What are you all staring at!" he barked as he tried to smooth the wrinkles out of his reddened forehead. "Our duty is clear. Find the Davenport and Rockland girls—that is our first priority. Forget all other projects. When we find them, Senator Davenport's countercult fangs will be effectively removed."

"Hey, Captain Caro! Over here!"

Caro looked around the large, ornate room of the Club Circular Militar. He broke into a lopsided grin as he recognized Steve Lancaster, the commercial attaché to Paraguay. He weaved his way through the throngs of splendidly uniformed Paraguayan officers to Lancaster's table by the huge curved window. "Hello, Steve. It's great seeing you. What's it been—three months?" He shook his hand.

"At least, Angel. Oh, this is Scott Rasmussen, geologist. He's into oil."

Caro sized up the big freckled American sitting across from him.

"Oil?" He shook the geologist's hand. "Here in Paraguay?"

"Oil exploration, Captain—out in the Chaco region."

"Oho! My home territory. I'm out at Mariscal Estigarribia. I'm in town on a weekend pass."

"Mariscal Estigarribia . . . hmmm. Yes, that's south of me," exclaimed the geologist. "I'm between you and a place called Colonia Gardún."

Caro sat up with a small jerk. "Colonia Gardún, Mr. Rasmussen? Have you ever been there?"

"No, but the Parachaco Corporation has its support and maintenance facilities there. Our drilling rigs are partly assembled at Colonia Gardún and trucked out to our drilling sites."

"Have . . . have any of your men been there . . . to pick up supplies or take equipment in for maintenance?"

Rasmussen cocked an eye and gave the captain a quizzical look. "You seem to have an inordinate interest in Colonia Gardún, Caro. Why?"

"A . . . a friend of mine is up there, and I've had a hard time . . . no, an *impossible* time, getting to see her. The colony is off limits."

The geologist's eyes probed into Caro's. "Captain, now that you've mentioned it, some of my men have complained about the same thing. They've taken equipment to the colony for repair or modification and they're stopped by armed guards at a roadblock about a half mile from the colony. They call for a driver and he takes the equipment in. My men either have to wait or come back and get the equipment when they get the word. It's a logistical nightmare. It's almost like the Parachaco people have something to hide."

Caro looked around the room. Their table was fairly isolated from the crowd of chattering Paraguayan military men. He spoke in a low voice—almost a whisper. "Colonia Gardun is the site of a religious cult, the Sacred Order of the Holy Garduna. Most of the members are young Americans brought in by submarine from the East Coast of the United States."

Lancaster looked around furtively and grabbed Caro's arm. "Look, Caro, I don't know how much you know about the Garduna, but it's Paraguay's business. Strictly an internal affair. Just keep what you know to yourself. We can't afford to offend *anybody* in this country, especially now."

"Now?" asked Caro.

"Yes, now!" emphasized Rasmussen. The big geologist leaned forward, his nose almost touching the captain's. "Right now, Caro, Paraguay—especially that wretched piece of real estate west of here—is going to be the most important hunk of real estate in the world."

"The Chaco?" Caro replied incredulously.

Rasmussen scanned the room. His eyes locked back into Caro's. "The Chaco, my good captain, is literally floating on an ocean of oil. It can be the West's declaration of independence from OPEC."

"Not to mention the economic warfare of the Soviet Union," added Lancaster. "That's why we're telling you this. The Sacred Order of the Holy Garduna is *the* power in the Chaco. Its roots and influence extend into every unit of government in this country—and perhaps into some circles in Argentina and Uruguay."

"Then you know about this cult, Steve?" asked Caro.

"Just that it's a power to be reckoned with, and that it's anticommunist. That's important to State."

Caro was growing annoyed at the evasive attitude of the two Americans. "There are two young women out there . . . one of whom wants out. Their fathers are very important people in Tulsa, Oklahoma. One's a well-known evangelist."

A look of despair spread over Rasmussen's freckled face. He hung his head and muttered, "Oh, shit!"

Lancaster's face turned white as the blood drained from it. "Who . . . what are . . . are the girls' names?" he stammered.

"Susan Rockland and Olivia Davenport. The Rockland girl gave me the whole story when their group stayed overnight at Mariscal Estigarribia."

"And they're at Colonia Gardún now—as members of the Holy Garduna?" asked the geologist, his voice quivering.

"Caro, have you told anybody else about this?" Lancaster asked.

"Just you two. I sent letters to the Reverend Rockland, but never received a reply."

The waiter arrived with the bill. The geologist picked up the tab and Lancaster grabbed Caro's elbow. "Angel, my car's out in the lot. Let's drive around Asunción. We've got a helluva lot to discuss."

An hour later, Lancaster nosed the embassy staff car into an isolated little park overlooking the muddy Pilcomayo River.

"This is totally unreal!" exclaimed Caro. "The men bankrolling oil exploration in the Chaco are Courtney Davenport and Joseph Rockland? They own the DAVROCK Development Corporation?"

"And much more," added Rasmussen.

"The ironic twist, Captain, is that *they* are in the forefront in fighting the influence of religious cults—all the way from the Senate level to religious revivals. The influence and power of these guys is enormous."

Steve Lancaster's expression became distant. He stared out

the windshield at the muddy water. "My son, Paul, attended Davenport-Rockland University after his discharge from the Marines. He was really messed up after his unit fought to keep the Straits of Hormuz open in 1987. He received multiple wounds—the whole bit. Anyway, he became 'born again' and now works for Davenport as an administrative assistant. He would do anything for the old boy, or his partner."

"Anything?" asked Rasmussen.

"Anything, Scotty. And he can justify with scripture, chapter and verse. He's also got a thing for one of the girls."

"Which one?" asked Caro, clearly concerned.

"Olivia—Davenport's daughter."

The Puerto Rican let out a small sigh of relief.

Steve laughed. "Then the Rockland girl is the one you've got the hots for, eh, Angel?"

The geologist interrupted. "Gents, we've got one helluva problem here, and the three of us have got to keep on top of it. The Chaco's full of oil—our country needs it—and the Holy Garduna controls it. If Courtney Davenport ever finds out that his daughter and Rockland's are involved in a cult down here, he'll come roaring down to Paraguay and tear this damned country up. I know him. When it comes to religious cults, he's totally irrational and self-righteous. When he feels that God is on his side, he's capable of doing anything."

"And that could mean good-bye Chaco oil and suck up to OPEC again," sighed Lancaster.

"I appreciate all of this information, guys," said Caro, "and I'll keep quiet about this. But I'm more determined than ever to get into Colonia Gardún, find Susan Rockland, and get her the hell out of there before the shit hits the fan."

A gentle rain and refreshing breeze hit Colonia Gardún at the same time, sending the small dried leaves of the jacaranda trees scurrying in brittle, little whisps down the cobblestone streets. Olivia Davenport ran to the shuttered window of the barrackslike building and flung them open. "Oh, look, Susan. Look. It's raining!" she said excitedly, holding her hands out the window and letting the water run down her arms, onto her blouse.

"Let me see," said Susan as she crowded into the window opening. She held out one hand.

"Oh, that feels good, Livvy. We haven't seen rain like this since we left Virginia. I wonder if this is the beginning of the rainy season."

Suddenly the speaker on the wall started to squeal.

"Damn, there goes that bitch-box again!" muttered Susan as she returned to her bunk bed and flopped dejectedly on the straw mattress.

"Attention! Attention! The following *chivatos* will report to the administration building in five minutes."

The names of seven female cultists, Olivia's among them, were read over the public address system.

They looked at each other, frightened expressions on their faces.

"Susan . . . I . . . I didn't think I'd be called so soon." Tears welled in Olivia's big blue eyes.

"Susan, I don't want to leave you. The others they called haven't come back. I . . . I don't want to go. I don't know what's going to happen to me. You know what we've heard."

Susan fought to keep her emotions from showing. "Yeah, I know, Livvy. This place is one big rumor mill. But selective breeding is hard to swallow, and this crap about the Holy Garduna trying to create a master race to populate the Chaco . . . it sounds too far out, even for old Estigarribia."

But there were gnawing doubts. The new *chivatos* who worked the cucumber fields near the eastern edge of the colony reported strange tales told to them by colony members who had been there longer—stories of assigned mates from the American cult members and, even more frightening, from among the contingent of Guaraní Indian men who lived in the colony.

Susan recalled, with a slight shudder, the cluster of buildings shaped like a swastika. She had since learned that Colonia Gardún had been started by the S.S. of the Third Reich and had been known as Colonia Alemán, the German Colony, of the Third Reich. She could remember enough of her history to know that selective breeding was part of Nazi ideology.

The seven *chivatos* were herded into a large, tastefully decorated room in the adobe administration building. A Guaraní aide to the Hermano Mayor motioned for them to be seated.

They sat and waited silently. The ancient clock on the paneled wall ticked away the anxious minutes. Olivia twisted and untwisted her scarf until it was a mass of knots and wrinkles.

The door opened and a short, slightly paunchy man in his early thirties stepped quietly into the room unnoticed. His black liquid eyes darted from one person to another, locking on the familiar forms of the female cultists. His brown friar's robe made a swishing sound—a sound which every *chivato* in the room had heard before.

Within seconds, the room was alive with the squeals of laughter and delight as the cult members clustered around the brown-robed man with the friar's haircut.

He put his outstretched arms around as many of the *chivatos* as he could embrace, his fingertips touching Olivia's shoulder, sending shudders of well-being throughout her body.

"My children, my children. It is so wonderful to see you again!" he cooed. He smiled as the attractive young women nudged in closer, eager for a touch of his fingers.

Julio Barrajas, the founder and prophet of the Garden Children, absorbed the warmth from the press of young female bodies as he joyfully anticipated his next assignment.

The Mercedes minibus sped northwest toward the undulating foothills of the Andes, where they intruded into the Bolivian-Paraguayan frontier.

Olivia was at peace with herself and her assigned role to further the kingdom. The Prophet Barrajas had explained it so beautifully—putting everything in the right perspective and allaying her fears. Her body was to be a vehicle—a transmission belt—a way station for the spirit children who would become flesh and inherit the Chaco and make it blossom into a garden.

The Lord's anointed knew what they were doing. Why did she even question the plan? They would, through divine inspiration, find the right mate for her, be he Caucasian or Guaraní. It really didn't matter. The important thing was to create the genetic and racial combination which would generate a soul noble enough to convert the barren Chaco into a second Eden.

The countryside became more scenic, the barren dryness giving way to lush ferns and numerous tall trees, palms among them. Spider monkeys chattered in the treetops, and multicolored parrots and hummingbirds darted among wild orchids.

Julio Barrajas sat in the rear seat, smiling to himself, as he observed the *chivatos* chattering excitedly as they marveled at the changing scenery. His dark eyes caressed the faces of two—an auburn-haired girl in her late teens and a brown-eyed blonde from California. His loins stirred slightly as he remembered the previous night when he sent for them in two-hour intervals. How willing they were to surrender themselves to divine penetration. Surely, the role of prophet of the Garden Children has its rewards.

His eyes ranged over the rest. Whom will he choose tonight? Who will be chosen from among these unplucked blossoms from the garden of the Almighty? His thoughts continued. It was his duty—his right—to taste the fruit of every flower.

As Olivia looked out the window, Julio Barrajas studied her profile: well-formed lips, slightly tilted nose, a slight thrust to her chin. She stood up and reached for some fruit in a straw basket in the storage rack above her seat. Her stretching revealed small but well-formed breasts which looked like hard rubber balls under her blouse. Her jeans revealed a tight, rounded bottom and well-shaped thighs.

As Olivia sat down, she glanced toward the back of the bus and caught Barrajas studying her. She smiled coyly, suggestively, and turned to continue looking out the window.

The minibus rounded a corner abruptly, sending a shower of gravel into the fern-shrouded shoulders of the road, and entered a wide, open area surrounded by vegetation thick enough to be called a jungle. A cluster of buildings was in the middle, and small cottagelike huts radiated in a circular pattern from the large center building. Beyond the huts to the north, and almost against a low hill, was another large building—long and low, with an aluminum smokestack rising from the center. Surrounding the entire complex was a chain link fence, a triple strand of barbed wire on top, which jutted inward. Unseen, but present, were remote electronic sensors, and guard dogs accompanied by armed Guaraní guards.

The bus stopped at the fence gate. Two men in camouflage military fatigues stepped on board. One was a Guaraní, and the other had the unlikely combination of swarthy, pockmarked skin and blond hair. Julio Barrajas ambled forward, notebook in hand, and conversed with the blond in rapid-fire Spanish. The blond glanced back into the bus, gave a little smirk, and handed some documents to the prophet of the Garden Children.

Waved on, the bus started up and inched forward, passing under the black wrought-iron archway over the fence's gate. The letters on the archway, hammered artfully in English in neat Germanic block lettering, spelled out the mission of the complex Olivia Davenport was entering. The same words were coined by Heinrich Himmler, chief of the Nazi S.S., some fifty years before, to describe the selective breeding process of the Third Reich: STRENGTH THROUGH JOY!

"Courtney, that's it! You're pushing me too far . . . too far! I can't go along with this. We're violating our trust with the government."

Joe Rockland paced the room of Courtney Davenport's huge, richly paneled office on the twelfth floor of the DAVROCK Building. He turned on his heel and pointed a finger at Davenport, who slumped in his leather swivel chair and stared at the window overlooking Tulsa. "Isn't it enough that we're killing people in this country . . . and now . . ."

"I'm not so sure we can classify them as people, Joseph," Davenport interrupted.

"Good Lord! Has it come to this, Courtney? Have we become so callous, so self-righteous, that we are dehumanizing our victims? They may be the agents of Satan but they're still people."

Davenport rubbed his chin nervously and stared out the window. Rockland continued to fume. He waved a piece of paper in front of Courtney's face. "How can you possibly justify this, Courtney? This shipping inventory lists enough armaments to equip a small army. Since when have we become merchants of death?"

Davenport stood up and banged his massive fist on the desk, sending a flurry of papers to the floor. "Since I learned that there are other Christian warriors in other countries fighting the same battles we are, dammit!"

"And just what are they fighting down there in Paraguay? Why would this—this Carlos Von Reinach need sixteen Saladin armored cars; twenty antitank rocket launchers, mounted on jeeps; an assortment of several hundred machine guns; and automatic rifles and hundreds of thousands of rounds of ammunition. Is this Von Reinach fighting cults or planning World War III?"

Courtney Davenport turned, his face and neck reddened.

"I learned that this is the second shipment, Courtney. Our flights to the Parachaco Development project have increased by one third. Don't you think that the State Department is going to suspect something?"

"The State Department be damned!" muttered Davenport.

"Now you've become a complete law unto yourself. That's dangerous . . . very dangerous, my friend."

"And why not, Joseph? There's no law worth a *damn* in this country anymore. I follow the laws of the Almighty."

"The Gospel as revealed by Courtney Davenport. That's the first step to apostasy."

"I won't stand here and be called an apostate!" thundered Davenport.

Rockland's tone became softer. "Courtney . . . the government has allowed us to fly our aircraft directly into Paraguay without clearing customs or accounting for our cargo. This is a sacred trust. By sending weapons to some—some Holy Order of Warriors which we know nothing about . . ."

"The Sacred Order of the Holy Garduna is a group of

dedicated Christians, consecrated to the task of purifying their country. If Señor Von Reinach tells me that he needs weapons to do the job, then I believe him. He's my brother in this struggle."

Abruptly, Davenport turned on his heel and left the office with a set look on his face.

Joseph Rockland reached for the buzzer on Courtney's desk and pressed it three times. Five minutes later, Paul Lancaster walked in.

The Pan American 747 rolled down runway number seven of Houston's International Airport and slid into the night sky. After the aircraft gained cruising altitude, Paul opened the envelope that Joseph Rockland had given him earlier that afternoon with his airline ticket to Asunción.

Paul,

When you get to Paraguay, find out all you can about a religious organization which calls itself the Holy Order of the Sacred Garduna . . . or perhaps it's the other way around—the Holy Garduna. They also label themselves as the Sacred Warriors of Paraguay.

I'm particularly interested in one of its leaders . . . a Carlos Von Reinach. Be discreet. Tell nobody about this, especially Mr. Davenport. Report directly to me when you get back.

May God be with you.

XIII.

The rain-washed sweetness of the Nevada desert filled the nostrils of the panting group of young people as they jogged along the dirt road. The early May sun was beginning to rise over the low purple mountains to the east, and shafts of light probed the sage-covered valley floor at oblique angles through the scattered clouds.

"C'mon, step it up! We've only got a mile to go," shouted Andrea Macranskia as she led the group. Her sweat-stained jogging suit clung in dark patches to her body.

A tanned, clear-eyed blonde broke from the pack and loped alongside of Andrea. "I'll race you the last half mile," she beamed, looking at the Hungarian with worshiping eyes.

"You're on, Patty!" she replied.

They raced along the hard, damp surface, their rubber-soled jogging shoes slapping rhythmically on the packed dirt. Andrea restrained herself, pacing her efforts. She panted dramatically as Patricia Benson pulled ahead and left her behind.

Ahead—in front of the honeysuckle-covered porch of the one-story rambling structure near the end of the dirt airstrip—Nick Portumo stood, stopwatch in hand.

"Come on, Patty! Pour it on. She's an old lady . . . over the hill. You can beat her!"

Andrea suppressed an urge to surge ahead, but she continued

to pace herself, letting the puffing, sweat-stained young blonde pound ahead until she fell exuberantly into Nick's arms.

"Thirty-seven seconds from the end of the airstrip. That's great, Patty! How do you feel?" asked Nick.

"Like making love!" She threw her arms around Nick's neck and kissed him on the cheek.

Andrea laughed. "Well, *well*, Miss Benson . . . you *are* making progress. All of your natural appetites are returning."

"With gusto, Andrea!" she replied with a chuckle as she walked inside the former brothel. Her arms encircled the waists of the Hungarian psychologist and the SAS captain.

An hour later, showered and refreshed, the group of ex-cult members sat down in the large kitchen and wolfed down gigantic quantities of pancakes, eggs, and sausages. The food was washed down with quarts of milk and orange juice.

Nick and Andrea stood in the kitchen doorway and watched the eating, chattering youngsters. Nick slipped his arm around her waist, kissed her on the ear, and whispered:

"Six weeks ago, I wouldn't have given a dime for the whole lot of them. You've done a remarkable job, Andi. These kids are ready to face the world again."

"Maybe," she said thoughtfully. "Except for the Benson girl . . ."

"Patty! She's made the most dramatic progress of all. She's the picture of health, and her performance this morning . . ."

"Physically, yes, Nick. We've brought her back from the land of the nearly dead to the land of the living. But she's simply transferred her dependency from the Church of the Son of the Morning to me."

"Yeah, I've seen how she looks at you. Almost as an object of worship. Like a personal savior."

In the past six weeks since the first group had arrived at the deprogramming center at Countercult One, Andrea had utilized the reverse processes of the Sverdlosk Institute.

The process of programming dissidents at the Sverdlosk and dozens of other "mental health" facilities in the Soviet Union and Eastern bloc countries was essentially the same. In the democratic West, medicine and psychiatry were dedicated to inducing mental health; restoring the body and mind to a point where they could function independently of artificial crutches, whether they were chemical or mental. Western psychiatry attempted to break down unhealthy dependencies and create autonomous, sovereign individuals who were capable of choices and actions independently arrived at.

In the communist world the inmates had taken over the institutions, it had seemed. Although the use of psychiatry had always been part of the communist process of controlling "hostile" populations, it accelerated with a vengeance under Premier Khrushchev in the 1960s, who professed: "Anybody who cannot see that communism is superior to any other system . . . is not a criminal . . . he's a lunatic, and must be treated as such!"

This apparently spontaneous statement, thundered at a regional party congress at Tashkent, was the essence of a national policy designed to curb the inevitable fallout from the de-Stalinization movement.

De-Stalinization was almost more than communist populations and the party faithful could handle. An entire generation was raised to revere the old dictator as a demigod, and the party dictates as gospel. When the Twentieth Party Congress denounced the "crimes of Stalinism" in Moscow, the old gods died with a thunderous roar. The floodgates of dissent were flung open . . . even officially encouraged for a short—very short—period of time, until the tide of dissidence threatened to destabilize the system, as it did in East Germany, Poland, and Hungary in 1953 and 1956.

Soviet tanks could crush entire dissident populations, as they had done repeatedly, but the chain of "mental health" institutes were designed to crush a smaller but more threatening population: those intellectuals, artists, poets, and religionists who had committed the ultimate heresy in the communist world . . . the heresy of somehow surviving the smothering conformity of the system. Instead they matured into independently functioning, autonomous individuals and declared the fruits of their heresy as good. Such examples could not be openly tolerated if the system was to survive and the power elite was to continue enjoying the fruits of power.

Psychiatry in the Sverdlosk and other institutes was designed to induce mental illness in healthy individuals through a systematic process of neurologically damaging drug therapy, psychological programming in "correct" thinking, and the destruction of individual identity. New identities in conformity with the "new Soviet man" were created and recycled into the dull grayness of the communist world.

As Andrea watched the ex-cultists chattering animatedly at the breakfast table, she shuddered inwardly as she remembered that at one time she was a cog in the machinery of the communist assault on mental health.

Reversing the Sverdlosk process worked well with the pilot group—and would work well elsewhere. Elaine Kearney and Bob Talbot would see to that, as they took their newly learned skills to the other deprogramming centers. Old dependencies were being broken, healthy identities formed, egos strengthened, and positive self-concepts created.

Andrea observed another phenomenon arising from the healing process of deprogramming . . . a phenomenon which baffled her; one which she wasn't at all certain how to handle. As the ex-cultists were restored to physical, emotional, and spiritual health, an awful anger consumed them: at what they were; at wasted time; at wasted lives; at the cult which trapped and manipulated them. Full of militancy and missionary zeal for their newly found identity and freedom, they wanted to strike out—to destroy that which they once dedicated their total being to.

Perhaps, Andrea mused, the channeling of this anger toward appropriate targets can be therapeutic. Perhaps a righteous violence can be part of the self-renewal necessary for complete recovery.

Suddenly Andrea's thoughts were propelled back to Budapest in 1988, when she returned from the Sverdlosk Institute ideologically shattered. Her faith in the old gods was totally destroyed, and her disgust in her role as programmer was personally devastating. The Second Hungarian Uprising, which began in Budapest in November, stemmed from a commemoration service for the thousands of students and workers killed in the 1956 revolution. It was Andrea's personal salvation. The speed and intensity with which she plunged herself into the uprising surprised all who knew her as a quiet scholar, a pampered child of the system, and a favored daughter of the Hungarian elite. She could still remember the torrent of released, suppressed rage she felt as she stormed the headquarters of the AVH, Hungary's Secret Police. With her fellow revolutionaries, she converted the ornate baroque building into a charnel house of bullet-riddled corpses and burning dossiers and microfilm records of her countrymen.

Two weeks later, as she escaped across the Austrian border, she was purified and cleansed. The sins of Sverdlosk had been washed away through the baptism of the revolution, and by the blood of her enemies. She had atoned for her sins. She would carry on the struggle elsewhere.

"Hey—hey, Andi!" Nick snapped his fingers in front of her face. "Come on back to the real world."

"Oh, I'm sorry, Nick. I was a million miles away." She slipped her arm around his hard waist, her thumb and finger gently pinching a roll of skin. She looked up into his dark eyes, smiling oddly.

Nick responded with a puzzled frown. "What's going on inside that beautiful clinical head of yours?"

Her smile broadened as she put her arms around his muscular shoulders and kissed him on the nose, oblivious to the stares and chuckles of the kitchen group. "I think that you, *Dr*. Portumo, will be conducting the next phase of our therapy."

It was a German band: a real oompah-pah type. The quality of the music was surprisingly good for a Latin American army. Since arriving in Asunción, Paul Lancaster was impressed with the order and cleanliness of the city. European faces, mostly Germanic, were numerous—especially among those in uniform. And the city was full of uniforms this day. It was May 5, the Cinco de Mayo, Mexico's Independence Day. The little country of Paraguay celebrated not only its own national holidays but those of other Latin American countries as well. It was an excuse for the nation's militarists to don their extravagant uniforms and strut down El Paraguay Independiente Calle to the Calle Palma, which was the city's main parade route.

Paul had learned little about his quarry, the Sacred Garduna, or Carlos Von Reinach. When he inquired, the people asked would avert their eyes or feign ignorance. Even his father, whom he dined with the night before at the embassy, was evasive and vague.

The military units, each wearing gaudy uniforms, as if trying to outdo one another, passed the reviewing stand. This was a celebration—a circus—not a display of military power. A battalion of young cadets from the military academy broke out into an exaggerated goose step as they passed the dignitaries and foreign diplomatic personnel, who stood in the hot sun in the reviewing stand. At the command they snapped an "eyes right" toward their country's leaders, as their German-style hobnailed boots thudded in pronounced cadence on the cobblestones. The attempt to appear martial was sheer comic opera. Even the senior military officers appeared embarrassed by it as they returned their salutes to the serious goose-stepping youngsters.

Abruptly the circus mood of the crowd changed. Expressions were hushed as the squeal of fifes and the slow cadence of drums were heard up the avenue—heard, but still out of sight. The music became louder. The drums beat a strange, almost menacing beat. Quiet expressions, whispers of awe and some of fear, rippled from the crowds into the reviewing stand. Paul craned his neck as he looked to his left down the flag-bedecked avenue. "Dad, what's going on?" he asked.

"I'm not sure, son, but *something* has changed the mood of the crowds."

A fife and drum corps of fifty musicians in tiger-striped camouflage fatigues was preceded by a group of horsemen. The quality of fifing and drumming was professional, the march step perfect. The musicians were all Guaraní Indians.

The equestrian unit clip-clopped by. There were thirteen men in flowing purple and white robes, similar to those worn by their predecessors long ago in their guerrilla war against the Moors in Spain. Riding in front, erect as a ramrod, was the white-haired, neatly bearded Prophet Estigarribia. A hushed reverence stilled the crowd as the old man pranced by on his dainty Paso Fino mare.

Paul turned to a Paraguayan naval officer to his right and addressed him in broken Spanish. "Pardon me, señor, who are the gentlemen on horseback?"

The officer, who was adorned with medals, smiled, revealing several stainless-steel teeth. He exhaled breath smelling of garlic into Paul's face. "Aha, señor. The white-haired *patrón* is the Prophet Francisco Estigarribia. The men behind him are his Holy Council."

"Prophet? Holy Council?" Paul frowned a question.

"Sí—of the Order of the Holy Garduna. The Sacred Warriors of Paraguay," replied the naval officer.

Paul sucked his breath in between clenched teeth as he shared the excitement of the crowd. The next unit was approaching the stand. It was led by a lone horseman: tall; impressive; a man with dark brown hair and electric-blue eyes; a man wearing the field uniform of a Paraguayan cavalryman. The uniform was devoid of decorations, and the rider was bareheaded—a nonverbal message to all who observed him that he was above the rules and regulations of his country's military establishment. The large white Arabian stallion he straddled skittered sideways, but the enigmatic horseman retained perfect control as he trotted past the reviewing stand.

The naval officer shot the horseman a sharp salute and held it until he passed.

"Uh . . . pardon me again, señor. Who is the lone horseman?"

"That is Colonel Carlos Von Reinach of Colonia Gardún," the officer snapped back, irritated at Paul's questioning.

Angel Caro didn't like it. The contingent of commandos from the Escuela para Comando should have been led by the school commandant and his staff, not an unknown colonel in the cavalry reserves. He stood at attention with the other advisers to the Paraguayan military establishment, as his

Guaraní Indian commandos marched by in perfect step to the music of the fife and drum corps.

It was apparent to all who viewed Caro's Indians that they were the real military power in the country. The no-nonsense uniform of tiger-striped camouflage fatigues and black berets; the Heckler & Koch assault rifles slung over their shoulders, or Uzi submachine guns pressed against their chests, contrasted sharply to the blatantly ridiculous struttings of the regular services.

Caro felt a mixture of pride and anxiety as the last of his troops padded by.

"Your people look good, Captain . . . damned good! I wish I had troops like that to work with instead of those clowns at the War College," whispered Colonel Elkins, chief of the U.S. Military Advisory Team to Paraguay.

"I didn't know your people had mechanized units," the colonel added.

Caro frowned and jerked his head to the left as he heard the armored cars rumbling down the cobblestoned avenue. Twenty-five Saladin armored cars, followed by rocket-mounted jeeps, roared in perfect formation past the stand. Caro squinted against the bright sunlight at the camouflaged, black-bereted soldiers in the vehicles. They were Guaraní, wearing the uniforms of his commandos, but he didn't recognize any of them—and he knew his troops. Where in the hell did they come from? Who trained them to handle such sophisticated machines of war?

Caro could feel the paranoia and hear the whispers of discontent of the Paraguayan military throughout the reviewing stand. It was an unwritten rule—a gentlemen's agreement in Paraguay—that no one service would gain a preponderance of power at the expense of the others. Weapons were to be parceled out equally, with the full knowledge of the rival services of what each was getting.

The black and green mechanized vehicles represented an awesome shift in the balance of power. Not only were the commandos the most disciplined in the nation; they were now the most formidably armed. The balance of power had shifted dramatically to the Sacred Order of the Holy Garduna . . . courtesy of Courtney Davenport.

Emil Günter wiped the small, clouded Plexiglas window of the DC-10 with his handkerchief as the plane circled low over Washington waiting for instructions to land. The city was at its best in early May, and this had been a warm, wet spring. The abundance of cherry blossoms throughout the capital were clearly visible from the air.

As the aircraft whined to a stop, the passengers crowded the aisle to deplane, ignoring the stewardess' instructions to remain seated. Emil waited until the last passenger, a nervous little man with a camera bag, shuffled by in small steps, as if he didn't want to jiggle a full bladder.

"Do you need any help, sir?" smiled the blond stewardess with white, even teeth.

"No . . . no, thank you," replied Günter as he slid the single aluminum cane-crutch under his armpit. Though one foot was bandaged, he hobbled expertly down the aisle.

Clearing customs at Washington National was as casual as Emil had ever seen, and his line of work took him through many customs procedures. As usual, the crutch was never touched. An Austrian businessman with a bandaged foot and a cane-crutch—especially an Austrian representing a ski supply industry—created the usual sympathetic chuckles from customs personnel in democratic countries.

"Well, Mr. Müller," chided a florid-faced official who exuded the smell of wine. "You're not the best advertisement for the skiing industry. Did you hurt your foot skiing?"

Günter had heard it a dozen times before, but managed to smile and respond in an exaggerated accent.

"Oh, *ja, ja!* My binding came loose on the Jungfrau near Salzburg. That's what I get for wearing my competitors' equipment."

As usual, this elicited good-natured guffaws from the customs people, and he was waved through the turnstile.

"In the Eastern bloc," he thought, "they'd have torn my baggage apart and would have disassembled my crutch and left me to put it back together again."

• • •

The black cabbie was unusually talkative, and for a member of an "oppressed" minority, openly critical of his government.

"Here you are, suh, Surratt Hotel."

Emil hobbled out, the cabbie holding his crutch as he steadied himself. An ancient bellboy was propelled from the revolving door and met him with a small luggage cart, on which he began to strap Günter's two suitcases. Emil slipped the cabbie his fare and tip.

"Thank *you*, suh!" He smiled, flashing white, widely spaced teeth. "Just one thing," added the cabbie. "Stay outa that park across the street after six-thirty. Fulla queers and muggers. Also, they deal a lotta dope over there . . . so watch it."

"Thank you for the warning, my friend. I shall stay in my room and watch television."

The room was plain but clean and had a good view of the street. Dr. Weishaupt demanded economy in his department, so extravagant expense accounts were discouraged—except for a few top operatives in high-cost areas. Besides, Weishaupt did not choose this hotel for Emil.

He spread his suitcases on the bed and laid out the crutch lengthways. With a few deft movements of his hand, he unclicked segments of the crutch and reassembled them into a single-shot rifle. He removed what appeared to be a bottle of talcum powder. He poured the white powder into the toilet bowl, flushed it, and cut the plastic bottle lengthways with his penknife. He removed a long gunmetal-blue cylinder. He screwed the silencer onto the end of the brushed-aluminum barrel and fit a mercury-tipped explosive bullet into the chamber, then closed the bolt. He worked the action several times before ejecting the cartridge. He shoved the weapon under the bed and put the suitcases on a canvas-strapped rack.

Günter lay down, arching his back to make a hollow in the lumpy mattress. He inhaled deeply from a half-smoked cigarette and blew the remaining smoke in nervous little puffs toward the ceiling.

The phone rang. Emil jumped off the bed and yanked the receiver off the phone.

"Hello? Mr. Müller? This is the front desk. You have a long-distance call from Oslo, Norway."

Günter's heart pounded. If only all of the right connections had been made . . .

"Hello? Hello, Lottie?"

He could hear his wife's voice clearly.

"Yes, it's me, Emil. Are you all right?"

"Yes, yes. Are Karl and Erika with you?"

"Yes, the children are here. We're fine."

"Where are you staying?" he asked, wiping little beads of sweat off his forehead.

The voice on the other end of the line sounded confused and agitated. "This is why I am calling, Emil. I was supposed to go to the Aeroflot Tourist Hotel. I was met by two men at the airport. I thought that they were from the embassy—they said they were—but they took me here."

"Where?" he demanded, his throat and chest tightening. He ground out the stub of his cigarette. He could hear his wife asking somebody in the room where she was. He strained to listen but couldn't hear the other voice.

"I'm at the Stänge House outside of the city. Emil. What's happening? I'm afraid!"

Günter felt the fear and anxiety drain from his body. He sighed deeply, almost feeling drowsy from the anxiety and tension of the past six months.

"Lottie, don't be afraid. Trust these men. Let me talk to the man in the room."

"Hello. Mr. Günter?" The voice was American. "This is Sam Reilly. We have your family. They're fine—confused, but fine. You're at the Surratt Hotel, I hope."

"He's supposed to be at the Garvey Hotel. What's happening?" his wife whined in the background.

"Mr. Günter, stay put. Bolt your doors. Don't leave. You'll be contacted tomorrow by a Wayne Porter. He's completely bald. Remember that. Your debriefing will start with him. Your family will join you in four days."

Günter smiled as he thought of Weishaupt's reaction to his

defection, and his inability to retaliate against his family. He would realize that his little Emil wasn't the meek, sniveling little mouse he thought he was.

One more task and the detailed planning of the past six months would be complete. He picked up the phone again.

"Front desk," the clerk answered.

"Yes, I want to direct dial," said Günter.

"A local number?" asked the front desk clerk.

"Yes . . . in Alexandria."

"Dial 8 and wait until the dial tone changes, then dial your number."

Günter hung up, waited, and picked up the phone and dialed 8. The dial tone went from a low bass to a tenor. He dialed his number. The ringing continued . . . three, four, five rings. Günter dabbed at his perspiration with a damp gray handkerchief. After what seemed an eternity, a deep voice drawled a hello into the receiver.

Günter breathed deeply. "Hello? Is this . . . Senator Courtney Davenport?"

XIV.

Patches Jackson worked the dinghy quietly along the brush-covered shore, staying close enough to the tall vegetation so he wouldn't be seen or outlined against the pale moon of early June.

He couldn't get too close. He had to have enough room to manipulate the eight-foot tongs. Also, most of the oysters he was stealing that night were at least three feet from shore. Lifting the long tongs expertly, Patches plopped them into the water. He felt along the shallow bottom for familiar clumps, until he finally hit something. He steadied the boat, stood on the stern, and opened the tongs. Closing them around the oysters, he lifted his precious cargo. He emptied seventeen huge seed oysters into a burlap bag on the bottom of the dinghy.

Feeling his way slowly along the eastern shore of Parramore Island, he came to a bend in the shoreline where a large bush protruded into the water. Beyond the bend there was a sudden blaze of lights, the sound of machinery, and men's voices. Patches quickly stopped, eased the small craft into the jutting bush, and peered around the bend toward the commotion.

The life of an oyster pirate was seldom exciting, but what Patches saw that early June evening made up for all of the nights of boredom. A small submarine, a French "D" class, 1968 vintage, was being secured to the boat dock of a large private estate. The powerful floodlights over the unloading area lit up the dock activity and the large stone mansion beyond the spacious, sloping lawn. As the crated boxes of the submarine's cargo were being lifted from the hold, a group of young women sat on the lawn waiting to board.

Patches had worked the string of other islands off the coastal tidewater of Virginia, but this was the first time he had worked Parramore Island. He had no way of knowing that this half of the island was owned by the Bouchegrave family, and that the huge estate in view belonged to Senator Calvin Bouchegrave, senior senator from the state of Virginia. Nor did Patches realize that the submarine cargo contributed substantially to the already immense fortunes of the Bouchegrave dynasty. The submarine was unloading the finest and the purest Santa Cruz Bolivian cocaine. An estimated street value of $50 million.

After the last crate was unloaded, the submarine captain motioned for the young women to board, young women who would soon become the new *chivatos* of Colonia Gardún.

His human cargo secured, the captain cast off the lines, and the sub skillfully warped itself away from the dock, diesels throbbing rythmically. It turned and headed for the open sea.

Back on the spacious lawn the last of the crates were sequestered inside the Bouchegrave mansion, and—one by one—the lights went out.

"I tell you, Phil, it was a *submarine*. A damned submarine. Not one of those new nuclear jobs, but an old one!"

"Patch . . . you're fulla shit! You've been belting that cheap wine agin. What'n hell would a submarine be doing at that estate? That place belongs to the Bouchegrave family."

"*Senator* Bouchegrave?" asked Patches as he folded one long leg over the other and lit a cigarette.

"Yeah, *the* Senator Bouchegrave. Now, what'n hell do you think he's doing, Patch? Starting his own navy?"

"Yeah? Well, let me tell you something else. They loaded a bunch of young gals on that sub."

"Young gals?" replied Patches's brother, his mouth open.

"Yeah, and not bad-lookin' from what I could tell. They

went on board and the sub headed for the open sea—on the surface."

The square-jawed man with the light gray eyes and the ragged army field jacket swirled the foam in his beer and appeared disinterested and nonchalant. In fact, however, he was drinking in the details of the conversation down the bar. It was a small bar—one of three in the little fishing village of Bellehaven. Crandall Donovan felt that finally something was about to break on the Davenport case. After covering the scores of grubby bars in the tiny fishing villages in tidewater Virginia, he felt that he had hit pay dirt.

"Hell, I'm gonna tell the sheriff," said Patches. "Fur all I know, there might be a reward for this kind of information."

His brother shrugged and followed him out to the battered, old Toyota pickup, which reeked from the smell of oysters.

Donovan slipped a two-dollar bill under his glass and also left the bar.

"You say you saw a *submarine* at Senator Bouchegrave's place?"

"That's right, Sheriff," replied Patches proudly. "I saw it."

"That estate's private—guarded by guards and dogs. How did you manage to get over the fence, past the guards, where you could see the dock?" the sheriff asked suspiciously.

"I saw it from the seaward side."

"What in the hell were you doing on the seaward side? I assume you were in a boat."

"Ummm . . . yeah," answered Patches. "I was fishing."

The sheriff caught the eye of his deputy, who had overheard the conversation, and made a slight motion with his head. The deputy nodded and left the room.

"Patches, I think the best thing you can do is keep this under your hat. This might be a secret government project of some kind," the sheriff said condescendingly.

"Yeah . . . I'll bet it's something like that. Hell, I don't wanna blow the whistle on a secret project. Sheriff, I'll keep this real quiet." Patches uncoiled his lanky frame and lifted himself out of the soft sofa chair.

The sheriff checked his watch. Ten minutes since the deputy left. That should be enough time.

"Thanks, boys. Get back in your truck now and forget what you've seen." He took a five-dollar bill out of his wallet and pressed it into Patches's hand.

"There—this'll take care of the gas and buy you boys a couple of beers. Thanks a lot for dropping in and remember—mum's the word."

As they came out of the sheriff's office, the deputy slid out from under the old Toyota and faded into the trees beyond the parking lot.

Donovan started up his 1985 Chevy Citation and nosed onto the road, keeping the truck in view. When they hit the next bar, he'd buy them drinks and pump them for information. They were the types, he thought, that would spill their guts for a pitcher of beer.

The old pickup bumped and yawed over the chuckholed county road, going a bit too fast for the condition of the highway. But there were no other vehicles on the highway, so Donovan could follow at a respectable distance.

Donovan felt the blast before he heard it. The old Toyota blew up with an earsplitting roar. If Donovan's windows hadn't been rolled down, the concussion would have shattered them. He swerved violently to the left to avoid a fender flying through the air.

The sheriff of Accomac County heard it, too, and smiled grimly at his deputy. "Glad you had a spare. Came in handy."

The deputy nodded his reply, picking his teeth with a paper clip. The sheriff picked up the phone, dialed, and let it ring three times. He then hung up, redialed the same number, and let it ring.

"Hello? Alex? Let me speak to the boss."

He waited several minutes until a cultivated voice answered.

"Hello? Senator Bouchegrave?"

"I'm sorry, Donovan, Senator Davenport can't be reached right now." Shirl Tucker didn't like Crandall Donovan, but had to admit that he was a competent and persistent investigator. He was arrogant, boorish, and crude—but he did his job.

"Look, Tucker. Ever since old man Davenport hired me to track down his daughter, I've run into dead ends. Now, I think this submarine business at Parramore Island may mean something. I've gotta talk to Davenport."

"He's out of town. I'm holding down the Washington office until he gets back."

For a research intern from Davenport-Rockland University, Shirl Tucker had an unusual amount of clout with Courtney Davenport. He also acted as a secretary as well as a researcher for the Senate Subcommittee on Cults, and kept track of the senator's whereabouts and appointments. He was also privy to information pertaining to the personnel and operations of the countercult forces, and with the kind of information he was receiving from Crandall Donovan, perhaps a Countercult Team Chief would act upon it more effectively—and less emotionally—than Courtney Davenport, who he knew could be quite impulsive and rash at times.

"Tell you what, Donovan. Give me the details, and I'll get it to the senator as soon as possible. That's the best I can do."

Wimpy little bastard. I could take him out in one swipe, thought Donovan, as he yanked out a large manila envelope from his briefcase.

Tucker extended a thin, languid hand and gently—yet teasingly—plucked it from the investigator.

Bet he's a fag, mused Donovan, as he rose to leave. "Okay, Tucker, see that Davenport gets that as soon as possible. Have him contact me as soon as he reads it."

As soon as the investigator slammed the door, Shirl Tucker grabbed the phone. "Yes, operator. Give me an outside line. Class one security."

The operator, a trusted member of the countercult administrative staff, cleared a secure line to an old stone farmhouse in rural Virginia, which was twenty miles north of Charlottesville.

Elaine Kearney answered the phone. "CC-3. Kearney speaking."

"Elaine. Shirl Tucker. Let me speak to Raúl Caro."

The woods around the Bouchegrave estate were as thick as the Yunque rain forest in eastern Puerto Rico, thought Raúl Caro as he cautiously approached the chain link fence. He crept through the vine-covered tangle and stopped before a cleared strip of brown earth outside the enclosure. The curled, dead vegetation which straddled the fence, ten feet on each side, told Caro that a herbicide had been used—probably to increase the field of fire from the guard's weapons.

Behind him stalked two other countercult commandos: Cliff Walters, formerly a sergeant in the ex-Rhodesian Police Anti-Terrorist Unit (PATU), and Stan O'Connell, who was on leave from the Australian Army's Special Air Service.

O'Connell took out a small radio receiver and put the earphone in his left ear. He twisted the channel selector slowly until he heard voice traffic. "Raúl, they've got guards in there . . . and transceivers."

"How many?" asked Caro.

"Can't tell. I picked up at least three different conversations—but the area's covered. I'd be surprised if they weren't armed."

"We've got to grab somebody from out of there and find out what in the hell is going on," said the Rhodesian.

"I agree," said Raúl. "All we know is what was in the Donovan report. He feels that the Bouchegrave estate is somehow involved with the Garden Children, the cult that Davenport's kid is locked into."

They stalked along the edge of the brown dirt strip until they came to a large tree with one thick branch jutting over the chain link fence into the estate grounds. Within minutes, the three camouflaged commandos had climbed the branch and dropped to the other side.

The estate grounds seemed to go on forever. Finally, Caro saw a clearing ahead and approached it carefully. He stopped in the dense shrub at the end of the clearing and peered ahead. The Bouchegrave mansion, like a medieval castle, loomed up ahead. In fact, it was rumored that an earlier

Bouchegrave had dismantled the ancestral manor in Burgundy, France, and reassembled it on Parramore Island, stone by stone, just after the Civil War.

Raúl heard footsteps crunching on dead sticks and froze. He quickly motioned to the others to hunker down. Suddenly a lone guard, a shotgun cradled in the crook of his arm, appeared some fifty feet away. O'Connell crept forward, reached in his fatigue pocket, and retrieved what appeared to be an aluminum marking pen. With a slight tug, the device telescoped open into a blowgun. He picked a small dart from a dummy cigarette case and inserted it into one end.

Phhhht! The guard heard it and felt the sudden sting on his neck at the same time. As his brain was trying to assess and process the threat, the fast-acting tranquilizer was already impairing his neurological reactions. Within seconds, he fell unconscious on the new spring grass.

O'Connell crept forward, dragged the body into the brush, and hoisted it onto his shoulders.

"Let's get him up to CC-3 and pick his brain," whispered Caro, and they pushed their way through the tangled vines toward the fence.

The following three days were like Christmas and a birthday party rolled into one. Caro and Elaine Kearney were amazed at how verbal and how knowledgeable the guard was. It seemed as if every other word uttered under the influence of sodium pentothal was a major revelation which tied the Bouchegrave operation to a host of feeder cults in the United States—and to a large master cult in faraway Paraguay.

Outside, a small Piper Warrior taxied from the adjacent grass airstrip to the old stone farmhouse. Nick Portumo, briefcase in hand, jumped out and bounced up the flat stone stairs. Elaine Kearney opened the heavy weathered door before he could turn the knob.

"Where is he?" asked Nick excitedly. "Is he still unconscious?" He began to leaf through a sheaf of papers, which was testimony taken from the guard. He hit his forehead dramatically with the flat of his palm. "Do you realize what we have here? This information is a series of keys which unlock a lot of doors we've been banging on. This guy"—he jerked his thumb toward the interrogation room—"has given us information which ties the Bouchegrave family to the biggest cocaine ring in the country, and to a cult in Paraguay called the Garduna. The cult processes the stuff and ships it to the States."

"Hey, if you need a volunteer to check it out, I'll go," offered Caro with a slight smile.

"Why the sudden interest?" asked Portumo.

"My brother's down there serving as an adviser to the Paraguayan Army."

"Really? That might prove useful later on. Let's get on top of the Bouchegrave thing before we do that, Raúl, but I'll keep it in mind. Meanwhile, let's brainstorm this problem out and reach some solutions. We've got to come up with a plan."

A 1954 Chris-Craft, the old yacht had seen better days, but it was suited for the mission. Its twin Packard diesels enabled her to plow through the slight swells of lower Chincoteague Bay with ease. Shirl Tucker had arranged for the old craft to be waiting for Nick at the little resort town of Chincoteague, on Assateague Island, in Virginia's Accomac County. It was solid and seaworthy, but, most important, it had modern, updated communications equipment. Its white lapstrake hull had been recently covered and bonded with fiberglass, and its engines were overhauled. Even in these swells, it could easily make twelve knots per hour.

Inside the mahogany-paneled upper cabin and down in the passenger area, the ten countercult commandos poured over maps, cleaned weapons, and attached steel-blue silencers to submachine guns and assault rifles. Weapons and equipment for every possible contingency were brought aboard. Nick wanted a zero-defects operation.

The Chris-Craft poked along the eastern shore of upper Parramore Island. The skipper throttled back his engines, now humming in a low, rhythmic throb, and nosed his boat into a small tree-shrouded cove. The laminated fiberglass-reinforced hull scraped against the sand, and the camouflaged figures jumped off and disappeared into the dense foliage. It was dusk and the sun's western rays spilled over the treeline, sending shimmers of light on the green sea beyond the beached pleasure craft.

"Raúl, how far?" asked Cliff Walters as he adjusted the sling of his SIG assault rifle.

"About seven miles, and it's all like this: vines, dense vegetation, and poison oak. The Bouchegrave family has owned the southern end of the island since 1820. The state of Virginia gave the land to one André Bouchegrave for using his own ship as a privateer during the War of 1812. The original Bouchegrave was a French sea captain who saw a way to turn a fast buck."

The ten black-faced commandos stole through the blackness of the forest—a forest that seemed to be still in its primeval state. The Bouchegraves had never permitted any logging or commercial exploitation of the island, except for fishing. Many of the trees were over two hundred years old.

Now, four hours after landing, Stan O'Connell, the point man, waved his small penlight in a sweeping arc. The other ten men froze in their tracks. O'Connell stalked back to the group.

"Raúl—the fence. Up ahead. We're right on target. There's the tree."

They crowded around Caro. "Okay, let's go over this once more. Anybody that's armed we shoot, if necessary. Use head shots if possible so they won't discharge their weapons. We want to take as many prisoners as possible by surprise."

Within ten minutes, the commandos were over the fence with their equipment. Later, they were positioned near the edge of the woods, where the lights of the huge stone mansion were in sight.

The Doberman stiffened, his short hair bristling and the ridge of his back arching as he uttered a low growl. The guard stiffened, too, looked around, and started to unsling his weapon. The hail of bullets caught the dog full in the chest, spinning him backward into the earth in a bloody heap. The deadly stream of lead, spitting silently from the treeline, stitched into the guard, sending him sprawling on top of his dog.

Ten figures raced from the trees toward the old French mansion and flattened themselves against the side of the structure.

"Raúl! Here's a door! I'll bet it's the servant's entrance," exclaimed a commando.

"Find some windows first," replied Caro. "Let's see what's inside. I don't want to bust in on a party—especially if they're armed."

Ten minutes passed, and Raúl returned from his reconnaissance. He ascertained that a skeleton staff was on duty inside the huge estate. He started to pick the lock of the heavy oaken door when Cliff Walters padded up to him.

"Raúl! Forget about the door!" he exclaimed. "Take a look out front."

The commandos stole around the side of the mansion until they could observe the sloping lawn and the waterfront below.

"Holy shit!" Caro sucked in his breath nervously as he observed the activity down by the brightly lighted dock. A dozen female cultists—all Garden Children—sat on the lawn waiting, as the cult's own submarine warped its way to the loading dock.

It had been two weeks since Olivia left Colonia Gardún, and Susan Rockland felt the emptiness. All of the Garden Children and members of other cults at Colonia Gardún had come to accept that which was painfully obvious: They were virtual prisoners and slaves of the Sacred Order of the Holy Garduna. Gone was the spiritual excitement of the Garden Children. The dull gray duty of work became the new religion. Everybody knew that exhortations to "build the kingdom" were simply commands to build up the economic power of the Holy Garduna. Any spiritual benefits were reserved for the Garduna members, not their slaves.

Susan's emptiness, however, did not consume her. She kept her spirit alive by thinking, living, and breathing thoughts of escape . . . and of Angel Caro.

• • •

"Sister Rockland, grind up these herbs into a fine powder and put them into these jars."

Dr. Hilda Von Ziegazar handed Susan a large bag of what appeared to be tulip bulbs. Susan scooped out a handful and put them into a stone bowl. With a smaller stone, she started the laborious process of grinding the herbs into medicinal powder.

Von Ziegazar, head of the infirmary, watched Susan with a slight smile. Her flat chest and masculine, angular body contrasted sharply with Susan's soft curves and sensual good looks, and the feminine softness of Susan Rockland excited Von Ziegazar. She had had her pick of others in the colony, and she would have Susan. Her power and authority in the Gardún structure gave her the right—and the opportunity—to choose any young girl she wished.

"Susan, *mein schönes Kind*, you have taken to hospital work very well." The doctor caressed Susan's blue-black hair with the back of her wrist. Susan shuddered, but managed a smile of appreciation. "I have heard reports from the Indians that you are a natural nurse. They like and respect you. You have also gone to the trouble to learn some of the Guaraní language. You will do well here if you work and obey. I have the power to grant you extra privileges if you obey . . . in every way. Perhaps you would like to accompany me out to the oil fields?"

"Oil fields, Sister Von Ziegazar?"

"It will be known to all soon. The Parachaco Corporation has found oil south of here, and there is much activity. Industrial accidents and disease have increased. I have been ordered to establish a small branch of our infirmary there."

"Where is the field located, ma'am?" Susan asked cautiously yet politely.

"South of here. Not too far from a place called Mariscal Estigarribia."

Susan's heart pounded as if it would leap from her chest. She tried to appear casual. "Oh, yes, that's where we stayed before coming to the colony. Isn't that an army camp of some kind?"

Hilda Von Ziegazar didn't answer. Susan took her silence

as an indication that the conversation was over. Perhaps she had overstepped her bounds. Perhaps she had shown too great an interest in Mariscal Estigarribia. Her mind raced—thinking, fantasizing of escaping to join Angel and flee to Brazil. She would do anything for the opportunity to be near Angel Caro. Could she manipulate Von Ziegazar into letting her go to Mariscal Estigarribia on some pretext if she became the doctor's lover? The thought was revolting, but the prospect of staying trapped in Colonia Gardún was even more revolting. The more she dwelled on escape, the harder she ground the herbs into a fine white powder. She ground with a fury, rotating the grinding stone until sparks flew.

"Susan!" Von Ziegazar's voice was like an electric shock. "Go to your barracks and pack some personal belongings. Get enough for three or four days, then load up the medical gear into the pickup truck. We leave for the oil fields at six in the morning."

The Indians called the little valley La Cuna de Dios: the Cradle of God. It was an appropriate name. The children born there were considered consecrated to the god of the Holy Garduna—that strange god which was a mixture of Jesuit, Nazi, and Guaraní beliefs.

The large aluminum building against the hill processed that which was considered the sacrament of God—at least to the hedonistic gods of the hundreds of cults in the Western nations of the world. They claimed that their sacrament, which was the purest, finest, Bolivian Santa Cruz cocaine to be had, enabled them to experience a type of rebirth. The aluminum shed was the processing center for the first-stage refining of the new Golden Triangle cocaine. Here the raw cocaine was transhipped to Fuerte Olimpo for the second-stage refining, and then shipped by submarine to Parramore Island.

Olivia was assigned to an attractive one-story thatched-roof cottage, one of ten which radiated from the central administrative building. She shared the three-room structure with two others, a green-eyed brunette from Denmark, and the brown-eyed blonde from California, the one that the Prophet Barrajas had taken to his bed the night before the trip to La Cuna de Dios.

The spiritual life at La Cuna was more structured and more fulfilling than that of Colonia Gardún. Here, during the last week, there were inspirational talks by those who worked directly under the Hermano Mayor. A feeling of love—of sisterhood—was growing among the girls. Even the stoic Guaraní Indians seemed to be more animated and more caught up in the spirit of La Cuna.

La Cuna was also a school, and classes were held daily. Olivia marveled at how truly ignorant she was of modern history. And why wouldn't she be? Like millions of others in the Western world, she was taught the "established truths" of Jewish Liberal dogma; of truths which denigrated the truly great men of history—men such as Adolf Hitler.

"Olivia . . . do you ever wonder . . . what it's like to get pregnant? I mean . . . what it feels like?" asked the brunette in a thick Danish accent.

"You mean . . . like having morning sickness and carrying around the extra weight?"

"Yes," replied the Dane, "and knowing that the father will never be part of the baby's life."

Olivia swallowed and fought a choking sensation as feelings of guilt and depression assaulted her. Her own father, Courtney Davenport, although authoritarian and rigid, was part of her life, even if some of the subparts were negative. He was her father, and part of her identity.

The California blonde spoke with a slight quiver. "I . . . I learned . . . yesterday . . . that after the babies are weaned from their mothers they take them away. You never see them again."

"From their *mothers*?" Olivia gasped.

"Hey, that's us, Olivia. We're the mothers—or will be," added the Dane, trying to be humorous.

Olivia stood and paced the room, her pale blue eyes blazing in anger.

"No! No! No! It's wrong! I've accepted everything else but that's wrong! If I have a baby, it will be *my* baby. Mine! I won't let them take it away!"

"Sssshhh!" hushed the blonde. "Don't let them know how you feel. If you feel that strongly, just avoid getting pregnant."

The Dane chuckled nervously. "And just *how* do you propose that we do that, dear girl? We have no access to the Pill or any other birth control devices, and they know our cycles. They have our medical records."

Olivia threw herself on her bunk and put her hands over her eyes, massaging her eyeballs with the tips of her fingers. Her migraine was excruciating, and she sought to alleviate the pain. Her mood swung from anger to passive depression.

It was at dusk when the Guaraní guard tapped on the cottage door. The blonde opened it, took the message, and went over to Olivia, who was sitting on her bunk.

"Olivia, are you awake?"

"Yes, but I'm sleepy. I think I'll go to bed early."

"You may—but you won't sleep," replied the blonde, her lips twitching in a half smile.

"What do you mean?" Olivia sat up, a puzzled expression on her face.

"Julio Barrajas. He wants you in his cottage in ten minutes. Prepare to spend the night."

"Does he . . . want to . . . ?"

"Yes, Olivia. Let me warn you—give him what he wants . . . *whatever* he wants."

"What do you mean?" Olivia asked the blonde, her face screwed into a puzzled frown.

"Are you a virgin, Olivia?" the California girl asked.

"No, there have been several times."

"Probably high school stuff. Julio is a man of—strange appetites."

"I would say kinky appetities," added the Dane without humor.

"What? Strange appetites? Kinky? What's this all about? What do you mean?"

Her cottage-mates averted their eyes. When they heard the footsteps of the Guaraní guard crunch up the gravel walkway, the blonde grabbed Olivia's arm.

"Olivia, you want to survive this. Be strong, but don't resist. Don't resist Barrajas. Give him what he wants!"

The bruised and battered body of Olivia Davenport was laid carefully on her bunk by two Guaraní Indians. The early June sun was poking its warm winter rays through the open window. Already, small flying insects and birds were stirring, some darting in and out of the window opening.

The Dane was the first to react.

"Is . . . she . . . dead?" she asked one of the Indians.

Olivia moaned loudly, answering the question. She wiped her mouth with the back of her hand, smearing the blood trickling from a cut on her lip.

"Oh, Olivia, Olivia!" cried the blonde. "What did he do to you?"

"He's . . . he's a false prophet! He's not a man of God. A man of God wouldn't ask me to do . . . what he asked. He's an *animal* . . . a filthy animal!" Olivia started to sob uncontrollably.

The California blonde held Olivia, rocking her back and forth. "Oh, honey . . . Olivia," she choked. "I told you to cooperate. Barrajas can't stand to be rejected. He reacts to it with violence."

Suddenly Olivia's expression changed as if an elastic band had snapped in her face. Her eyes became vacant and glazed. There was a strange, twisted smile on her face. "My daddy will take care of *him*. Daddy can make me better. He can make the hurt go away. He will punish Barrajas. Daddy! Kiss my hurt away."

The two girls looked at each other with shocked but knowing glances. They shook their heads slowly as Olivia continued to babble.

"My daddy can fix anything. He'll take me back to Tulsa. He's a very important man—he can fix the people who hurt me."

Olivia Davenport curled up in her bunk bed in a near fetal position, pulled the blanket up over her head, and moaned herself to sleep.

XV.

Courtney Davenport knocked four times—two rapid, a ten-second pause, and two more. He looked in both directions down the dingy hallway of the Surratt Hotel, hoping that nobody had heard him.

"Senator Davenport?" piped a high-pitched voice, in a thick German accent, from behind the bolted door.

"Yes, it's me, Mr. Günter." Davenport patted the .25-caliber Beretta in his coat pocket for reassurance.

The door squeaked open and the dim light revealed a mousy, almost cringing, little man in his middle forties. His patchy baldness contrasted somewhat with his small but thick mustache.

"Please come in, Senator Davenport. Forgive me for asking you to come to such a miserable hovel as the Surratt."

"That's all right, Mr. Günter, I'll go to the pits of hell to get information about my daughter."

During the next hour and a half, Courtney had heard it all. Günter had left nothing out. His story was accompanied by documents and photographs of key personnel in the AVH/KGB organization of Section VI.

"What you have here, Emil—may I call you Emil?" Davenport slapped Günter's knee.

Günter smiled and nodded, relieved and grateful that the tall Oklahoman seemed to believe his story.

"What you have here would be of *some* interest to my

government, but it would be of greater interest and value to me and the people who work for me. I'm offering you and your family a chance to live in safety and work within my organization."

"But I was supposed to meet a Mr. Wayne Porter tomorrow from your CIA. He was to take me to a safe house where I would meet my family."

"I'm not without influence with the CIA. I am one of a handful of senators on the Roberts Committee fighting to keep the CIA intact and potent. The CIA owes me a few favors."

"Another thing, Senator," Günter began timidly. "I . . . I was supposed to kill you if I had the opportunity."

Davenport felt for the small automatic as Günter reached under the bed and pulled out the crutch-rifle.

"What in the hell is *that*!" boomed Davenport, relaxing his grip on his automatic.

"It started out as a cane-crutch, but it is actually a very efficient silenced rifle." Günter showed the weapon to Davenport and worked the action.

"These mercury-tipped bullets explode within the target, Senator. A death shot is assured."

With a few deft movements, Günter reassembled the weapon back into a crutch.

"That is how I got it through customs, Senator Davenport . . . along with the diversion of a bandaged foot."

"Amazing, truly amazing. I'm afraid that our CIA is out of *that* kind of business now—thanks to the Roberts Committee."

"It is inconceivable in the Eastern bloc, Senator, that such a committee can actually be organized to dismantle your intelligence organizations. There are many in the AVH/KGB who refuse to believe it. They think it is a clever ruse to deceive us."

"Oh, I assure you that it's true, all right, Emil. The climate in our country is one of defeatism and guilt. Any attempt to defend ourselves is looked upon by many as endangering world peace and reviving the Cold War. America has lost her instinct to survive."

"And that is what makes our work in Section VI so easy,

Senator. So easy that we expect a ploy of some kind; but I guess it *is* true,'' Emil commented dejectedly. ''This state of affairs has saddened even some people within our organization. They are people who want to play the game, but secretly do not want America to be defeated.''

''Well, Emil.'' Courtney stood up, his massive frame towering over the diminutive Günter. ''This time tomorrow you'll be safe at my ranch in Oklahoma. Get your things and let's be out of here.''

''But my wife . . . my children . . .''

''As I said, Emil, I'm not without influence with the CIA. They'll be with you within a few days.''

The Piper Warrior circled low over the Davenport ranch, which was cradled in a shallow valley in eastern Oklahoma's Boston Mountains. It dipped its wings in acknowledgment of the permission to land, which was given by the Cherokee Indian shooting a purplish-red flare. The aircraft touched down on the grass strip and sped by the nervous, neighing Paso Fino horses behind the white slat fences. The plane was secured by two Indians, and Nick and Andrea stepped out and made their way to the large log-and-rock ranch house.

''Nick . . . Andrea! So good to see you again,'' drawled Davenport as he walked gingerly down the flagstone walkway, the golden oil derrick symbol gleaming from his belt buckle. He took Nick's hand in his and put an arm around Andrea, hugging her tightly. Andrea felt the warmth and appreciation of this gracious, if not impulsive, man. His enthusiasm and resources were enabling her to fight her own private war against Martin Weishaupt, and she was deeply grateful.

As they entered the large living room with the hunting-lodge decor, Andrea froze in her tracks.

''Emil! Emil Günter!'' she cried. Her voice was fearful. She was shaken.

Günter smiled an embarrassed little smile.

''Hello, Andrea. It's been a long time. I suppose you are wondering what I am doing here.''

''I think it's pretty obvious, Emil,'' Andrea replied, breathing deeply to regain her composure. "You have defected, leaving that despicable bastard, Weishaupt, and all of his toadies in Section VI. I thought if anybody else would defect, Emil, it would be you. You were his whipping boy. I didn't know how much more you could stand."

"I am here to tell you everything, Andrea. As much as I know about Section VI. I have already told the senator about his daughter joining a cult named the Garden Children, but he already knew about it. The Garden Children is one of ours. It came under our jurisdiction a year and a half ago."

Nick stepped forward and shook the little defector's hand. "Mr. Günter. I'm Nicholas Portumo."

"Ah, yes, the SAS captain. You are the one that Dr. Weishaupt is particularly afraid of. Your approach in dealing with our section is not to his liking. We would rather deal with organizations like the Roberts Committee."

They all laughed and took seats around the huge oaken coffee table. Davenport spread a variety of documents and photographs on the table.

"This is remarkable information!" gasped Andrea. "The section has been totally reorganized and staffed since my defection."

"That is why Weishaupt hates you so much, dear Andrea," smiled Günter. "Even with the little knowledge you brought out, he took no chances. Your defection cost the section millions of dollars and thousands of man-hours."

"And your defection, Emil, will entail even more drastic changes," drawled Davenport.

"This means that we have to act fast—with tremendous speed—to eliminate these key people"—Portumo thumped on the coffee table for emphasis—"before changes can bc made."

Andrea's deep green eyes probed into Emil's.

"Emil. You know what we'll have to do. We are going to have to kill these people. How do you feel about that?"

Günter stiffened and drew his slight frame up to its fullest height. "The people in my section are swine! They are the dregs of the AVH and KGB! They are men and women without conscience. They deserve any punishment you will mete out. Believe me, they would do it to *you*—and will, if the opportunity arises."

Davenport turned to Nick. "Is it a total effort on Weishaupt's organization then, Nick?"

"Yes, Senator, and quickly before Weishaupt has the chance to reorganize. Most of his people are in Western Europe and the United States. Two are also in Canada. I believe that we can take them all out in a week. I can place Jean Trucdeau and Paul Redecker in position tomorrow, or the day after. They have teams that can be fully operational for this, and they are familiar with most of the cities in Western Europe. Weishaupt's people might have false identities, but they are highly visible and accessible. We can take them out in less than two weeks. Full termination."

Andrea shuddered inwardly at Nick's cold and technical evaluation of the need to terminate other human beings. How unlike her own personal killing spree in the AVH headquarters building in Budapest during the 1988 revolution. To expend one's energies and pent-up rage on their enemies seemed more moral than the systematic, unemotional planning to terminate one's enemies.

Andrea rose, her face flushed, her movements agitated. "Why don't you say it like it is, Nicholas! We are not 'terminating' people, we are *killing* them! Let us say what we mean. Let's not use polite words for ugly deeds. It doesn't make the deed any less ugly if we camouflage it with bureaucratic terms. I can live with the idea of killing my enemies. It justifies the action emotionally. To use polite terms for what we are doing is . . ." Andrea turned to the wall and started to sob. Davenport worked his jaw muscles rapidly and played with his huge silver and turquoise ring.

Portumo got up and put his arm around her shoulder and squeezed it. He had never seen Andrea cry before. At times, he wasn't sure if she was capable of crying. It frightened him, and yet reassured him that she was vulnerable—a female trait that suddenly made him feel protective of her.

"Ah, *mein Gott*!" Günter sighed. "We are engaged in a

business—on both sides of this conflict—which is eroding our humanity. I'll be happy when I'm out of it for good."

A station wagon squealed to a stop outside the ranch house. Davenport looked out the window and smiled broadly. "Emil, you have guests."

Davenport opened the front door and ushered in a confused-looking, dumpy little hausfrau, followed by two chubby children—a boy of eleven and a girl of nine.

"Lottie! Dear Lottie!" cried Emil as he rushed toward his wife, arms extended. She fell into his arms, crying excitedly, and the children jumped up and down, clutching their father's tweed jacket.

Andrea observed the reunion and smiled through her tears. If Emil Günter succeeded at anything in this life, it was as a loving husband and father.

Martin Weishaupt sipped from the thimble-sized glass slowly. The absinthe coursed down his esophagus and into his stomach, where it burst into a hot glow, spreading its warmth to his loins. He had long been a secret addict to absinthe, a drink outlawed many years ago in most of the civilized countries of the world after it was rumored that the French Army in the Franco-Prussian War was incapacitated by the massive abuse of the liquor among the troops.

Weishaupt didn't care. Absinthe seemed to alleviate his impotency—at least temporarily. The drink, made from the oil of the root of the wormwood tree, which grew in Morocco, was dubbed the elixir of perpetual erection. Perhaps it *was* all psychological. Weishaupt smiled to himself. For him it worked.

An hour later, Weishaupt's secretary left the inner office through the back door. Weishaupt locked it and put his clothes back on, carefully knotting his tie. He went to the medicine chest in the small bathroom and took four aspirin. He always developed a severe headache after sex. Perhaps it was the absinthe. More likely it was Carla. She was so young; so vigorous. Her appetites were so insatiable.

He sat down on the large leather chair and read over the report from agents Faith and Hope in Tulsa. He still marveled that his little Emil, sniveling, cringing little mouse that he was, had defected. His disdain for his ex-aide was replaced by a kind of smoldering respect and an awful anger. Emil Günter and his family must be made examples of.

His agents had located them. It wasn't too difficult to find out where he would defect to. The American government was no longer an effective protector of defectors. Since the Roberts Committee had gained in strength and influence, the U.S. Government had consistently caved in to Soviet demands to return defectors as criminals.

Yes, little Emil had planned well. He would find more security with Davenport's countercult apparatus—and in a safe house on the Davenport ranch. But nobody was beyond the long arm of Section VI.

Peter Chomsky and Sylvia Froenze, code-named Faith and Hope, drove the Jeep CJ5 over the rolling back country of Oklahoma's Boston Mountains as the purple dusk slid behind the hills, giving way to darkness. The radio-teletyped photographs of Emil Günter and his family were etched into their minds. The mission given to them was the most important, so far, of their careers. Their training at Cuba's Island of Pines had been rigorous and intense, and enabled them to carry out other missions—even assassinations—with dispatch. But they had never been asked to kill an entire family before. Before they had left, it was agreed that Peter would kill the children and Sylvia would dispose of Emil and Lottie.

They parked the jeep in a slight depression in the landscape and covered it with brush. The two Section VI agents climbed the slight sandstone bluff, wriggled under the three-strand barbed-wire fence, and darted from scrub oak to scrub oak until the complex of buildings of the Davenport ranch was in sight.

"Are you sure that this place isn't guarded, Peter?" the girl asked nervously.

"I'll tell you again, Sylvia. All they have out here is two young Indians patrolling the fences, and that's to keep stray cattle from breaking out. Don't worry, this place wasn't built as a secure installation."

The guest cottage was on the edge of the field—about sixty meters from the water tank. A light was on in a small room, probably the bathroom, thought Chomsky as he stalked toward the cottage. Emil frequently had to get up in the night to empty his bladder.

Faith and Hope checked their weapons—silenced Walther P-38s—and crept up to the stone and wood cottage. They pressed themselves flat against the native rock wall, near a window that was partially open. There were voices.

"Emil, while you're up, would you get me something for my stomach? Perhaps some of those Seltzer pills that Mr. Davenport gave me."

"Where are they, Lottie?"

"I put them in the white medicine chest above the sink."

Emil emerged from the bathroom, a fizzing glass in hand, when Weishaupt's assassins broke through the door. Before Emil could cry out, Sylvia Froenze leveled her Walther at him and fired repeatedly. The heavy hollow-point 9mm slugs tore through the top of his head, lifting part of his skull off and splattering gray brain material and blood over the wall.

Lottie managed to let out a piercing scream before Sylvia cut her down in her bed. She had been in the process of placing her dentures in a glass on the nightstand before the bullets caught her in the chest, shattering her heart. Her dentures clattered to the floor and bounced into the corner as she slumped in a heap onto the mattress, the gaping chest wound gushing blood.

"The children's room!" whispered Peter excitedly. "This must be it." He yanked open a door. Nothing. A storeroom.

As Peter Chomsky yanked open the second door, Erika was pushing her brother out the window. Chomsky cut the little girl down in a hail of lead and ran to the window and leveled his automatic at the fleeing boy, bracing his arm against the window frame.

"Mr. Portumo! Mr. Portumo!" little Karl screamed as he raced toward the ranch house.

Two well-aimed bullets caught the boy in the back of the neck, ending his escape.

Nick was out of bed at the first of Lottie's screams. He pulled on his cords, grabbed his Sterling submachine gun, and ran outside. As he bolted out the front door he saw the flash of pistol shots from the children's room. At the same time he heard the boy and saw him gunned down from the cottage window.

The bile rose in Nick's throat as he fought the urge to vomit. How could this have happened? Where were those two damned Cherokees that were supposed to be guarding Emil and his family?

Portumo reached the live-oak tree just as Faith and Hope emerged from the front door and sprinted toward the bluff.

Nick knew why they had come. Emil and his family had been executed for their defection. His instincts told him that he would find them murdered when he entered the cottage.

He raised his Sterling and sighted it slightly in front of the first target and squeezed the trigger, working the chattering submachine gun to the left. The stream of bullets caught Chomsky in the abdomen. It stitched the woman across the upper thighs as she was scrambling over a water pipe.

Nick ran to the boy. He was dead, his small head almost severed from his body. He raced into the guest cottage, ignoring the writhing bodies of the Section VI agents. It looked like a slaughterhouse. The 9mm bullets rendered the face of Emil unrecognizable, and the upper torso of Lottie was shattered pulp. Four bullets into the chubby frame of little Erika had almost cut her in half.

"Those pigs! Those filthy, fucking pigs!" screamed Nick. He ran outside and straddled the twitching body of Peter Chomsky. He rammed the end of the Sterling's barrel into his mouth, breaking and shattering teeth in the process. "Now, you bastard! Child killer! I'm going to blow your bloody head off!"

Chomsky pleaded—his pleas muffled by the cold blue barrel crammed in his mouth. The muffled pleas were cut short by the burst of fire from the Sterling. Chomsky jerked upward from the blast, the slugs tearing off the back of his head and splattering skull fragments over the grass.

Nick whirled just in time to see Sylvia Froenze struggling

to aim her Walther at him. Nick fell to the ground as two rounds cracked over his head. He squeezed off another burst, catching the agent in the wrist and shattering it.

"No . . . No more! I give up!" she shouted.

"Throw your weapon over here!" Nick responded.

The Walther sailed in an arc and thudded three feet from Nick. He jumped to his feet in a catlike manner and sprinted to the wounded woman. He worked the barrel of his gun into the cleavage of her breasts and worked the bolt menacingly. "Your turn, sweetheart."

"No. No, Nick! She'll be useful!" Andrea ran up and grabbed Nick's arm. Courtney Davenport was puffing behind her.

"Good Lord!" exclaimed Davenport, surveying the carnage. "Who are these people?"

Andrea knelt down beside Sylvia and yanked her into a sitting position. The agent screamed from the pain.

"You're from Section VI, aren't you? *Aren't you?*" She slapped the woman hard across the face.

"Whoa! Settle down, Andi," said Nick, his composure regained. "First you save her, then you try to kill her."

"Let's get her into the house before she bleeds to death," exclaimed Davenport.

"What about the rest of the bodies? We've got five dead bodies here," said Nick.

"Emil . . . his family . . . all dead?" cried Andrea.

"Dammit! We didn't anticipate anything like this!" added Davenport. "If I'd known, I would have let the CIA guard them."

They carried the wounded woman into the ranch house and treated her wound. Nick took a hypodermic needle and inserted it into her upper arm.

"There. That will take care of your pain for a while and put you to sleep. You'll get better medical attention when we get to the farm," said Nick, referring to the deprogramming center in Arkansas.

Sylvia Froenze fell into a comalike sleep, a small amount of blood still seeping from her splintered, bandaged wrist.

"Nick, don't worry about the bodies," said Davenport.

"We've got a burial spot here on the property. It's an old pioneer cemetery. We'll give Emil and his family a proper Christian burial. The other one we'll dump into a hole, and may his black soul rot in hell! Leave everything to me."

"Senator . . . you're not safe here anymore," said Nick. "I'm going to bring in a security team from Westwind One."

"That might not be such a bad idea, Nick." The senator breathed deeply. "I don't want to be put away before my mission is accomplished."

"All right, that's settled. Let's get this one"—Andrea pointed to the sleeping agent—"to Countercult Two. She's got a lot to tell us."

"And after?" asked Nick, a strange smile playing on his lips.

Andrea's thoughts flashed back to the cottage and the slaughterhouse scene which assaulted her.

"Then the devil take her . . . wherever he will."

Sylvia Froenze didn't need sodium pentathol. She revealed everything she knew about Section VI in the hope of saving herself. Her testimony corroborated Emil's and filled in many of the details of Section VI's Western operations. This new information was sped to field teams—those of Trucdeau and Redecker in Europe and those in the United States.

Martin Weishaupt was not asleep. His operational teams were soon fielded and the wire services of the major networks were humming with reports of pitched battles between clandestine groups in the major cities of Western Europe and the United States. Assassination followed assassination. The police in Paris, Rome, Brussels, New York, Los Angeles, and Toronto were reporting finding the bodies of unidentified men and some women; bodies whose fingerprints could not be found in the data banks of the FBI or other investigative agencies. Their fingerprints *were* on file, however. Not in Washington, D.C., but in the agent personnel section of the AVH/KGB, Section VI, in East Berlin.

• • •

The hard, baked ground trembled slightly, as if the vibrations from the powerful diesel engines were transmitted to the earth itself. The vibrations were also transmitted to the heavy galvanized structural steel of the derrick until it reached the intensity of a small earthquake. Suddenly the black liquid, which was forced up by the immense pressure of steam and natural gas mixed with the crude oil, exploded from the top of the drilling rig in a high arc and fell in huge drops. It drizzled on the exuberant crowds below.

"Halle-lujah!" cried Rasmussen. "Fazzio! We did it! We punched through that quebracho layer and hit pay dirt! I haven't seen a gusher like that in years!"

Scores of DAVROCK and Parachaco workers danced and gyrated around the booming, vibrating oil derrick, as if they were worshiping a black liquid deity. The cascading oil turned them into blackened silhouettes. Even the stoic Guaraní joined in the excitement, dancing in the black rain with the others. They slipped and slid ecstatically in the blackened mud.

Dr. Hilda Von Ziegazar and Susan could see the black oil spout from a mile distant as they bounced toward the drilling site in their Toyota pickup.

"What in the world is *that*?" boomed the masculine female doctor as she stared at the gusher. "A tornado?"

"No, ma'am," answered Susan, her heart pounding excitedly. "That's a gusher! I've seen a few in Oklahoma, but not that big. That's a whopper!"

The pressure of the gusher increased until the structural steel of the upper portion of the huge derrick weakened, and the inevitable happened. The weakened derrick started to disintegrate under the pressure. The force of the gusher carried pieces of angle iron and structural steel aloft with the power of an explosion. The steel rained down upon the oil workers like shrapnel, cutting and bruising flesh and shattering bones. Only the hard hats of the workers saved them from massive head injuries. Some of the bareheaded Indians were not so lucky, and lay in the blackened mud, their blood mixing with the falling oil.

"*Mein Gott!*" cried Von Ziegazar as she braked to a

slippery stop on the oil-soaked ground. "It looks like a battlefield!"

Susan wasted no time, nor did she wait for instructions from the doctor. She slung her first-aid kit over her shoulder and raced for the wounded men who were being dragged by the uninjured to a dry area out of the falling petroleum. She noticed that there were more wounded who were writhing in pools of oil near the base of the derrick. She ran into the rain of oil and steel, shouting commands in broken Guaraní to the Indians who stood traumatized by the gusher. She dragged several to safety, completely disregarding the deadly hail of the gusher. Within minutes, Susan's authority was established. Confidently barking orders in English, broken Spanish, and Guaraní, she sprinted around the injured workers bandaging, splinting, and giving comfort. Soon a small emergency center was established—operating out of the back of Von Ziegazar's enclosed pickup truck.

Rasmussen and Fazzio ran puffing to the truck. It was easy for them to see who was in charge. The sweating, bloodstained girl with the blue-black hair was clearly in command. Hilda Von Ziegazar worked quietly, resentfully, tending the wounded.

"Ma'am! Ma'am!" Rasmussen shouted over the roar of the gusher. "We won't be able to get this thing capped for another couple of hours. We've gotta get these men out of here!"

Susan shouted back. "That's right! They need to be hospitalized." Suddenly her mind snapped to a decision. "How far is it to Mariscal Estigarribia?" she asked the geologist.

"Only twenty-three miles and they have a small army hospital there."

"Good!" Susan could hardly contain her excitement. "Bring as many vehicles as you can over here. Load up the wounded! The doctor will stay here and tend to the ones that aren't so bad. I'll accompany the rest into Mariscal Estigarribia."

Von Ziegazar did not resist, but deferred to Susan's authority—her resentment smoldering into hatred.

After the injured were loaded into five of the trucks, Susan jumped into the lead vehicle. The small convoy lurched ahead, bumping over the dirt road and swerving to avoid the pieces of shattered derrick which littered the area.

Rasmussen leaned against Von Ziegazar's truck and then slumped against the rear tire, exhausted. Fazzio ran up to the big geologist and squatted in front of him.

"Ras . . . you're gonna crap when I . . ."

"I already have," he interrupted. "This has been one *hell* of a day. This wouldn't have happened if my men instead of those damned Indians had rigged the derricks and did the drilling."

"It ain't over yet, my friend. I've got one more bombshell for you."

"Come on, Fazzio! I can't handle another," Rasmussen said wearily.

"That little gal—the one who tore into the wounded like a tornado . . ."

"You mean our little Florence Nightingale-on-the-spot? Yeah . . . where in the hell did *she* come from? Talk about an angel of mercy."

"Tulsa," answered Fazzio.

"What? What in the hell are you talking about?"

"You asked where she came from, Ras. I'm telling you. She's from Tulsa. I've seen her in the oil fields with her father. It's been a few years, but I'd recognize her anywhere."

"Who is her father?" asked Rasmussen, his interest jarred.

"This will blow your mind, Ras. Her father is none other than Gypsy Joe Rockland."

"You mean—*the* Joe Rockland . . . part owner of DAV-ROCK?"

"Yeah. The same."

"Uh-huh!" the geologist murmured, the facts learned during the past few weeks jarring into place. "Now I know why that girl is so anxious to get to Mariscal Estigarribia. It all fits!"

"What'ya talking about, Ras?"

"Look, Fazzio." Rasmussen grabbed his lab technician's arm. "Keep this quiet—not a peep to *anybody*. Understand?"

Fazzio nodded, his face knotted into a puzzled frown.

Inside the enclosed pickup, Dr. Hilda Von Ziegazar kept

still and listened, her mind processing the information she had overheard. She thought of how she would use it against Susan Rockland.

The exhaustion finally hit her, but Susan couldn't relax. She still marveled at her boldness in taking charge of the disaster at the drilling site. It wasn't the first time. There was the dormitory fire at Bryson. It seemed as if a dormant mechanism within her simply clicked on in times of crisis and gave her a command presence.

Her exhaustion was replaced by an inner glow, a feeling of accomplishment, and a knowledge that within a few minutes she might be in the arms of Angel Caro.

The communications center had heard. News of the gusher and the disaster which followed exploded in Mariscal Estigarribia like a hand grenade. A Guaraní commando trotted up to Angel Caro and saluted smartly. "Captain Caro, the gusher has shattered the derrick and has hurt many workers. They are bringing them here to the hospital!"

"How many were hurt?" asked Caro.

"Thirty . . . forty. I am not sure. Five trucks are bringing them in. There is talk about an angel from Colonia Gardún who ministered to the wounded. She is a young one. Not one of the blond *Aryanos*. More like a Guaraní, I have heard."

"A dark one . . . from the colony?" Caro's heart was thumping.

"Sí, she was called the dark one over the radio. As you know, most—if not all—of the female *chivatos* are *Aryanos*."

"Angel, what's all the excitement about?" Paul Lancaster stumbled out of the visiting officer's cottage, rubbing the sleep out of his eyes.

"Siesta time's over, Paul. Your trip to the oil fields is going to be postponed."

"What do you mean?" asked Lancaster.

"The oil fields are coming here. About forty injured workers . . . and news of Susan."

"What?" bellowed Lancaster. "Where . . . how?"

Caro related the story of the accident and the radio report of the dark angel. The Guaraní commando stood by, uncomprehending.

"Angel, what's the relationship between this place"—he waved his hand in the direction of the Escuela para Comando—"and the Garduna?"

Caro grabbed Paul's elbow and walked him around the corner of a stucco warehouse. "Paul, I'll need your help before they get here," he said, ignoring his question.

"How?"

"When Susan gets here, she mustn't see me or talk to me until I can get her alone. I don't want the locals to know that we . . . ah, know each other."

"She knows me, too, Angel."

"Yeah, but with you, old buddy, she'll control her chemistry and play it cool. Now, if she was Olivia . . ." Caro smiled and smacked Paul's back with the flat of his hand.

The commotion outside the main gate told Caro and Lancaster that the convoy of wounded was approaching. The clouds of heavy red dust almost hid the trucks as they sped toward Mariscal Estigarribia.

Angel peered around the corner of the warehouse as the lead truck roared by after being waved through. He saw her through the swirling dust as she sat on the passenger's seat next to a grim-faced Guaraní driver. His heart pounded as he made out her features in spite of her sweaty, oil-stained appearance.

The convoy rounded the corner and squealed to a stop outside of the small hospital.

It had been a grueling two hours, but Susan forced herself to tend to the injured workers in the small but well-equipped hospital. The two Paraguayan army doctors were demanding, but unstinting in their praise of Susan's efforts.

"Señorita Rockland, your assistance here has made the difference between the life and death for several of these men, and your work in the field has prevented severe injury. I want you to be assured that we are grateful for your efforts."

"Is there anything else you need me for, Doctor?" asked Susan.

"No, my child. You go and clean up. I am going to give you a dress to wear that I bought for my daughter in La Paz. You will be the guest of our staff at the officers club this evening. There is a bathroom down the hall."

Susan hobbled down the hall, almost staggering from fatigue. Her mind reeled from the events of the past eight hours. Suddenly she heard her name whispered from inside an empty patient room.

"Pssst! Susan! Susan Rockland!"

She froze, then responded eagerly.

"Angel! Is that you?"

"It's Paul Lancaster. Remember me?"

As she entered the room, Paul closed the door behind her and locked it. He adjusted the bamboo shades so that the light filtered in, allowing them to see each other.

Susan rushed forward and impulsively put her arms around Paul's clean blue sport shirt, smearing it with grime. "Paul . . . I can't believe it! You . . . here . . . in the Chaco? I know! The gusher. You're here with DAVROCK!"

"Susan, listen. There isn't much time. Angel Caro told me . . ."

"Angel! Where is he?" she almost shouted.

"Sssshhhh! He knows you're here but you mustn't show anybody that you know him until he can get you somewhere alone. If you pass him somewhere in the fort, *don't* recognize him. It's too dangerous."

"Oh, damn! I don't know if I can do that. I've waited so long. I've had these wild fantasies about throwing my arms around him . . . kissing him. I . . . I don't know if I can control myself if I see him."

"Even if it means putting his life in danger?"

"Since you put it that way, Paul, I have no choice—do I?"

"Susan, where's Olivia?" The tone in Paul's voice was almost desperate.

Susan was caught off guard. She had known of Paul's feelings for her friend, but wasn't prepared for his question.

"Paul, she was taken from Colonia Gardún . . ."

"The headquarters for the Sacred Order of the Holy Garduna . . . right?"

"Yes. It's a prison, Paul, not a religion. Olivia was taken to a place where . . . where the . . . breeding takes place."

"Breeding?" Paul shot back.

Pools of tears formed in Susan's light brown eyes. How could she tell him that Olivia was considered little more than breeding stock, fit only for breeding a super race for a Fourth Reich in the Chaco?

"When I saw her last, she was physically healthy, but I'm worried about her mind. She was depressed. She didn't want to go."

"Señorita. Señorita Rockland. Where are you?" A voice called from the hallway in broken English.

"Paul, I've got to go. I know I'll see you later. I'm going to be at the officers club tonight. Can you and Angel be there? I'll tell you more . . . what I can."

Susan quietly left the room and padded toward the bathroom.

Like all of the other officers clubs throughout Paraguay's military establishment, the club at the Escuela para Comando at Mariscal Estigarribia was the largest, most ornate building at the fort. The large dining room was specially decorated for the occasion. The commando officers were dressed in their finest uniforms to honor the angel of mercy from Colonia Gardún. Nobody knew who she was except for Captain Angel Caro and his American guest.

The two Guaraní women assigned to Susan made the last adjustments to the jacaranda blossoms in her shining hair. The dress, which was loaned to her by the doctor, fit her perfectly. She looked beautiful. The pale blue and silver Indian-style squaw dress was slightly tight, revealing her well-formed breasts. The plunging neckline was adorned by a large silver and jade necklace. Her hair was tied back in a bun, which accentuated her high cheekbones, and was garlanded with fragrant blossoms. The two Guaraní maids fussed over her for three hours. After scrubbing the oil and grime off her, they turned her into an object of exquisite beauty.

The small orchestra broke out into the "General Stroessner" polka, an old but popular tune, which honored the former president of Paraguay. This was the signal for Dr. Félix

Pacoima to escort the guest of honor into the crowded dining room.

As she entered, her hand clutching the doctor's arm, the assembled officers rose and applauded. Susan did not want to appear anxious or obvious as she gazed around the room looking for some sign of Angel. She locked onto the envious, hate-filled eyes of Hilda Von Ziegazar—eyes that mingled hate with lust, as the lesbian doctor was aroused by the exotic beauty of Susan.

The Paraguayan doctor led her to the place of honor at the head table and seated her next to a reserve colonel in the Paraguayan Cavalry. He was strikingly handsome, with dark brown hair and electric-blue eyes.

Susan recognized Carlos Von Reinach immediately. She bowed slightly as Von Reinach took her hand and pressed it to his lips. She lifted her head and his eyes captured hers. She could not help staring at the magnificent blueness of his eyes.

Von Reinach stared back, his blood rushing to his cheeks and turning them brick red. When he was told of the extraordinary heroism of this young cultist, he had called Colonia Gardún to find out more about her. This girl, Susan Rockland, was the dark one—the Cherokee from Oklahoma. And to think, he had almost ordered her elimination.

He had read about the Cherokee Indians since that day at Fuerte Olimpo when the *guapo* convinced him to let her live. How similar the Cherokee were to his Guaraní. The Cherokee, a remarkable Indian tribe in the American Southeast, learned the white man's ways so well that they became superior to them, creating a superior hybrid culture and their own power . . . and the seeds of their near destruction as a people.

The American government reacted against the Cherokee in the 1830s, like the Spanish and the Inquisition reacted against the Guaraní and their Jesuit allies in the late 1700s. The massacres, the destruction of their villages, the death march, which was called the Trail of Tears, to the wastelands of Oklahoma did not destroy these superior people. Like the Guaraní, they thrived on adversity. Then, early in this century, Providence smiled on the Cherokee. Oil! Huge reserves of oil were found on their land; land thought worthless by the government who had forced them onto it.

And the God of the Guaraní and the Holy Garduna, their protector, had blessed them in the same way. Was it more than a coincidence that this beautiful creature, the perfect racial representative of the remarkable Cherokee, would be led to him in such a fashion, through a feat of extraordinary heroism in an oil field?

Von Reinach could not help but notice Susan's resemblance to an earlier Indian beauty, the beautiful María Ynsfrán, who was his mother. It was at his mother's knee that he learned of the former greatness of the Guaraní: of their myths, traditions, and former martial glory.

The meal over, Von Reinach toasted Susan and praised her heroism. Caro sat stiffly at his table, trying not to stare at her. Susan had seen Angel soon after starting the meal. Their eyes had met and then averted. Both tried to conceal their excitement as they chewed their way slowly through their meal and endured the effusive testimonies of the workers who were pulled to safety by Susan.

Hilda Von Ziegazar could not help but notice the attention that Von Reinach was showering on Susan. The little bitch, she fumed inwardly. How she'll pay. But first she would feel the full fury of her lust. She would purge the little tramp of her impurities. She would purify her!

Angel noticed, too. Von Reinach could not take his eyes off her, and Susan responded eagerly. She seemed to be enjoying his attention. During her animated conversation with the Gardún leader, she would steal a quick glance toward Angel, then turn back quickly to Von Reinach, smiling and chattering brightly.

Suddenly Von Reinach rose and raised his glass to again toast his beautiful guest. After a lengthy and flowery speech, he concluded:

"Unfortunately my duties take me out to the drilling site and the scene of the accident. But, as far as I am concerned, this lovely lady has the run of the fort until I am back in five days. Since she is an American, I think it is only appropriate that I assign another American, also an honored guest here at Mariscal Estigarribia, to be her escort. Captain Caro, will you please come up here?''

Angel Caro wove his way stiffly through the tables and approached Von Reinach. He stood there staring at Susan as if she were just a beautiful stranger. She stood in front of him, a slight smile—almost a teasing smile—curling the corner of her lips.

Von Reinach took Susan's slim hand and put it in Angel's. ''Señorita Rockland. This is Captain Angel Caro of the Special Forces of the American Army. He is from the American colony of Puerto Rico.''

''I'm *delighted* to meet you, Captain Caro. It's so nice to meet another American.''

''It's my pleasure, Miss Rockland. It's my hope that I can be of service to you . . . in some small way,'' he said stiffly, looking to Von Reinach for instructions.

''Captain Caro, from now on, until I return, you are completely at the señorita's disposal. Her wishes shall be your commands.''

Susan's eyes flashed mischievously as Caro smiled in acknowledgment.

''So . . . go. Enjoy the hospitality of the fort.''

Von Reinach kissed Susan's hand with a low, gallant bow. ''Until I return then, my brave little Cherokee.''

Susan and Angel walked slowly and casually out of the club as the crowd dispersed. They kept walking, not daring to speak. They fought to control their emotions as they stepped out into the tropical night. Down the walkway they came to the chapel, the same one they met in during their clandestine meeting several months before.

Wordlessly they walked behind the chapel and stopped. The sound of the insects seemed to diminish. They just stood and listened. Silence. They were completely alone. Susan slipped her arms around his neck and pressed her lips softly to his. The dam broke, and in seconds she was smothering the Puerto Rican with her kisses.

XVI.

When Calvin Bouchegrave was in one of his black moods, he was not one to be trifled with. He tromped on the gas pedal and his new Lincoln Mark VII limousine lurched ahead. He was daring, just hoping that a state trooper would pull him over for excessive speed as he traveled down the Old Dominion Freeway toward his estate on Parramore Island. There was little chance of that. Every policeman in his home territory knew his car and license plate. In fact, most of them owed their jobs to the senator.

During the past several months, Bouchegrave had been growing more and more anxious about his participation in cocaine trafficking; and yet it was his financial salvation. Four years ago, he was on the verge of bankruptcy—of losing it all: his mansion, his property, and other properties, including coastal and tourist investments in Haiti and the Dominican Republic. Unwise investments, and the recession of 1986 had all but wiped out the liquid assets of the Bouchegrave family fortune. Only the family name, his position as a United States senator, and his ability to influence legislation had enabled him to secure loans at astronomical interest rates.

That problem was behind him now. The loans were paid off, and his investments, once on the verge of being sold to pay off his loans, were his once more—and prospering. Cults and cocaine had been good to Calvin Bouchegrave.

It was four years ago that a representative of the Paraguayan

Embassy asked to meet with him. The diplomat was a member of the Holy Garduna. He offered the panicky Bouchegrave a deal he couldn't refuse: the use of his island mansion and his plantation at Port Concepción on the Dominican Republic's northeast coast.

His percentage from the cocaine traffic had pulled him out of the red. The legislation which he had introduced in Congress, at the request of his benefactors, had resulted in what amounted to a "Bill of Rights" for religious cults. The payoff for that particular favor had been generous. When he was successful, his new friends were extremely generous. But when he failed, and up until now his failures were minor, there were veiled threats to expose him.

This morning had been a failure, a massive failure. His efforts to have a bill passed by Congress legalizing the use of cocaine had been blocked by the efforts of Courtney Davenport and his allies, who were a growing power in Congress. Indeed, the mood of Congress and of the entire nation was growing more conservative. With the assassination of cult leaders, the destruction of their physical resources, and the barrage of propaganda against them in the media lately, key individuals in government and society became emboldened to speak out against their excesses. And a new phenomenon had arisen: Squads of militant ex-cultists, many recently deprogrammed, were confronting, discrediting, and attacking cult members wherever they were found . . . at airports, train stations, the streets, and even in the halls of Congress itself. Nor were the supporters of cults safe. They, too, were targets.

Yes, the national mood was changing. Calvin Bouchegrave wanted to change with it, but he couldn't without alienating his "new friends" and putting his reputation, and perhaps his life, in danger.

Bouchegrave's huge Lincoln approached the chain link fence which surrounded his Parramore Island estate. A guard appeared from behind a huge ancient maple tree, unlocked the gate, and waved the senator through. Bouchegrave inched his limousine forward and peered at the guard over his bifocals. He didn't recognize him. Must be a new man, although security necessitated that personnel rotation be kept to a minimum.

He drove slowly along the treelined gravel road leading to the manor house. There wasn't a guard in sight. Something was wrong. There were usually two or three guards among the trees when he drove in. Bouchegrave picked up his CB microphone, flicked the switch to send, and spoke:

"Mourning Dove to Neptune. . . . Mourning Dove to Neptune. . . . Come in, Neptune."

Nothing. No response from the manor house. The senator made his decision quickly. He tromped on the gas pedal and spun around skillfully in a clearing which flanked both sides of the road. In the middle of his turn, three shots rang out and three of his tires went flat. Camouflaged commandos ran from the treeline and pointed their automatic weapons at the senator in the immobilized limousine.

"Senator Bouchegrave," said the tall one with the sandy-colored hair, "please remove yourself from your vehicle . . . *slowly* . . . with your hands in the air."

"Just *what* in the hell is going on? Who are you men? What are you doing on my property?" the tall, slim, aristocratic-looking senator said indignantly as he emerged from the car.

A commando spun him around roughly and shoved him against the fender. "Feet spread apart . . . lean over the fender . . . touch your nose to the hood."

Bouchegrave was sweating profusely. He spread his hands on the Lincoln's shiny black hood and touched his aquiline nose to the metal. Beads of perspiration puddled on the car. His mind was fearful and racing as the armed men searched him and rummaged through his car. Were they drug-enforcement people? Mafia? A rival cult? Where were the regular guards, the ones provided by Barrajas and the Garden Children?

A pickup arrived from the direction of the mansion, and the senator was hustled aboard, his hands tied behind his back. Two grim-faced commandos sat with him in the back as the truck lurched and crunched over the gravel, back toward the manor house.

Bouchegrave was marched into his own home, flanked by

the two gun-toting guards. From the huge picture window in the living room, he could see the submarine still moored under the covered pier, the camouflaged netting obscuring the outline of the craft from the seaward side.

Raúl Caro strode into the room. A .45-caliber pistol dangled from his webbed belt. He stood with his hands on his hips in front of the cowed senator and stared at him. His eyes flashed malevolence. Rivulets of sweat coursed down Bouchegrave's forehead, over his nose, and dripped onto the plush carpet.

"Well, well, *Calvin*," Caro said mockingly. "This isn't the kind of homecoming you expected, is it?"

"Who . . . who are you people?" the senator said weakly.

"Why, we're your friends, Calvin. We're here to offer you a deal you can't refuse. We've taken over your little weekend retreat so we can negotiate," remarked Caro.

It took only ten minutes to convince Calvin Bouchegrave that this strange armed group of men had enough evidence against him to land him a thirty-year jail sentence, plus the confiscation of his property.

The commandos brought out the submarine captain, who blurted out more information, further implicating Bouchegrave in the cult cocaine-smuggling network.

Bouchegrave sank to his knees in a near faint.

"Take the captain back to his quarters," barked Caro. "Lay the senator on the couch."

Minutes later Bouchegrave revived, his glazed eyes slightly out of focus as he spoke.

"Please . . . please . . . don't turn me in. I'd . . . I'd lose it all. Everything I have . . . everything."

Raúl leaned over, his nose almost touching the senator's. "That depends on you, Calvin. You're going to have to do an about-face in the Senate and cooperate completely with us."

"Cooperate? What do you mean?"

"What I mean is that we're going to stay here and continue to operate your estate as if nothing happened. We'll accept the Garden Children, but instead of sending them to Paraguay, we'll send them to our little rehabilitation camps. Meanwhile, you'll be in the Senate doing *our* thing, and you'll have a tutor to help you introduce correct legislation and act in appropriate ways."

"A tutor? Who . . . is . . . it?" asked Bouchegrave timidly.

A slight smile flickered across Raúl's rugged face. "An old friend of yours, Calvin. One who will lead you out of the darkness and into the valley of light," Caro said dramatically. Then he added, "Senator Courtney Davenport."

"Are you sure about all this, Paul? Are you absolutely sure?"

"Yes, Brother Rockland. I was there. I saw Susan. I talked to her. I know what the Holy Garduna is and what kind of power it has. And now that we've brought in that gusher . . ."

Gypsy Joe Rockland sank into his big leather chair as if he wanted to merge with it and forget the written report which was the fruit of Paul Lancaster's investigations in Paraguay.

"I never expected to learn something like this. This is unbelievable!" He shook the report in the air. "And Olivia is to be used . . . as a breeder . . . in some kind of racial experiment?"

Paul nodded. "If they don't dispose of her first, Reverend. As I told you, Susan informed me that she wasn't too stable."

"And Susan . . . she'll be all right?" Joe Rockland's eyes pleaded for an affirmative answer.

"I believe so, sir. Susan is the 'Woman of the Hour' down there after her heroism in the oil field. She'll use her head and survive until we can get her out of there."

Rockland sat down, his swarthy face a mask of anxiety. Suddenly he brightened. "Paul, I want a meeting in two days with Nick Portumo and Andrea Macranskia. Get Rasmussen up here from Paraguay; and, oh, yes, Raúl Caro, too. Caro's in eastern Virginia on assignment. Call CC-3 to contact him. And, Paul, not a word of this to Mr. Davenport."

"I understand, sir."

"One more thing, Paul. Courtney is back in Washington. He'd blow this situation sky-high and create an international incident if he found out that his 'brother-in-Christ,' Carlos Von Reinach, is responsible for his daughter's captivity by some insane neo-Nazi cult that intends to use her as breeding stock."

Two days later, Nick, Andrea, Rasmussen, and Raúl sat around the big oval table in the boardroom of Tulsa's DAVROCK Building. Joe Rockland sat at the head, nervously shuffling through a pile of papers. Paul Lancaster sat slightly off to Rockland's right, away from the table, his attaché case on his lap. Gypsy Joe had conducted the initial briefing, with Paul and Rasmussen filling in details.

"And this Von Reinach character has suckered the old man into believing that this Holy Garduna is some kind of benevolent Christian organization?" asked Raúl Caro incredulously.

"Yes, and more. He has been bankrolling Von Reinach into turning the Holy Garduna into a formidable private army," added Rockland.

"The Commando School at Mariscal Estigarribia—where Angel is stationed—is, for all practical purposes, the training school for the Garduna. Its officers, down to the company level, are members of the cult. Susan told me that she saw a vehicle park of almost twenty-five armored cars, and jeeps with rocket launchers, at Colonia Gardún," said Paul.

The meeting dragged on. Nick, who had been scribbling notes, finally said, "Okay, we've got enough data here to come up with some kind of plan. Let's take a look at what we're up against. First, the oil found in the Chaco must not be lost to the West under any circumstances . . . right?"

The others nodded in agreement.

"Second," Nick continued, "the Holy Garduna is *the* controlling power in the Chaco . . ."

"And soon, perhaps, in the entire country," interrupted Paul.

"Is there an alternate source of power which is anti-Garduna and anticommunist which we could work with—perhaps the country's generals?" asked Andrea.

Paul chuckled. "I anticipated your very question when I was down there, Andrea. The senior officers are hopelessly corrupt. The Garduna has involved them in the cocaine trade to the point where most of the Officer's Corps, and many in the civil government, have been compromised."

"Geez! It sounds like the damned Mafia!" exclaimed Raúl.

"In a way it is, Raúl, but they use evil methods to bring about a so-called righteous and a resurrected, glorified, and powerful Paraguay," Paul continued.

"Let's not forget the girls," said Andrea. "It sounds like Susan is temporarily safe, but Olivia's situation is desperate."

Paul stood, and unrolled a map of Paraguay and her neighboring countries, and pinned it on the corkboard which lined part of the wall.

"Right here"—Paul pointed to a section of eastern Bolivia—"is located a small guerrilla group, known as the Socialist Christian Action party of Paraguay. They have been harassing the government for years. It's anticommunist, although mildly socialist . . ."

"We can live with that," interrupted Nick.

"And anti-Garduna," continued Paul. It has attracted some of the best minds in the country. There's perhaps more sympathy for their party program, and respect from the ordinary people for this group, than for many of the other parties contending for power. Their problem is that they've never been able to put their act together militarily."

Raúl tapped his pencil thoughtfully on the table. The others turned and looked at him, anticipating his reaction.

He smiled. "Looks like SCAP needs an adviser. Right, comrades?"

They all laughed. Taking his question as an acceptance, they were relieved.

"The buildup of the Christian Action party will have to be coordinated with my brother," said Raúl. "Once these people get moving, Angel's commandos will take to the field and, from what Paul tells us, they're crack counterguerrilla troops."

"Mr. Rockland," said Rasmussen. "I'm going back to the Chaco with some new equipment. I can get to Angel. I'd like to be in on this. Let me coordinate the details between Raúl and Angel. I have more freedom to maneuver down there."

"Fine. Do it, Ras," Joe Rockland said. "Paul, I hate to

ask you to use your father, but would he have *any* information on who the Christian Action people or their sympathizers are in the capital?''

"That's possible, sir. Let me explore it.''

Raúl stood, stretched, and then walked over to the map. He pointed to a spot almost at the top of the country.

"Right here, up the Paraguay River, is an inland port, Fuerte Olimpo. This is where the submarines come in, unload the Garden Children, and pick up the processed cocaine. If the Bolivian connection with La Cuna . . .''

"Where Olivia is kept, right, Raúl?'' asked Andrea.

"Yes. If the Bolivian connection with La Cuna and Fuerte Olimpo were smashed, the economic power of the Garduna would be ruined.''

"Until they replaced it with oil,'' said the geologist.

"How do you propose to get to Fuerte Olimpo?'' asked Andrea.

"Submarine,'' answered Caro.

Nick leaned back in his swivel chair, playing with the ends of his newly grown mustache. "Intriguing idea. Explain, Raúl.''

"We have the crew intact. They're in it strictly for the money. They'll cooperate because they have no choice. We have all of the ship's codes and signals used to communicate with Fuerte Olimpo and the refueling and resupply station at Puerto Concepción in the Dominican Republic; and, most important, we have Calvin Bouchegrave and his estate in our hip pocket. We've inherited the entire Garden Children cocaine network. All we have to do is operate it for our own use.''

"When the sub pulls into Fuerte Olimpo, they're going to be expecting a group of Garden Children. Do we have any spares?'' asked Paul.

Andrea and Nick exchanged knowing glances.

"Yes, we have a few in mind,'' answered Nick.

The Senate Hearing Room was designed for larger meetings, but what the group present lacked in numbers, it made up for in importance and influence.

There were twenty-three top officials from the State, Treasury, Health and Welfare, and Drug Enforcement agencies, plus some of the top state and city police officials in the nation.

Courtney Davenport arrived with Secretary of State Roger Benson in tow.

"I don't know why you dragged me here, Courtney, or involved State. Cults and drugs aren't my area of jurisdiction."

"What about your daughter, Roger?"

The secretary's face suddenly became a mask of sadness. "She's not part of my problem anymore. She became lost to me years ago. Her involvement in drugs and that damned cult was the culmination of years of rebellion against everything I and her family stood for."

His expression changed to bitterness. "Patty's beyond help. She's created a living hell for herself. It was her choice. She chose it with malice aforethought."

Courtney shared Benson's pain as he took his seat at the chairman's section in the middle of the curved counter in front of the assembled group.

The hearing was totally unprecedented. Most of the witnesses were young ex-cultists, who gave personal testimonies of their experiences and the personal destructiveness of cult membership. The linkage to organized crime and foreign governments, especially Section VI, was particularly revealing. Elaine Kearney and Bob Talbot testified, after several of the ex-cultists, on the success of deprogramming. They avoided any reference, however, to Courtney Davenport or his countercult movement.

The star witness arrived—a young woman under indictment in several large cities for leading militant attacks on cult meetings. The Denver chief of police took the witness stand before her. He testified of the near paralysis of his city by cult activities until countercult militants, led by the young woman in the audience, swept his city of their presence. Although officially under indictment for leading riots, no jury in the country would have condemned her or her young vigilantes. The mood of the country was definitely in their corner.

Roger Benson studied the tanned, athletic-looking blonde with the clear blue eyes sitting halfway to the rear of the room. He took off his glasses, rubbed his eyes, and then cleaned them with a tissue before putting them on again. He wasn't sure. He wanted to believe it, but was afraid to. He looked helplessly at Courtney, who flashed him a wide smile before he called the next witness.

"Miss Patricia Benson."

Patty Benson's testimony took thirty minutes; and they were, perhaps, the proudest thirty minutes in Roger Benson's life. She was forceful and articulate, revealing the scope and influence of cult activities in the United States. Clearly, Patty Benson had become more than a militant. She had become an expert on cults. She outlined what roles citizen paramilitary groups, such as hers, could do outside of the law. Her proposals were frightening, perhaps, but these were unusual times, frightening times, and old formulas and existing institutions were either overwhelmed by the influx of cults or unwilling to deal with them.

When the meeting adjourned, Patricia Benson walked over to her father and impulsively put her arms around him, hugging him tightly and kissing his tear-stained cheek. It had been years since she had done that. It seemed as if they had been strangers forever—since her involvement with drugs at fourteen.

"Patty . . . Patty, honey, I . . . I don't know what to say." A beaming Roger Benson fumbled for words. "You . . . you were absolutely magnificent on the witness stand! Patty, I'm so proud of you."

Her father's words were almost the words of a stranger. As long as she could remember, she had never heard her father's praise. The ex-Harvard professor of international relations was a man of exact standards—impossible standards—and if one didn't measure up, he or she was shut out of the inner world of Roger Benson.

At fourteen, Patricia stopped trying to buy into her father's private world, a world where love and approval were dispensed as rewards for "correct" behavior and excellent grades. She had found an alternate world, the world of drugs and cults: a destructive world, but one in which she did not have to perform to gain acceptance.

Patty turned to her father and took both of his hands in hers. She gazed steadily into his eyes, eyes that pleaded for her return.

"Patty, your mother and I would like to have you come home and . . . . and start college. I know we can get you into Amherst. I know the dean of . . . oh, oh, there I go, dictating your life again. I'm sorry, honey. We'd like to have you home, no matter what you want to do."

"Daddy, there's nothing I'd rather do than return to my old room . . . go through my things, and pick up the threads of my life, the life that unraveled for me at fourteen." She glanced at Courtney Davenport and back at her father. "But I've got a mission to perform. For the first time in my life, I've got a cause—a crusade, if you want to call it that, and I've got to follow this through, Daddy. I'm too involved to drop it now. I've got too much of myself invested."

Roger Benson was disturbed. He was a rational man, an intellectual—a gentle cynic. He felt uncomfortable around crusaders and true believers; and yet that was what his daughter had become and that was what had caused her transformation.

Patty sensed her father's uneasiness. "Daddy." Her clear blue eyes probed into his. "Would you rather I'd be . . . the way I was?"

His mind was jolted back to memories of an earlier Patricia. "No, Patty," he said softly. "Complete your mission. Your family will be waiting for you when you return."

Dr. Benito Salazar longed for the classroom and students to teach. That was his first love, and the ten years he taught political science at the National University in Asunción were the happiest of his life. He took out his briar pipe and tamped in a load of his custom tobacco, the one luxury he allowed himself since taking up the role of guerrilla chieftain of the Christian Action party. The doctor was not a guerrilla tactician, not a good one anyway, but he looked the part with his carefully cultivated Pancho Villa mustache, which had become a source of pride. He absentmindedly twisted the long handlebars as he gazed down from the little rise on which he was perched.

The men and few women of the guerrilla camp were clustered around the roaring fire, which did little to alleviate the cool dampness of the eastern Bolivian jungle. The greenwood smoke sent clouds of acrid spirals filtering through the double canopy of trees. Salazar walked down and called his guerrillas into formation. They formed into a ragged line, some armed with World War I bolt-action Enfields; some with no weapons at all. Their bandoliers, worn haphazardly around their chests in a diagonal pattern, were only partially filled with bullets.

The professor's troops were hardly a match for the ineffectual Bolivian Army. His dark brown eyes reflected discouragement, bordering on despair. What will happen, he wondered, when the elite counterguerrilla troops of Mariscal Estigarribia take to the field against them?

Suddenly a volley of shots rang out, and several dozen bullets plowed up the earth between the guerrillas and Salazar. Everyone scattered, some firing wildly into the green darkness of the jungle. His troops lay panting—frightened—on the open ground, their weapons pointed in a variety of directions.

Salazar cocked his pistol and waited. He knew in his guts that those firing the shots could have killed him and all of his little band if they wished. In the past month, strange things had been happening. Several of his patrols had been ambushed by an enemy firing blanks. They were never seen. In another situation, two of his sentries had been rendered unconscious by some sort of a chemical aerosol, and the unseen enemy had sneaked into their camp and stolen important documents and the only automatic weapons they had. And then, in the most frightening situation up until now, Salazar had woken up with a note pinned on his shirt which read: "Bang! Bang! Amigo, you're dead!"

Every time one of the guerrillas moved, a shot rang out, kicking up the dirt near him. They were trapped; their position was hopeless. A voice bellowed from the jungle beyond.

"Soldiers of the Christian Action Movement, leave your

weapons on the ground! Remove your bandoliers and pistol belts and stand in the same formation you were in before the firing!''

The guerrillas looked in Salazar's direction for instructions. The professor's cheek was pressed hard against the sand. His tears of frustration dampened the granules, making small indentations in his cheek. He clutched his weapon tightly, knowing that if he didn't surrender, his gallant but ineffectual soldiers would be slaughtered. He also knew that if the invisible enemy were Paraguayans, then captivity would be worse than a quick death on the jungle floor, especially if they were members of the Holy Garduna. But they might be Bolivian rangers. If that were the case, then the worst they could expect would be long prison terms, and the firing squad for him.

Benito Salazar made his decision quickly, after several more shots rang out and a bullet plowed the earth inches from his head. ''All right! We will do as you say!'' shouted Salazar.

''Then do it, amigo . . . and quickly!'' responded the voice from behind the thick green ferns.

The dejected guerrillas formed into pathetic, listless ranks with Dr. Salazar in front. The ground was littered with weapons and equipment. They stood waiting. After five minutes, no one had yet emerged from the jungle. There was absolute silence. Finally, Salazar could stand it no longer.

''Isn't it enough that you have captured us? Do not mock us! Show yourselves!'' he cried, the tears running down his cheeks.

Suddenly five camouflaged commandos emerged from the trees, assault rifles pointed at Salazar's little army. As they surrounded the little band, Raúl Caro walked up to the professor and saluted smartly. ''Raúl Caro at your service, Dr. Salazar.'' He extended his hand.

The confused guerrilla chieftain extended his awkwardly and cautiously. ''I . . . I do not understand. Who are you men? Are you enemies?''

''We are friends, Dr. Salazar. We have been trying to

point out the vulnerabilities of your group over the past few weeks."

"*You* were responsible for the sentries—and the note on my shirt?"

Caro smiled, nodded, and helped the commandos stack the guerrillas' weapons by the treeline. Salazar's troops were commanded to sit.

It took only ten minutes for Raúl Caro to explain who he was and what he proposed to do.

"We have followed the history of your movement," explained Caro. "You are brave. There is no doubt about that, but you are ineffective fighters, and you have absolutely no sense of security."

"Yes, you have proven that several times. Your proof leaves what is left of our dignity in shreds," Salazar murmured. He stood, and Caro walked over and put his hands on the shoulders of the crestfallen guerrilla chieftain and looked steadily into his eyes.

If Salazar was not a great warrior, he was a judge of men, and a man's eyes were the mirror of his soul—his character and his intentions. In the eyes of Raúl Caro he saw a mixture of humor and pity; but most of all, concern for his ragged little group.

Salazar put his hands on Caro's shoulders, the two men gazing at each other. The doctor was the first to speak.

"Señor Caro. I trust you. We are in your hands. We thank you for coming to us. Teach us what we must know to liberate our fatherland."

"Dr. Von Ziegazar, do you have the medical records of the Davenport girl?"

The masculine female doctor flipped through several folders and yanked out Olivia's record and handed it to Julio Barrajas.

Barrajas was the chairman of the Strength Through Joy Committee at La Cuna. Every month, those selected for breeding would be examined medically. If found fit, they would be assigned a mate and isolated in a Cottage of Joy. Here they would live together until the first sign of pregnancy. The girls would then be assigned to light duties, usually in the first-stage cocaine processing plant until delivery time.

"I have examined Olivia Davenport, Brother Barrajas, and find her physically fit to breed. There is nothing organically wrong with her," said the doctor.

"But her mind, Hilda. She has detached herself from reality. She lies curled up on her bunk most of the day. Her friends bring her food. Often she does not eat. There have been times when she doesn't even get up to go to the bathroom. She relieves herself in her bed, and her friends have to clean her up."

The doctor smiled to herself as she visualized the perversions that Barrajas had tried to force upon Olivia weeks earlier. She had learned the details from the Dane and the girl from California. No, not everyone could handle the strange tastes of Barrajas—let alone a psychologically fragile girl like Olivia Davenport.

"It is my recommendation to the committee that the girl, Olivia, be given a treatment of rehabilitation. Her mental affliction is temporary. She will revive. When she is functional again, give her light duty in the refinery."

The committee was surprised at Von Ziegazar's proposal. Usually she was the first to advise disposing of the unfit, especially if they were young and pretty.

Barrajas cocked a suspicious eye and chuckled. "Why the sudden compassion for this little *chivato*, Hilda? Are you saving her for yourself when she recovers?"

The swine! The filthy Latin swine! thought Von Ziegazar. She fought the urge to lash out at him, but swallowed her desire.

"No, my dear Julio," she cooed sweetly. "Evidently, a night with you has ruined her for me—or for anybody else. My criterion for retaining her is based solely upon her genetics, and not upon her ability to perform in bed. Olivia Davenport is genetically superior to most of the girls here at La Cuna. Even in her mental state, she is capable of conceiving and giving birth to a child of quality. We must not waste her."

Another committee member, a young Guaraní Indian man, spoke up. "I believe she is right, brothers. We have received reports that the feeder cults in North America have been cruelly hurt by anticult forces. Even the supply from the Garden Children has been curtailed. This situation may be temporary, but until we are sure, the Davenport girl must be utilized."

The committee voted, with Barrajas casting the only negative vote. Olivia was not to be killed. She would be rehabilitated until she was functional, and then impregnated.

After the meeting, Von Ziegazar walked over to Olivia's cottage. The other girls were gone. Olivia lay on her bunk bed, sleeping soundly. The doctor sat beside her and stroked her hair. "Do you think I saved your miserable ass because you are worthy? No, *mein schönes Kind*. I must keep you alive until I decide how I can use you to destroy your little Cherokee friend."

The jeep left the red dust behind in little swirls as it began to climb into the foothills. The soil, like the flora and fauna, seemed to change abruptly as Angel and Susan sped up the incline. The red baked clay of the Chaco gave way to the greenness of the Andean foothills, which were about fifty miles south of La Cuna, near the Bolivian border.

The disaster at the oil field had taken a week longer than Carlos Von Reinach had expected, and Susan was left at Mariscal Estigarribia almost forgotten. The days alone with each other were beyond Susan's and Angel's expectations. Angel was, for all practical purposes, without a job temporarily. His commandos were drafted by orders of the Holy Garduna to report to the oil fields and help repair the damage and erect new, reinforced derricks. Carlos Von Reinach felt a new sense of urgency to develop the fields and create a new, more stable economic base for the Garduna. Reports had been filtering into his headquarters that the market for cocaine among cults in North America might be threatened by new attitudes and new legislation.

Angel and Susan took advantage of the confusion to be together constantly. The heroic actions of Susan and the way in which she handled herself that night at the officers club gave Angel more than a clue that she was a remarkable and unusual young woman. The last two weeks gave him greater insight into this Cherokee-Negro *chivato*. She was a person of depth, intelligence, and warmth. Many of her actions during the past several years could be explained by her devotion to Olivia, and her desire to keep her from harm's way.

"I know a spot that'll blow your mind, Susan," said Angel. "It's a place that my troops found while conducting an exercise up here a couple of months ago."

She smiled broadly and put her hand on his knee as he wheeled the jeep off the dirt road and onto a tree-covered jungle pathway. "Wow! This is almost like going into a tunnel of love!" exclaimed Susan as the cool green of the ferns slapped against the side of their vehicle.

Several minutes later, Angel braked to a stop. "Let's get out. We've got to walk about a mile."

He took his machete and parted the wide ferns as he probed through the dense vegetation. Finally, they heard the rushing of water ahead.

"What's that?" Susan whispered as she clutched his arm.

"Nothing to be afraid of, you'll see."

They walked a little farther, and as Angel parted the last of the wide fern leaves, they came upon a beautiful parklike setting: tall green grass; smooth boulders; and a small waterfall, which cascaded off a ridge almost thirty feet high. The waterfall emptied into a large clear pool, and white sand formed a half-crescent beach on the approach side of the pool. On the opposite side of the water were huge smooth rocks which kept the jungle at bay. The spray from the falling water formed a permanent mist near the falls, creating a rainbow. The hot tropical winter sun was filtered and cooled by the trees overhead. Wild palms shot out at odd angles, lining the creek below the pool.

"It's a paradise!" gasped Susan. "It's too beautiful for words! Angel, let's go swimming!"

"Yes." He held her tightly, feeling her wildly beating heart against his chest. "It's our little Shangri-la. I doubt if even the local Indians know about this place. Did you bring a bathing suit?" His question was accompanied by a leer.

Susan smiled slightly, and threw her head back and laughed. "No. Today I'm a child of nature, and I'm reverting to my childhood!" She giggled mischievously as she peeled off her clothes. Moments later, she stood before Angel completely naked and unashamed.

Angel sucked in his breath, overwhelmed by her magnificent body. He took off his fatigues and shorts, and began the tedious task of unlacing his combat boots. Susan knelt down in the gleaming white sand and started to unlace the other.

"Do you always take off your clothes before your boots?" she teased. "Do you realize how silly you look sitting in your birthday suit and wearing a pair of boots?"

Angel felt ridiculous and blushed, causing Susan to laugh even harder.

"Just hurry up with that boot so we can get into the water," he said.

When she had finished, they stood, their bodies pressed together. Susan reached up and put her arm around his shoulder, drawing him to her, and kissed him deeply. They fell gently to the sand and lay there as the warmth of the sun played over their bodies.

Susan's light brown eyes, which were alive with sensual expectation, locked into his. "Angel, these past two weeks have been the happiest of my life. If the Garduna crucified me tomorrow, I'd die happy, just knowing that you love me."

They had spoken of love before, but had never been in a place—or had the time—to express their love.

"Susan," he whispered, "the Garduna is *not* going to crucify you. Nobody is going to harm you. I'm going to get you out of this wretched country—and soon. I'm putting you in storage until I can leave, and then . . ."

"And what, sweetheart?" she asked, kissing his cheek.

"And then we'll be married. If you'll take an army officer."

Susan's eyes filled with tears. She blinked tightly and held him, squeezing her arms around his waist.

"I . . . I wanted to hear that. Yes! I'll marry you. I'd like nothing better. The thought of being your wife is the most beautiful thing I can think of."

"Think of the stories we can tell our kids, Susan, when they ask how Mommy met Daddy."

Suddenly Susan frowned. She raised on one elbow and looked oddly at Angel.

"What's wrong?" he asked.

"Olivia."

"Olivia?"

"Angel, we've got to get her out of La Cuna before I . . . I mean . . . before we can do anything. I couldn't leave the Chaco . . . or marry you, knowing that I left my best friend to those animals."

"I knew you would say that. I would have been disappointed in you if you hadn't." With the back of his hand he brushed her blue-black hair, which had cascaded down the sides of her face and framed it. He traced the outline of her nose, throat, and breast with his finger, stopping at her nipple. He raised her nipple with the tip of his finger and kissed it. She pressed his mouth to her breast, sighing slightly. He moved toward her lips and kissed her fully—his tongue probing for hers. She responded eagerly and slid her leg over his hip. They pressed their pelvises together until Angel's hardness found her furry softness.

Later, delicious with exhaustion, they fell into a deep sleep in each other's arms.

Angel felt the cold water dribble the length of his sun-baked body. He recoiled in shock and opened his eyes. Susan laughed playfully as she wrung out the last of the water from her blouse onto Angel's back.

"All right, little Miss Nasty Ass!" he shouted. "You've had it!"

Squealing with laughter, Susan ran the length of the beach. Angel pounded after her. Suddenly she wheeled, dove into the sparkling pool, and swam for the waterfall.

Angel dove in after her, but upon surfacing, discovered she was nowhere to be seen. "Susan?" he shouted. Nothing. Just the roar of the waterfall. He swam underwater toward the fall. There, behind the cascading water, was a pair of shapely, tanned legs treading water. He managed an extra surge of power and grabbed them. Susan squealed and broke away, swimming in long, powerful strokes toward the center of the pool. Angel caught up with her and dunked her repeatedly. Laughing loudly, they bobbed to the surface and kissed.

Angel felt their presence first, before Susan saw the group of armed men sitting on the boulders. Several more appeared on the beach. One was sorting out the clothes they had left on the sand.

"Please . . . finish your swim." The one with the large handlebar mustache smiled. "It pleases me to see you young folks enjoying yourselves."

"Yes, like Adam and Eve in the Garden, frolicking in your innocent nakedness," chuckled another.

Wordlessly Angel and Susan walked out of the pool and onto the beach. They dried themselves self-consciously and slipped into their clothes. Angel noticed that his pistol belt with his loaded .45 was gone.

"I suppose it would be a waste of effort to ask who you gentlemen are and what you want," said Angel.

"On the contrary, my dear captain. I am Comandante Benito Salazar."

"Of the Christian Action party . . . right?" interrupted Caro.

"Yes! Very good!" The professor smiled, showing large white teeth under his mustache. "As the adviser to the commandos who will soon take to the field against us, I'm sure that you have done your homework on our little band."

"Yours . . . among others," Angel responded sullenly.

"Enough!" The professor's expression changed suddenly. "You will come with us. We have a rendezvous with our adviser."

They snaked single file through the dense jungle for an hour before coming to a small clearing. Angel's trained eye could tell that it was a temporary camp. He discerned that the guerrillas were fairly well trained, confident, and had a grasp of the essentials of security. The automatic weapons they had were new Heckler & Koches with a sprinkling of Belgian FALs and Uzis. They were logically uniformed in jungle-striped fatigues and new combat boots. They might be a formidable enemy, Angel thought, if I ever have the opportunity to take to the field against them.

"Captain Caro . . . Susan Rockland!" called the *comandante*. "You will wait here until I contact our adviser." The guerrilla chieftain had a mysterious twinkle in his eye as he slipped into the jungle.

Salazar reappeared with five black-bereted commandos. The leader approached the couple, who stood in the clearing.

Susan frowned as she noticed the similarity between Angel and the leader of the strange armed men.

Angel's mouth flung open with surprise. "Son of a bitch!" he whispered, and broke out into a grin.

The commando leader gave him a tight *abrazo*, then stepped back smiling. "Hello, brother!" exclaimed Raúl Caro.

XVII.

The late July heat was stifling. Usually a slight breeze blew in from the seaward side of Parramore Island in midafternoon, and it was often accompanied by brief but violent thundershowers. But not so this afternoon.

Nick lay languidly in the striped canvas-duck hammock strung between two of the white pillars of the back porch of the Bouchegrave mansion. He sipped his gin and tonic slowly and deliberately, and Andrea leaned against the south pillar, watching the frenzied activity on the large sloping lawn below.

"Don't you have any pangs of guilt, Captain Portumo? Relaxing up here while those poor kids are working themselves to death?"

Nick grinned widely, his white, even teeth flashing under his now-full handlebar mustache. "No way, milady. Those youngsters down there are going through a character-building experience. They'll be the better for it when they complete their training."

Fifty-three young men and women, all deprogrammed ex-cultists, struggled and tumbled on the lawn as they went through their kick-punch karate drills.

It had been an excruciating eight weeks. The young people who were selected for the raid on Fuerte Olimpo had to complete a rigorous cycle of training which exceeded even the requirements of Marine Corps boot camp. Nicholas Portumo had created the curriculum of the course, the skills to be mastered, and the instructional aids to assist the trainees in learning their tasks.

Andrea sauntered over to the hammock. She was wearing a pair of tan midthigh shorts, and a braless halter top. She seemed to be tanned all over. She leaned her thigh against Nick's shoulder and teased his tousled dark brown hair. He smiled up at her and ran his hand up the back of her leg.

It was getting easier for Nick and Andrea to speak of love. And, as it was now mentioned more frequently than before, they spoke of commitment. They might be caught up in the bizarre world of the countercult movement, but the bedrock values of Nick and Andrea were solidly old-fashioned. Both were the products of traditional societies, Andrea's communist upbringing as thoroughly conservative and traditional in its way as Nick's structured life in the military. The episode on the bean-bag chair at Countercult Two several months before had taken both of them by surprise. Neither was particularly promiscuous or loose. It just happened. But it didn't happen again. The experience had been an equalizer; a barrier had been broken through, and an understanding had started to develop. Their passions became inflamed at times when alone, but their loins were disciplined. There was the beginning of a realization that they were entering into a relationship which might become permanent and honorable, which was consistent with their value systems. They did not want to be burdened with regrets later on.

"Nick, have they shown any resistance to weapons training?" Andrea asked.

"Those who did have been weeded out, Andi. We'll let them bash heads here at home. The kids we send to Paraguay have got to *believe* that the people down there are the enemy. They can't hesitate to waste 'em. If they do, they'll pay the price. One thing we have going for us with these kids is zeal."

"Fanaticism?" queried Andrea.

"Call it that if you like. But if those youngsters down there didn't believe that they were engaged in a titanic struggle between the forces of good and evil, they couldn't pull it off."

• • •

Building commandos out of fifty-three young ex-cultists at the countercult centers and the Bouchegrave estate was not a difficult task. All were in superb physical, mental, and emotional condition—thanks to the untiring efforts of the deprogramming centers. All were burning with a near-religious fervor to wreak vengeance on those forces which had destroyed a portion of their lives. They had plunged into their training with an enthusiasm which startled even Nick, who was a veteran of SAS training. The team of instructors, all ex-terrorist fighters, taught these youngsters the deadly secrets of their profession. The fifty-three survivors, those who had weathered the storm of physical and mental torture which was their training schedule, were fit for the rigors of the Puerto Concepción and Fuerte Olimpo assaults.

"Nick, it's one thing to watch those kids rough-and-tumble down there on the lawn, but the acid test is whether or not they can actually *kill* somebody. Aren't you afraid that some of them will lose their nerve when it comes time to . . ."

Nick interrupted. "That's why they've got to pass their final exam before they can board that sub."

"Final exam? Nick! I'm almost afraid to ask!"

"Next week, all of our students will be assigned a target in either New York, Philadelphia, or Washington."

"A target? You mean . . . a person?"

"If you want to call them people, Andi. I know I'm dehumanizing the enemy again . . ." Nick smiled grimly. "But these people *are* bad. They gave up the right to call themselves human long ago. They've laughed at the law for years. Now they're going to pay the piper."

"Who are these people, Nick?"

"Notorious pimps, who are responsible for the ruin and death of countless young girls; drug traffickers; some local left-to-communist agitators, who have been untouchables so far. We've spent considerable thought and effort in compiling our hit list. We haven't gone into this thing willy-nilly."

"How . . . how . . . will they do it?"

"Knife."

"Knife?"

"Yes. The contact must be personal . . . and bloody after they close with their target."

"Nick! That's awful!"

"No. It's good psychology. If they can kill a bona fide bad guy close enough to see his death expression, and hear the blood gurgle in his throat, then they've broken through a gigantic mental barrier. That's how we were trained, and it works, Andi. Those who make it will have a better chance of surviving the coming ordeal."

Andrea screwed her face into a frown. "Is that how the SAS trained you?" she asked, almost fearfully.

"Yes. We had to take out known terrorists. Some were IRA, some were Palestinians. It was done with a knife. After my first, the rest were easy."

Andrea breathed deeply. "Nick, these targets . . . Any . . . any females?"

Nick gave her an understanding smile. "No, Andi, no females."

"Well, hurray for our side!" She sighed uneasily. "Nick," she continued, "have you ever thought of what we're going to do with them after this is all over? I . . . I mean, will they be any good for the things that . . . that we want to do on a . . . Dammit! I'm not saying it the way I want to! I'm thinking in Hungarian and trying to express something very deep in English. I just can't mesh my gears!"

Nick laughed and took her hand, caressing her knuckles with his thumb.

"You mean like marriage and kids, and the vine-covered cottage down the lane? The nine-to-five routine?"

"You *know* that's what I mean!" she said in frustration.

Suddenly the humor went out of Nick's expression as he surveyed the activity on the lawn.

"I don't know what they'll be good for, Andi, after this is all over."

The police of New York, Philadelphia, and Washington, D.C., were baffled, but pleased. In New York City, over a four-day period, nineteen of the city's most vicious pimps and dope dealers—not common criminals by any means—were found murdered.

Sixteen were found murdered in Philadelphia in the same time span. Again, the victims were well-known pimps and drug traffickers who had slipped through the judicial process time after time, making a mockery of the law.

In Washington the victims were a mixed bag: pimps, drug dealers, left-wing agitators, and two well-known Mafia figures.

In all three cities the M.O. was the same: a single thrust under the left ear by a slim, long-bladed, double-edged knife . . . then a slash, cutting the throat almost to the upper spinal column. In all cases, the murders were extremely bloody affairs.

The police of all three cities made token investigations and quit. No clues.

The fifty-three apprentice commandos had passed their final examination.

It was August 5 when the countercult strike force boarded the submarine. Patty Benson checked off the last of the passengers and yelled down to Nick. "All on board, Nick. The weapons and equipment are stored in the forward compartment. Say your good-byes and let's get this show on the road!" She smiled from the blackened deck.

Andrea looked up at her, a knot forming in her stomach as she thought of the dangers which awaited. Patty Benson was strong and tanned, a far different person from the pasty-white near corpse that was brought into Countercult One in the Nevada desert. She wore, as did all of the other fifty-two ex-cultists, a pair of cut-off fatigue pants. Her shapely muscular legs were bare from her midthighs to her black tennis shoes. Her lightweight jungle fatigue shirt fit her loosely, and was cinched at the waist by a canvas-webbed pistol belt. The olive-drab bush hat was rumpled and sat on her strawberry-blond hair at a rakish angle. A silenced Uzi submachine gun was slung casually over her shoulder. She looked like an Israeli woman soldier from an earlier war in the Sinai.

The twin diesel engines started to throb steadily, the twin propellers throwing a trail of violent bubbles from behind the sub. Andrea slipped her arms around Nick's waist and hugged him tightly, laying her head on his chest. She looked up into his eyes. Hers were filled with pools of tears. It suddenly dawned upon her that she was seeing her man off to war, and that he might not return. "Be careful, Nick. Try to get word to me as soon as the Puerto Concepción operation is over. I want you back."

"I will, Andi." He wiped away a tear rolling down her cheek. "Don't worry, darling. I have two good men with me. Redecker and Trucdeau are my team chiefs, and the kids are superbly trained. The opposition at Puerto Concepción will be light—primarily local guards."

Nick kissed her a long, hard kiss and boarded the submarine. The craft backed away from the pier, skillfully handled by a skeleton crew who were selected carefully from the regular crew, which had switched loyalties. Nick and Patty stood on the deck. They became distant specks to Andrea, as the sub slid away toward the purple-red horizon to the east.

Nick was wrong. At that very moment, a motor launch was pulling away from a Soviet naval frigate bound for Cuba. The craft turned and headed southwest toward the stone jetty at Puerto Concepción. Inside the hull were fifteen heavily armed men, all agents of Section VI. In the wheelhouse a bald man with Coke-bottle lenses in his glasses pored over a map of the Dominican Republic.

Things had been going badly for his section, and Martin Weishaupt was determined to set things straight. He was taking care of this operation himself. He himself would ensure that the Paraguay-Parramore connection would remain intact. There had been troubles in the United States. His puppet in Washington, who dangled from his control strings, had not been dancing his tune lately. All Weishaupt had been getting from Bouchegrave was excuses, and the senator continued to act and to vote contrary to his dictates. Even the threat of exposure didn't seem to worry him anymore.

The palm-fringed beach closed to meet the speeding craft, which bounced over the swells. The old stone jetty, a cattle-hide loading platform built by colonists left behind by Columbus, stabbed into the surf like a long, pointed finger.

Weishaupt stared vacantly at the jetty as it came closer. Yes, he would reorganize Puerto Concepción. And later, he would visit Parramore Island and confront Calvin Bouchegrave. If necessary, he would dispose of the senator.

In three days his agent-in-place from Colonia Gardún would arrive. He would ensure that the Sacred Order of the Holy Garduna became more closely integrated into the global operations of Section VI.

"Here's the list, son. You realize the consequences for the embassy if these names fall into the hands of the *pyngares*." Steve Lancaster handed his son a blue-and-white-striped computer printout with the names of almost six hundred men and women.

"*Pyngares*? What's that?" asked Paul.

The commercial attaché to Paraguay laughed nervously and brushed back his graying hair with the flat of his hand. "It's a Guaraní word which means those with hairy feet. It's a nickname for the government secret police who prowl softly all over the city. Paul . . . what do you . . . or should I say DAVROCK"—he looked at his son slyly—"want with the names of members and sympathizers of the Christian Action party? They're hardly a force to be reckoned with in this country."

"I just follow orders, Dad. Whatever Mr. Rockland wants, I get. I don't ask questions. I would imagine that he wants information on anybody with any real or potential political clout in this country, now that oil has been discovered out in the Chaco."

Steve Lancaster stared absently at his son. His seemingly mindless commitment to anything connected with Davenport-Rockland, Inc., worried him. Paul's total dedication to DAVROCK had turned him, by Steve Lancaster's standards, into an automaton . . . a robot . . . who might even kill for his masters. At times he wondered if Paul *had* killed for DAVROCK. He certainly had the skills after being trained as a Marine Recon Commando. And then, there was the campaign to keep the Strait of Hormuz open. Paul didn't win his Silver Star and two Purple Hearts for sorting laundry in a rear-area supply depot. No, his son was capable. He could tell by Paul's silence that he would not tell him why the list was needed.

"Okay. Keep me in the dark. Just remember, if anybody asks where you got that"—he jabbed a well-manicured finger toward the computer sheet—"we'll deny it if it's traced back to the embassy."

Paul folded the paper, inserted it into a large manila envelope, sealed it, and stuck it firmly into his suitcoat pocket. He shook his father's hand. "Lord be with you, Dad."

Paul Lancaster walked into the bright sunshine and the busy streets of Asunción humming a few bars of "Amazing Grace."

Carlos Von Reinach wiped his uniform sleeve across his perspiring forehead. He breathed deeply, more easily now, as the two structural-steel high riggers signaled that the last of the derrick towers had been bonded.

"Well, Mr. Rasmussen," he said in his overcorrected English, "we have welded the last of the towers that my men have erected. The bonding process is complete. Can we resume the drilling process now?" Von Reinach's question was in the tone of an anxious command.

Rasmussen had been impressed. The Guaraní commandos had learned the techniques of derrick construction and rigging, angle iron by angle iron, and welded them to withstand the pressure of another gusher, in a remarkably short period of time.

Eight derricks had been emplaced strategically in a trapezoidal pattern in and around the suspected oil find. It was now mapped out even more accurately with the aid of supersensitive seismic equipment and computer-graphic maps. Rasmussen's game plan was to drill four wells at approximately the same time near the original gusher site, to relieve the pressure. He had used a similar technique in Western Australia two years ago, and it had worked.

"Yes, Señor Von Reinach," replied the big freckled geologist. "We'll position the drilling bits this afternoon, and tomorrow we can start drilling, and perhaps even start storing crude."

The hard, baked red clay was littered with hundreds of large, deflated rubberized-vinyl bladders which would store the new crude oil. They would be loaded onto flatbed trailers and, when filled, trucked to the Pilcomayo River, where they could be towed and floated to the refinery on the River Plate in Argentina.

Von Reinach was a disciplined man, and not too proud to engage in manual labor along with his Guaraní soldiers. He violated the code of the *patrón* mentality by getting his hands dirty and working with the enlisted ranks. That is why I will succeed and the others of my caste will fail, he often mused. I am willing to work at whatever task is necessary to build a greater and stronger Paraguay. Perhaps it is the German in me, he pondered, that sets me apart from the rest.

His thoughts during the past weeks had been constantly on Susan Rockland. Her face, her beauty, her Cherokee purity were a constant vision before him. How much like his mother, the beautiful María Ynsfrán, she was!

His loins stirred for her. Von Reinach had always disciplined such stirrings in the past, but this was different. He had never succumbed to sexual temptations, although he could have any female *chivato* in the colony. To him, up until now, at least, sex was a tool, a weapon to be utilized in the struggle to improve the population stock of his country. His ideological hero, Adolf Hitler, refrained from sex during his mission and, even after his marriage to Eva Braun in the bunker during the Battle of Berlin, he refrained from consummating his marriage in that manner.

But, unlike Hitler, Von Reinach planned to live and propagate himself, but only through a vessel of righteousness and purity. Yes, Susan Rockland would be his queen—his co-ruler over a resurrected and powerful Paraguay; a Paraguay which would soon absorb its weaker neighbors to the east and west, Bolivia and Uruguay. Seaports on both the Atlantic and Pacific oceans would create a nation which would cinch the continent of South America like a pistol belt. Powerful friends in Brazil and Argentina, who were members of the Holy Garduna, would ensure the noninterference of these countries when Paraguay began to make her moves. And now, with the assurance of supplies of Chaco petroleum for these two oil-starved giants, Paraguay's future was assured.

But before Von Reinach could choose Susan Rockland to be his bride, he must hasten to Colonia Gardún and tell his uncle, Francisco Estigarribia, and receive his blessings.

"I don't like being placed in the role of a field marshal, Mr. Revvim. I'm a man of God, not a military man."

Eli Shem Revvim drummed his fingers on the large oval oak conference table in Gypsy Joe Rockland's executive boardroom. He could tell that the Reverend was becoming more and more anxious as the time for the coordinated assaults on the Holy Garduna drew near.

"Mr. Rockland, I don't think you have to consider yourself a field marshal, but you *are* the chairman of the Strike Committee, and we need your presence. You have a handle on what impact our operational planning will have on the DAVROCK exploration project in the Chaco," Eli said.

Joe Rockland had been feeling like a lamb in a den of wolves during the past several weeks. His involvement with Revvim, Detlefs, and some of the other professional mercenaries who were hired by his partner had left him in a state of constant anxiety. Clearly, these were not his kind of people; but they were necessary, it seemed—although he had his doubts—to carry out the Lord's program in cleansing the world of cults. Who else would do it—and so thoroughly—than these professional soldiers of fortune?

"Reverend Rockland, perhaps it's a blessing that Mr. Davenport is supporting the Holy Garduna," added Puerter Detlefs.

"And how's that?" Rockland asked, his swarthy face screwed into a frown.

"If you were in Von Reinach's place, would you suspect DAVROCK of complicity in the assaults on Fuerte Olimpo and La Cuna if it was supplying you with oil drilling equipment and weapons? It's doubtful that the Garduna would associate us with DAVROCK. We could rig up enough evidence to tie in our assaults with the Christian Action folks. And if we really want to be bastards, tie the assaults to a government unfriendly to the West."

Rockland brightened. "Like Cuba?"

"Too obvious," replied Detlefs. "Cuba gets blamed for everything in Paraguay. It's a case of right-wing generals crying wolf too often. I was thinking of Nicaragua."

"Good choice!" exclaimed Revvim.

"They've proven that the Sandinistas were responsible for Somoza's assassination in Asunción nine years ago. The former dictator of Nicaragua was General Stroessner's buddy before he got zapped. Paraguay retaliated by unleashing its *pyngares* against the Nicaraguan diplomatic personnel."

"*Pyngares*? What's that?" asked Revvim.

"Oh, pardon me. I picked that term up in a radio message from Paul. It's an Indian word which means hairy-footed men, or secret police. Anyway, there's bad blood between the two countries," said Detlefs.

"Excellent! Excellent!" Rockland exclaimed nervously. "Nicaragua it is. It'll serve them right. They've expelled all of our missionaries and confiscated the mission property. Gentlemen, I'll leave the details to you." He rose and excused himself, and left hurriedly from the room.

It was to be an extremely complex military operation. If not global in scope, it was at least hemispheric in attempt.

Portumo would lead the assault on Puerto Concepción. Redecker and Trucdeau would act as team chiefs. It would be an amphibious operation. Small rubber boats loaded with forty-seven ex-cultists would land on an isolated coral beach about a mile and a half west of the plantation. The force would enter the jungle, then cut east until they came to the sugarcane fields. They would then approach the plantation complex from the south—the landward side. They would be preceded by a special underwater detachment of six, who would approach the stone jetty from the seaward side, swimming the half mile from the submarine. They would create a diversionary attack after the jetty and beach guards were disposed of.

No prisoners were to be taken. It was unfortunate and not to Nick's liking, but there must be no survivors to complicate the continuing operation of Puerto Concepción. A skeleton staff would be left, and it would continue to function as if nothing had happened. It would still serve as the communication link between Colonia Gardún and Parramore Island.

An airborne assault by parachute from low altitude was scheduled at the same time that the Portumo force attacked Fuerte Olimpo. The thirty-five commandos were led by Revvim and Detlefs. It should take no more than two weeks for the submarine to sail from Puerto Concepción to the port on the upper Paraguay River. The coordinated attacks between the two assault forces must be timed to the hour. Contact between La Cuna and Fuerte Olimpo must be broken immediately.

The assaults on La Cuna and Fuerte Olimpo were dependent on several conditions. First was the creation of an urban guerrilla force in the capital city of Asunción. That was Paul Lancaster's job, and he was to receive adequate support from the agents of Benito Salazar. An urban uprising and attack on key military and communications installations in and around the capital city would neutralize any support to the second target, the commando complex at Mariscal Estigarribia.

Fifteen miles outside of Asunción was a small operational air force base near the small road-junction village of Hato Mayor. The aircraft of the Paraguayan Air Force were old: U.S. T-6 trainers from World War II and six Douglas F3D jets, which were leftovers from America's involvement in the Korean War. But they were operational, and in the urban wing of the Christian Action party were pilots who could fly them. The bombs, rockets, and napalm, which would render any support from Mariscal Estigarribia to the final and primary target, were stored there.

The primary target was Colonia Gardún. It was to be a three-pronged attack: overland from Fuerte Olimpo by commandeered vehicles; an airborne attack by the La Cuna raiders; and, sweeping from the foothills of the Andes, the guerrillas of the Christian Action party.

During the turmoil, an intensive propaganda campaign would commence, by secret transmitters and rumor, that the urban insurrection was an attempt by the Holy Garduna to take over the reins of power by a coup d'état. Another conflicting propaganda campaign would tie responsibility to a Sandinista-inspired plot, which originated in Nicaragua and was controlled by their embassy in Asunción.

Besides the destruction of the Holy Garduna, the rescue of Olivia Davenport from La Cuna and Susan Rockland from Colonia Gardún would be of paramount importance. Susan would remain in place during the assault and be responsible not only for herself but for the safety of the other *chivatos*.

The Tower of Power at the Davenport-Rockland University would continue to broadcast the Word of God. The messages of hope and salvation would be similar to previous messages; however, there would be a slight difference. The word structure might sound unfamiliar to those who were regular listeners. What would sound stilted, and even incorrect grammatically, would be, in effect, coded messages to the three assault forces. The word of Joseph Rockland's God would be the operational and coordinating instructions to the Lord's own countercult force: 150,000 clear-channel watts of Christian electronic power, a beacon guiding the forces of light against the forces of the Evil One.

The Prophet Estigarribia was disturbed. A frown of disapproval wrinkled his brow as his nephew told him of his desire to marry Susan Rockland.

"But what do you know of this little *chivato*, my son? I mean what do you *really* know about her?"

"I only know, my uncle, that the forces of a benevolent providence have conspired to send her to us. She represents a group of humanity, and an industry, which the Almighty has raised up for the survival of our country."

"Have you approached her on this matter?"

Von Reinach shook his head.

"I knew that someday . . . that you would want to marry, Carlos. In fact, at times I was fearful that you would neglect the duty of marriage and raising a righteous posterity because you were so immersed in your work. I . . . I was hoping

. . . that your choice would be from among our own people, but I will give my blessing to this union if you so desire."

Carlos Von Reinach knelt before the Hermano Mayor of the Sacred Order of the Holy Garduna. The white-bearded old *patrón* draped a purple and white robe over his nephew's shoulders, a robe supposedly worn by the earliest Garduna members when they fought the Moors in Spain.

The old man took an ancient silver horn from an ornately carved quebracho wood chest and poured a portion of the oil within it on his nephew's scalp. He then placed his hands upon his head and blessed the future marriage of Carlos and Susan Rockland.

Hilda Von Ziegazar felt acute pangs of anxiety as Francisco Estigarribia gave her the details. "You mean, Hermano Mayor, that he actually wants to make this little *chivato* his wife?"

The Prophet of Paraguay arched his slim white eyebrows. "You disapprove, my good doctor? Was the report you filed on her activities in the oil fields accurate?"

"Yes, Hermano Mayor . . . but . . ."

"But *what*, Hilda? You were there! Your report corroborated what dozens of others have testified: The girl Susan is incredibly brave! Her actions were as commendable as those of our warriors."

A fire was raging inside the doctor as she fought to control her emotions—emotions which mingled hatred of Susan with fear of this young cultist, who assumed a position of power. If she told Estigarribia that she was the daughter of one of the DAVROCK owners, it would confirm Von Reinach's obsession that she was sent by a divine providence.

"There are some suspicions I have, Hermano Mayor, of the girl's genetic qualities," the doctor added hastily. Von Ziegazar knew that genetics was the magic word in the Holy Garduna. Any hint, any suspicion, of genetic inferiority was to be immediately investigated.

The old man stood up abruptly. "What?" he bellowed. "You have had suspicions?"

He leafed through Susan's file. "I see nothing—*nothing*—

which suggests genetic irregularity. If you had suspicions, why did you not report them to me?"

Actually, the doctor never had any doubts about Susan's claim to be a full-blooded Cherokee. As far as she was concerned, all Indians and most Latins were *Untermenschen*, or undermen. But now, she knew, there would be a covert investigation of Susan which might halt, at least temporarily, the marriage.

Estigarribia put his hands to his head as if he were trying to cope with a migraine. "You have put me in a most untenable position, my good doctor," he muttered softly. "I have given this proposed union my blessing."

Von Ziegazar's mind raced, groping for a course of action which would thwart the marriage. "Hermano Mayor, send me to America for a week. Let me confirm or deny my suspicions."

The Prophet sighed wearily. "Yes, it must be done. Withdraw what funds you need from the treasury and do your duty. Report directly to me when you return."

"It's been a great five days, brother. I hope I haven't been missed too much . . . and I hope nobody's ripped off my jeep."

Raúl grinned widely. "We wouldn't let you walk, Angel. We have two guards posted near it."

"You thought of everything."

"We try. You're too important to us to abuse. We've got to take care of you."

Angel, Raúl, Susan, and Benito Salazar walked over to a pile of smooth, rounded rocks. Each one picked a rock as a seat.

"Let's recapitulate our game plan, Angel," Raúl said. "We're working against the clock so we have to be sure we all understand what's expected of us."

"You realize that I'm putting my military career on the line by getting involved with you flakes?" exclaimed Angel.

"Look at it this way, amigo," said Salazar, poking his large, charred briar pipe with his custom tobacco. "If our little operation works, I'll be the new President of Paraguay and I'll make you a field marshal."

"Oho! And I can supplement my salary with all the cocaine I can smuggle."

Salazar's countenance suddenly clouded.

"No, amigo. That is a practice which will change drastically. The Armed Forces, especially the Officers' Corps, must be a model of service and respectability."

"Susan, what's your mission?" Raúl interjected.

"Raúl, we've been over this a dozen times!" she complained.

"Again! One more time!" It was a command.

Susan sighed wearily. "Okay. I'm to get into the vehicle park . . ."

"Before that, Susan. Before that!" Raul said impatiently.

"Develop a group of trusted *chivatos*—those who will help me in various acts of sabotage and confusion when the attack takes place."

"And then?" demanded Raúl.

"And then I get into the vehicle park where the armored cars are parked, pour sugar into the gas tanks—about a half pound per vehicle"

"Why a half pound? Why not a whole bag?" asked Raúl.

"As you mentioned before, Raúl"—Susan's brown eyes flashed with irritation—"a half pound will allow the armored cars to be driven about twenty-five miles before the engines burn out."

"Angel? Your mission?"

"Okay, brother." Angel picked up a pointed stick and sketched in the sand.

"Develop a group of trusted enlisted men at Mariscal Estigarribia. Benito has given me the names of five who might serve as the nucleus of our little group." He absently scratched five little lines in the sand. "Just before the assaults on La Cuna and Fuerte Olimpo, my men will sabotage the communications center."

"How will you know that the assaults are about to take place?" asked Raúl.

"The Tower of Power—God's message to a dying world!" Angel replied in a mocking tone.

Susan shot him a sharp, disapproving glance.

"All right, wise guy. What about the Tower of Power?" Raúl demanded.

"Listen to the nightly eight o'clock broadcasts on KDRM. I've got the codes." Angel tapped his breast pocket. "We've gone over them fifty times."

"And prior to the assaults?"

"Spread rumors linking the Officers' Corps, especially those who are associated with the Garduna, to a Nicaraguan-inspired plot to take over the country by coup d'état."

"I still can't believe all this is happening!" exclaimed Susan. "It scrambles my mind to think that my father and Courtney are involved in planning military operations against cults. And my dad! Gentle, pacifistic soul that he is, getting involved with a bunch of mercenaries! It blows my mind!"

"You disapprove of us, Susan?" asked Raúl, arching his eyebrows.

"No . . . No!" She hastened to exclaim. "It's only that . . . that . . . I didn't think my father would ever go this far for . . . for . . ."

Tears started to form in Susan's coffee-colored eyes.

"For you, little *chivato*?" asked Salazar. "Where one's daughter is involved, a loving father will go to any lengths, even associate with demons from the pits of hell, to save her. That is the depth of your father's love."

Susan choked back more tears, but they came anyway and rolled down her cheeks. "Yeah, I've got a lot of fences to mend with my father—that is, if I get out of this with my skin."

Angel put his arm protectively around her. "Hey, little one, this lovely skin is mine . . . remember? I'll make sure we get out of this with both our skins."

The little group arose and hacked their way through the ferns along the jungle path and back to the jeep.

Santiago, in the north-central part of the Dominican Republic, had the nearest commercial airport to Puerto Concepción, and even its runways were too short to handle regular jet airliners. Most of the airliners which landed in the pretty little jewel of a city, which was nestled in a kelly-green valley surrounded by extinct volcanic mountains, were twin-engine prop jets.

A reconditioned but entirely serviceable DC-3, an ancient American aircraft of the early 1940s, which was still used by Cubana Airlines for its short feeder routes, yawed and bounced over the low hills adjacent to the runway. The pilot skillfully crabbed into the wind to compensate for the brisk breeze that always blew across the west end of the runway. He landed roughly after two or three bounces. Evidently the pilot was Russian-trained and was familiarizing himself with this near-antique but venerable American airplane, thought Martin Weishaupt as he anticipated meeting his agent-in-place from Paraguay.

The aircraft taxied over to the small, squat concrete-block passenger terminal. Two attendants in white and blue coveralls pushed a battered aluminum and chrome loading ramp up to the passenger exit. On the other side of the plane, attendants were removing luggage and refueling the Cubana DC-3.

Weishaupt scanned the passengers as they emerged. He smoothed out the wrinkles in the forefront of his bald scalp, a sign that he was wrestling with his chronic anxiety.

His agent was the last passenger to emerge, as Weishaupt knew he would be. The man had a penchant for sitting in the rear of airplanes, as well as buses, trains, and restaurants. It gave him the opportunity to survey that portion of humanity nearest to him, especially the female portion. And then he would choose. He seemed to have an unerring talent for choosing those who shared his strange and unusual appetites in bed. Perhaps there is a similar chemistry between those whose desires were "elevated" above the masses, he often pondered, which allowed his man from Paraguay to home in on his targets with such accuracy. He seldom failed in his choices. And when he did, as he did in the case of Olivia Davenport at La Cuna, he reacted to this rejection with violence and brutality.

The short, portly fellow with the trench coat and shaggy wig over his friar's haircut waddled down the ramp and met Weishaupt. They shook hands briefly and then piled into the rented Ford Escort and pulled out of the airport complex.

Within minutes, Martin Weishaupt and Julio Barrajas, prophet-founder of the Garden Children, were on the secondary highway headed for Puerto Concepción.

There was a Teutonic cleanliness to Tulsa which impressed Hilda Von Ziegazar. The wide, uncluttered boulevards, the orderly flow of traffic, and the quiet but businesslike demeanor of its citizens, who strode purposefully on its unlittered streets, told the doctor that Susan Rockland's hometown was a community of order.

She steered her rented Citation to the central city area and saw the fifteen-story DAVROCK building. The huge block letters D-A-V-R-O-C-K were arranged in a perpendicular fashion between the fourth and the twelfth floors along the east side of the building. Half a block from the building she found a parking space, slipped two quarters into the parking meter, and turned the dial. The arrow popped to the two-hour mark. More than enough time, she thought.

The tall, mannish-appearing doctor walked in long, anxious strides to the revolving door of the building. A gust of air from the inside caused her short blond hair to fly up. She smoothed it down with her palm and went into the lobby. There, on a large black and white directory panel, was her quarry: Joseph J. Rockland, Foreign Operations Division, DAVROCK Development Corporation, Room 1210, Twelfth Floor.

The elevator doors slid open with a hiss, and the doctor entered. She was the only passenger. She punched the 12 button and swallowed hard, as the speed of the elevator caused her stomach to jump. At the second stop, floor number 12, Von Ziegazar found herself facing a large beige-colored corridor. A row of mahogany doors flanked each side of the hallway, and at the end of the corridor, facing out, was another door with a large brass plate. Von Ziegazar entered boldly and walked into a spacious reception room. There she stood before the secretary, who greeted her pleasantly.

"Hello," Von Ziegazar said, "I'm Leona Brammer, technical sales representative with Pastracher Medical Specialties. I have an appointment with Mr. Rockland at eleven o'clock."

The secretary smiled sweetly, her slightly freckled nose wrinkling in the process. "Oh, yes, Ms. Brammer. Mr. Rockland is in."

"I hope I didn't cause a change in his schedule. When I called for an appointment from New Orleans three days ago, I was hoping I could catch him between business trips."

The secretary smiled again, showing full, sensual lips over her white, even teeth. Von Ziegazar's loins stirred slightly as she noticed how attractive and wholesome-looking she was.

"You said the magic word when you mentioned medical specialties and complete portable field hospitals. Mr. Rockland has a great interest in extending the blessings of Western medicine to the Third World."

In the short time she had available to her, Von Ziegazar had done her homework thoroughly. The information she gleaned from the DAVROCK branch office about Joseph Rockland's interests were starting to pay off.

The secretary buzzed Mr. Rockland's office and announced the visitor.

"Mr. Rockland will see you now," she said.

When the swarthy man behind the large ebony-topped desk got up to greet her, Von Ziegazar knew! She just knew! She had been trained not only as a medical doctor at Württemberg University in West Germany, but also as a specialist in racial genetics. She knew all of the specific racial characteristics, and there were enough Negroid features apparent in the face, skull dimensions, and eye structure of Mr. Joseph Rockland to determine that he was undoubtedly a mulatto—perhaps as much as one-third Negro.

Von Ziegazar composed herself after the initial shock and held out her hand in greeting.

An hour and a half later, Von Ziegazar left the DAVROCK building elated. A windfall had plopped right into her lap! When she began this investigation she had hoped to find something—*anything*—she could use against Susan Rockland to discredit her in the eyes of Von Reinach. The *most* she had hoped for was evidence of some youthful indiscretion: drugs, promiscuity, anything but racial inferiority. She smiled a smug, victorious smile to herself as she walked in a masculine, almost swaggering manner down the busy street toward her rented car.

Joseph Rockland talked and talked. Dr. Von Ziegazar was a skillful interviewer and knew how to manipulate conversations; indeed, she could be disarmingly charming, exuding an aristocratic, old-world charm when she had to.

A discussion on medical problems in Africa led naturally to the problems of race and minorities in the United States. Von Ziegazar lied and said she understood, since she was one-fourth Jewish and had had a grandmother who survived the death camp of Ravensbrück during World War II.

It was then that Rockland dropped his bombshell and offered the information that his own father was a social outcast. He was an alcoholic, an ex-convict, and black! *One hundred percent Negro*. His mother was a half-breed, Cherokee and white, and his deceased wife, who was killed in a light-airplane accident shortly after Susan's birth, was also a Cherokee-white half-breed.

So, Von Ziegazar smirked to herself as she opened the door to her car, the little bitch was a quarter Negro, and had been passing herself off as a full-blooded Cherokee at Colonia Gardún all these months! That alone was enough to cause her beautiful body to be a feast for Von Reinach's piranha.

The doctor made two more stops: one to the office of vital statistics in the County Building, and one to the local newspaper, *The Tulsa Record-Searchlight*.

She was in luck. The County office had records of those born not only in one's home county but in the entire state of Oklahoma back to 1873. The advent of microfilm had revolutionized record keeping in the state. In forty-five minutes Von Ziegazar was able to obtain photocopies of the birth records of Susan, her father and mother, and most important, her grandparents.

A trip to the *Record-Searchlight* closed her case on Susan Rockland. Again, with the blessings of microfilmed records, the obituary of one Jesse W. Rockland, with a photo taken several years before his death, was procured.

Jesse Rockland had died in 1948, the obituary read, and his death was under investigation by the state medical examiner. Dr. Von Ziegazar knew that usually meant that a person died of unnatural causes.

Jesse W. Rockland, Joseph's father, was a black man, no doubt about that. The picture was proof. He left several children as survivors, one of whom was Joseph Jesse Rockland.

Von Ziegazar had copies made of the evidence, patted the photocopied documents, and placed them in her attaché case. She walked briskly to her Citation, nosed out of her parking spot, and headed for the Tulsa International Airport.

Now, you little tramp, we'll see who's superior. When old Estigarribia and Von Reinach see these, you'll provide a banquet for their little friends in the well. But, first, you'll provide a banquet for me.

"Mr. Rockland? This is Jean Crowley down at the Vital Statistics Office in the County Building."

"Yes, Jeannie. How are you? Are you calling to get your old job back? I told you when you left it's yours anytime you want it."

"No, thanks," the clerk said, laughing, "but I think you should know that a lady, at least I *think* she was a lady, was here asking for birth records of you, your daughter, Susan, and, in fact, your entire family. Her name is . . . let's see . . . Leona Brammer. I didn't handle her request or I would have called you first. One of the other clerks helped her."

Alarm bells went off in Rockland's mind. He thanked the county clerk and placed the phone absently in its cradle. He knitted his brow in thought, then in anger. He picked up the phone and called the *Record-Searchlight*. After a short chat with the microfilm clerk, his suspicions were confirmed.

"Race . . . genetics . . . breeding! That's what the Holy Garduna is all about," he muttered between clenched teeth. "She deliberately manipulated me into giving her my genealogical history. I can see it now! Damn her soul to hell! She works for them! I'll bet on it—and I've put Susan's life in jeopardy."

He jabbed at the intercom buzzer. The freckle-nosed secretary bounced in. "Cathy. That . . . that representative that came in . . . ?"

"Yes. A Ms. Brammer from the Pastracher Medical Specialties Company of West Germany."

"Cathy, find out what you can about the company and Ms. Brammer."

Twenty-five minutes later, the secretary returned. Her pert, pretty face was screwed into a frown. "Mr. Rockland, there isn't any Pastracher Medical Specialties in West Germany or anyplace else!"

Rockland dismissed her and sighed wearily. He picked up the phone and called the switchboard and asked for the special countercult circuit.

"Yes, operator. Give me Paul Lancaster in Asunción as quickly as possible. I'll hang up and wait for the call."

He pressed the buzzer again. The secretary came in within seconds.

"Cathy, call the travel clerk. I want to take the next plane to Asunción via New Orleans."

XVIII.

They came from the sea: twenty-three armed men wearing night-blue combat fatigues and navy-style knit watch hats. They were a day ahead of the countercult commandos, whose French "D"-class submarine was now submerged and throbbing its way toward them.

The armed band departed in silence from their Hovercraft, which had pounded across the Mona Passage from western Puerto Rico to this remote beach west of Puerto Concepción. They penetrated the plantation complex with ease, disposed of the guards, and after a brief but vicious firefight, killed all but three of Martin Weishaupt's Section VI agents.

Just as silently as they arrived, the strange force left, and sped back across the water to Mona Island with their three captives.

Weishaupt and Barrajas had been in the capital, Santo Domingo, during the raid. Both had the need to satisfy their appetites. Barrajas satisfied his in the secure comfort of a brothel which catered to the bizarre and unusual. Weishaupt's quest was more difficult as absinthe was scarce in the Caribbean capital. But a determined search and a hundred-dollar bill turned up a quart of the outlawed liquor.

When they returned to the plantation after a weekend binge, they found the bodies of their guards and agents in a state of putrefaction. They had been laid out in a row at the edge of the building complex. It had appeared, at first, that they had been lined up and executed, but the bullet holes on the sides of the buildings told a different story. The bodies had been dragged to their present location after a battle.

Weishaupt and Barrajas lost no time. They didn't even attempt to retrieve their personal gear. They fled the plantation and drove, at breakneck speed, to Santiago to catch the first plane off the island.

At sea the countercult commandos were making a final check of their equipment and plans in preparation for the assault the following night on Puerto Concepción.

At 11:30 P.M. the submarine rose to the surface, the cold waters of the Atlantic cascading off the blackened conning tower. Nick was the first to exit from the hatch. He stepped out into the moonless, inky night and saw the rhythmic flash of the lighthouse at Point Lobos. He took his bearings. They were right on target. The landing beach was about a mile to the south.

"Paul . . . Jean. Help me get the inflatables on deck," whispered Nick.

Redecker and Trucdeau passed up five large rubbery bundles. Nick laid them together along the forward deck. The countercult commandos followed. Their weapons and gear barely clanked as they climbed up the steel ladder from the submarine's dimly lit interior and stepped on deck.

Nick yanked the CO_2 cartridge lanyard on each bundle and they hissed into the shapes of twelve-man inflatable boats. The commandos slid them into the water and stepped carefully inside, hauling their weapons and paddles in after them.

A final check showed nothing amiss. All was in order. Nick, Redecker, and Patty Benson stepped into their assigned boats and shoved away from the sub's hull. They paddled silently toward the shore, disappearing among the slight swells of the sea.

Trucdeau and his underwater assault team stayed below and checked over the air tanks and array of underwater breathing apparatus, which would enable them to complete their mission.

• • •

Nick was worried. The beach landing was unopposed, as he felt it would be. However, the trek inland to the plantation's southern boundary was made effortlessly and without contact. It was too easy. At the very least, there should have been some sign of roving patrols, or even dogs if the guards at Puerto Concepción had any sense of security.

They were at the jungle's edge, where the stumps of the harvested sugarcane met the treeline. There, beyond the cane fields, were the squat adobe buildings of the plantation complex. Their whiteness was barely visible this moonless night.

Nick turned the frequency selection dial on his portable transceiver to the special countercult frequency. "Jean, we're at the edge of the plantation. The buildings are about a hundred meters north. What's your position?"

Beyond the plantation, along the ancient stone jetty, Trucdeau's assault swimmers pulled themselves hand over hand along the stones. The three team members who scaled the jetty reported nothing on top. No guards, no equipment—nothing.

Trucdeau didn't like it either. It was too quiet, and too dark. There were no lights or noise from the direction of the plantation buildings or the small warehouse at the landward end of the jetty.

The slight breeze shifted, and the fetid, pungent odor of the putrefying corpses wafted into Nick's group like a cloud of phosgene gas. Redecker smelled it, too. They both knew the smell of death, and their gut instincts told them what awaited their group at the plantation.

Portumo, Patty, and twelve others darted across the cane field. It was now, thought Nick as he ran, that any opposing force could catch them in their searchlights and cut them down. There were no shots: just silence.

The first of the buildings was reached, and the stench became unbearable. There, lined up in a row, were the bullet-riddled corpses; the remains of Weishaupt's force.

Trucdeau's swimmers met Nick in the middle of the complex. A brief reconnaissance of the plantation turned up nothing. Puerto Concepción was deserted.

"What do you make of it, Nick?" asked Patty, who was disappointed that she was cheated out of battle.

"It's obvious that somebody got here before us. The question is, who? We'll have to wait until daylight to look for clues."

"We'll have to bury the bodies," exclaimed Redecker.

"We can dig the graves now," replied Nick, "but we'll have to wait until daylight before we can bury them. We've got the unpleasant task of searching the corpses, taking pictures of their faces, and taking fingerprints. I want to know who these blokes are."

The hot tropical sun came up over the eastern sea too soon, and by eight in the morning the plantation was a steaming caldron of sun and humidity.

The grisly job of photographing, fingerprinting, and searching the bodies was completed, and they were shoved into deep pits, which were easily dug in the soft, rich tropical soil.

"There's enough evidence here," Trucdeau said, pointing to an array of documents on the ground, "to tie these gentlemen to Section VI. They are clearly Eastern European—not Dominicans or Latins. The weapons over here"—he picked up a small submachine gun—"are Czech Skorpions, the operational weapons of Section VI."

"The battle was clearly one-sided," added Redecker. "These people were caught by surprise. If they were Weishaupt's agents, they were pros, so the attacking force must have been very professional."

"A rival cult?" asked a commando.

"Somehow I doubt it," replied Nick thoughtfully. He turned to the assembled group and barked, "Okay, everybody comb the area and look for clues. Pick up anything which will tell us something—spent brass, pieces of equipment—anything that doesn't fit into the normal life of the plantation."

After two hours of searching, it was clear that the attacking force had cleaned up any telltale signs before departing. The absence of spent cartridge brass meant only one thing: that their automatic weapons had brass-catching bags over their ejection ports. But in a nighttime operation, something is usually left behind—and something was.

Three of the ex-cultists brought pieces of evidence to Nick.

"Hmmmm," murmured Nick as he examined the spent .45-caliber cartridge case.

"Forty-five caliber, U.S. Government. Doesn't mean anything conclusive except that the only folks I know using forty-five-caliber automatic weapons are the clandestine forces of the American government. Most other groups use nine millimeter."

Nick looked at the second piece of evidence: a regulation-style U.S. Navy blue-black knitted watch cap. It was apparent that the specification label inside the cap had been cut off.

"Take a look at this, Nick. This was found down near the beach," said a freckle-faced commando.

Nick examined a dark blue vinyl pack and slit it open. Inside were small packets of dehydrated food, chocolate, and powdered coffee. The outside of the packet read:

FOOD PACKET, LONG RANGE PATROL
BEEF WITH RICE—MENU NO. 4
U.S. NAVY EMERGENCY RATION

Paul Lancaster discovered, after a week of following up on his contacts, that the Armed Forces of Paraguay were similar, in many respects, to the military structure of other Latin American nations. The army, the largest and most senior service, was also the most conservative. The officers were drawn from the landed aristocracy. In the case of Paraguay, the large immigrant population, especially Germans, added to the corps of army officers.

The Paraguayan Navy and Air Force, although minuscule, selected their personnel from the nation's small but influential middle class. These were the technical services, and the officers and enlisted men were several cuts above their counterparts in the army in technical skills, education, and general intelligence. Many of them had been trained at the U.S. School of the Americas in Panama.

Paul also discovered that the navy and air force were

seething with discontent. They had played a nonexistent role in Paraguay's last conflict—the Chaco War. The glory had gone to the army, and from then on, the bulk of the national defense budget had gone to the army also.

The Paraguayan Government was careful not to neglect the navy and air force altogether. Their budgets were lavish in proportion to their function and utility. The government issued the officers and enlisted men expensive uniforms. There were constant and numerous opportunities for them to receive training in foreign countries, particularly the United States, Israel, and South Africa. This was done primarily to get potential subversives out of the country, particularly junior officers who were captains and below. The theory was that if navy and air force personnel were constantly rotated, then personal loyalties to their commanders would not develop. As every Latin American leader knows, this is the first stage of revolution.

The government lavished medals and decorations on these services, which the men wore with a sense of embarrassed pride. The medals looked splendid on their ornate uniforms, but they signified nothing.

The Paraguayan Navy was especially irate when the submarines it had fought to obtain for so many years were taken from them. The three French "D"-class boats, 1968 vintage, were sold to the Parachaco Corporation. The navy was given an old American Landing Craft Infantry (LCI) and five transport helicopters. Of course, everybody in the naval Officers' Corps knew that the Parachaco Corporation was synonymous with the Sacred Order of the Holy Garduna.

As Paul contacted the individuals whose names were provided by the embassy, a surprising but important pattern began to emerge. All of the contacts, so far, were highly educated or skilled people. Many were junior officers or senior enlisted men who were placed in strategic positions.

The Paraguayan Government had a wise and positive policy of recycling its discharged or retired military personnel into government services. The technical ministries of telecommunications, transportation, aeronautics, and supply were liberally sprinkled with former navy and air force technical people. Many of them held key spots in the government and were in a position to facilitate a coup d'état and, most important, were sympathizers, if not clandestine members, of the Socialist Christian Action party.

Brigadier General Ramón Torrejos looked disdainfully at the antigovernment posters spread out on the intricately carved table before him. As chief of the Ministry of National Security, which was the secret police, or *pyngares*, any subversive activity, especially in the Asunción Military District, was reported directly to him.

His black lizardlike eyes, which were sunken in little pouches of fat, gave him the look of a wild boar ready to charge. His scraggly mustache, grown to prove that he was more Spanish than Indian, looked ridiculous and out of place on his squat head. But he did look like a policeman—one whose authority transcended even the nation's military in matters of national security. Being the brother-in-law of General Ayala, Paraguay's president for life, put Torrejos in a position in which he answered to no one except the President.

He picked up a poster which showed the silhouette of a worker with an upraised fist, a broken chain dangling from it, and a Russian AK-47 assault rifle clutched in the other hand. The caption underneath read: "Break the bonds of those who oppress you through armed struggle."

"We found them all over the city, sir," said the *pyngare* captain as he stood at attention.

"At ease, Rodríguez. Did you get them all?" asked Torrejos.

"Yes, sir. But as soon as we tore them down, others were put up. We caught one young boy in the act. He was paid to do it by a group of students. We interrogated the boy gently, in deference to his tender years. What we could learn from him was that the sponsors of these posters were of the Sandinista faction of the Communist party."

"Sandinistas?" bellowed the general. "I thought we had rooted out those pigs!"

"We have heard rumors floating around the capital during the past few weeks that there has been a new flurry of Sandinista activity. We . . . we have heard something even

. . . even more disturbing, my general. It's only a rumor but—but if true, it's of devastating consequences."

"What, my man? What?" The general pounded the palms of his hands on the table.

"Again . . . it's only a rumor and I . . ."

"Out with it, Rodríguez!"

The *pyngare* captain swallowed hard, as if trying to choke down the words that were forcing themselves out of his throat. Finally he blurted.

"There is evidence that a conspiracy exists between the Sandinistas and the Holy Garduna to take the country over by force."

Torrejos's double chin dropped on his sloppily knotted tie. His cruel little mouth flung open in surprise. "A Sandinista-Garduna conspiracy? Surely you are joking, Captain!" roared the general. "Such a thing is not possible; and you said rumor, not evidence, did you not?"

"I was reluctant to present you with this information, sir. More than reluctant; I was afraid. I know what power the Holy Garduna has."

"Yes," the general muttered thoughtfully, his beady eyes flashing from cushions of fat. "Perhaps too much power. Perhaps they are not content with the power they have and are making a pact with the devil to obtain more."

"If I may show you these, sir."

"What are they?" asked Torrejos impatiently.

"These are secret inventory lists of armored cars, rocket-mounted jeeps, and other weapons which have been sent to Colonia Gardún."

"We are aware of those weapons, Captain," growled the general. "They were shipped down by the DAVROCK Corporation to Von Reinach to protect the oil fields."

"Shipped by DAVROCK is correct, sir. But they were purchased secretly by the NICUBA Trading Corporation, a front for the Cuban-Nicaraguan economic and political penetration of Latin America. The money supplied came from Libyan petrodollars. NICUBA has been using DAVROCK as a conduit, since their aircraft fly directly to the Chaco from the United States without inspection."

The secret-police general picked up the incriminating document. His hand was trembling with anger as his eyes scanned the inventory and the damning information. Suddenly his scowl was replaced by a smiling sneer.

"The two most troublesome groups in this country are the Sandinistas and the Holy Garduna. The Sandinistas we can deal with. They are only the enemy; but the Holy Garduna has been operating under the guise of patriotism and religion. So far, Captain, they have been untouchable, and their power has expanded at the expense of the national security organs and the regular services. This"—he waved the document angrily in the air—"proves beyond the shadow of a doubt that they are traitors to the homeland! We must find a way to crush the Garduna and the Sandinistas once and for all!"

The documents which were planted in the *pyngare* informant network by the disinformation branch of the Christian Action party had sown their deadly seeds of subversion.

The fort looked deserted. The guards were on duty, but Mariscal Estigarribia seemed to have lost something, thought Angel, as he and Susan drove through the front gate. With the bulk of troops and their officers in the oil fields, a laxness had settled over the Chaco military post. Angel braked the jeep to a stop in front of the school commandant's office and stepped inside. Within minutes he emerged, a troubled look on his face.

"What's the matter?" asked Susan.

"The troops are coming back tomorrow. You're to go back to Colonia Gardún with a Dr. Schutzler at six in the morning. He came down to pick up some supplies."

"Did . . . did anyone miss us, Angel?"

"I doubt it. This place is in the doldrums. When the officers leave, the enlisted men goof off. Nobody was looking for us."

Angel cast her a perplexed glance. "I've got to figure out how I'm going to make contact with you in Colonia Gardún. I'm . . . I'm not sure how I'm going to put this all together before the assault." He smiled grimly. "We don't have too much time to organize a revolution."

Caro backed up the jeep and then pulled forward and headed for the infirmary.

The next morning dawned hot and dry, and Susan dejectedly piled her belongings in the same Toyota pickup that Von Ziegazar drove down. She glanced over toward the officers' quarters and choked back her tears as she saw Angel looking at her out the window. Dr. Heinz Schutzler, a balding little man with a beaklike nose which made him look like a bird of prey, slid in next to her, ground the gears, and lurched ahead slowly out the main gate, heading north toward Colonia Gardún.

"Dr. Schutzler," Susan said pleasantly, "where's Dr. Von Ziegazar?"

Schutzler rolled down the window to capture some cooling breeze. "Ach! She was called on assignment elsewhere and I was sent down to replace her, pick up medical supplies for the colony, and go back. We have a functioning aid station in the oil field now, so my duty is complete."

The ride going back was pleasant, and the doctor was a talkative little man. He clearly enjoyed Susan's company.

About thirty miles from Colonia Gardún, Dr. Schutzler dropped his bombshell.

"So, *mein schönes Kind*. You are so lucky. You must be excited."

It didn't register. Susan knitted her forehead into a puzzled frown. "Excited? About what?"

"To have been chosen by Señor Von Reinach to be his wife," the little doctor beamed.

Susan stared ahead at the road, which was straight and narrow, through the flat scrublands of the Chaco. Her silent response was the response of a cold numbness mingled with fatigue. It coursed throughout her body. Her knees became weak and she fought the urge to vomit. But, oddly, she didn't feel any sense of panic. Her being chosen in this manner—without her consent or knowledge—was so typical of the Garduna. Women were never consulted. They were ordered, assigned, and expected to obey and perform.

Perhaps my lack of anger, indignation, or even great surprise is an indication that I am becoming conditioned to their value system. Without any emotion, Susan asked flatly, "And . . . and when is the wedding to take place?"

"That is unknown, my child. What is known is that Señor Von Reinach sees you as the mother of his children and his co-ruler over a greater Paraguay. What an honor is yours, Susan!"

Susan squinted thoughtfully out the side window, her chin resting in the cup of her hand.

Von Reinach was old enough to be her father; and yet there was a magnetism—a dynamic attraction to the Gardún leader. Her mind spun a series of fantasies and what-ifs.

What if the revolution planned by Salazar didn't succeed?

What if I married Von Reinach? Would I be in a better position to get Olivia out of La Cuna?

What if we married? What kind of power could I wield to moderate—to humanize—the Garduna? Could I reform it from within?

What if . . . A cold chill ran through Susan. *What if we married and Von Reinach discovered that my grandfather was a black man? If we had a child, would he kill it? And me?*

She looked up at the concrete archway as the truck slowed down to enter the colony, and read the inscription: "The Glory of God Is Obedience."

Angel slept fitfully all night. He was worried about Susan and wondered just how she was going to carry out her awesome part of the conspiracy. She was so young, so inexperienced in these things. The responsibility thrust upon her was mind-boggling. Her success in sabotaging the armored cars at Colonia Gardún was the key to the success of the revolution. When he thought of the task she was faced with, he felt a mixture of helplessness and anger at Salazar and his brother, Raúl.

His thoughts were interrupted by an unfamiliar sound at Mariscal Estigarribia, the *whumpity-whumpity-whump* of helicopters. He pulled on his fatigue pants and rushed outside, as did the few troopers left at the fort. Overhead, ten Brazilian-made troop-carrying helicopter gunships were circling, awaiting their turn to land on the parade ground in the middle of the commando school complex. The red, white, and blue circle of the Paraguayan Air Force was clearly visible on the fuselage of the helicopters.

Grounded and secured, the helicopters, main rotors still spinning slightly in the breeze, disgorged their crews. Caro sized them up as they sauntered over to the commandant's office to report in. They weren't Guaraní, that was for sure. They were young, cocky, self-assured: typical of the young officers in a Latin American air force who have mastered difficult technical skills. Most of the pilots were warrant officers, a recently created rank in the Paraguayan military to accommodate the newly trained technical ratings.

One of the officers, the one clearly in charge, detoured from the group and walked casually toward Angel. The others relaxed on the wide shady porch of the commandant's building, smoking their cigarettes and waiting for the building to open. The slender, dark-haired pilot, not more than twenty-two, walked up to Angel.

"Pardon me," he said in a Spanish which was tinged by an immigrant's accent, "I'm looking for the American adviser to the Escuela para Comando."

"You're looking at him," said Caro. "Captain Angel Caro, U.S. Army Special Forces." He held out his hand to the pilot.

"Chief Warrant Officer Filippo Gaduti." He shook Angel's hand with a firm grip. "My squadron is on permanent change of station to provide transport to your commandos. We're the rapid part of your rapid-reaction force."

"Come on in. My room is a mess, but have a seat, Mr. Gaduti. Can I give you some coffee? It's instant, but it'll get your heart started."

Gaduti relaxed in the occasional chair in the corner, sipping his coffee slowly to avoid burning his lips. He looked around the room. He noticed Angel's fatigue jacket. The name CARO was clearly visible on his name tape above the left breast pocket.

"Give me a few minutes to shave and I'll join you. Have you and your men had breakfast yet?"

The pilot shook his head.

"Good. I'll take you over to the mess hall." Caro shut the bathroom door as he finished the comment.

Gaduti reached over and took Angel's wallet off the dresser. He ignored the money, but rifled through the identification documents: green U.S. Army I.D., driver's license, Social Security card, Fort Bragg Officers Club card. He was convinced that this was, indeed, Angel Caro. He put the wallet back on the dresser.

Caro emerged from the small bathroom minutes later and was surprised to see the door locked and Gaduti peering out the window through the bamboo blinds.

"Problems, Mr. Gaduti?" Caro asked suspiciously.

The pilot turned his face. He was wearing a serious expression, and Angel tensed.

"Captain Caro, I have been in contact with your friend Paul Lancaster, in Asunción."

Angel held his breath and waited, still tensed.

"I'm your contact with the Christian Action party, Captain. My men and I are at your disposal."

Caro exhaled and collapsed on the bed. "Wow! An hour ago I felt totally alone in this little caper, and now I have an entire helicopter squadron!"

"And more, Captain. I have the names of at least seventy-five of your commandos who can be trusted to join us. They are the men of families who have been bled white by the Garduna through taxes, threats, and harassment."

"Do . . . do you have any men in place in Colonia Gardún?" Angel asked anxiously.

"We will. Five of our helicopters are going up there to support the armored cars. Don't worry. We'll keep an eye on your little *chivato*." Gaduti winked.

"Lancaster briefed you very thoroughly, my friend. Did you know that Susan's mission is . . ."

"To sabotage the armored cars, Captain?" the pilot interrupted.

"You people know everything!" Caro marveled.

"We have been in radio contact with Comandante Salazar and your brother, Raúl. We know of your affection for Susan

Rockland. My men want to be in a position to protect and extricate her if she's in danger."

A sense of peace and well-being descended on Angel.

Outside, driving through the barbed-wire gate, the Brazilian-made Fiat army trucks roared into the compound, bringing the commandos back to Mariscal Estigarribia.

"The United States has become a dangerous place, Julio," whispered Weishaupt. "The political climate has changed radically in the past year."

Barrajas and Martin Weishaupt snapped on their seat belts as the DC-8 circled Washington National, awaiting clearance to land.

After fleeing the carnage of Puerto Concepción, they took the first plane out of Santiago. It was one which flew to Jamaica, and it left minutes after they arrived at the airport. From Kingston they went to Miami. Contacts were made there with several of Weishaupt's agents who were inactive because of new and stringently enforced federal legislation curtailing the activities of religious cults. After several days in Miami, Weishaupt and Barrajas enplaned again, this time for Washington, D.C., to contact and confront their man there, Senator Calvin Bouchegrave.

"You know I never get involved in politics, Martin," said Barrajas as he leered at the wriggling bottom of the stewardess, who was prowling the aisle checking seat belts. "I'm a prophet, remember? Political affairs are not included in my job description."

"You may have no job, my phony friend, if Senator Courtney Davenport continues his countercult activities. What he's done in Tulsa has been expanded to other cities. I'll swear on Lenin's tomb that the force which destroyed our operation at Puerto Concepción was the work of his countercult commandos. We have to tell Bouchegrave about this and get him to act. That damned Davenport! He's untouchable! Do you realize that there are noises in the American political system to nominate him as a presidential candidate in the 1992 election? The American people are beginning to appreciate his direct methods in purifying their fatherland."

Barrajas's interest perked. "Martin, this Davenport . . . why is he so zealously against cults?"

"There are several reasons, Julio. He was saved and 'born again' twenty-seven years ago. The person responsible for his conversion was his business partner, an itinerant faith healer named Gypsy Joe Rockland. He's what they call a Christian Fundamentalist. What really got him started was . . ."

It hit them both at the same time. Rockland? Davenport? Weishaupt condemned himself for not following up on this before; but there were other pressures and priorities, such as the decimation of his agents in the cities of Western Europe after Günter's defection.

Of course! Olivia Davenport and Susan Rockland were part of the contingent of Garden Children that left Parramore Island last winter. Barrajas remembered Olivia Davenport and felt a mixture of anger and humiliation as he thought of how she rejected him at La Cuna. *So that little blond bitch is Senator Davenport's daughter. And to think, if it wasn't for Hilda Von Ziegazar, she'd be dead. Our supreme bargaining chip would have been thrown away!*"

Barrajas looked at Weishaupt, his chubby face wreathed in a silly grin. Weishaupt stared back, his eyes appearing huge through his thick eyeglass lenses.

"Your stupid little smile is telling me something, Prophet. I hope it's what I want to hear."

Barrajas nodded, his grin fixed.

"Don't play games with me, Barrajas! Where is she?" Weishaupt demanded.

"What's the senator's daughter's name, Martin? Just to make sure we have the right girl."

"Olivia. She's a slender blonde with big blue eyes. I have a complete file on the Davenport family with photographs," explained the Section VI director.

"Yes! Yes, she's the one!" Barrajas chuckled. "A true believer—or at least she was until our little encounter."

"You . . . you didn't hurt her?" asked Weishaupt, alarmed.

"Not her body. Not permanently." Barrajas's mouth became set. "But she wouldn't play my games, and she had the honor of being chosen!" His voice became louder.

"Ssshhh! The main thing, Julio, is that she's alive! We can—and we will—use her to put the screws to Davenport."

"How will we reach him, Martin? Do we just burst into his office and say, Senator Davenport, we are holding your daughter hostage in a breeding station in the jungles of Paraguay. Her mind is scrambled but her body is still functioning. Will you cooperate with us?"

Weishaupt smiled, wrinkling his scalp to the crown. "No, my dear prophet. We'll be much more subtle than that. We'll work through our man in the Senate."

"Bouchegrave?"

The DC-8 touched down at Washington National. White yachts on the muddy Potomac flashed by the rear windows where Barrajas and Weishaupt were sitting, anticipating the impact the information about Olivia would have on Courtney Davenport.

Susan stood fidgeting nervously with a lace handkerchief as she waited in the richly paneled office of the Hermano Mayor of the Holy Garduna, Francisco Estigarribia. When she got back to Colonia Gardún yesterday, she had found a note pinned to her pillow instructing her to appear at the office the following morning, in her "finest attire." Her "finest attire" was the beautiful squaw dress which was given to her by Dr. Félix Pacoima the night of the reception in her honor at the officers club at Mariscal Estigarribia. He had never taken it back to his daughter, but insisted that Susan keep it.

Susan fixed her hair, jacaranda blossoms and all, exactly as the Guaraní Indian women had done that night.

The door opened and the Prophet Estigarribia stepped in. He stared at Susan and was taken by her beauty and her resemblance to Carlos' mother. Yes, he could see why his nephew was enthralled by this *chivato*. Surely, Hilda Von Ziegazar must be wrong.

Von Reinach followed, dressed in beige whipcord riding breeches, brown high-topped boots, which were shined to a brilliance, and a white loose-fitting cotton tunic, which featured a high collar. The outfit complemented his dark complexion and bright blue eyes. He looked like a Russian cossack in a vodka advertisement, thought Susan, as he walked toward her, smiling broadly.

"Ah, my dear little Cherokee," he beamed, taking her hand and pressing it to his lips. "You are just as lovely as that night I last saw you at Mariscal Estigarribia. I trust that you were not too bored during the past two weeks?"

Susan smiled graciously. Several images of her time with Angel flickered in her mind. "Oh, not too bored, Señor Von Reinach. I managed to keep myself occupied."

Francisco Estigarribia ruffled through some papers in his desk drawer, retrieved an envelope, and started for the door. "I will leave you two alone. I would like to say before I leave that you are indeed a beautiful sight to behold in this barren wilderness, Señorita Rockland. You symbolize what the Chaco will look like after it has been blessed and beautified."

Susan smiled nervously as the door closed behind him. She and Von Reinach were alone.

"Sit down, Susan, please." He motioned toward the couch.

Susan sat, hoping that her shaking knees were not too obvious. She smoothed the wrinkles from her lap.

"Susan," Von Reinach began haltingly. "The life of a man with a sacred mission to perform is a lonely life—a life fraught with hardship and sacrifice. God puts many tests and trials in the path of such men; test and trials which must be overcome to prove our worthiness before Him."

Susan listened, nodding her understanding.

"A woman . . . that is, one which can share the life and mission of such a man, must often wait until the most appropriate time, and she, too, must be proven worthy, as you were in the oil field accident."

Von Reinach took her hand in his and moved closer, his electric-blue eyes gleaming, almost hypnotizing Susan. Her eyes were captured by his as she felt his hot breath on her cheek.

"When I saw you that night at Mariscal Estigarribia, I felt the whisperings of the Great Spirit of the Chaco that you, my sweet *chivato*, were to share in the glory which awaits me.

When I learned of your bravery and your Cherokee purity, I knew that a wise and benevolent Providence had sent you to me to be my wife."

The word "wife" cut into Susan like a saber thrust. To marry a man like Carlos Von Reinach, the leader of a vicious religious cult which would use young girls like Olivia as breeding stock, was a gross violation of everything she desired in a husband. But his words were not a proposal of marriage, they were a command—a foregone conclusion on his part that she would be overjoyed at the prospect of sharing his glory.

Without another word, Von Reinach slipped his arms around her and kissed her hard, fully and sensually on the lips.

The suddenness of his move took her by surprise, but she found herself responding to his passion.

Carlos felt an inner glow at her response, taking it as an affirmative answer to his description of the glories which awaited them as man and wife—and as co-rulers over a powerful and greater Paraguay.

XIX.

They came from the sky: twenty-three armed men, wearing leaf-patterned camouflage jumpsuits and camouflaged berets under their hard nylon helmets.

Their unmarked blue-black C-130 had flown over the vastness of Brazil's Mato Grosso jungle at a low altitude, barely skimming the treetops to avoid radar detection, turned westward, and climbed to twenty thousand feet. The strange armed band had jumped at that altitude in a HALO—high-altitude, low-opening approach—and landed expertly in a small jungle clearing twenty-five miles north of the Gardún breeding station at La Cuna.

They folded their chutes, buried them, and disappeared into the thick greenness of the Andean foothills. With the ease of experienced jungle fighters, they slipped their way toward the complex.

The submarine had entered the wide estuary of the River Plate, steering a middle course on the surface. The lights of Montevideo to the east and Buenos Aires westward and farther upstream acted as navigation aids to the countercult skipper.

The skipper had approached the Paraná River delta cautiously. Like threading the eye of a needle, he aligned his craft with a broad avenue of water from among the network of waterways which laced the delta.

The submarine sailed on the surface at night, except when approaching the cities and towns which lined sections of the river in Argentina's Entre Ríos province. It passed the large Argentina cities of Rosario and Santa Fe by August 18, and had slid by Corrientes and entered Paraguayan waters by August 20.

At Asunción, where the Pilcomayo and Paraguay rivers form the junction to create the Paraná, the submarine went straight north on the Paraguay. By August 23 it had crawled underwater at a shallow depth, scraping the mud bottom at times, and passed the dingy, little river port of Puerto Sastre—less than one hundred miles from its target, Fuerte Olimpo.

At a remote, abandoned oil drilling site at Campo Grande in the southern Brazilian highlands, the radio operator tuned in to KDRM, the Tower of Power from Tulsa, Oklahoma. It was odd to hear a religious message broadcast in English to a Portuguese-speaking country, but the audience wasn't Brazil. It was much smaller than that. Every fifth word of the stilted prepared sermon constituted the disparate elements which, when put together, formed the instructions for the countercult raiders who were to attack La Cuna.

Deciphering the message, the operator handed it to Eli Revvim. Revvim read it, smiled wryly, and repeated it to Puerter Detlefs and the thirty-five commandos who were crowded into the weathered old barracks which was one of the three buildings left at the old DAVROCK drilling site.

"All right, people! This is it. We jump into the vicinity of La Cuna on September thirteenth. We'll land about ten miles southeast. We make our assault on the fifteenth at 0430."

Radio operators aboard the submarine, in the capital city, in the Andean foothills with Benito Salazar's guerrilla group, and Angel Caro at Mariscal Estigarribia also heard the message. In a little over two weeks, the Christian Action/Countercult assault on the Holy Garduna and the government of Paraguay would begin.

• • •

"I think it's a splendid idea, Captain Caro." The beefy, red-faced Paraguayan army colonel smiled from behind his desk in the school commandant's office.

"Thank you, sir," said Angel. "I feel that if our rapid-reaction force is to get off the ground, and do so in any size, then a force of fifty to seventy-five of our best troopers could serve as a prototype. We could iron out a lot of operational difficulties with a group that size. The five helicopters we have left can transport the men and their equipment. Each helicopter can take fifteen men."

"Just how realistic do you plan to make their training, Captain?"

"Extremely realistic, sir." Caro smiled. "As you may know, sir, the Socialist Christian Action party has been somewhat active during the past few weeks. We're going to search and hopefully make contact with some of their units."

"*Somewhat* active, Captain! This is an understatement. They have come from nothing—*nothing*—to a potent, professional guerrilla force; and they're getting more recruits every week. Take a look at this map, Captain Caro." The colonel pointed to a multicolored, dot-studded map of the Chaco on the wall. "Here . . . here . . . here and here!" He jabbed his pointer at four large dots on the map. "At Fortín La Faya, Fortín Garrapatal, Fortín Madrejoncito, and Fortín Hernandarias: all small army outposts west and north of here. They have been raided by the Christian Action guerrillas. They have become very expert, Captain. The small garrisons at La Faya and Garrapatal surrendered after putting up token resistance. They joined the guerrillas and took their weapons with them! I know that the Christian Action pigs are receiving assistance from the procommunist Guevarist party in Bolivia."

Caro rubbed his chin thoughtfully. "I had no idea that this group was now raiding Paraguayan territory."

"Yes, and it doesn't stop there. My agents in Asunción report the formation of an urban guerrilla movement there. I *know* it's Christian Action! Just try to tell those pig-headed *pyngares*! All they see these days are Sandinistas and threats from the east."

"From the east?" Caro arched his eyebrows.

"From Uruguay. The Tupamaros, a communist urban guerrilla group par excellence in the late 1960s and early 1970s, have reappeared as a legitimate political party. They are still communist and maintain their guerrilla organization, but they feel that they can take over Uruguay in a legitimate election. And they're right! Uruguay is ripe for a communist takeover.

"That is the situation, Captain, and it's a desperate one for our country: Tupamaro power in Uruguay; the Che Guevara party, now a legitimate power in Bolivia; the Sandinista resurrection in the capital; and the Christian Action guerrillas in the Chaco. Only the army, Captain, and especially our commandos, can save our fatherland from its enemies. What you develop with your rapid-reaction force will enable us to be mobile and stamp out the many brushfires that are being lit by our foes."

Caro emerged from the school commandant's office with mixed feelings; feelings of guilt about his betrayal to the government he was advising, and feelings of acute anxiety about Susan's fate.

The population of the Chaco is small, and word travels fast—especially news of a proposed wedding of a person as prominent as Carlos Von Reinach. If the wedding date was to be before September 15, he would have to act fast.

Angel walked briskly to the far end of the Escuela para Comando complex. There, at the edge of the school, isolated in two barracks, were sixty-seven enlisted men, whose anti-Garduna sentiments were uncovered by Caro and Filippo Gaduti.

Nearby, parked neatly in a row, were five of the Brazilian-made helicopter transport gunships.

Soon, very soon, the nucleus of the rapid-reaction force would take to the field, but not against the Christian Action guerrillas of Benito Salazar.

The first day of September dawned bright, clear, and surprisingly chilly at Colonia Gardún.

Susan yawned and stretched her lithe, tawny body in a variety of directions until she heard her joints snap. A cool, dry breeze blew into her room. The smell of dried leaves brought back a few nostalgic memories of Bryson Academy, the snappy autumns of the Virginia countryside, and football weather. How desperately she wanted to return to America, tie the threads of her life together, and lead the existence of an ordinary American woman—preferably a housewife. Or, as she thought of Angel—an army wife. But that was not to be. Susan Rockland, an ordinary eighteen-year-old from mid-America, was to be married to the leader of a powerful religious and military cult. Indeed, the marriage was to be almost a coronation.

She looked around the room trying to focus her eyes. It was difficult without that first cup of coffee, a rare drink in the Chaco where yerba maté tea was the national beverage.

It was a nice room. More than nice, it was luxurious by Chaco standards. The room had been Hilda Von Ziegazar's, but Von Reinach had claimed it for his bride-to-be. He had the doctor's furniture and personal items moved to a stark, sterile room in the infirmary, and had the doctor's old room and bath redecorated. At Colonia Gardún a person's rank and position were determined by one's dwelling, and certainly Susan's move into Von Ziegazar's room told those at Colonia Gardún where she stood in the Gardún hierarchy.

She had heard of the wedding date, September 13, from Heinz Schutzler. A gossipy little man, he had become Susan's confidant and source of information. As usual, the plans were made by the leaders of the Holy Garduna without her input or consent.

She patted the empty spot on her bed by her side and wondered who would share it a month from now—Carlos or Angel. What kind of lover would Von Reinach make? she wondered. Would he be as sensitive and satisfying as Angel? The thought of Von Reinach on top of her, kissing her roughly, his hard face contorted with passion, was not at all unpleasant. She suddenly felt pangs of guilt as she remembered Angel and the discussions they had had about marriage.

Susan was beginning to wonder if her instinct for survival was turning her into an opportunistic little slut. When she thought of her responsibility to create a small cadre of conspirators, from among the *chivatos*, and sabotage the armored cars, she felt overwhelmed; overwhelmed and totally alone in her efforts. There was nobody at Colonia Gardún to coordinate her actions with, or even share her feelings with. Perhaps her best course of action, she often thought, was to marry Von Reinach—as if she had a choice—and make the best of the situation. Clearly, the power of the Sacred Order of the Holy Garduna was too pervasive, too great to overthrow. Perhaps God had put her in this position to be a moderating and humanizing influence on her husband-to-be and the Garduna.

Suddenly her fantasies were interrupted by the sounds of helicopter rotors chopping the cool Chaco air. She opened her window, rubbed the sleep out of her eyes, and gazed to the south, from where the noise came. The five helicopters of Filippo Gaduti's rapid-reaction force were circling for a landing near the vehicle park where the armored cars were located.

Calvin Bouchegrave appeared completely unruffled as the bald-headed man in thick glasses stood before him and pointed an accusing finger.

"You have failed us *miserably*, Bouchegrave. We've counted on you to hold up this end, and you've done so, admirably, until the past few months. We've given you instructions and advice on what pieces of legislation we wanted introduced and defeated in the Senate. You haven't even made the attempt to draft rough copies of those bills we want. Our people in Washington have informed us that you have a thousand excuses; and as for Parramore Island, you won't even allow any of our people in there anymore. I want some answers, Bouchegrave, and they'd better be good!"

Bouchegrave ran the back of his hand across the bridge of his aquiline nose, and then started to explain in a casual, almost disinterested manner.

"Ah, Dr. Weishaupt." The senator smiled. "The paranoia of the times is affecting you, as well as everybody else in Washington." He waved his thin hand airily in conversation. "I'm in a holding pattern right now, Weishaupt. I dare not make too many rash moves. I'm trying to maintain a low profile until this countercult madness subsides."

"You mean Davenport?" wheezed Weishaupt.

"Yes, Davenport. He's the man of the hour in Washington right now. What he's done in Tulsa, he's done in other cities. The followers of Davenport are called the Ramrod Rights, and it's a mass movement, a purifying and cleansing force which is wreaking havoc on cults. Do you realize that there is a ground-swell movement to nominate him as a presidential candidate in 1992?"

"Don't worry about Davenport." Weishaupt smiled a scalp-wrinkling smile. "He'll be taken care of, Bouchegrave."

"What do you mean, Weishaupt?" The senator sat up straight in his chair, his face a mask of concern.

"We have his daughter in Paraguay—at La Cuna."

Bouchegrave's face turned ashen. "At . . . at the breeding station?"

"I won't go into details, but we have this fellow right by the balls; and when you have someone by the balls, their heart and mind will follow, eh, Bouchegrave?"

Weishaupt stood up abruptly. "Tomorrow is Saturday, Bouchegrave. Your calendar is clear; we've checked with your secretary. Barrajas and I will be visiting Parramore Island at ten o'clock. We want you there, and we'll want some answers to some questions we've had for some time. We can't do anything here in your Georgetown town house. We want to talk to some of Julio's people at Parramore so we'll kill two birds with one stone."

"Barrajas is here?"

"Yes, my dear senator. If you don't start cooperating, we can get you fifty years at Leavenworth. Don't make us play nasty."

Weishaupt started to shuffle toward the door. Bouchegrave followed, his thin lips pressed together in a slight smile. "Very well, my good doctor. Parramore it is. This will give me the opportunity to play the perfect host."

Bouchegrave watched the director of Section VI get into his rented Pontiac Phoenix and drive down the tree-shaded Georgetown street to the traffic light and turn right on Wisconsin Avenue.

He walked to his bookcase, removed two thick volumes of

constitutional law, and pressed a button where the books had been. The reel-to-reel tape recorder behind the paneling stopped playing. The senator from Virginia picked up the phone and dialed the special countercult circuit. The phone rang twice, and the operator answered. Bouchegrave responded: "Give me a direct line to Senator Davenport, please."

Paul Lancaster bit his lower lip nervously as Joe Rockland paced the floor in front of him, his swarthy face clouded with anxiety.

"You mean I came all the way down here to Asunción only to find out that *nothing* can be done, Paul? I can't accept that! Right now, for all we know, this woman could be telling the Garduna that Susan is partly Negro and . . ."

Outside, the bright sun was almost directly overhead, bathing the attractive Paraguayan capital city in its heat. It was two o'clock in the afternoon—siesta time—and the pace of life in Asunción, like the traffic outside the DAVROCK branch office, slowed to a crawl.

Lancaster knew about the proposed wedding and the date, which was September 13. Paul knew that he had to tell Rockland, but was afraid of the response.

"Mr. Rockland, I . . . I know that Susan is safe and . . . and well taken care of right now."

Joe Rockland cocked a dark eye. "How do you know that, Paul?"

"We have agents in Colonia Gardún—helicopter pilots—who are watching her. One of them is my radio contact."

Rockland stared, his eyes pleading for more answers. Paul swallowed hard, his hands fidgeting with a small model oil derrick on the desk. His voice was almost a whisper.

"Susan is marrying Von Reinach on September thirteenth."

Joe Rockland stood up as if an electric shock had prodded him. "What? What did you say?"

"Susan is marrying Von Reinach. It's to be the social event of the year in this wretched country. It'll be in all of the newspapers soon."

Rockland sat down again, his hands gripping the arms of the chair until the knuckles were turned white. He then rubbed his forehead with the heel of his hand, tears forming in his eyes and rolling down his cheeks onto his jacket lapels.

"Paul, I've . . . I've failed in the most important task the Good Lord has given me. Courtney, too, has failed. We've saved tens of thousands in His name and reversed the trend in the growth of cults, but we've failed our own daughters. I've lost Susan forever!"

Paul sat silently on the edge of the desk, his foot swinging nervously. He was embarrassed by Rockland's outburst and fumbled for an appropriate response.

"I could attempt to have the timing for the assaults moved up two days or . . . or the raid on Colonia Gardún rescheduled."

Paul knew that this was impossible. The multifaceted operation to bring down the Holy Garduna, the government of Paraguay, and to place Benito Salazar in power was incredibly complicated. Any attempt now to tamper with the finely coordinated mechanism of insurgency would create chaos.

"I've got to clear my head and think this out, Paul. The Lord will give me an answer. I'm going to walk downtown to Independence Square and visit the National Cathedral. Perhaps I'll get some inspiration near a house of the Lord."

"But you're a Southern Baptist, sir. The National Cathedral is Catholic." Paul smiled, trying to be humorous.

Rockland responded with a tight-lipped smile of his own. "I don't know what denomination the Lord is, Paul, but the cathedral was built by honorable men who dedicated it to Him. That's where I'll seek Him out, and hopefully, that's where I'll find Him."

He then opened the door and stepped out into the bright, deserted streets of Asunción.

Hilda Von Ziegazar did not rush back to Paraguay with her evidence. She had decided to let Susan and Von Reinach stew in their own passion for a while. There was time. The wedding was almost two weeks away. She had been in constant telephone contact with a female lover in the capital, who kept her informed. She had twelve days in which to act.

Von Ziegazar wanted to hurt Von Reinach. She had never liked him and the feeling was mutual. She could never understand the mentality of the German-Guaraní mixed bloods. How could a man like Von Reinach, with his noble Germanic heritage—his father's legacy at least—find *anything* worthwhile in the Guaraní? She often wondered if Von Reinach was prouder of his mother's legacy, the Guaraní, than his father's.

Those early Nazis of the 1930s, Hilda often thought with contempt, were too eager to cement their relationships with the native stock in order to create a safe haven for Nazi influence and refugees. It had created a short-term answer, but in the long racial view of history, it had created genetic havoc and polluted the bloodlines of her people.

Von Ziegazar felt superior to all of those German-Guaraní who infested the Holy Garduna. After all, she was a grandniece of the late Dr. Josef Mengele, Paraguay's most famous guest from the Hitler era. As a youth, Hilda had often sat at the old doctor's knee, in his hideaway near the Brazilian border, and learned of her racial heritage—the "heritage of pure blood."

She left her lover, another German woman, and climbed into the high seat of her rented Volkswagen microbus. She drove aimlessly around the capital, her mind probing for possible ways in which to confront Von Reinach with the evidence and create the greatest humiliation. Would he accept it or was he too emotionally involved with this *chivato* slut to believe it?

Von Reinach detested Hilda. He hated her because she was a lesbian, and because his uncle, the Hermano Mayor, gave her employment over his objections. Her great-uncle, the late Josef Mengele, was an old friend of Francisco Estigarribia. He talked the Prophet of Paraguay into accepting Von Ziegazar as a staff physician at Colonia Gardún. As the resident geneticist, she would have vast influence over the racial policies of the Garduna, among those to decide which of the *chivatos* were racially pure enough to breed.

Hilda drove toward Independence Plaza, which was always a pleasant place to sit and think. She nudged her VW into a tree-shaded parking spot and sat, her thoughts turning to fantasies of revenge against Von Reinach and Susan.

She first saw Joseph Rockland as he walked across the plaza, diagonally, toward her car. Her heart leaped. In a fit of panic she fumbled for the ignition key. The walkway led directly to the red brick sidewalk to the left of her car. She started her car and began to back out, but he stopped and sat on one of the many green benches which dotted the plaza. She shut off the engine. Her flat chest heaved deeply.

"What's he doing here?" she gasped to herself. *Did he find out who I am? How could he? Of course! He's down here on DAVROCK business. Perhaps he's here to give the bride away!* She relaxed, smirking at her own humor.

Her heart leaped again when Rockland got up after spending fifteen minutes in what looked like either meditation or prayer. He walked away from her toward the huge baroque National Cathedral. He entered, and Von Ziegazar waited thirty more minutes until he emerged. His countenance had brightened and he had a slight spring to his step.

Von Ziegazar started her engine, eased out of her parking space, and slowly followed him. He walked three blocks to the Asunción Hilton. *Of course! Where else would a man of his means stay in this backwater national capital?* She waited five minutes, parked her car, and walked cautiously into the plush lobby. No sign of Rockland. She sauntered casually up to the front desk. The portly clerk smiled pleasantly, exhaling garlic breath. Hilda blanched.

"Pardon me. Do you have a Mr. Joseph Rockland from Tulsa, Oklahoma, in the United States, registered here?"

"Oh, sí, señora. In fact, he just came in and went up to his room. Shall I ring him for you?"

"Oh, no," she said sweetly. "He must be tired from his trip. I'll catch him later. What is his number in case I want to call?"

"Room 512," the clerk answered.

Von Ziegazar stepped into the hot street and swaggered toward her car. She was almost consumed by feelings of victory. She stepped into a phone booth and called Hermann Rathner, a well-known bullyboy in Asunción's German colony. Rathner would arrange anything from an assassination to a kidnaping for the right price, and he owed Hilda many favors. She steered much of the Garduna's business of that nature to Rathner.

The details were agreed upon. Tomorrow, she would charter a plane to Colonia Gardún and have her way with Susan. She wanted to sink her teeth into that beautiful flesh before old Estigarribia's piranha did, and they would, when he and Von Reinach found out that Susan had deceived them.

Hilda could hardly contain her emotions as she thought of Von Reinach's humiliation when she confronted him with the evidence of Susan's heritage. *Every important person in Paraguay, including President Ayala, will be there. I will present the evidence at the height of the ceremony, before they say the I-do's. It is my right! In the case of genetic inferiority, especially when marriage is concerned, it is my duty*. Her thoughts were now becoming quite audible.

"If Von Reinach does not accept the documentation I obtained in Tulsa as proof, I will present my star witness. In fact, I will present him anyway—kidnaped and handcuffed—at the wedding ceremony."

"I've never seen a forest like this before, Julio. In Germany we have teams of foresters clearing out the underbrush and thinning trees. This is like a jungle."

Weishaupt marveled at the primitive thickness of the pristine forest of Parramore Island as they approached the entrance to the Bouchegrave estate. The ancient, gnarled maples and elms which lined the road bent overhead and touched, creating a magnificent archway.

Barrajas slowed down as they approached the chain link fence gate. Two armed guards, part of the countercult commando force left on the island, opened the gate. One of them cradled a shotgun. "Julio Barrajas? Martin Weishaupt?" he asked.

"Yes," answered Weishaupt.

"Senator Bouchegrave is expecting you at ten," the guard said.

Several minutes later they reached the huge stone mansion.

"Ach! The senator lives *very* well!" exclaimed Weishaupt. "All this for one man? Does he have a family?"

"No. He's a bachelor," answered Barrajas. "He is perhaps the most selfish man I've ever met. He doesn't want to share this with anybody."

"A typical capitalist!" snorted Weishaupt. "Such people are only fit to be used and discarded."

They walked up on the front porch and rang the doorbell. Bouchegrave himself appeared.

"Ah, gentlemen." He smiled graciously. "You *are* punctual. It's ten o'clock straight up. Come in, please."

They entered the magnificent living room, which was paneled with pecan wood, and sat down. Weishaupt spoke first.

"I can see that your involvement with our organization has enabled you to maintain your lavish life-style, Bouchegrave. I'm having a difficult time understanding why you would jeopardize all of this by ignoring our directives. Your attitude baffles me. You know what we can do to you!"

Bouchegrave raised his arms and waved his thin hands in the air, gesturing his helplessness. "You won't believe me, gentlemen, but I'm helpless. I've been converted to a power stronger than yours."

"Have you been 'born again,' too, Calvin?" smirked the Prophet of the Garden Children.

"In a way," Bouchegrave said deliberately. He snapped his fingers. Immediately, armed men rushed into the room and grabbed the pair, searching them for weapons. Two pistols were removed. Weishaupt was forced to the floor by two commandos. His jaw was pried open and a pair of pliers was shoved roughly into his mouth. Within seconds, the cyanide capsule, which was implanted in a false tooth, was yanked from his bridgework.

"What . . . what is this, Bouchegrave!" Weishaupt blurted, his gums bleeding profusely. "Are you mad? Are you absolutely mad?"

"Not quite, old boy, but I've seen the light, so to speak. Oh, by the way, I'd like you to meet some new friends of mine."

Weishaupt's eyes grew huge in his lenses as he recognized the pair walking into the living room. He rubbed his aching, bleeding jaw and muttered, "Andrea . . . Andrea Macranskia!"

He adjusted his glasses on the bridge of his nose and focused his eyes. He recognized the tall Oklahoman from the photographs in his file and from the attempted assassination of Andrea at the airport. His knees became weak and he sagged slightly.

Barrajas saw the gleaming oil derrick on Davenport's belt buckle and guessed who he was. The color drained from his plump cheeks as he thought of Olivia at La Cuna.

"A pair of vipers if I've ever seen any," snorted Davenport, looking disdainfully at the pair. "Sit down! Both of you! Keep your hands on your lap!"

Weishaupt and Barrajas did as ordered.

"You know who I am?" Davenport asked gruffly.

They both nodded.

"I'll waste no time then. Several months ago, my men penetrated Bouchegrave's operation here at Parramore. We had the senator in our pocket and promised to obliterate any evidence of his connection to your Section VI, Weishaupt; or to your filthy cult, Barrajas."

Weishaupt had partially regained his composure. "You seem very sure of yourself, Senator Davenport."

"I am, Weishaupt. The people of this country are sick and tired of halfway measures. What I've done in Tulsa and elsewhere, they want done in America. It will be a different country when I'm elected."

Davenport reached over and picked up the Polish Radom 9mm pistol from the coffee table. He toyed with the weapon as he talked. "Do you have any more clips for this, Weishaupt?"

Sheepishly the director of Section VI reached into a secret compartment of his jacket and produced four fully loaded magazine clips. "You may have them. Without my pistol, they won't do me much good."

Davenport turned to Barrajas, his face contorted in disgust. "Julio Barrajas, the Prophet of the Garden Children; the one son of a bitch responsible for the ruin of more young people than any other in this cesspool of cults."

Barrajas sat quietly, shaking inwardly.

Suddenly Davenport leveled the pistol at Barrajas and cocked the hammer.

"My daughter, Barrajas! She's at La Cuna, isn't she?"

Barrajas choked down his fear and nodded.

"And what's her condition, *Prophet*?" Davenport sneered.

"She's . . . she's fine. Fine . . . I assure you."

Davenport's face became livid with rage. He aimed the pistol at Barrajas' head and pulled the trigger. The gun barked and a 9mm bullet clipped Barrajas's ear, tearing out a half-moon chunk.

The Prophet screamed and held his bloody ear. He pointed to Weishaupt and blurted, "Davenport . . . there is the mastermind behind the cults. He's . . . he's the one! The rest of us are mere pawns. We do what he says!"

Weishaupt stood up, smiling contemptuously at Barrajas. Davenport barked an order.

"Sit down, Weishaupt!" He leveled the gun at his thick midsection.

Weishaupt chuckled, his tongue feeling the empty space where his false tooth had been. "You may go straight to your fundamentalist hell, Davenport."

Courtney blanched, his finger tightening on the trigger.

Weishaupt drew himself up to his five feet seven inches. "I'm a soldier, Davenport. You can understand that. I wage my kind of war against those whom I consider my enemies, just as earnestly as you do. Like you, Davenport, I was 'born again' to an ideology which will sweep the earth and bring about universal peace—not through the mumbo-jumbo belief in a supreme savior, but by man's scientific approach to solving the world's problems."

Weishaupt turned and pointed his stubby finger at Andrea. "Ah, Davenport. You should have seen our little Andrea when she was a true believer at Sverdlosk. She was magnificent! Had she kept her head and caught the vision of the movement, she would have ultimately replaced me as the head of Section VI."

Andrea's suppressed rage exploded like a volcano. She threw herself on Weishaupt. She knocked him to the ground—scratching, biting, tearing. Weishaupt lay still and laughed, unresisting. Two commandos pulled her off the bleeding, battered Weishaupt. Davenport watched Weishaupt stagger to his feet, still smiling slightly. The senator had a puzzled expression on his face.

"You're wondering why my attitude in the face of certain death is so inappropriate, Davenport? You feel that I should be begging for mercy, turning to your God for final absolution, don't you? No, Senator. I decided a long time ago that if I ever found myself in this situation, I would go like a soldier, shouting my faith in *my* gods—Marx and Lenin! I'll not give you the satisfaction of seeing me whine and whimper for salvation. Your intelligence people have served you well. Very few knew of the cyanide capsule, so you have cheated me out of a self-inflicted death. I'll have to accept whatever you have in store for me."

"You're a brave man, Weishaupt," said Davenport. "I wouldn't have expected that."

"No, not brave, just fatalistic—and practical. I respect you, Davenport. You operate as we do. You're the only worthy opponent your country has raised up in the past twenty years. In deference to that, I'll give you a few facts about your daughter's condition."

Barrajas turned white and closed his eyes as if waiting for a physical blow to descend upon him.

In the next few minutcs, Weishaupt related in graphic detail the kind of perversions which Barrajas inflicted upon young female cultists. He described, from the boasts of Barrajas to him, what the Prophet of the Garden Children tried to do to Olivia, and the psychological state she was in at La Cuna. An enraged Davenport glared at Barrajas, cocking and recocking the Polish pistol.

"She'll be dead before you can do anything about it, Davenport. The Holy Garduna will not tolerate dysfunctional vegetables. She'll be discarded upon their trash heap," snickered Weishaupt.

Davenport breathed deeply and turned. His gray-blue eyes burned into the pair. "Right now, Weishaupt . . . right now, there are several countercult task forces descending on Paraguay with the intention of overthrowing the Garduna and the dictatorship of General Ayala."

Andrea's jaw fell in surprise. Davenport smiled at her.

"Are you surprised I knew, Andrea? I've known for some time—ever since Bouchegrave was assigned to me as my pupil. He knew a great deal more than you thought, and was willing to spill everything in order to get out from under this mess. He told me about Von Reinach, Estigarribia, and the cult-cocaine network. Joe Rockland was right, Andrea. I felt like going down to Paraguay and tearing that damned country apart, hanging Von Reinach and his whole filthy crew by their testicles in the process."

"Why didn't you, Courtney?" asked Andrea.

"Pride, for one thing. I would have admitted openly that I had been taken in by Von Reinach. Also, I didn't want to jeopardize Chaco oil to the West. A superior wisdom than mine convinced me of that."

Davenport pushed an intercom button on the wall and spoke. "Roger. Want to join us?"

Within minutes, Roger Benson, secretary of state, walked in. Weishaupt looked him over through his thick lenses and recognized him. "Ach! You have involved your government, Davenport. A precursor of things to come after 1992, I presume?"

Davenport's lips compressed into a tight smile. "You're looking at my running mate—the future vice president."

"And Bouchegrave?" added Weishaupt, a slight sneer curling his lip.

"Secretary of state. Bouchegrave has his weaknesses, but he's an able, if not gifted, politician."

Courtney draped an arm around Benson's shoulder. "Roger is my source of wisdom and my restraining influence. He's put the State Department's intelligence apparatus at my disposal. By focusing on Paraguay and the Garduna, we've learned enough to take care of that little problem down there."

Davenport continued, his revelations stunning Andrea. "Joe's secretary is my deceased wife's niece. She learned of your meetings in Tulsa. She has her ways, believe me, and gave me the information. She's a born snoop. Her intelligence apparatus is almost as good as Roger's.

"It grieves me, Andrea, that you and Nick didn't trust my judgment enough to confide in me. I was hurt; hurt enough to decide to do things my way."

Weishaupt laughed "Do you really think your puny countercult force can overthrow an entire nation?"

"No. That's why Rockland's people have built up the rural and urban guerrilla forces of the Socialist Christian Action party of Benito Salazar."

Weishaupt's face clouded, recognizing the tremendous attraction the principles of the Christian Action party had in Paraguay. "You've added military power to powerful principles. Very good, gentlemen. That's a winning combination."

"The raid on Puerto Concepción? Your countercult commandos, Davenport?" asked Weishaupt.

"No. Those are my people, Weishaupt," answered Benson. "They're SEALs."

Weishaupt removed his glasses, revealing beady, myopic eyes. He cleaned the thick lenses thoroughly and replaced the glasses, his eyes reappearing as huge blobs of blue. "Ah, yes, SEALs. U.S. Navy Special Forces. An acronym for Sea-Air-Land. Splendid troops. They were very professional."

"The best," smiled Benson. "They're going to attack every target my daughter Patty is assigned to. I don't want to see her wasted on one of your crummy cults. I'm going to preempt all her targets with my SEALs."

"You've taken quite a risk, Benson, using government SEALs for your own private war against us. It's unconstitutional, you know," said Weishaupt, smiling wryly.

"In this case, the means justify the end," Davenport snapped.

"Oho!" Weishaupt laughed, pointing a finger at Andrea. "You've uncorked quite a genie, Andrea. You're not going to get this one back into the bottle after your countercult obsession is exhausted. When this fellow becomes president of your precious republic, after a few years of his administration you won't be able to tell your country apart from a country in the Eastern bloc. Bravo, Davenport! More power to you!''

''It won't last forever,'' added Benson reassuringly. ''The SEALs will simply attack a few targets and go home. After Concepción they left for La Cuna. They're in place right now. They'll destroy the station, the refinery, and rescue Olivia and the other cultists. Patty will come home with them. They'll see to that!''

''How did you learn of our schedule of assaults, Mr. Benson?'' asked Andrea.

''From Joe's snoopy little secretary, and from KDRM, Courtney's Tower of Power. We broke your amateurish little code. It took only five computer runs by our cryptanalysis people at the National Security Agency and we had it.''

Andrea swallowed hard. ''I feel compelled to tell you that . . . that your daughter's team is to raid Fuerte Olimpo—not La Cuna. She's probably in Paraguayan waters right now.''

The color drained from Benson's face. ''You're lying, Andrea! We've deciphered your messages! My people have already jumped into a clearing near La Cuna!''

''Why would I lie? I would feel more secure if your SEALs were supporting Nick Portumo—the man I hope to spend the rest of my life with.''

Weishaupt leaned his bald head back and laughed.

''Damn your rotten communist soul to hell!'' roared Davenport, firing a shot at Weishaupt. The bullet creased his arm, causing it to bleed profusely.

''Shoot! Kill me, Davenport!'' he shouted. ''I don't think you have the balls to kill me!''

Bouchegrave winced as the second bullet splintered the imported pecan-wood paneling in his living room.

''Take them outside!'' bellowed Davenport.

Weishaupt and Barrajas were marched through the forest to the Bouchegrave family cemetery deep in the woods. Two fresh graves had been dug.

Barrajas turned, tears filling his frightened brown eyes. ''No, Davenport, no! Please! I'll work with you! I'll help you destroy the Garduna! Don't kill me!''

''Oh, shut up, *Prophet*,'' snapped Weishaupt. ''You've

had a fulfilling life as a 'beacon of light' to your children. You've lived several lifetimes in the five years you worked for me. Don't give these swine the satisfaction of seeing you whine for mercy."

"Please . . . please, Davenport. I'll tell you all I know about Section VI. I can help you destroy Weishaupt's organization!" whined Barrajas.

Weishaupt's lips curled into a twisted smile. "Andrea, you're a clinical psychologist. Have you ever wondered how an *Untermensch*, an inferior underling like Barrajas, becomes a certifiable grade-A pervert?"

Barrajas put his hands over his genitals, his eyes now ablaze with fear and indignation. "No, Martin, no! Leave me some shreds of dignity, I beg you!"

Andrea began to comprehend.

"Have him stripped naked, Davenport, and behold the organless wonder! Now you'll know why your daughter's mind was scrambled."

Davenport nodded, and two of the commandos wrestled the screaming, kicking Barrajas to the damp earth and tore off his clothing. They yanked him upright, pinning his arms behind him. Andrea, Davenport, and the others stared at the hairless blank triangle between Barrajas's chubby thighs, and understood. Andrea was flooded with pity, momentarily, toward this hapless morphadite, and was ashamed at the raucous laughter of the commandos.

The humiliated, broken Prophet Barrajas fell to his knees sobbing. "My rosary, please! In the name of God, let me have my rosary!"

The commandos released Barrajas. He removed an ancient pewter rosary from the pocket of his coat, which had been thrown to the ground.

"Look how they all resort to their old supersuitions when they are threatened," sneered Weishaupt with contempt. "Five hours ago he would have denied his God and all of the Christian saints just for one little female cultist to perform upon."

• • •

The late morning sun filtered through the treetops and sent little shafts of light into the cemetery clearing. The birds were chattering brightly in the late summer air.

"Ach! It's a beautiful day for an execution, Davenport. Have your commandos shoot us and be done with it," smiled Weishaupt.

"What makes you think they're going to do it, Weishaupt. I might treat myself. Or, perhaps little Andrea wants the honor." His face wore a strange, twisted smile as he handed the pistol to Andrea.

She put her hands behind her back, shrinking from the weapon.

"Oh, come now, Andrea," said Davenport. "All these months I've heard nothing except how evil Weishaupt was and what you'd like to do to him. Here's your chance, girl! Gun him down!"

Slowly, Andrea took the pistol and aimed it at Weishaupt. She lined up the front and rear sights with a spot between the director's thick lenses. She licked her dry lips and fought waves of nausea as her finger started to squeeze the trigger.

"Shoot straight, Andrea. Make it clean," said Weishaupt.

The gun wavered and Andrea dropped her arm by her side, her trigger finger untensing.

"What's the matter, Andrea," barked Davenport. "Lose your nerve? You've killed before!"

"This . . . this isn't Budapest, Courtney. It's . . . it's not the same," cried Andrea. She handed the pistol back to Davenport.

"Then I guess I'll have to do it myself," sighed Davenport.

"You're full of surprises, Davenport, but I still don't think you have the balls to personally kill me," said Weishaupt.

"Your intelligence people missed one phase of my life, evidently, in putting together my personality profile, Weishaupt."

The director said nothing. He just stood in front of the pre-dug grave, a cynical smile playing across his face.

"In the Marine Corps I was a machine gunner during the Korean War."

"I'm aware of that, Davenport." Weishaupt now had a bored expression on his face.

"What you didn't uncover is that I enjoyed it immensely." Courtney's eyes developed a savage gleam.

"My buddies were fighting for their lives, their units, their friends. Not me. I was fighting a holy war! My fifty-caliber piled up the Chinese communists like cordwood! I felt no guilt then, nor will I now. You people are beyond the pale of humanity!"

"Oh, spare me the war stories and get on with it," said Weishaupt wearily.

Davenport aimed the pistol—first at one, then the other. Barrajas stood in his soft, chubby nakedness mumbling and fondling the old Hungarian rosary.

The front sight lined up with the hairless triangle between Barrajas's legs. Davenport concentrated on the small button of flesh which was either a miniature penis, an oversize clitoris, or a combination of both.

"You freak! You filthy, subhuman freak!" snarled Davenport.

The pistol roared, reverberating through the woods. The pubic triangle turned crimson. The Prophet screamed, one hand clutching the rosary, the other making the sign of the cross.

"Hail . . . hail . . . Mary, full of grace . . ."

A second and third shot shattered his kneecaps. Barrajas fell to the grass.

"The . . . the Lord is with thee . . . with thee."

A fourth shot plowed into his left shoulder. Barrajas dropped the crucifix onto the bloodstained grass.

Davenport swung the pistol to the right and fired two shots, shattering Weishaupt's kneecaps. The director winced and fell to the ground heavily, smiling slightly.

"You . . . you do have the balls, Davenport. You know, you're really more like us, you born-again phony."

He turned his thick neck toward Andrea, Benson, and the transfixed commandos.

"You lose, Andrea!" Weishaupt shouted triumphantly. "He's one of us. Do you understand? Your creation, Andrea . . . your genie! What we would have created in your country, had we been victorious, you're going to get in 1992. Good job, Andrea!"

Another shot plowed into Weishaupt's shoulder.

The mutilation slayings of Barrajas and Weishaupt sickened Andrea as she buried her face in Benson's jacket. The secretary of state was in a state of confused shock.

Weishaupt laughed shrilly, his right arm held out rigidly in front of him, his middle finger extended toward Davenport in an obscene gesture of defiance.

"Accept the Lord, Weishaupt! Before you die, accept Jesus!" shouted Davenport.

"See this, Davenport?" The director laughed. "It means the same thing in my country as it does in yours."

Next to the finger-flipping Weishaupt, the mutilated morphadite was chanting in Latin, calling for divine deliverance and crossing and recrossing himself.

Irrational with rage, Davenport emptied the magazine at the pair.

"Your marksmanship has deteriorated since Korea," shouted Weishaupt, who was now bleeding profusely from multiple wounds.

Courtney ran screaming toward the kneeling pair, ramming a fresh clip into the pistol. He shoved the Radom into the back of Barrajas's neck and pulled the trigger, shattering his upper spine and killing him instantly.

He reached over and yanked Weishaupt's head backward and to the left by the ear, the pistol barrel shoved in the other ear.

"No balls, eh!" rasped Davenport.

"Go to hell, Davenport!" wheezed Weishaupt.

Courtney Davenport pulled his hand away from Weishaupt's ear just before the bullet emerged from his brain. The director's extended finger curled inward and his arm dropped. The slight contemptuous smile remained on his face.

The man who would be president of the United States in 1992 kicked, unceremoniously, the mutilated bodies into their prepared graves.

XX.

The shallow valley, as seen from the bluff overlooking Colonia Gardún, was a blaze of colors. Purple and white, the colors of the Sacred Order of the Holy Garduna, predominated.

There were flags everywhere: the Paraguayan flag with its red, white, and blue horizontal stripes; and the purple and white Garduna flags. The Garduna flag had three broad bands—purple on the top and bottom, with a broad white band in the middle. The symbol of the Holy Garduna was in the middle of the white band: a Trojan horse superimposed upon an ornate Christian cross, which was the Cross of the Cordovan Virgin of Spain.

Myth and tradition had it that a sanctified hermit named Apollinario, in the wild country of the Sierra Morena in Spain, was visited by the Holy Virgin, who, at the time, had come from the city of Córdova. She presented the hermit with a button which she herself had removed from the robe of her crucified son. The button had miraculous powers, and from it bands of Spanish Christians, now fighting the Moors, would draw strength and inspiration. From this early encounter with the Virgin, the Holy Garduna was born, with the hermit as its prophet and founder.

The cross of the Cordovan Virgin had four buttons on it, symbolizing the influence of Christ in the far corners of the earth. The Trojan horse was symbolic of deceit and surreptitious entry: the operational modes of the Holy Garduna in the name of their brand of Christianity.

Carlos Von Reinach parked his vintage 1938 Mercedes-Benz convertible on the vantage point on top of the bluff and got out, holding the door open for Susan. She stepped out, grasping Von Reinach's hand for support. They walked to the edge of the bluff and gazed down at the valley, which was transformed by color.

"It looks so beautiful from up here, Carlos. It's amazing what a little color will do for the Chaco."

He slipped his arm around her shoulder and kissed her under the ear. "All of this is for you, my Cherokee queen. The Chaco will be your backyard in which to play—to do with as you wish."

Susan's countenance grew pensive. "In my yard back home, I had a sandbox when I was a child. I would pour water in it and make sort of a clay and create miniature cities and towns."

"And here in the Chaco, as my wife, you can do the same, my love, but on a much larger scale, with real people as your subjects." Von Reinach turned Susan toward him and tilted her chin. He bent his head and kissed her fully, tenderly on the lips. A shiver of excitement ran through her, and she found herself encircling his hard, slim waist with her arms.

She turned and surveyed the valley below. There were flags as far as the eye could see. They lined the four roads leading from the colony. Purple and white tents and canopies covered all of the vacant ground within the colony, and for several acres outside, to accommodate the thousands who would be arriving for the festivities. In the center of Colonia Gardún was a huge, ornate, circus-type tent—again in the same colors. It stretched over the entire plaza. The administration building facing the plaza was bedecked with purple and white bunting; and an ornate altar, a relic from the Spanish Colonial period, was assembled on a wooden platform in front of the stairs—the very stairs where the Hermano

Mayor stood a few months ago and ordered the whipping of the rebellious Garden Child who slugged the *guapo*.

"In two days, Susan, only two days, you and I will be kneeling at the altar down there, in front of thousands, swearing our love and loyalty to each other. I intend, my love, to elevate you to a status far above the other women of the Garduna. I will have you ordained a Magistri. No other woman of the Garduna has been given such an honor!"

"A *what*, Carlos?" asked Susan, arching her dark eyebrows.

"A Magistri." Von Reinach smiled. "A supreme ritualistic priest, or, in your case, a priestess. I do not intend for my wife to be a passive observer. You will be a cocreator, not only of our children but of a new civilization in the Chaco—a civilization built upon the infallible foundation of pure blood."

The words "pure blood" sent a chill through Susan. "Carlos, in my country, the bride's parents always participate in the wedding ceremony. Don't . . . don't you have any curiosity about my parents? Do you know anything about my family?" she asked almost fearfully.

His bright blue eyes bore into hers with a near-hypnotic effect. "Susan, please do not misunderstand what I am about to say. When you came to us of your own free will, you had forsaken your family. The Holy Garduna is now your family. As the Prophet Barrajas has taught the Garden Children, the natural family is an enemy to God. Your new family is now a larger, more complete family. No, Susan, I do not want to know anything of your prior family."

Susan felt a twinge of anger, but also a feeling of relief. She almost relished the thought that the Negro blood of her grandfather would pollute the previous bloodlines of the Garduna. To bear Carlos a child would be her first act of rebellion.

She stood, nestled against Von Reinach, her right arm encircling his waist. She stared at the panoply of color and activity below, and felt an eager anticipation. She almost hoped that the uprising would be aborted. Her new status had isolated and elevated her from and above the *chivatos*. There had been no contacts made, or even attempted, by the agents of Benito Salazar. The armored cars were off limits to the *chivatos* and impossible to reach, let alone sabotage with sugar. What a ridiculous idea! She felt totally abandoned and alone; she had decided several days ago to make her peace with the Holy Garduna and accept her fate. After all, Von Reinach was not unattractive and things could be worse, she rationalized. She could be assigned to La Cuna—with Olivia.

Hermann Rathner had been observing the daily routine of Joe Rockland for several days. It had become a consistent pattern. He left the Asunción Hilton at 9:00 A.M. and walked five blocks to the American embassy, where he would stay until 11:00. After a leisurely lunch at Rubio's, a Basque restaurant near the ornate capitol building, he would walk briskly through the commercial district, a teeming quarter of the city, which was full of stores and small shops, to the DAVROCK branch office. At 4:00 P.M. he would leave, stroll through Independence Plaza, and return to his hotel. Rathner determined, correctly, that Joseph Rockland was a man of predictable habits; a man who rarely broke with routine.

September 11 dawned brightly and clearly, with just a few high clouds scudding in from the west. Rockland had spent much of the night on his knees petitioning his God for answers on how to avert Susan's marriage to Von Reinach. He thought he had received an answer several days ago in the baroque quietness of the National Cathedral. It was dashed when he was told by the American ambassador that the United States would do nothing to endanger its relationship with the regime of General Ayala or the Holy Garduna. The flow of Chaco oil to America took precedence over everything—especially over a teenage cultist who had gotten herself into this situation with malice aforethought.

Rockland almost shuffled toward the branch office this morning in a state of depressed anxiety. The usual bounce to his step was missing; he plodded slowly through the commercial district, which was now almost devoid of activity because of the afternoon siesta—a ritual in Asunción. His way was blocked by two burly Europeans carrying a large, unrolled Persian carpet from an empty store to a waiting van. He stopped, absently examining the intricate pattern on the rug directly in front of him.

A third man, unseen by Rockland, jumped down from the van ostensibly to help the others. He turned quickly and emptied an aerosol spray into Rockland's face. In seconds Rockland collapsed, his attacker catching him before he hit the sidewalk. The other two spread the rug out quickly and, within half a minute, it was over. The unconscious Rockland was rolled tightly in the rug, placed in the van by Rathner's men, and driven away to a secret location in Asunción.

Susan heard the gravel on her window and sat up. She glanced at her clock—2:30 A.M. She stalked cautiously to the ground-floor window and peered outside. Blackness. It was an inky, moonless night. She raised her window approximately a foot and listened.

"Susan Rockland?" a voice whispered.

Her heart beat faster as she raised the window some more. "Yes," she answered softly.

A uniformed figure appeared from the blackness, darted to the side of the building, and sidled up to the half-opened window. It was one of the helicopter pilots who had arrived several days before. "I'm Alfonso Vitali," he whispered, his Italian accent hardening his halting Spanish.

"Arc . . . are you from Angel Caro or Salazar?" Susan asked, fearing an affirmative answer.

"Sshhh! Not so loud, señorita. I am, yes." He spoke now in broken English.

"How is Angel?" she responded.

"He is fine. He gives you his love. Susan, we know the position you are in now. We heard of the announcement of your wedding. Your part in the uprising has been changed. The . . ."

"Will there be an uprising?" she asked anxiously, interrupting the pilot.

"Oh, yes, to be sure. The armored cars will be taken care of. Do not attempt to do anything. Just go along with their plans."

Susan sighed in relief. "When . . . when is the attack and what do I do when it happens?"

"Unfortunately, you will already have been married to Von Reinach. We cannot change that. The assault is for the fifteenth—in the early morning."

"Oh, fine," exclaimed Susan, pouting sullenly. "I'll be on my honeymoon with a man old enough to be my father. If the attack succeeds, I'll descend from the Queen of the Chaco to a refugee on the run."

"What's that, señorita?" the pilot asked.

"Oh, nothing," she answered dejectedly. "Right now I'd settle for the sandbox in my backyard in Tulsa!"

Vitali shrugged his shoulders. "You have many private thoughts that you are dealing with, Susan. I wish that there was somehow a way that we could move up the attack. Your wedding has both complicated things and made things incredibly easier."

Susan frowned. "How's that?"

"There will be over thirty thousand people at your wedding and for the three days of festivities which will follow."

Susan gasped. "That's—that's fantastic! I've always wanted a big wedding, but *that* is ridiculous! It's a spectacle!"

"It's the biggest social event in our little country in years. Yours is a very real Cinderella story," added Vitale.

"I can see how my wedding will upset your timetable, but how will it make things easier?"

The pilot smiled grimly, as if he were envisioning the carnage resulting from the September 15 attack.

"The entire hierarchy of the Holy Garduna will be here. You will be amazed, Susan, at the multiplicity of rank and offices they have. Hundreds of the Garduna leaders from Paraguay, Argentina, and Brazil will be concentrated right here! General Ayala and the ranking members of his government, as well as the senior officers of the Armed Forces, will be here also. We'll have all of the fish in one net!"

"Except the biggest—my husband-to-be," sighed Susan.

"Could you find out his plans for after the wedding, Susan? If we know what they are, perhaps we can adjust our operations to rescue you."

"Yes. I'll try to find out. When will you . . ."

The pilot had disappeared, slipping away through the bushes.

Von Ziegazar arrived at Colonia Gardún at 5:30 in the morning. It had been a short night flight in the Parachaco courier plane which flew in twice a day from the capital to the small airport outside the colony.

The transformation of Colonia Gardún as seen from the air in the early dawn boggled the mind of the lesbian doctor. "All of this for that little *Untermensch* slut!" she hissed. "She'll have her day, all right, but it'll be different—much different from what she expects."

She walked past the purple and white tents and the multitudes of Paraguayan and Gardunian flags which seemed to sprout from the ground. She reached the long, low building, with the red-tiled roof, where her room was located, and inserted her key in the outside door. Hilda reached inside and fumbled for the light switch. The first indication that something was different was the texture of the wallpaper around the switch plate. Hers was a rough texture—this was smooth. Did she have the right room? She backed away and looked at the room number. No doubt about it, it was hers. The second hint of change was the aroma of perfume that seemed to fill the room. It perplexed and excited Hilda. She entered quietly and slipped into the bathroom. She closed the bathroom door and turned on the light. She then opened the door a crack—just wide enough to send a shaft of light into the main sleeping room. It was hers, but it had been completely redecorated.

There was a slight stirring from the bed. Von Ziegazar turned off the light and slipped into the bedroom, allowing her eyes to adjust to the increasing dawn light. There, on her bed, was the seminude body of Susan Rockland. She lay on top of the sheets with only a pair of panties on.

The doctor felt a mixture of overwhelming anger and lust. Only Von Reinach had the power to take away her room—her sanctuary from the *Untermenschen* who infested Colonia Gardún. Now the most polluted of the *Untermenschen* lay on her bed!"

She padded over to Susan and sat on the bed. The weight

of her body caused Susan to stir and roll over on her back, arms in back of her head, exposing her magnificent breasts.

Susan felt the hard, thin lips on her neck and throat and stirred slightly. She was in a state of semisleep, but her instincts and experiences told her that it wasn't Angel or Von Reinach. She opened her eyes and looked downward and saw the short blond hair of Von Ziegazar. In a flash she rolled off her bed, slipped on her robe, and flicked on the light.

"What—what are you doing in my room?" demanded Susan.

"Your room?" Hilda breathed deeply, her former passion turning to anger. "No, my future Queen of Paraguay, this is *my* room! Or it was until Von Reinach had it fixed up for his little bride-to-be."

"I—I think you'd better leave, Doctor. There have been many changes since that day in the oil field. I—I don't work for you anymore. I'm to marry Carlos Von Reinach the day after tomorrow. Surely you must have heard?"

"Oh, yes. I've heard of the wedding. Who hasn't? It will be the social event of the year. You must be very proud of yourself, Susan." The doctor lurched toward Susan, her eyes flashing malevolence. She backed her into a corner and pressed her angular body against Susan and tried to kiss her on the lips.

Susan's mind froze into panic. It flashed back to a similar experience at Bryson Academy, a year and a half ago, when one of the girls in her dorm—a suspected lesbian—cornered her in much the same manner. Susan reacted as she had then. She grabbed a handful of Von Ziegazar's short blond hair and yanked her head back. Her right fist smashed into Hilda's face, causing her head to snap back sharply. Blood spurted from her nose. She wiped her hand across her face and stared unbelievingly at the blood.

"You—you dared to strike me? Me? You little—little *Untermensch!*" Von Ziegazar rushed toward Susan, hands outstretched. She grabbed her throat. The muscular doctor started to squeeze, her face contorted into a twisted mask of hate. "There won't be enough left of you, you little she-bitch, to fill Von Reinach's bed when I get through with you!"

The fear had left Susan. Her survival instincts took over and the rage and frustration she had felt during the past months exploded. She clasped her hands together into a double fist and held them close to her stomach. By shooting them straight up, they had the effect of a battering ram. Von Ziegazar was caught on the jaw and reeled backward. Susan followed up her attack with a kick to Von Ziegazar's stomach. Hilda fell to one knee, stilled and gasping for air. Susan ran to her dresser drawer and yanked out a long, wicked-looking, rusty butcher knife she had stolen from the kitchen two months before. She kicked Von Ziegazar in the side, rolling her over on her back. Susan leaped on her, straddling her chest, her knees on her upper arms. The knife was held at her throat.

The doctor looked into Susan's light brown eyes, which were now flashing with anger, and recognized the desire to kill.

"One of the first things I'm going to do, *Doctor*, when I become Carlos' wife, is have your filthy lesbian ass nailed to the door. Do you understand, you freaky bitch?"

Susan pressed the tip of the rusty blade against Von Ziegazar's slightly protruding Adam's apple.

Hilda tried to nod. Her voice squeaked. "You . . . you must forgive me, Susan, I—I was upset that my room had been taken. That's all I meant. I—I want us to be friends." The doctor was overwhelmed with fear. She knew that if Susan plunged the knife into her throat and killed her, Von Reinach would do nothing. Susan could claim self-defense and go unpunished.

"Let me go and I'll never bother you again. When you marry, I'll find work elsewhere. You'll never see me anymore—I promise!"

Susan got off her slowly, but still held the knife straight out in front of her. Von Ziegazar staggered to her feet, still in a state of shock.

"I hope you didn't leave any bruises on me, Hilda," snapped Susan. "Von Reinach wants an unblemished offering, and I'd hate to have to tell him that you attacked me. I've heard that he tends to overreact to such things."

Von Ziegazar said nothing. She headed for the door, her fear now turning to an overwhelming desire to destroy Susan and her father. A slight smile curled her hard, thin lips as she stalked back to the airport, fantasizing about the exposure of Susan's racial inferiority at the height of the wedding.

When the facts were known of Susan's deceit and racial pollution, she would demand the ultimate penalty—death by piranhas. It was her right—her duty as the Garduna's chief geneticist—to protect the Holy Garduna from impure blood. The thirty thousand spectators who came to see the wedding of the year won't be disappointed. They will witness the execution of the year.

It was quiet at La Cuna. It usually was. The young female cultists who were unassigned to mates were returning from the cocaine refinery. Their hair was still damp from the showers they had to take at the end of their shift to wash off the white sticky powder which clung to their skin and clogged the pores. The indentations on their faces from the respirators they wore were still apparent.

Olivia was functioning. A compassionate *guapo* had assigned her to the nursery where the babies and children up to the age of five were kept. This was therapeutic. The children became her link with sanity and the real world. Olivia was smiling again and talking, but only to her roommates and the children.

September 12 ended like any other day at La Cuna, and by eleven o'clock in the evening all of the *chivatos* and children were asleep. The only signs of activity were the movements of the eight guards on duty that night.

Outside the La Cuna compound, the SEALs had located all of the unmanned sensors and neutralized them. They tested the fence surrounding the breeding station. It was not electrified. Ten minutes of snipping with heavy wire cutters had created a hole large enough for them to enter. A special team split from the main body, sought out the guards, and killed them with silenced weapons. In twenty minutes all of the Garduna guards and administrative people were dead.

The SEALs stalked through the cottages and nursery and sprayed an aerosol mist into sleeping faces. Now they would sleep longer—sounder.

"This one is the Davenport girl," whispered the task force commander. "Get her and the others into the trucks."

Satellite photo reconnaissance had shown a vehicle park of nine trucks which were used for hauling processed cocaine to Fuerte Olimpo. They would be sufficient. The trucks were fueled, and the sleeping cultists and their children were passed into the rear of the vehicles.

Timed explosive charges and incendiary devices were placed in every building.

The convoy crawled down the Andean foothill road. An hour and a half later the terrain leveled and the trucks turned off into a wide grassy plain. The blackened silhouettes of two C-130s were etched against the night sky. Medevac teams leaped from the waiting aircraft and helped the SEALs unload their sleeping human cargo and place them into the planes. The cargo doors slammed with a thud after the last of the SEALs were aboard. The C-130s roared into life, sped down the level field, and lifted off. At an altitude of two thousand feet they leveled off and circled toward the direction of La Cuna.

The devastation was complete. The Andean foothill country was completely devoid of any light, manmade or natural, except for the inferno of La Cuna. Huge clouds of acrid smoke, the fiery residue of several hundred million dollars' worth of cocaine, boiled from the refinery.

The two aircraft turned and headed north toward their first and only refueling stop at the U.S. Naval Air Base at Coco Solo, Panama.

It was an impressive little army. The Caro brothers stood on a slight rise overlooking the two thousand well-equipped and camouflaged troops of the Socialist Christian Action party. Raúl and Salazar had done a good job. They were blooded, tested soldiers with a string of impressive victories to their credit. They were confident and aggressive. To the right of the guerrillas were the defecting soldiers of the rapid-reaction force, whose helicopters were parked behind them.

Another special assault force was lined up to the left. They were the men and women who would be bused, at Garduna expense, along with thousands of others from various parts of the Chaco, to Colonia Gardún to attend the wedding and the festivities to follow. They were dressed in their finest peasant attire, which was fitting for feast days and special holidays. All wore the traditional *capo pañolón*, the combination cloak and shawl which would protect them from the night chill and hide their weapons.

Tomorrow, September 12, the peasant infiltration force would board some of the many buses brought in from as far away as Asunción and travel to Colonia Gardún. The regular guerrilla force would filter into the ravines and gullies of the rough bush country behind the bluffs overlooking the colony and prepare for the final assault. The rapid-reaction force would be held in reserve to provide reinforcements or to block any Paraguayan army units coming from Asunción or Mariscal Estigarribia.

It would be a bloody battle. There was no way to escape it. The sheer numbers in the colony would ensure that. Von Reinach would be one of the primary personnel targets, and Susan would be in close proximity unless they left on the fourteenth for a honeymoon trip.

Angel fought the urge to persuade the guerrillas to rescue Susan. It would be a relatively simple task to have one of the helicopter pilots at the colony—perhaps Vitali—lift her out and bring her to Salazar's camp.

But that was not to be. Susan's role of Von Reinach's bride-to-be had made her the bait which would concentrate all of the fish in one pond. The guerrilla force would catch not only the entire Garduna hierarchy at the wedding ceremony but the leadership of the entire nation, including General Ayala.

Salazar and the guerrilla command believed that Susan's wedding on the thirteenth was an act of divine intervention

. . . and so it seemed. She would have to stay in place and play out her role in this drama until the assault forces could rescue her.

"I tell you, I can't nose through this muck, Mr. Portumo. The river channel has shifted and the silt from the tributaries upstream has blocked our approach. Dammit, a submarine was not made for a river. It's an oceangoing vessel! We'll have to sail on the surface from Puerto Guaraní to Fuerte Olimpo. The upper reaches of the Paraguay are very unpredictable. I told you that before we left Parramore. From here on, it's either walk to Fuerte Olimpo or sail on the surface."

Nick Portumo pounded his fist into the palm of his hand in frustration. "Damn! Damn! Double damn!" he muttered. "I didn't come all this way in this stinking tub to be cheated out of attacking Fuerte Olimpo!"

The countercult commandos crowded around Nick in the cramped crew's quarters and awaited his decision. Nick stared back, searching the face of each one. They were eager and shared his frustration, but they knew the risk of sailing on the surface. Gunboats of the Paraguayan Navy regularly patrolled these waters.

"Take her up. Let's look around. We need some air to clear the cobwebs out of our brains and help us think this out," said Nick.

The skipper shrugged his shoulders and gave the order to surface. First the periscope then the conning tower appeared, rising from the brown silt-laden river.

When the sub was fully out of the water, a series of grappling hooks sailed through the air from the nearby Paraguayan naval craft, an LCI, which was a landing craft infantry ship of World War II vintage. The lines were made secure. Two machine guns, a 37mm cannon, and the individual weapons of sixty Paraguayan marines were trained on the submarine.

Nick emerged from the crew hatch and saw the large shallow-craft vessel alongside. "Oh, shit!" he cried. "It's all over!"

The bearded ship commander, who was dressed casually in a Paraguayan naval officer's uniform of white shorts and short-sleeved shirt, stood on deck smoking a large cigar. Portumo looked up into his full, rugged face, and then at the multitudes of weapons pointed at them.

"Want a tow to Fuerte Olimpo, señor?" asked the smiling captain in halting English.

Nick swallowed hard and said nothing.

"Get all of your people on deck. Leave your weapons below. We want to look you over."

Nick ordered the crew and commandos on deck. The marines lining the railing of the LCI tensed as the raiders formed into a ragged formation, which stretched the length of the sub's deck.

"Which one of you is Nicholas Portumo?" asked the LCI commander.

Nick sullenly raised his hand.

The naval officer climbed down a swaying rope ladder and jumped gingerly onto the sub's deck. He walked up and down the ranks of commandos and stopped in front of Nick.

"A fine looking assault force, Señor Portumo. They're ready and eager for action, eh?" the commander smiled.

Nick continued to stare back. Occasionally he glanced at the weapons which were trained on them.

"We picked you up on sonar back at Puerto Casado. Following you was no problem. We could tell where you were by your bubbles. We knew you wouldn't be able to make it to Fuerte Olimpo on the bottom. If you surfaced, it would be here where the tributaries silt up the channel. We were waiting for you, señor."

"And now?" asked Nick.

"And now"—the captain clapped his hand on Nick's arm good-naturedly—"we join forces and take you upstream. This is a Christian Action assault force, Señor Portumo. We've been informed by your Paul Lancaster that you people were coming. Didn't you get the message about joining us through KDRM?"

Before Nick could answer, the marines were swarming on the sub's deck, laughing and embracing the confused but happy commandos.

XXI.

September 12 was the day of purification. Susan was to be cleansed inside and out before she could enter into marriage with the Gardún leader.

When the chapel bell struck midnight, Susan was escorted by thirteen young women, in flowing purple and white robes, to the isolated eastern edge of Colonia Gardún. The women were *serenas*. The ex-*chivatos* now functioned as minor administrative and religious personnel of the Holy Garduna.

The *serenas* were met by three ancient men, known as *fuelles*. The group shuffled past other officers of the Holy Garduna who lined the path to thc low concrete building near the narrow, muddy river east of the colony. Assembled along the processional route were the *floreadores*, the muscle-bound strong-arm men of the Garduna, as well as the *ponteadores*, the swordsmen; *guapos*; Capataz; and Magistri.

The concrete buildings along the river were the very earliest buildings constructed. They were the core buildings of Colonia Alemán, the German colony built by Hermann Von Reinach, Carlos' father, back in 1938. They were the buildings that Susan had observed from the bluff the day she entered Colonia Gardún months ago. The buildings joined together in the shape of a swastika.

In the center of the Casa del Swastika, Swastika House as the locals called it, was a three-story fortified stone tower, which was located where the twisted arms of the swastika came together. As the procession approached the ornate entrance to the Casa del Swastika, they were met by the Hermano Mayor. The old man smiled a toothy gold-capped smile and bid Susan to kneel on a purple pillow. She complied, and the Prophet Francisco Estigarribia hovered over her, chanting in rapid Spanish. He held a silver horn of holy oil high above his head. The officers of the Garduna joined the Prophet in the chant, which soon became a hymn.

Susan tried to show no emotion as the Hermano Mayor parted her hair with his thumb and forefinger and exposed a bit of scalp. Three drops of oil were placed on the exposed flesh. The Prophet and the three ancient *fuelles* placed their hands upon her head, pronouncing her worthy to enter the rite of Purification.

Three *serenas* escorted her into the long, low, twisted building complex, through the maze of quebracho-wood-paneled corridors, to the very center of the complex where the stone tower jutted skyward. The four women ascended the winding staircase noiselessly, past the first two stories which held the colony's weapons and ammunition, to a cell-like chamber on the third floor. Here Susan was to be cleansed, purified, and readied for the wedding. This was the Core Center of the Nazi swastika.

The ritual demanded that the physical body be cleansed internally as well as externally. When the *serenas* told her that she must be given a garlic enema and then came at her with a hot-water bottle, rubber tubes, and a garlic solution, Susan almost bolted and ran. She could remember her only stay in a hospital. She was only four and had endured all of the preliminaries bravely: the blood tests, the needles, and the strangeness of the hospital environment. Her parents were so proud of her. Then came the nurse with the grease-smeared insert for her tight little rectum. She became a screaming maniac as the nurse and two orderlies held her down for her pre-op enema. As a child she vowed "never again" and kept her promise—until now. She submitted meekly, exposing her shapely bottom, and praying that the insert was well lubricated. After that ordeal, which proved to be rather painless, but humiliating as she eliminated in a wooden bucket, she submitted to the ritual washings of her body by the three women. This was followed by the rubbing in of scented oils.

Just before dawn, she was dressed in a loose white gown and instructed that the rest of the day was to be spent in fasting, meditation, and prayer. The purged and purified Susan Rockland breathed a sigh of relief when the *serenas* left, and she bolted the door behind them. She was left alone with her thoughts for the rest of the day. Her husband-to-be was enduring the same ritual somewhere else in the colony.

The sturdy stone tower must have been an observation post of some kind in the early days, pondered Susan. The four semicircular windows gave her a commanding view of the entire colony complex. She could hear the constant roar of buses and trucks bringing in peasants from all over the Chaco. Some were assigned tents, but the vast majority staked out a spot on the hard red earth as their temporary home for the next four days.

The golden-orange dawn was indescribably beautiful from Susan's chamber. She watched the huge orange orb climb from behind the purple bluffs. The broken clouds, turned reddish silver, filtered the early morning sunlight, sending shafts of light stabbing into the valley floor. Susan smiled wistfully. Riding on the memories of her childhood, she recalled a colored print from an old Sunday School manual, which portrayed an Old Testament scene of Moses breaking the tablets of stone, perhaps on Mount Sinai. The shafts of light were similar.

She pulled up several large pillows and curled up by a window and looked out over Colonia Gardún. From her vantage point, everything looked so different, so alien. And yet, this was to be her home, perhaps forever, after her marriage to Carlos Von Reinach.

Suddenly Susan was flooded with regrets and longing; longings for the things and people she so casually rejected and left behind. As she looked out over the hundreds of Paraguayan and Garduna flags flapping listlessly in the morning breeze, she felt an overwhelming desire to see an American flag. Strange she hadn't really thought about her native land until now; and now she desperately wanted to see her nation's flag and to hear her country's national anthem.

She curled up tighter, staring vacantly out the window. Her voice croaked out the first few bars of "The Star-Spangled Banner."

Oh, say, can you see
By the dawn's early light
What so . . .

What's the rest of it?

She stifled a sob and started singing again.

Amazing Grace
How sweet the word
That saved a wretch like me
I once was lost
But now I'm found
Was blind but now I see

No, dammit! Susan Rockland, you're blind and lost! Trapped in the center of a Nazi swastika in some kinky country. Did you ever think your early arguments with your father, your rebellion, your running away would end up like this? Tomorrow, old girl, your tit is really gonna wind up in a wringer. There are thousands of people out there that are gonna watch you make a supreme ass of yourself as you marry Von Reinach. When you screw up, Susan, you leave no stone unturned.

Other thoughts tormented Susan. She should be starting college this month back at DRU. *Hell! I didn't even graduate from high school. I blew it when I left Bryson and joined the Garden Children. A high school diploma didn't mean a damn thing then. I wanted freedom and adventure. Well, you got it, dummy! There aren't too many eighteen-year-olds trapped in the center of a swastika with an aroma of garlic to their bowels. How exotic did you want your fantasies, Susan Rockland? Is this exotic enough? How about a gigantic wedding which approximates a coronation? Isn't that what Von Ziegazar called you: the Queen of the Chaco . . . or was it*

Paraguay? It doesn't matter. When the oil comes in, the Garduna and your future husband will be the real power in this crazy little country. Wow! If anybody told me a year ago I'd be in this predicament, I would have had them committed to the funny farm. Now I'm to be the queen of one gigantic funny farm and all of the strange little animals out there in their purple and white robes.

A sly smile flitted across Susan's full lips. *Susan Rockland: the mulatto queen of a neo-Nazi cult based on pure blood. Boy, if they only knew! Wouldn't that frost the gonads of those clowns down there! Rest well, Grandpa Jesse, little Susan's gonna get you your revenge!*

Her sobs started as a series of sniffles and soon cascaded into a torrent of tears. Memories filled Susan's mind; her father, the revivals, fleeting pictures in her mind of her mother before she was killed. All of this was her heritage, her birthright, which she sold for a mess of pottage. Like so much excess baggage, it was thrown out and away—never to be recovered. Her family was out of reach. Those purple and white freaks out there with their absurd theories of racial superiority were to be her new family—her only family. She could never accept that! If she could only see her father once more, she might be able to endure the trials which awaited. But her father, like the other parts of her life which were jettisoned, was beyond her reach.

Susan curled up into a tight little ball on the large pillows. Twiddling a long strand of her glossy black hair, she cried herself to sleep.

"Señorita! Señorita! Wake up! Today is your wedding day!" Susan stirred slightly and rolled over toward the stone wall. The *serena* shook her again.

She opened her eyes and focused on the mortar between the large stones which served as the tower's inside wall. She had slept fitfully, off and on between crying spells, all day yesterday. She had been purged now of tears, as well as everything else. There were no more to give. Last night, the night of the twelfth, she had slept soundly. She must have gotten thirteen hours of sleep during the last thirty hours. She felt rested and confident that she could face the coming ordeal.

Then she heard the music. A small orchestra was playing in the direction of the colony's central plaza. She got up, yawned, and sauntered over to the window. She looked out and stiffened in shock.

"Good Lord!" she gasped. The size of the crowd overwhelmed her. The thousands of spectators were in place, waiting for the wedding ceremony to start.

Eli Revvim could see the smoke from the forward slope of the hill. The cocaine refinery was still smoldering after the SEALs' attack.

"That's not the smoke of their normal operation, Puerter. They've got a fire down there."

The countercult commandos snaked down the mountain trail toward the small valley which cradled La Cuna. From a closer vantage point they could discern the devastation.

"That's more than a fire, Eli. La Cuna's been had! Somebody's wasted our target!" wailed Puerter Detlefs.

An hour later, the commandos were sifting through the ashes and rubble looking for clues to the attackers' identity.

"Spent forty-five-caliber brass, Eli. Who uses forty-fives in this part of the world? I thought South America was nine-millimeter country," said Detlefs.

"It is, Puerter," answered Eli as he nudged a dead guard with the toe of his boot. "Could be an organization using surplus American ammunition. There's a regular war between rival groups down here for the control of the cocaine traffic."

"So what's our next move, Eli?"

Eli shrugged. "All we can do is notify our man up at Campo Grande. He'll contact KDRM. We just sit here until we hear from Nick after the attack on Fuerte Olimpo."

The valley reverberated to the roar of a cannon fired at the western edge of Colonia Gardún. The music started almost at once. It was a piece from the Baroque era, Vivaldi's *Four Seasons*.

The large ornate altar dominated the plaza. Below it was

the stage where the wedding would take place. An orchestra pit, divided into two sections, flanked the processional aisle and held a small but excellent concert orchestra, which was bused in from Asunción.

All of the principal leaders of the Sacred Order of the Holy Garduna were there. Resplendent in their robes, they flanked the aisle.

The weather was perfect, thought the Hermano Mayor, as he stood in front of the altar. Surely all of the omens pointed to a day that had been sanctified by the Almighty. From his vantage point, his old and crafty eyes surveyed the vast throngs under the canopy which stretched over the plaza. The sides had been rolled up and the crowds spilling into and out of the colony were partly visible. Loudspeakers had been installed at strategic locations throughout the colony and into the fields beyond so that all could hear the ceremony.

At ten o'clock the chapel bell struck the hour. The wedding of Susan and Carlos was about to commence.

"What do you mean we cannot pass? This is a vessel of the Paraguayan Navy!"

The smaller boat, which blocked the narrow waterway, bobbed in the slight swell caused by the LCI's throbbing engines.

"I'm sorry, Commander, but Fuerte Olimpo is off limits to all vessels except those of the Parachaco Corporation. Surely you know of the agreement between our company and the government," shouted the *guapo* from his small patrol craft.

The bearded officer turned to Nicholas Portumo, who was leaning on the bridge's railing beside him. "Well, I guess that this is where it begins, amigo," he said, compressing his lips into a grim smile.

He nodded to his waiting gun crew. They ripped off the canvas cover in swift, deft movements and cranked the 37mm cannon in the direction of the Parachaco boat.

The *guapo* in the bow stared helplessly, unbelievingly, as the cannon swung toward him. An order from the Holy Garduna or the Parachaco Corporation was the law in the Upper Paraguay. Surely the LCI commander knew that.

The last earthly vision that the *guapo* and his small crew experienced was the bright orange-red flash of the cannon. Had they lived a millisecond after the explosion of their small vessel, they would have heard the roar and felt the heavy machine-gun slugs ripping the muddy river water, ventilating their mutilated corpses.

Well, this is it stupid, Susan thought aloud as she stood in front of the huge double doors of quebracho wood. Beyond the doors was the beginning of a five-foot-wide purple carpet which ran the five hundred feet across the plaza to the altar. She knew her part well. The three *serenas* had drilled and rehearsed her.

I can see my wedding announcement now—if I had one. Local girl marries cult leader in Paraguay: Becomes Queen of the Chaco.

Where's the Chaco? they will wonder.

Oh, some God-forsaken spot of dry brush in the middle of South America. Susan Von Reinach's little queendom.

Well, Susan Rockland, you finally did it! You are about to screw your life up completely. As soon as these doors open, you're going to step into another world. No place to hide, Susan. You've gotta tough it out and fake it all the way. You're good at that.

Outside, three trumpets blared a fanfare. The heavy double doors were slowly pulled open by two sword-bearing *ponteadores*. Susan choked back her fear as she stood framed in the open doorway and looked across the carpeted plaza to the altar. She felt completely alone in this drama. It seemed as if she had to play her part without her leading man.

To the two ancient *fuelles* who flanked her, Susan muttered, "Why couldn't they have loaned me a father figure to lead me down the aisle?"

Uncomprehending, they took her by each elbow. Susan stepped off the doorsill and onto the purple carpet. It was as if she were leaving the security of her space capsule and stepping onto the soil of an alien planet. It was a gigantic step. There was no turning back.

The thirteen *serenas* who escorted her to the Casa del Swastika fell in behind her and slowly, to the tune of Handel's "Judas Maccabaeus: See, the Conquering Hero Comes," she started her journey down the carpeted aisle.

The crowds murmured their approval as they beheld Susan's beauty. A lace mantilla framed her face, giving her the countenance of a madonna. Her wedding dress was a mixture of the traditional Colonial Spanish wedding gown and the priestly robes of the Garduna. The *serenas* held the long purple and white train which flowed behind.

Susan marched in dainty half steps to the slow cadence of the music. The baroque altar loomed ahead, dwarfing the robed figure of the Hermano Mayor. Beside the Prophet Estigarribia was her husband-to-be, dressed in the purple and white regalia of his office.

Her head was not allowed to turn, but her large brown eyes, which were now saucers of anxiety, darted from side to side, surveying the huge throngs. She started to think bizarre and absurd thoughts in order to quell her rising fear. *I wonder if I could leap on the stage, grab the mike, and lead them in a few bars of "Amazing Grace"? Heck, I'll bet these clowns don't even know the words, let alone the tune.*

She shuffled closer to the altar. *I wonder if they'd go for an old-fashioned revival, the kind that Daddy used to give when we had the old circus tent. Maybe one of those give 'em hell, fire, and brimstone jobs. I could give an altar call and when they rushed on stage to be saved, I'd skedaddle and take off with Angel.*

Susan could now make out the anxious smile on Carlos's face. The early morning rays of the sun caught the gold caps on the teeth of the Hermano Mayor. It seemed as if he were eating little shafts of lights.

I wonder if Angel is in the crowd watching me? Perhaps he's clutching a submachine gun, waiting to shoot Carlos before he claims me as his bride.

One of the *fuelles* squeezed her elbow, causing her to snap out of her fantasy. She stopped abruptly in front of the stairs leading to the altar, falling slightly forward in the process. She looked up into Carlos's sky-blue eyes. She was ready to ascend to the stage and be claimed by the Gardún leader.

• • •

A city is built on the basis of faith that those utilities which provide essential services will be sacrosanct—untouched by violence—as everybody benefits from their operation. The power relay station located west of Asunción, along the right bank of the Pilcomayo, was one such utility. It served a dozen neighborhoods and provided light and power for tens of thousands. Unfortunately for these consumers, it also provided relayed power to the Ministry of Telecommunications, the Armed Services Radio Network, and the *pyngare* communications systems. The relay station was part of an old, outmoded system which was built by the British in the 1920s. It was spliced into a modern telecommunications system built for the Paraguayan Government in the 1970s by a West German firm. The Pilcomayo substation, however, was the strategic weak link in the central capital system. It absorbed the raw power from many generating sources and distributed it according to need. One transformer did the work of dozens. It was the key within the key.

The raiders knew that. They quickly overwhelmed the few guards and technicians and planted their explosive charges. Seconds after the explosion, hundreds of communications technicians throughout the city and beyond were huddled over their lifeless equipment. They turned dials and calibrating instruments, but it was useless. The source of life had died in the explosion.

Diesel technicians in almost a dozen buildings rushed downstairs to basement rooms to start up the emergency power generators. Fifteen huge diesels throughout the city were reduced to useless, smoking derelicts within minutes. The metal shavings, thrown in the fuel and lubricating oil by unknown saboteurs, had done their work well.

Carlos descended to meet Susan halfway, his hand outstretched. Susan took it, trembling slightly, and climbed the remaining steps with her husband-to-be.

A slight breeze stirred the purple and white bunting hanging from the buildings surrounding the plaza. There was silence now, except for the flapping of the hundreds of flags throughout the colony. The plaza was filled with several thousand spectators, with the fifty rows of chairs in front reserved for the VIPs of the Garduna and the Paraguayan Government. Just behind the orchestra pits were the splendidly uniformed senior officers of the government. General Ayala sat ramrod straight in his cushioned high-backed chair in the very front. His rust-colored eyes gleamed with approval as he observed Susan's beauty.

The Hermano Mayor stood before the couple. A microphone on a floor stand was between them. He spoke Spanish in his high nasal voice. "Brothers and sisters of the Holy Garduna. Honored and respected members of the government and Armed Forces of our great republic and honored guests. We are gathered here, at the very center of creation, the site of the original Garden of Eden, to witness another creation—the creation of a union of two of God's noblest souls, into a marriage which was foreordained by the Almighty. The candidates for this union have been cleansed and purified. They have been blessed and pronounced clean and worthy of union by myself and those ordained to discern such things."

Estigarribia's eyes probed into Susan's. "The *chivato* Susan has been found to be morally, physically, and racially pure and suitable . . ."

A cold chill ran through Susan and she shivered slightly.

". . . to be a righteous vessel of the Lord and the Holy Garduna, and to produce a noble posterity with her intended husband, Carlos. She has been deemed worthy, in every way, to be ordained a Magistri. She is the first female to be accorded this honor."

There was slight murmuring from the multitudes of Gardún officials in the crowd.

"With this priestly rank, she will assist her husband in carrying out the secular and religious duties of the Garduna. If anyone has evidence as to why this union should not take place, let them come forward and publicly state their reasons."

The Prophet scanned the throngs below looking for and dreading some sign of Hilda Von Ziegazar. There was silence.

The old man took the hands of Susan and Carlos and joined

them. Susan looked into Von Reinach's eyes and tried to smile graciously. It wouldn't happen. Her face was an expressionless blank.

Estigarribia raised his hands high above his head and tilted his face to the sun. His eyes were shut tightly, causing his brownish-red forehead to wrinkle into a frown.

"Lord of the Garduna! Holy Virgin of Córdova! Sanctified and most holy Apollinario! I, the Prophet and Hermano Mayor Francisco Estigarribia, your humble servant, submit the bodies and minds of two of thy children, Carlos and Susan. They have been cleansed and purified and, through our imperfect means, have been deemed worthy of union as man and wife, within thy Holy Order, the Sacred Garduna, the Holy Warriors of God. We beseech thee, O Mighty One, for some sign that this union meets with thy approval."

The sun continued to shine and the flags continued to wave listlessly in the slight breeze. All was well with the gods of the Garduna.

"Then kneel, my children, and prepare to receive the sacrament of union."

They knelt on the purple pillows in front of the Prophet, Susan's left hand in both of Von Reinach's. The old man placed his gnarled hands on their heads. His eyes remained tightly shut, his face tilted heavenward.

"By the powers invested in me by the Republic of Paraguay and the Almighty and his servants, the Holy Council of the Garduna, I place my hands upon these, thy sanctified children, and pronounce them worthy of union in the sight of God, the Holy Virgin of Córdova, and the Holy Offices of the Garduna."

At the far southern edge of the colony there was a slight stirring of excitement. The agitated voices and automobile engine noises were not loud enough to be heard by those on the stage or directly in front of the altar.

"You, Carlos Von Reinach, son of Hermann von Reinach and María Ynsfrán, have chosen this woman, Susan Rockland, to become your wife, partner, and priestess of your own free will—is that not so?"

"It is, Hermano Mayor," Carlos said proudly.

The excitement of the crowds to the southeast was now apparent to the spectators outside the huge canopy. The honking of several vehicle horns could be heard as the throngs parted to let the vehicles roar through.

"Will you, Carlos Von Reinach, take this female *chivato*, Susan, to be your wife? Will you love and cherish her and take care of her needs throughout prosperity and adversity for the rest of your natural life?"

"I will, Hermano Mayor."

The old Prophet's eyes darted to the left. Something was happening beyond the canopy's rolled-up side. The crowds seemed to be surging back and forth. There was noise and confusion and the sound of angry, agitated voices.

The ceremony continued. "Will you, Susan Rockland, take this man, Carlos Von Reinach, as your lawfully wedded husband, to honor, obey, and satisfy for the rest of your natural life?"

Carlos squeezed her hand and smiled into her blank, expressionless eyes.

Carlos and Susan heard the commotion. Much closer now. It was clear. Approaching vehicles gunned their engines as they pushed through the crowds toward the canopy. Their horns blared. There was a murmur of excitement as the crowds parted. General Ayala and his officers jerked their heads to the right, looking for the source of the noise. Some of them fumbled for hidden weapons.

Susan shut out the noise. Her mind and mouth were immobile and frozen. She tried to voice the words, but they wouldn't come.

The old man repeated the words, frowning. Carlos squeezed her hand repeatedly—anxiously.

"I . . . I . . ." stammered Susan.

A volley of shots rang out. The crowd in the center of the plaza scrambled in panic as two jeeps and a van roared under the southern flank of the canopy. Blue smoke and the smell of cordite wafted over the agitated throngs. The vehicles braked to a stop in front of the altar. Chairs were askew as the VIP spectators spread out in anger and confusion. The purple-and-white-robed officers of the Garduna yanked out concealed pistols and trained them on the vehicles.

Susan turned. Her face hardened into a mask of horror as she recognized the figure standing in the back of the jeep. Von Ziegazar was holding on to the rear roll bar!

All eyes and dozens of weapons were trained on the doctor. There was a stunned silence. The woman spoke in a booming, masculine voice, which carried throughout the plaza.

"Stop! This wedding must *not* take place!"

The Prophet's worst fear had been realized, but he *was* a prophet and high priest of the Garduna. He regained something of his composure and drew himself erect. "By what authority, Dr. Hilda Von Ziegazar, do you burst into a sacred ceremony of the Holy Garduna and disrupt it?"

The old man's voice was without indignation or emotion. He knew the answer to his question.

Carlos leaped to his feet, his face contorted in uncontrollable rage. He screamed into the microphone.

"Kill her! Shoot them all! How . . . how dare you disrupt my wedding!"

Hermann Rathner's man pointed their automatic rifles into the crowd from the back of the jeeps.

"Even you, my impulsive, hot-blooded friend, would not turn this ceremony into a bloodbath, especially in order to protect an *Untermensch*—a mulatto slut!" shouted the doctor.

The words cut into Susan like a rapier. *She knows! The bitch knows! I am doomed!* She tried to get up from the pillow, but her knees were locked in fear. She fell sideways against Carlos. He grabbed her and held her, trying to comfort her.

The doctor got out of her jeep and swaggered to the stage. She boldly grabbed the microphone. Carlos held Susan tightly, his hate-filled eyes staring at Von Ziegazar.

"As the chief geneticist of the Holy Garduna, it is my sacred duty to protect our people against the infusion of impure blood. You should thank me, Carlos. I have taken a great risk to prevent you from making a terrible mistake," Von Ziegazar said calmly in a patronizing voice. "I am laying my life on the line to carry out my duties. This little *chivato* slut has deliberately wormed her way into our society in order to pollute it. She is guilty of racial sabotage!"

Susan heard the words. They pounded into her as she clutched Carlos tightly. She felt his arms relax around her as the doctor continued her indictment. He was beginning to waver! Perhaps to believe her! Susan's survival instincts took over. She felt the rush of adrenaline, and staggered to her feet.

"She is a liar!" Susan screamed, pointing a shaking finger at the smirking lesbian. "She is a damned perverted liar! She is accusing me of these things because I spurned her filthy, unnatural advances several nights ago. She tried to seduce me and I almost killed her for it! I wish I had! That is why she is trying to destroy me!"

"Do you deny, Susan Rockland, that your paternal grandfather was a full-blooded Negro?" Von Ziegazar smiled as she waited for the reply.

Carlos turned to Susan and looked at her helplessly. His eyes pleaded for a negative answer.

She knows! She must have had her agents in Tulsa dig up the information. But could she prove it? It was her word against the doctor's.

"Of course I deny it! My grandfather was an elder of the Holy Council of the Cherokee nation. He was a full-blooded Native American!" Susan lied.

"Aha! I was waiting for that, Susan! You have just condemned yourself to the piranha tank. You have lied to the Garduna after submitting to the ritual of purification!"

The doctor thrust a sheaf of documents at Estigarribia. "Read these, Hermano Mayor. These are the fruits of my visit to Tulsa."

Trembling, Susan jerked herself straight, locking her knees so she wouldn't collapse. *That treacherous bitch had been to Tulsa! Well, I will deny everything. Perhaps nothing will happen until the uprising. The revolution! The day after tomorrow! Surely there will be an inquiry of some kind that will ensure my survival until the fifteenth.*

Susan realized that her status as Carlos's bride-to-be would ensure her of a hearing and trial. Anybody could fake official papers with today's technology. She knew her only hope was to accuse Von Ziegazar of forging the documents in order to discredit her and embarrass Carlos. Perhaps the doctor instead of Susan would provide the banquet for the piranha.

Susan stepped up to the Prophet and spoke clearly and confidently. "May I see these, Hermano Mayor?"

The old man stared at her with suspicious eyes. His trembling hand gave her the photocopies.

Susan made her move. She spoke into the microphone forcefully and addressed the silent throngs in her best Spanish.

"My brothers and sisters, and you *are* my brothers and sisters, as I have traveled many thousands of miles to join you of my own free will. I have accepted you, the Garduna, and your values and have made them my own. I have forsaken former family and friends to be among you. I have chosen, voluntarily, to live among you, and to honor and obey my intended husband. *You* are my family!"

The crowds murmured in approval.

"Does anybody here think that I would dare to stand in front of the entire Garduna and claim to be . . . to be anything but what I am unless I was totally innocent of the charges of this . . . this woman?"

Susan slurred the last two words. The portion of the crowd that could observe the doctor's masculine features laughed softly.

"In today's world, my brothers and sisters, documents are forged, created and altered to serve the wicked. Dr. Von Ziegazar has crashed this wedding with so-called evidence which could have been—which *was*—manufactured in a printshop somewhere."

She held up one of the photocopies.

"Here's an obituary notice of a Jesse Rockland of Tulsa, Oklahoma. There is a picture, a photocopy from a photograph from a newspaper. It details the man's life. It wouldn't take much imagination or skill to create this."

The crowds were with Susan. The little *chivato* who had shown such bravery in the oil fields was, by her raw courage, turning the tables on Dr. Von Ziegazar.

A man screamed from the audience: "Death to Von Ziegazar!"

Several more, then a chorus of voices took up the cry: "Kill the lesbian heretic! Feed her to the piranhas!"

A Gardún officer started to climb into the second jeep. One of Rathner's men hit him alongside of the face with his rifle butt, sending the purple-and-white-robed figure sprawling onto the cobblestoned plaza.

Carlos walked up to Susan and put his arm around her waist. She sagged slightly, then steadied herself, grabbing at Von Reinach for support. He took the microphone with his left hand, a twisted, victorious smile on his face.

"Brothers of the Holy Garduna! My wife-to-be has again demonstrated her incredible bravery and worthiness in the witness of thousands. If she were of polluted racial stock, could she rise to such an occasion? Would she dare to confront us and plead her innocence if this were not so?"

"No!" roared the thousands of spectators.

"She!" He pointed at the doctor. "She is the one who is guilty! She is the one who has used her position and authority to settle a personal vendetta with Susan Rockland! When Susan spurned her filthy advances and her unusual desires, this female—at least I *think* she is a female . . ."

The crowds laughed as the nervous Von Ziegazar turned crimson.

"She resorted to these falsifications and this insane act of rebellion against the anointed of God. For this, she must die! I demand retribution here and now!" Carlos bellowed.

The crowd roared its approval.

"Give me a pistol! Let me kill her while God has given me the will! It is my right! It is I who have been insulted and humiliated."

A Gardún leader leaped to the stage and thrust an automatic pistol into Von Reinach's hand.

Von Ziegazar's eyes were orbs of fear as they locked onto the orifice of the pistol held in his hand. Von Reinach grabbed the doctor's short blond hair with his left hand and yanked it sideways, holding the barrel to her temple.

• • •

The shawled peasant had a commanding view of the stage from the second-story window of the red-tiled warehouse, which flanked the west plaza. The side of the giant canopy was rolled high enough so his view was unobstructed. Two other "peasants" were busy assembling parts which were taking the shape of a .50-caliber machine gun. The peasant in the window trained his binoculars on Susan and spoke into a portable transceiver with the other.

"As long as I live, Señor Caro, I will never forget what I am seeing. One minute your Susan was about to be condemned and executed. Now she has manipulated the feelings and emotions of the crowds. Von Reinach has a gun to the doctor's head. What a woman you have, amigo!"

Seven miles away, to the west of Colonia Gardún, in a deep gully behind the sandstone bluffs, Angel Caro lay in the dense bushes, his transceiver glued to his ear. His expression was one of fear mixed with pride. Several hundred camouflaged guerrillas lay hidden in the ravines nearby.

"That's my girl, Eduardo! She'll get herself out of this. I hope Von Reinach has the guts to pull the trigger. Keep an eye on her. Let me know what happens if there's a turn for the worse."

The peasant clicked off the transceiver and stepped away from the window, allowing his comrades to emplace and sight the now-assembled machine gun on the stage across the plaza.

Von Ziegazar didn't expect this. She hadn't counted on Susan's sudden boldness or her ability to manipulate the masses in the plaza. Chilling fear ran through her angular body as she felt the cold blue of the barrel against her temple. The snarl on Von Reinach's face told her that she had just seconds to live.

"Hermano Mayor! Wait! I have one more piece of evidence. Let me present it. If it does not satisfy you, then I will accept a bullet."

Von Reinach's finger tightened on the trigger.

"Stop!" cried Estigarribia. "Lower your weapon and stand back. That is an order!"

Reluctantly Von Reinach lowered the gun. He released the tufts of hair held tightly in his hand.

The doctor breathed deeply, relieved by the reprieve. She yelled to her colleagues in the jeep. "Bring out our star witness!"

The double doors of the van swung open and two of Rathner's men jumped down. A third occupant shoved a hooded man, hands tied tightly behind his back, out the rear. The other two caught him and marched him roughly through the silenced crowds, up the stairs, and onto the stage.

Susan stared, her face in a frown. Who was Von Ziegazar's prisoner? Did they capture Angel? Raúl? Salazar? She wondered who it could be. Whoever it was, what could they prove?

Von Ziegazar grabbed the bound and hooded hostage and pushed him in front of the Hermano Mayor. She spun him around, his front facing the audience. "This is the only proof I need!" she screamed into the mike. She yanked the hood from the prisoner's head. The battered but recognizable face of Joe Rockland stared vacantly and fearfully at the throngs below. His mulatto features were the first thing that Carlos and his uncle noticed.

Her father's eyes locked onto Susan's. She stared back in transfixed horror as she observed the tortured features of her father's face. Oblivious now to everyone around her, Susan rushed to the bound and battered hostage. She threw herself into his body and wrapped her arms around him, burying her head in his chest. The microphone picked up her every word, carrying her sobs to the thirty thousand spectators as she spoke to the mulatto prisoner through her tears.

"Daddy! Daddy! Oh, Daddy! What have they done to you? Oh, Daddy!"

XXII.

"Through the swamps, Nick?"

"Through the swamps, Patty." Nick grinned as he slipped on his small pack and adjusted the harness straps. "Did you expect us to just sail up to the dock and walk down the gangplank and say 'Here we are, blokes'? We've got to be somewhat more subtle than that!"

"Are . . . are there snakes in there?" asked Patty Benson, pointing to the clumps of mangrove trees and tangled vines lining the shore.

The bearded commander joined them on the railing and laughed. "Yes, my little warrior, but they are not poisonous. What they lack in venom they make up for in size. They are constrictors."

"How . . . how big do they get, Commander?" asked Patty, wide-eyed.

"They took out one that was twenty-five feet long not too many years ago. His circumference was almost three feet! It took ten men to carry him."

"Wow!" responded the Benson girl. "What do they eat?"

"Teenage girls!" The LCI skipper laughed. "Blondes are preferred."

Patty fondled her submachine gun, flicking the selector switch on and off.

"And there's to be no shooting. We've got to approach

Fuerte Olimpo silently. If you see a snake, use your knife," Nick said, laughing.

Patty's expression grew more serious. "Why are we stepping up our attack schedule, Nick?"

"The last message we picked up from KDRM before leaving the sub was that Eli's group had gone into La Cuna and found it wasted—totally destroyed. We don't know who did it, or what the reaction of the Paraguayan Army or the Garduna will be when they find out. We've decided to hit Fuerte Olimpo several hours early while everybody's concentrating on the wedding. They'll be glued to their radios, and many of their key people will be gone to Colonia Gardún."

The shallow-draft LCI nosed into a dry spot of land and lowered a gangplank. The countercult commandos and Paraguayan marines scampered off and slid into the dense green.

"I'll stay put until I hear that Fuerte Olimpo is secured, then I'll steam majestically in and claim credit for the victory, amigo," the commander said, and chuckled.

Nick smiled and waved, motioning his force into the swamp.

Joe Rockland looked somewhat more presentable since his treatment at the dispensary. Dr. Schutzler had been kind. He was not a racist. He dabbed the mulatto's face with iodine and applied gauze and tape with a concern that would have been given to the Prophet.

Rockland's hands were no longer bound, but the blue-black rope-indented bruises were still visible on his wrists. He and Susan stood quietly, almost sullenly, in Estigarribia's office. Von Ziegazar, the Hermano Mayor, and ten *fuelles* from the Holy Council sat in a semicircle around them. Carlos sat on the end, a defeated expression clouding his handsome features. He stared straight ahead, avoiding Susan.

"Your life among us here at Colonia Gardún has been one gigantic lie, Susan Rockland!" hissed the Hermano Mayor. "You knew the requirements of our Order and the genetic commandments and yet you perpetrated your deception until your perfidy was unmasked by the courageous doctor. Only an agent of the adversary could have done this with such consummate skill; skill which deceived all of us so easily. You have committed the most grievous of sins, child, and you *are* a child—a child of Satan, a mistress of deception! He has even infused you with bravery to gain our confidence and blind my nephew. The adversary is cunning! He will use every stratagem to destroy us—but we will triumph! The Garduna will destroy his agents before they can harm us!"

Von Ziegazar spoke with a softness that belied her hatred of the Rocklands. "Hermano Mayor, perhaps this near-disastrous incident can be turned around and be made into a learning experience."

"You speak in riddles, Hilda," the old man snarled.

"Thirty thousand people have come to see the wedding. Instead, they have seen the Holy Garduna humiliated! If they leave without seeing the resolving of her crime"—the doctor jabbed a finger toward Susan—"then their opinion of the Garduna will be diminished. The power we generate is based on fear; the fear of swift and painful retribution on those who thwart or oppose us."

"Speak plainly, doctor. What are you proposing?"

Carlos stared at Von Ziegazar helplessly. The spark had left his once electric-blue eyes. The familiar gleam was replaced by the vacant dullness of fear—fear of what the doctor was about to suggest.

"The spectators must see justice done before they leave. They must witness how the Holy Garduna deals with traitors! The mulatto and her *Untermensch* father must be put to death. We must show them out there"—she pointed out the window toward the plaza—"that the Garduna has fangs!"

The Hermano Mayor rubbed his beard thoughtfully, a slight smile tugging at the corners of his lips. "A public execution! Yes! That would satisfy them. Even Ayala and his cronies would stay for that!"

A *fuelle* chuckled, "Especially Ayala."

Everyone seated laughed, except Carlos.

Suddenly Joe Rockland spoke up, to the surprise of everyone. He had been ordered to remain silent.

"There are some things you should know, gentlemen, before you . . ."

Von Ziegazar lunged from her chair and struck him hard across the face with an open hand.

"You are to remain silent, pig!" she spat.

Rockland absorbed the punishment and continued. ". . . before you kill us. The doctor has kept certain things from you."

"Let him speak!" barked the Hermano Mayor.

Joe Rockland breathed deeply and began. "You have heard of Courtney Davenport, Señor Von Reinach?"

Carlos looked up quickly in surprise. "Of course! He's my brother-in-Christ. How did . . ."

"The armored cars, the rocket launchers, the weapons that have made your Garduna the most powerful force in the country . . ."

"Silence him, Hermano Mayor! He speaks lies!" cried Hilda, clenching her fists in anger.

The Prophet held up his hand for silence. Von Ziegazar shrank back into her seat.

"Who do you think has been working with Davenport on your weapons project, Von Reinach?"

Carlos' eyes developed their familiar gleam. "You . . . you are . . ."

"Yes, Carlos. I am the 'Rock' portion of DAVROCK. DAVROCK is an acronym for Davenport-Rockland Development. I am Courtney Davenport's business partner. If I was an enemy of the Holy Garduna, would I have allowed these weapons to be shipped down here?"

The Prophet Estigarribia rubbed his temples. The migraines were starting again.

"Do you feel that you can execute us without hurting yourselves? Do you realize that I have helped you in other ways, Señor Estigarribia?"

"How is that?" asked the old man, a bewildered expression on his face.

"Davenport's daughter is among you. Olivia is up at La Cuna."

There was a stunned silence. Even Von Ziegazar realized the importance of that statement. She had no idea that the human vegetable she visited and planned to use against Susan was the daughter of the one man responsible for the Garduna's tremendous economic potential in oil and its formidable military might.

"I have known of this for some time, but have chosen to keep silent. I did so because I feel that the Garduna is an inspired movement and South America's last chance to defeat the inroads of communism," Rockland lied.

Von Ziegazar saw her victory slipping from her. She reacted predictably, with hysterics. "Do not listen to him!" she screamed shrilly. "An *Untermensch* is an *Untermensch*—no matter what they do! He had done these things to gain power for America, not to help us!"

Von Reinach smiled for the first time since the doctor unhooded Joe Rockland. "Are you afraid, Hilda, that you won't be able to show off the effectiveness of your piranhas before the masses? Would you put personal revenge before the power of the Garduna?"

Rockland spoke again. "As far as I am concerned, gentlemen, I view this whole episode as a tragic misunderstanding. I can appreciate your concern for discipline. To be honest, I cannot subscribe to your racial theories, for obvious reasons, but that is a matter of doctrine which you will have to wrestle with. Many religious groups have had to make compromises between doctrinal purity and practical necessity: in your case, to execute us and adhere to doctrine, or work with us and watch the power of the Garduna multiply. Believe me, gentlemen, our stake in Chaco oil is so great that I am willing—I am obligated even—to forget everything which has happened here."

"He speaks wisdom," voiced a *fuelle*.

"Our power base is of paramount importance," added another.

There was heated discussion among the council members. Von Reinach sat straight in his chair, a slight smile on his lips. His eyes, which were filled with hate, darted to Von Ziegazar. When he turned toward Susan, they softened in sympathy, but she avoided his glances.

The Prophet stood and spoke. "We must decide, brethren. Those who will have them executed, raise your hand."

Von Ziegazar's hand shot up.

"Those who would forgive and forget, but would banish Susan Rockland from our midst forever?"

All except the doctor concurred. Susan squeezed her father's hand. She was going home!

"Then it is my decision that we . . ."

There was a frenzied knock on the door. A *fuelle* opened it, and a *guapo*, a messenger from the north, burst in. "Hermano Mayor!" he panted breathlessly. "The station at La Cuna! It has been destroyed!"

The countercult commandos and Paraguayan marines broke out of the swamp after a five-hour ordeal of mosquitoes, snakes, and lizards. The spongy terrain gave way to stands of quebracho trees and rolling grasslands. It was getting toward late afternoon. They had traversed the swamp during the heat of the day, and the hot, dry breeze dried their clothing quickly. The small force snaked along an old logging road until it came to a large grove of trees overlooking the river.

"We'll hole up here for a while, mates. Take off your boots and socks and set 'em in the sun—away from the road. Let 'em dry out," said Nick.

An hour later, the whine of a straining automobile engine was heard down the road to the west. Patty Benson scrambled up to the edge of the rise and peered down the road. Approximately a half mile away was a Toyota Land Cruiser. She focused her binoculars on a roving patrol of four armed men. Nick joined her.

"Well, young lady, you're going to get your first taste of combat!" He smiled grimly.

A dead log was dragged to the middle of the rutty dirt road. Patty and three other commandos attached silencers to their Uzis and hid among the bushes.

The Toyota appeared over the rise, bounced along the ruts, and lurched to a stop. Four Guaraní Indians armed with Heckler & Koch automatic rifles scrambled from their vehicle. After some initial cursing, the four Indians set to the task of wrestling the heavy, dense log off the road.

Perspiration burned Patty's eyes as she lined up her front

and rear sights with the backs of the struggling Guaraní. She had killed once before, as part of her superb training by Nick and Andrea, but never in the heat of combat. She squeezed the trigger. The clicking of the Teflon-covered bolt was the only indication that the weapon was functioning. In the road, however, there was chaos and death. The 9mm slugs from the silenced Uzis ripped into the guards. After a brief but violent dance of death they collapsed in ragged, bloody heaps.

Patty ran to the convulsing figures. It was so easy! She resisted the thought that she had enjoyed killing, but she had! She rammed in a fresh magazine clip and fired four bursts into each twitching target. She smiled and flashed a "V" sign to Nick with her fingers.

Nick raised his fingers into the familiar "V" in return, but his thoughts were troubled. She looked like a triumphant hunter posing with her trophies. What demons had he and Andrea unleashed at the deprogramming center? They had returned a broken Patty Benson to the land of the living, but had uncorked the bottle which let out a killer genie. Nick stared quizzically at the smiling warrior as she stripped the guards of their weapons. *After she experiences the battles of Fuerte Olimpo and Colonia Gardún, how does one get the genie back into its bottle?*

Under the administration building at Colonia Gardún was a complex of cell-like cubicles which functioned as the colony's detention and interrogation center. All of the usual paraphernalia of interrogation was there: the rubber truncheons, electric-shock generators, whips, tongs, and irons. It looked like a standard *pyngare* torture cell, as it might well have been. A *pyngare* member of the Garduna had installed it several years ago, modeling it after the larger *pyngare* establishment at Asunción.

Susan and her father were chained by their hands to the wall. The Hermano Mayor, Von Ziegazar, and three of the senior *fuelles*, who were the high priests of the Holy Council, faced them.

"It almost worked, Señor Rockland," slurred a *fuelle*. "We would have believed you if we did not receive word of

La Cuna. We were fortunate to have the good doctor send a radio message to Asunción and learn of your association with Paul Lancaster. Lancaster has been suspected by the *pyngare* to have been in contact with the Sandinistas. We also learned from our contacts in the *pyngare* apparatus that DAVROCK is in conspiracy with the NICUBA Corporation, which is a front group for Cuban-Nicaraguan penetration of Latin America. It is all so clear, Rockland. You have been supplying our enemies with arms, and the raid on La Cuna is the first of several assaults planned by the Sandinistas—is that not so?''

Rockland shook his head wearily. ''Sandinistas? NICUBA? I don't know what you're talking about. We haven't dealt with any of those organizations.''

''Your lies are useless, you mulatto swine!'' hissed Estigarribia. ''This information comes directly from the headquarters of General Ramón Torrejos! We have our agents everywhere!''

Susan was engulfed by nauseating waves of fear. Her eyes, now reflecting pools of despair, swept over the instruments of torture on the wooden tables. Would she die down here screaming, unheard by the guerrillas in the crowds?

The Gardún officials were leaving. Estigarribia turned and pointed a gnarled, arthritic finger at the chained pair. ''Enjoy your evening. It is almost your last! At ten in the morning on the fifteenth, you both shall die. We are going upstairs now to the platform and announce our decision to the masses.''

The radio station was the first to fall. It was located away from the refinery and the dock complex of Fuerte Olimpo. The two guards were quickly dispatched, and the lone radio operator was shot while he sat reading a magazine and sipping a cup of steaming yerba maté. The power station was next. Three technicians and three guards were slain silently. They didn't know what hit them as the silenced weapons took their toll.

It was 8:30 in the evening of the thirteenth, and still light. The refinery workers and Parachaco administrative staff, as well as many of the guards, were huddled around a large radio in the administration building. They were listening to the high, whiny voice of Francisco Estigarribia which was coming over a special Garduna frequency:

". . . and they will be executed on the fifteenth for their evil actions against the anointed of God. At ten in the morning, the day after tomorrow, the execution will be witnessed by the thousands that would have seen the fruits of their treachery had the hand of the Almighty not intervened . . ."

The Prophet droned on.

The *guapo* José spoke, "I can remember this *chivato*, brethren," he said excitedly. "I was taken in by this wench and her blond companion. They came by submarine last summer and would not be separated. The dark one claimed to be a Cherokee Indian from the American state of Oklahoma. Von Reinach wanted to kill her, but I talked him out of it. May God forgive me!"

Estigarribia's voice continued over the slight static. "The execution of the prisoners will satisfy justice and be a lesson to all that the Sacred Order of the Holy Garduna cannot be, and will not be, trifled with! The method of execution will be conducted in the traditional way."

"Oho! What a pity. That beautiful body nibbled and gnawed raw by our little destroyers. What a waste of good flesh! It would be better if we made her last hours a little more entertaining before the piranhas got her!" continued another *guapo*.

Suddenly the animated conversation was replaced by another sound—that of windowpanes being broken as several hand grenades sailed into the crowded room. Within seconds the shrapnel and phosphorus of the countercult grenades turned the recreation room into a blazing inferno. Patty Benson and the countercult commandos burst in through both doors, their Uzis chattering.

It was slaughter, and the Benson girl reveled in it. She had become the countercult force's most proficient killer. She did her work well. Elsewhere in Fuerte Olimpo, the Paraguayan marines mopped up pockets of resistance.

In an hour it was all over. It was a lopsided victory, made easy by the concentration of Gardún personnel in the recreation building. The proclamation of execution by the Hermano Mayor had served the countercult force well.

The bodies of the slain were dragged to the dockside and tossed into the river. Within seconds a fifty-foot stretch of water was a mass of agitated activity, as the piranhas of the Upper Paraguay assisted in destroying the evidence of the attack.

In the waning minutes of sunset, the LCI appeared from around the little mangrove island downriver. It warped its way to the dock. "Everything looks normal here, Señor Portumo," said the skipper. "Has there been a battle?"

"You should have been here thirty minutes ago, my friend. We were up to our eyeballs in Gardunians! Luckily for us, they were concentrated like fish in a barrel. They were listening to an edict of execution for the Rockland girl. The speaker said she would die by the traditional methods—whatever that means."

"Piranhas!" exclaimed the commander, his expression hardening. "The Garduna way is to lower their victims slowly into a tank or well, then pull them out from time to time to show the spectators their handiwork. They are bastards!"

Nick toyed with his submachine gun nervously. "We've got to get out of here and join up with Revvim's group at La Cuna before the assault. How in the hell are we . . ."

Nick's thoughts were interrupted by the sudden sounds of clattering, whirling rotors. Five helicopters of the Paraguayan Navy came skimming along the muddy river, almost touching the water.

"You didn't think I would leave you stranded, amigos? You have our entire naval air force at your disposal. Those helicopters will transport your people, but I keep my marines. I'll have more business downriver when the uprising begins in earnest."

"You are an extremely efficient person, commander," said Nick. "You anticipate everything."

The helicopters hovered for a landing beyond the refinery as the skipper lit a large cigar. He inhaled deeply and sighed out a cloud of blue smoke. "I'm an old hand at this, Nicholas. In my fifteen years of naval service, this has been my fourth revolution . . . and"—he winked—"I always pick the winning side."

• • •

Susan and her father lost all track of time. One hour slid into the next, without the sun to create a frame of reference. The only source of light visible to the chained pair was a bare light bulb which hung from the ceiling by a frayed cord.

At 7:30 in the morning on the fourteenth, they had their hands unchained, and were escorted to a bathroom down the hall one at a time. The hallway and bathroom were as dimly lit as their detention cell. They were chained back on the wall after they had relieved themselves.

At noon, Dr. Von Ziegazar slipped almost unnoticed into the room. She was carrying a large open-mouthed jar. "Well, well, well," she cooed mockingly. "Our two star attractions for tomorrow's double feature."

Joe Rockland looked up with bloodshot eyes, a week's growth of beard on his face. "Why don't you leave us in peace, Von Ziegazar. At a time like this, I prefer the company of my God. Let us be!"

"Oh, shortly, shortly, *mein Untermensch* friend. I thought it would be appropriate if you met your executioners. After all, the two most important people in the world are the ones who brought you into this world and the ones who will take you out of it. Is that not so?"

Susan looked beyond the doctor toward the door, a helpless expression on her face.

"Ah, but in this case, we're not talking about a him or her. We're talking about an *it*. Meet my little friends, Hermann and Heinrich." Von Ziegazar held up the large jar. Inside, two small yellow fish with black and green stripes darted erratically around in the water. Susan and her father stared uncomprehendingly at the fish.

"Your little executioners, Susan! These two, along with hundreds of their professional colleagues, will reduce you both to basics."

"They're . . . they're . . ."

"Yes, Susan." The doctor smirked wickedly. "They're piranhas."

Joe Rockland squinted at the jar, trying to focus his eyes in the dim light.

"Oh, forgive me," said the smiling doctor. "Let me shed some light on them." She flicked a switch and the room was flooded with a bluish fluorescent light. The sharp and vicious teeth on the little fish were now plainly visible.

"These are not just ordinary piranhas scooped from the river. Oh, no. These are specially bred in our aquarium here at the colony. Did you ever see our aquarium, Susan? We have several five-hundred-gallon glass tanks where old Estigarribia raises a variety of aquatic life common to Paraguay. Actually the old man is quite a scientist in his own right. This particular breed of piranha is his pride and joy. They are smaller but more vicious; and if you'll observe, they have a mouth one half as wide as they are long."

Von Ziegazar held the jar up to Susan's face. She stared at the fish with horrified eyes. They seemed to be wearing a toothy grin and reminded her, oddly, of a prominent political figure from America's past. She couldn't make up her mind whether it was ex-President Jimmy Carter or Eleanor Roosevelt.

"These little fellows can eat twice their body weight. I have given them a name in my bastardized Spanish which explains their sole mission in life. They are my *voracianos*, the voracious ones. Watch, Susan!"

The doctor ran her finger around the outside of the jar. The piranhas followed, swimming in frantic circles, their teeth clicking rhythmically against the glass as they tried to bite her finger.

"You're sick—sick, Von Ziegazar!" shouted Joe Rockland. "You're pure evil!"

The doctor laughed. "Ah! Such lovely compliments so early in the morning.

"Oh! You are probably wondering why these little fellows were bred to be so small. Well, we had size and intelligence in mind. They are small enough to wiggle into every little crack, crevice, and opening in the human body and clean it out. They'll complete what your garlic enema started to do, Susan. After these little fellows get into you, you will be truly purified." Von Ziegazar wrinkled her face into the beginning of a chuckle, anticipating her own joke. "You see, we have trained our little friends to make 'orifice' calls. Get it . . . 'orifice' calls?'' She winked.

Susan sagged in her chains, her knees almost touching the floor.

''Let me give you a little preview of what to expect, Susan.'' The doctor grinned, her eyes reflecting a savage gleam. She reached down and grabbed Susan by the underarms and yanked her into an upright position. Grabbing a handful of her blouse, she ripped it off, taking her bra with it and exposing one hard, pointed breast. She grabbed Susan's hair and yanked her head down; the one breast dangled toward the floor.

Susan didn't comprehend what was happening until Von Ziegazar cupped the mouth of the jar over her exposed breast, immersing it in the water. Susan felt the tail of one of the fish brush against her nipple. A burst of adrenaline caused Susan to wrench upward. She reached up and grabbed the two iron rings which held her chains. In one movement she lifted the lower part of her body, her knees against her chest, and placed the soles of her feet against the doctor's stomach. With one mighty shove, she lunged out with her entire body, expending all of the energy she had for that one final effort.

Von Ziegazar shot backward, crashing against the wooden table. The table overturned, spilling the instruments of torture all over the stone floor. The jar fell to the floor and shattered. Von Ziegazar followed, slashing her face on a large jagged piece of glass. Her blood mingled with the water. The excited piranhas that were thrashing among the glass shards on the floor went for the bleeding face. One bit her on the ear, tearing off a small piece of her lobe. The other was closer and, frenzied by the taste of blood and lack of water, locked onto her cheek. Screaming and cursing, Von Ziegazar pulled herself up and tugged at the determined but doomed piranha as it held on to its morsel of flesh.

Two guards burst into the room and stared unbelievingly at the carnage. Susan and her father were still chained, but ten feet away there was chaos: blood, water, and instruments of torture littered the floor. The lesbian doctor was gyrating in a grotesque dance, the piranha dangling from her cheek.

One of the guards grabbed a rag and wrapped it around the writhing little fish, pulling it off—a large piece of Van Ziegazar's cheek between its teeth.

They led her from the room as she bled, cursed, and mumbled incoherently.

Susan fell to her knees and pitched forward in a dead faint, her chains preventing her from hitting the cold stone floor.

XXIII.

"Daddy?" There was no response from the wall alongside Susan. "Daddy?"

There was a slight clanking of chains as Joe Rockland shifted his weight. A rat scurried across the damp floor, running over Susan's bare feet. The cell was pitch-black. The guards had turned off the single naked light bulb for the evening.

"Are you awake, Daddy?"

"Yes, Susan, I'm awake."

"Daddy, I'm . . . I'm . . ." Susan started to sob uncontrollably.

"That's all right, honey. This is the time to cry."

"I'm so sorry I got you into this. It's so unfair that you . . . you should . . ." Susan choked on her tears.

"Should have to die, Susan? That's what life is all about, child—preparing to die. I can handle that and I hope I raised you to handle it, too."

"Yes, Daddy, I can die. But . . . but I don't know if I can stand the pain. The thought of those piranhas! Daddy, I . . ." Susan started to sob again.

"I've told you the story of the young prisoner who was executed in the Manchurian prison camp before, haven't I, Susan?"

"Yes. Tell me again."

"Honey, these barbarians have taken away all of our freedoms except one. We can choose the way we'll die. We can go to our deaths screaming, begging, thrashing in the water, or we can go as the early Christian martyrs went in the Colosseum in Rome to die among the lions. I'll never forget that young prisoner thirty-nine years ago. He chose to go with a testimony of his God on his lips. That was the only shred of freedom left to him. I'm going to take advantage of that. I'm going to show those bastards how a true Christian meets his God.'' Rockland's voice softened.

''Susan, you . . . you still believe, don't you?''

''Yes, Daddy. I still believe. I don't think I ever stopped. I—I just got sidetracked. I was in the Garden Children for kicks and for Olivia; but, yes, I believe.''

Joe Rockland could hear Susan shuffle in her chains. His brave words belied the despair he felt. How could he watch his daughter be dipped in a tank of piranhas which would strip her of her flesh and provide entertainment for thousands? All he could offer were brave words.

Susan breathed deeply, fighting for strength.

''Daddy?'' Her voice was stronger. ''Sing with me.''

Joe Rockland's voice squeaked out the first few words.

Amazing Grace
How sweet the word

Susan joined in, her voice strengthening his.

That saved a wretch like me
I once was lost
But now I'm . . .

The fluorescent lights flickered on, blinding the chained pair. Their eyes took almost a minute to adjust and focus on the figures in front of them. Von Ziegazar, Estigarribia, three *fuelles*, and four guards stood in a semicircle. ''Unchain them!'' the Prophet barked. ''It is time.''

The crowds in the plaza were in an expectant and festive mood. The flags, the bunting, and all of the decorations for the wedding were left intact. Nothing had changed except the expectations of the crowds.

The colony's maintenance crew had done a superb job. One of the large aquariums had been pumped out and moved to the stage in sections. It was composed of a large wooden frame with slotted uprights for its many sheets of heavy plate glass. It was a complicated device and, when erected, was not meant to be moved. The workmen had done their job well. They disassembled, moved, and reassembled the many pieces of framing and glass. When finished, it was completely caulked and watertight. Then came the water—nearly two thousand gallons. The hundreds of piranhas were trucked over and dumped by the bucketful into the large wood and glass edifice which dominated the stage.

The enclosed plywood orchestra pits on the plaza were directly below the aquarium. On one side of the aisle sat General Ayala and high officials of government. On the other were ranking officers of the Holy Garduna. Both sections of the pits were filled to capacity. They were situated in such a way that they would witness every shred of activity.

On each end of the tank was a large vertical wooden post extending fifteen feet above the top of the aquarium. A heavy horizontal bar jutted out eight feet from the top of each post—out over the water of the large aquarium. Ropes and pulleys attached to a hand crank on the bottom of each post allowed the executioners to lower or raise the victims at will.

Susan and her father were shoved and dragged roughly up the stairs to the main floor of the administration building, and then taken to the front door facing the plaza. Von Ziegazar approached the trembling pair, her swollen, bandaged cheek still oozing a little blood through the gauze.

"Out there, my *Untermensch* friends, are thousands who are waiting to be entertained. They want to hear you scream and beg for mercy. Do it for them, Susan, and I'll make it quick."

Susan did not reply. She stared numbly at the heavy door separating her from the stage.

A *fuelle* pulled the door open and the light blinded the captives. As they were led out, they saw the apparatus of execution and the hundreds of vicious *voracianos* darting around in the water.

Seated to the rear of the huge tank were the senior members of the Garduna. Carlos sat in the middle, his face waxen. His features were frozen into a nonexpression. He refused to look at Susan, who was taken with her father to the opposite end of the aquarium where the fifteen-foot posts were bolted to the stage floor.

Susan looked out over the vast throngs of spectators as the guards ripped her clothing from her body. In seconds she stood completely naked before them. The crowds hooted and whistled in approval as they leered at her magnificent body. Susan scanned the orchestra pit and saw the savage gleam in the eyes of General Ayala and his cronies. She looked beyond the orchestra pits. Her eyes widened in shock as she looked into the familiar face of Raúl Caro, who was not more than fifty feet beyond the pits! He was dressed as a peasant, a ubiquitous shawl over his ragged clothing. But it was he! Her observation was confirmed when he flashed her a "V" sign with his fingers and put his finger to his lips for silence. She didn't miss it. The guerrillas were in the crowd! They would not let them die!

"Whip them! Draw blood!" snarled the Hermano Mayor.

Susan and Joe Rockland were tied to the uprights on each end of the aquarium, their backs facing out. Two large black coils of leather were brought forward and given to two burly Guaraní guards.

"Let me!" shouted Von Ziegazar. "It is my right!" She took one of the whips and walked up to Susan, smirking. She grabbed her hair and wrenched her head backward. "Just a few stripes, my dear girl. Just enough to draw blood so that our little friends in the tank can have an appetizer before the main course."

Susan's courage welled up inside her. She spit into the lesbian's face. Von Ziegazar turned crimson, and more blood seeped into her bandage. "You little mulatto slut!" she screamed, raking her long fingernails down Susan's smooth, tanned back, leaving long bloody grooves.

The crowds booed and hissed their disapproval of the doctor's irrational action.

"Enough, Hilda!" shouted the Prophet. "Let it begin!"

Von Ziegazar took several steps backward, uncoiling the whip as she walked. Susan trembled as she waited for the lash to crash against her back. Her face was pressed against the side of the post, her eyes staring into the aquarium. A little group of piranhas congregated around her nose, which was pressed against the glass, and stared back as if in sympathy with her plight.

The sudden shock of pain caught her by surprise and she screamed loudly. From behind, she could hear Von Ziegazar laugh.

"Don't . . . don't give them the satisfaction, daughter!" she heard her father yell from the other side. "Remember the young prisoner in Manchuria!"

Beads of perspiration covered Von Ziegazar's face and ran into the cheek wound, the salt from the sweat causing the wound to burn. She continued to lash Susan. The sharp spines of the ceputo cactus, which were embedded in the last few feet of the whip, started to shred the back of Susan.

With every crack of the lash on Susan's back, Carlos Von Reinach stiffened as if trying to absorb the blows for his former fiancée.

"Enough!" cried Estigarribia. "Blood has been drawn!"

Susan's thongs were cut and she started to slide down the rough wooden post. Her back and shoulders were a crisscross of bloody welts and cuts. After her first scream of surprise, there were no more. She had endured the first stage of her execution well. She sagged slightly, her knees buckling, but caught herself. She jerked herself erect. She glared defiantly at the guards who pulled her hands in front of her and attached the ropes to her wrists.

A ripple of applause started cautiously in the audience and reached a crescendo as Susan struggled. She kicked a guard in the groin as he wrestled her up to the side of the plate glass.

The ropes from the pulleys were lowered from both scaffolds and pulled to the front of the tank, where they were fastened to the victims' wrists. A Guaraní turned a hand crank. Joe Rockland rose, his body sliding against the glass of the gigantic fish tank. Von Ziegazar operated the crank which controlled Susan's pulley. In a matter of minutes, father's and daughter's hands were touching the pulley, and they were positioned directly above the water.

The blood ran in little rivulets down Susan's back, on down to the bottom of her legs. Susan watched with morbid curiosity as the water started to froth some ten feet beneath her. The piranhas fought and thrashed at the smell of blood. She and her father hung suspended from the vertical scaffolding, and faced each other in their nakedness. The crowds were absolutely silent. Susan glanced to the left. The Holy Council of the Garduna stared at the suspended pair, now turning slightly at the end of their ropes. Below them was a caldron of frenzied activity.

Carlos stared straight ahead, an immobile expression on his handsome face. Von Ziegazar and the Guaraní stood rigidly at attention at each end of the tank, their hands clutching their crank handles.

Suddenly, to the side of the stage, the small orchestra, which had been displaced from its original position in the orchestra pit, broke into a melody. The Baroque piece, Pachelbel's Canon in D, was an exquisite little touch arranged by the doctor, who remembered stories of Auschwitz. Her late great-uncle, Josef Mengele, told her how inmate orchestras would play classical music as they accompanied naked Jews to the gas chambers. It was a fitting parallel.

The pulley above Susan started to creak, and she felt a slight downward jerk. Von Ziegazar was lowering her toward the water—toward the hundreds of little jaws which would shred and devour her and her father. Desperately she looked out over the crowd. To her right were the amused and leering eyes of General Ayala and his ministers, who almost constituted the entire government of Paraguay. There was no sign of guerrilla activity. No sign of Raúl Caro. Only thousands of upturned faces waiting for the spectacle to begin.

There was another jerk on Susan's rope, followed by a

smooth and slow descent toward the water. Von Ziegazar was toying with her, alternately jerking the rope and lowering her.

Susan's eyes probed into her father's, searching for strength. He appeared serene and almost peaceful as he smiled at her.

"Remember, Susan, the only freedom we have is to choose how we will die. Don't give them the satisfaction of hearing you scream for mercy. Endure, girl, endure. It'll be over and we will both be in God's peace!"

The pulley stopped squeaking and the descent was more steady and faster. Susan's feet were within five feet of the frothy water. Her head jerked to the right. She frantically scanned the crowd. Where were they? Where was Raúl? Angel? Benito Salazar? In despair she craned her neck and looked beyond the plaza. Nothing. She continued to descend. The only sounds were the thrashing of the fish snapping at the dripping blood, and the strains of the Canon in D.

Joe Rockland sensed his daughter's panic. She musn't cave in. Not now! The barbarians of the Garduna must be denied this last victory! His voice becamc heard above the sound of the piranhas and the orchestra. It was a hymn; an old hymn learned in his youth; a hymn which sustained him in that Manchurian prison camp so many years ago.

> Lead kindly light, amid the encircling gloom
> Lead me thou on
> The night is dark and I am far from home
> Lead thou me on

Susan remembered and joined her father, singing lustily, almost frantically, her spirit merging with his.

> Keep thou my feet; I do not ask to see
> The distant scene—one step enough for me

Suddenly a shiver of panic coursed through her naked body. Her feet were being bombarded by the tiny bubbles of thrashing water. A shower of pain assaulted her as her toe touched the surface. A piranha leaped up and snapped at her, his little razor teeth gashing her big toe. Her father's feet were almost to the waterline. Her head fell on her chest in despair; her eyes transfixed on the frenzied water below. The spectators in the orchestra pits were sitting on the edges of their chairs, anticipating the slaughter.

A long burst of .50-caliber machine-gun fire was the signal for the revolution to begin. The tracers arched across the plaza and stitched their way along the bottom of the aquarium's plate glass. It was totally shattered, the weight of the water completing the destruction. The bloody, piranha-laden water cascaded into the enclosed pits, completely engulfing the Paraguayan and Gardunian leaders.

In the pits there was unrestrained chaos. Scores of gaudily uniformed officers and purple-and-white-robed Gardunians thrashed wildly about as the piranhas snapped and gnawed frantically. General Ayala slipped, stumbled, and disappeared beneath the water, only to reappear again, one side of his face completely chewed away. The gleaming whiteness of his cheekbone shone. Scores of piranhas clung to his uniform; others had their teeth firmly embedded in his flesh.

Submachine-gun fire raked the bodies in the water and in the crowds. Hundreds of shawls were discarded in the plaza, and old peasant clothes shucked off, revealing camouflaged guerrillas.

One of the Garduna guards raised his pistol and aimed it at Susan. A volley of 9mm bullets caught him in the throat, spinning him backward to the fish-strewn stage.

There was absolute pandemonium. Robed figures raced around frantically grabbing at hidden holsters. They fired wildly, blindly, into the crowds.

Carlos was in command, a smoking pistol in his hand. "Everyone who can hear me . . . into the administration building. To the weapons room!" He glanced up at Susan, who was dangling above him. He raised his weapon but did not point it at her. Her frightened but soft brown eyes locked into his and pleaded.

"Shoot her! Shoot her, nephew!" screamed the Hermano Mayor.

Carlos grabbed his uncle's arm and shoved him into the

building without looking back. He then bolted the heavy wooden doors.

The scene was indescribable from Susan's vantage point. To the right looked like a watery Dante's Inferno. The water had filled the orchestra pits like the moat of a castle. The little doors on the aisle side prevented most of the water from seeping out.

In one fell swoop, much of the leadership of the Garduna and the Paraguayan government had been slaughtered. The guerrillas' bullets continued to plow the water. Some of the refugees from the pits managed to scramble over the chairs and vault over the small plywood wall. They were ludicrous figures; running blindly, screaming maniacally, piranhas dangling from their flesh.

The small *voracianos* worked fast. The bubbling caldron inside the orchestra pits was already displaying the whitened bones of its victims. General Ayala was one of the first to die. The small fish had reduced most of the dictator to skeleton without devouring his uniform.

In the plaza, yelling, cursing, and screaming crowds ran amok, stampeding away from the submachine-gun-firing guerrillas. Blood ran in small streams down the cobblestones, causing the masses to slip and slide in their own gore.

A rescue team of five guerrillas vaulted onto the stage. Firing their weapons with one hand, they released the crank mechanisms with the other. The pulleys ran free and Susan and her father plummeted toward the stage. Susan screamed as she fell toward the glass-strewn floor which was littered with twitching, gnashing piranhas. Her screaming stopped abruptly as two strong arms caught and cradled her. Without opening her eyes, she put her arms around her savior and kissed him repeatedly. She opened them and blinked into the smiling eyes of Angel Caro.

Inside the administration building, a confused and angry knot of Gardunians clustered around Von Reinach. Von Ziegazar, her bandage off and her cheek wound bleeding profusely, screamed insults at the Gardún leader.

"This is your doing! Those are your people out there who have rescued the mulattos!"

"This is no time for recriminations, Hilda," panted the Hermano Mayor. "We're under attack and we have to get out of here. What do you suggest, Carlos?"

Von Reinach slipped a bandolier of submachine-gun magazines over his shoulder and picked up his weapon, a World War II German MP-40. He unlocked the door to a small weapons room and passed out guns and ammunition to those present.

"To Core Central. We'll take the tunnel to the warehouse and fight our way there. We'll radio Mariscal Estigarribia for help, then to the capital!"

The group fled to the basement, past the interrogation cell where Susan and her father had been chained, and to the far end of the corridor. Carlos and two Guaraní slid a heavy metal door out on rusty hinges. They entered the darkened tunnel and groped their way downward, under the plaza where the carnage was taking place. Ten minutes later, they reached a flight of stone stairs. They ascended and reached another heavy metal door. Slowly, carefully, Carlos and the two Guaraní put their shoulders to the door and pushed. It gave grudgingly and they entered into another basement—the basement of the building where the .50-caliber machine gun was emplaced.

The Gardunians climbed the steps to the ground-level floor and slipped into a large room filled with boxes and packing crates. To the left they could hear the sound of voices, which were interrupted by the chatter of the heavy machine gun. They stalked their way toward the weapon, guns drawn.

"Aughhh!" gasped Von Ziegazar. She had almost stumbled over the bodies of two guards, their throats slit from ear to ear. The rough plank floor was colored with dried blood. They had been dead two days and were beginning to putrefy.

"Silence, Hilda!" warned the Prophet. His white beard was now full of the drool of fear. "It is lucky for us that their weapon was firing when you screamed!"

From the slightly opened door, Von Reinach could see the

backs of the two guerrillas. One was feeding the ammunition belt, the other firing. There were no more in the building.

Carlos burst in, weapon spitting death. He silenced the gun crew, who died instantly, without even a death twitch. Outside the window, he had a commanding view of the plaza and the stage. The scaffolding erected for the execution was empty. Susan and her father had escaped. He was glad for that.

In the plaza the crowds had now fled to wherever they could find cover. Small groups of combatants on both sides were firing at each other from behind barricades. The plaza was littered with corpses and, by this time, the water had seeped from the orchestra pits—facilitated by the hundreds of bullet holes in the plywood structure.

"Señor Von Reinach!" shouted a guard. "Three of our armored cars have broken through to the right of the building. They have the insurgents pinned down with their machine guns!"

"Run for the cars! They will provide cover for our retreat to Core Central!" replied Carlos.

The Gardunians sprinted from the buildings and ran two streets over to the armored cars and a detachment of crouching soldiers, weapons at the ready. Several whipped their FALs around, covering the group as they approached.

"Don't shoot!" yelled a sergeant. "It's Señor Von Reinach and the Hermano Mayor!" The old Prophet was the last to arrive, limping and panting.

"Who's in charge here?" barked Carlos.

"I am, Señor Von Reinach. Sergeant Villa at your service."

"What have you learned of the insurgents, Sergeant? Who are they?"

"They are the guerrilla army of the Christian Socialist Action party. We found identification on one of their dead."

Carlos's eyes widened in surprise. "They—they are not Sandinistas? Christian Action? Damn! Damn those swine! How dare they!" muttered Carlos.

"What's our situation, Sergeant?"

"Desperate, Señor Von Reinach. It is truly desperate! The main security force is cut off from the plaza. We were able to break through, but their forces sealed us off. Guerrillas, hundreds of them, are breaking through from the surrounding countryside."

Two loud explosions nearby punctuated the plight of the defenders.

"Mortars!" cried a trooper. "They are using mortars against us!"

Carlos peered down the street, the one leading to the small river. "We are going to hole up at Core Central at the Casa del Swastika. The armory and radio transmitter are there. We can radio for help and hold out for a week if need be." He motioned to the sergeant. "Turn these vehicles around. Provide cover for us."

The armored cars roared into movement and rumbled down the cobblestoned streets, their machine-gun turrets traversing—spitting death at the insurgents who were starting to infiltrate the colony from the outskirts.

The cars came to a slight rise overlooking the muddy river. The swastika-shaped building was below, the three-story stone tower jutting skyward from the center of the twisted cross like a grotesque phallic symbol. It was still in Gardunian hands. Slightly to the left, lining the bluff, were hundreds of squat vinyl bladders. They were filled with the new, light Chaco crude oil which was starting to flow from the oil fields. They were stacked on pallets, ready to be rafted down the river to the Pilcomayo when the waters were swollen from the rainy season.

Inside of Core Central, a member of the security contingent scanned the slight bluff with his binoculars. He stopped and adjusted the focus. Von Reinach's face came into view.

"It's Señor Von Reinach and the Hermano Mayor!" he shouted excitedly. "Provide covering fire for them if they need it!"

The ugly snout of a machine gun projected from the semicircular window of the stone tower, the upper room where Susan had been cleansed and purified before the wedding had been transformed into a war room. The windows had been broken out and machine guns emplaced. On the top of the tower was an 81mm mortar. A variety of other weapons was stored in the armory below, along with the colony's ammunition and explosives.

The armored cars rumbled off the ridge and sped toward the Casa del Swastika as Carlos and his group hung on the sides. As they were halfway to the building complex, a group of guerrillas appeared on the bluff and began firing at the escaping vehicle. The machine gun from the tower spit at them, pinning them down, rendering their fire ineffective. Several well-aimed mortar rounds exploded along the rise, sending Salazar's men scurrying in all directions.

The cars roared into the protective, twisted arms of the swastika, and were positioned to provide maximum covering fire toward the bluff and points up and down the river.

Carlos and his group strode rapidly through the darkened corridors of the swastika-shaped complex toward Core Central. He was gratified to see that so many Gardunians, caught in the initial burst of the uprising, had the presence of mind to make it to Core Central. He entered the first floor of the stone tower. An officer of the security force rose and saluted smartly.

"Captain Castillo at your service, Señor Von Reinach. We have followed your progress from the bluff. We await your orders, sir!"

Upstairs, two stories above, they could hear the chatter of the machine guns and the *whump-whump* of the mortar.

"Have you radioed Asunción and Mariscal Estigarribia?" asked Von Reinach.

The captain's face clouded. "Communication with the capital has been cut off. We did receive a brief message from one of our people that an uprising had occurred in the capital. Troops of the air force and the navy have taken over the buildings of the Ministry of Telecommunications and Defense. The army is wavering. The commanders are waiting to see who will assume power since the death of General Ayala . . ."

"General Ayala—dead?" whispered the Prophet.

"Yes, Hermano Mayor. He and all of his ministers died on the plaza by . . . by the little fish." The officer stumbled on the words. "There are those here who were able to escape the slaughter on the plaza, but they saw it all. It was horrible!"

Von Ziegazar stared numbly at the captain, her handkerchief to her cheek, as she tried to stem the flow of blood.

"Then . . . then this is part of a national revolution?" asked Carlos.

"It is, sir. And the worst part is . . ."

"What could be worse than what is happening right here?" wailed the bearded Prophet.

The captain recoiled slightly, and spoke. "An assault force has attacked Fuerte Olimpo. Everybody is dead. Everything is burned to the ground. The refinery, the stored cocaine, everything!"

The group stared at the officer uncomprehending—unbelieving.

"Surely there is some mistake. They—they wouldn't dare!" sputtered the Hermano Mayor.

"They would, and they did!" snapped his nephew. "Is there any *good* news, Captain?"

"Yes. We have radioed the garrison at Mariscal Estigarribia. They are sending a relief column."

"Thank God!" said the old man as he slumped, then collapsed into a chair.

"So! Now it's a waiting game," muttered Carlos thoughtfully. "We hold out until relieved by the troops from Mariscal Estigarribia. The fate of the Holy Garduna is in their hands."

Susan examined the loose-fitting camouflage fatigues which draped her body in front of the full-length mirror in Estigarribia's office. She smoothed out the creases and turned, examining her reflected image from several angles.

"Would I look more chic with a beret and a gun hanging from my shoulder, Angel?"

Caro laughed. "You're lucky you're wearing anything. We set aside the smallest pair our quartermaster had, and even those are too large."

"But not by much. I'm thankful for anything after hanging in front of those creeps out there in my birthday suit."

The medicated bandages covering her back gave Susan

limited motion. Her arm and shoulder movements were stiff and awkward.

"I'd be happy with a hair shirt and burlap," piped Joe Rockland cheerfully as a guerrilla medic plastered his wrists with medicated cream.

"There. That should do it," he said in broken English. He finished taping the last piece of gauze in place.

Estigarribia's office soon became a command center. Benito Salazar, the Caro brothers, and several platoon leaders gathered around a hastily drawn situation map.

"Colonia Gardún is ours, gentlemen, except for some very important pieces of real estate," said Salazar. "The vehicle park here"—he jabbed a pointer at the map—"and a building complex by the river, which they call Core Central. It's their redoubt—their citadel. They can hold out there for some time."

"Comandante!" saluted a platoon leader. "We intercepted radio traffic between Core Central and the army garrison at Mariscal Estigarribia. The army has agreed to send reinforcements to relieve the Holy Garduna; in fact, they are on their way now!"

"Mother of God!" Salazar slapped his forehead with the heel of his hand. "The radio down there was supposed to be neutralized!"

"Evidently it wasn't. If the commandos at Mariscal Estigarribia link up with the armored cars in the vehicle park here, they can relieve Core Central," exclaimed Raúl.

"Can't . . . can't you just wait them out and when they see how desperate things are they'll surrender?" asked Susan.

"Time is of the essence, dear girl." Salazar smiled condescendingly. "The longer the leaders of the Garduna hold out, the more likely the armed forces of Brazil and Argentina will intervene. These two oil-poor giants have a great stake in keeping the Garduna in power. They see it as the guardian of Chaco oil, which is reserved for them. I am sure that the wisdom of intervention is being discussed right now in Brasília and Buenos Aires. We must eliminate what's left of the

Garduna right away and establish ourselves in Asunción as the new government.''

Suddenly all heads jerked skyward toward the sound of helicopters overhead.

''What . . . what the hell?'' sputtered Angel as he rushed outside. ''I didn't give Vitali or Gaduti permission to take off!''

''They're not ours. They're incoming!'' shouted Raúl over the din of the rotors.

They looked up and to the west. Five helicopters of the Paraguayan Navy were hovering for a landing. The Caros and Salazar hopped in a nearby pickup truck and sped off to the landing site.

The aircraft were ringed with suspicious guerrillas. Their weapons pointed at the countercult commandos as they emerged from the helicopters.

As the pickup slid to a stop, Raúl recognized the familiar faces of Nick Portumo, Eli Revvim, Puerter Detlefs, Jean Trucdeau, and Paul Redecker.

''This makes the party complete!'' shouted Raúl as he embraced Portumo. ''Hey, amigos! These are our reinforcements from the States. Sling your weapons!''

Raúl introduced the countercult team leaders to Angel as they roared back to the administration office.

''Your work down here training the commandos at the Escuela para Comando is well known at the Pentagon and Fort Bragg, Captain Caro,'' said Nick. ''We've been monitoring your efficiency reports ever since we conceived of this operation. For our sake, I hope you didn't do *too* good a job.''

There was nervous laughter from the group.

''I ripped off the top students for my rapid-reaction force. They're all anti-Garduna as well as my best men. I'm hoping that their loss will take some of the initiative out of the rest.''

The truck lurched to a stop in the plaza.

''It looks like there's been one hell of a bash here, Angel,'' exclaimed Portumo as he scanned the carnage. Beyond, toward the bluff, the sounds of battle could be heard.

''That was the easy part,'' said Angel. ''They weren't

ready for us. Now we've got to attack a fortified position called Core Central, which is down by the river. It's gonna be a son of a bitch to crack."

"Not to mention the rest of the colony's security force and the armored cars. If they link up with Core Central or the relieving force coming up from Mariscal Estigarribia, we're in deep shit! We can expect the Argentinian and Brazilian armies to stick their collective noses into our little revolution to act as mediators, of course," added Raúl.

"Of course," echoed Revvim. "So speed is critical in reducing Core Central and preventing the relief column from reaching Colonia Gardún, right, gentlemen?"

They tromped into the richly paneled office, and the new arrivals were briefed on the current situation.

Salazar studied a communiqué just handed to him by a courier. He read aloud: "Mariscal Estigarribia has mobilized soldiers from all of the outlying garrisons for the assault on Colonia Gardún. There are almost three thousand troops on the way."

Raúl rolled his eyes in a gesture of dismay. "That tears it; we *are* in deep shit!"

"Unless—unless something happens here, and we are awaiting the word," said Salazar dramatically.

"Where?" chorused several voices.

"Right here!" replied Salazar. He stabbed his pointer to a spot on the map, which was fifteen miles north of Asunción, at a small road-junction village called Hato Mayor.

Captain Luigi Palermo was a first-generation Paraguayan, the son of Italian immigrants who came into the country as part of a swarm of Italians after World War II. And, like many of the sons of immigrants, he was infinitely more ambitious than his native countrymen.

As the commander of the small backwater air base of Hato Mayor, he had reached the zenith of his military career. The system was rigged against him. All field-grade promotions—major or above—were reserved for those of Spanish or Guaraní descent. Of course the rules were always bent for the Germans. This dusty little base at the road junction of the tiny farming village of Hato Mayor would be the graveyard of his military career unless he received a phone call from a Mr. Paul Lancaster by one o'clock this afternoon.

Yesterday, the fourteenth, all communication had been cut off from the capital. The radio operator had picked up a mixed bag of radio traffic, mostly from army regimental commanders asking each other which political faction had sabotaged the communications facilities in the city. With General Ayala and his ministers out of town, no military commander wanted to take the awesome responsibility of marching his troops into Asunción to find out what was happening—or even to restore order, if necessary. Such a move would be construed by the other commanders as an attempted coup d'état, so every commander sat on his hands and waited.

Palermo jumped when assaulted by the double sounds of the wall clock chiming 1:00 and the ringing of the telephone. He breathed deeply and answered in an official manner. "Base commander's office, Captain Palermo."

"Is this a secure line, Luigi?" the American voice asked on the other end.

"Mr. Lancaster?"

"Yes, Luigi. Is it secure?"

"Yes."

"It is done. General Ayala and his entire staff have been killed at Colonia Gardún. The army regimental units are waiting to see who will step into the power vacuum. Everybody is afraid to move except the garrison at Mariscal Estigarribia. Our sources report that at this moment a relief column is driving out the main gate and heading for Colonia Gardún."

"And my mission remains the same?"

"Yes, Luigi. Interdict the column. Time is more critical now. I just received word from our Buenos Aires office that your neighbors are planning an intervention. There has been an ominous shifting of helicopter squadrons in both Argentina and Brazil toward your border. It is imperative that Dr. Salazar is proclaimed president of the new government within a few days—in the capital, if possible."

"And . . . and the agreement is the same?"

"Yes, Luigi. You will be chief of staff of the air force under Salazar's government. His word is his bond. Now, my friend, get cracking! Get some photo reconnaissance of what's happening out there and hit 'em! Remember, time is critical!"

The captain smiled slightly and hung up the receiver casually. He stood in front of the full-length mirror and examined himself. His sky-blue uniform looked so bare, so naked of medals or decorations. The Paraguayan Air Force, more than any of its sister services, had been denied martial glory. That would change! He took out a sketch pad and outlined an ornate military decoration, complete with propellers and palm fronds. It was the one that he would have made and award himself and his pilots for the Mariscal Estigarribia campaign, the battle which would save the fatherland!

He stood in front of the mirror again and stared disdainfully at the captain's bars which shone dully on his blue epaulets. He reached inside his desk drawer and removed a small plastic box, which was a gift from Paul Lancaster just last month. The captain repeated a ritual which had become an obsession during the past thirty days. He unpinned his captain's bars and replaced them with the two small gold stars of an air force vice-general, and stared admiringly into the mirror. He sighed, took off his jacket, and removed the stars. Not yet, but by this time tomorrow—or the day after—he would be able to stop playing games. No more fantasizing or playacting. The promotion would be real.

Palermo walked over to the public address system on the wall and flipped on the switch. He grabbed the microphone excitedly and spoke, his words reverberating from the several loudspeakers throughout the base complex.

"All pilots and armorers report to hangar number one immediately. God save the fatherland!"

Within minutes the sleepy little aerodrome of Hato Mayor was a flurry of activity. Aircraft were wheeled out of hangars. Rockets, bombs, and napalm canisters were affixed to the wings of the aged but functional and effective planes.

Inside of hangar number one, Captain Luigi Palermo—the future leader of Paraguay's air force—was explaining, in a dramatic scenario, the glories which awaited the pilots of Hato Mayor.

XXIV.

Nick adjusted the focusing knob on his binoculars and scanned the complex of low gray buildings down by the river. Guns jutted from every window. More armored cars had broken through the guerrillas and found sanctuary in the protecting arms of the twisted concrete cross. By midafternoon, most of the effective combatants of the Holy Garduna had found their way to Core Central and had brought their weapons with them. It had become a formidable, if not impregnable, fortress.

"Why didn't we have some intelligence on the bloody place?" moaned Puerter Detlefs, automatically flinching as a machine gun cut loose nearby.

Salazar ran up in a half crouch and flopped down beside them. His large bristling mustache was caked with red dust. "Gentlemen, I have some news which you will not want to hear." His brown eyes were large and anxious.

Portumo leaned his head on his elbow and squinted at the guerrilla chieftain. "Whip it on us, mate. Bad news is better than none at all."

"We have received word from Asunción that our people have a very tenuous control over the key facilities they have captured. If I cannot declare victory here and proclaim my presidency, the Fourth Infantry Regiment will march in and declare martial law. Colonel Ramírez, the commander, has been promised assistance by Argentine forces."

"And those blokes down there"—Nick jabbed a finger at the Casa del Swastika—"are mucking things up for us."

"That's not all," Salazar panted. "We had a report from a patrol south of here. The relief expedition from Mariscal Estigarribia is speeding north toward us. An estimated three thousand combat troops are in the column."

"Motorized?" asked Detlefs.

"Yes. All in trucks, jeeps, and armored cars."

"Do they have air cover or a helicopter reconnaissance capability?" the South African asked again.

"No." Salazar's big mustache twitched into a smile. "'That is one thing we have going for us. Angel saw to that. We have five of their helicopters here, and the other five are with the rapid-reaction force held in reserve a few miles from here."

Several mortar rounds fired from the stone tower exploded along the bluff and scattered Salazar's troops.

"Damn!" muttered Portumo. "What's the situation at Hato Mayor? Do we have an air force yet?"

"No word. Radio communication has been chaotic between here and the capital," replied Salazar.

Eli Revvim and Patty Benson slid in beside the trio on the edge of the bluff.

"Wow!" exclaimed Patty, looking at the fortified complex. "We didn't exactly figure on this, did we?"

"No, dear girl, we didn't," answered Nick through clenched teeth.

"How . . . how are we going to take it, Nick?" asked the blue-eyed blonde, her hair falling around her cheeks. "Frontal assault?"

Salazar rubbed his chin thoughtfully, a faraway gleam in his eyes. "I see no other way. A frontal assault by determined men would create confusion in their ranks and cause them to panic."

"That's sheer madness!" blurted Detlefs. "You would sacrifice hundreds for nothing!"

"For nothing, señor?" Salazar's eyes were now blazing with indignation. "Our army is forging a new and better nation. Our casualties, so far, have been ridiculously low. A final cataclysmic struggle to save the fatherland demands a heroic attack. A revolution without martyrs is shallow. We must show the world that we are not afraid to die!''

The foreigners exchanged disgusted glances. Salazar's strange logic was an affront to their rational military minds.

''What about a night attack, Dr. Salazar?'' Eli asked softly in a controlled voice.

''A night attack? Approach the enemy like thieves in the night? No! The enemy and the world must witness the bravery of our troops! We will not go skulking around in the darkness!''

''You might want to confer with Angel and Raúl before doing this, comandante,'' responded Detlefs.

Salazar exploded in anger, his mustache bristling like the fur on a frightened cat. ''The advisory phase of our movement is over! We are eternally grateful to the Caro brothers for their assistance; but now it is *I*, the future president of Paraguay, who must provide the generalship for the final struggle. It must *never* be said in the future history books of our nation that I left the winning of the last battle to foreigners.''

The once-gentle ex-professor of political science stood up and struck a near-Napoleonic pose as bullets from the fortified complex plowed the dirt less than fifty feet away. His eyes developed a hypnotic stare, almost as if they were envisioning the climactic battle to follow. ''It must be said by my countrymen, forever, that I, Benito Salazar, General of the Revolutionary Armies, was the sole savior of the fatherland.''

To the two guerrillas perched on the forward slope of the hill near the narrow pass, which flanked the Mariscal Estigarribia–Colonia Gardún road, the motorized column looked like a gigantic writhing snake.

''It seems to go on forever, Captain Caro,'' said the younger of the pair into the mike of the portable field radio. ''I estimate that they are twenty miles away. From up here I can barely make out individual vehicles with the naked eye. It looks like one continuous line.''

The other guerrilla swept the column with his binoculars.

"There are over a hundred and twenty vehicles from what I can see. Tell him that," he said.

The radio operator repeated the words and signed off.

Angel switched frequencies on his radio and grimaced slightly. He would soon be giving the order for the attack on his former students—by his former students. He sighed slightly and pushed the send button on the microphone. Thirty miles away, tucked into a protective ravine, Filippo Gaduti tuned in Angel's voice.

"Gaduti? Caro here. This is the big moment for our rapid-reaction force."

"Great!" responded the helicopter pilot enthusiastically. "We're tired of sitting on our asses while you fellows are having all of the fun. The men are primed and ready to move out. The news of the defeat of the Garduna has had a tremendous impact on the men."

Angel swallowed hard and winced, leafing through the hurriedly written reports, brought by panting messengers, on the buildup of power in the concrete fortress. "Well, let's not proclaim victory just yet, my friend. There is still a lot to be done. Vitali's squadron will join you. Your ten helicopters should be enough to transport the men . . ."

"To the same coordinates we agreed upon, Captain?"

"Yes. Just north of the pass. You can make the approach and land without them seeing you. Your men can be in position within fifteen minutes after landing."

"Fine. We've gone over this operation a dozen times. Each man knows his duty, Captain.

"For God and fatherland!" barked Gaduti on the other end of the communication.

"Yeah," slurred Angel wearily. "For God and fatherland."

Major Hermano Busch stood in the turret of his vintage British-built Saladin armored car as it crunched over the gravel toward the pass between the stunted hills some five miles distant. He looked back and adjusted the camouflaged silk scarf around his neck. He poked a stray corner of his scarf into his black leather German-style tanker's jacket. His brownish-green eyes showed the pride with which he viewed the long line of vehicles stretched out behind him. There were trucks, jeeps with rocket launchers, and armored cars. It was his first battle command.

He thought of his grandfather, a former tank commander of Rommel's Afrika Korps. How similar the Chaco must be to North Africa, he pondered. His gaze fell on the barren, slightly inclining dry scrubland, which tilted toward the low hill ahead of the convoy.

Hermano Busch had often had fantasies of himself as a latter-day Rommel. *And why not? The Chaco was created for armored warfare, and I, Major Hermano Busch, could be its greatest practitioner if Paraguay had its own version of an Afrika Korps. After the relief of Colonia Gardún, I will have my chance. When the powers-that-be see how skillfully I deploy and utilize the armored cars in support of the commandos, they'll listen to my request for armor. It is recognized by all who studied the Chaco War that if either side had tanks in that bloody stalemate they would have been decisive.*

The latter-day Rommel turned and stared at the pass which loomed before him. It was less than two miles away now. He took out a flare pistol and fired in the air. A purple puff of smoke blossomed about a hundred feet above his vehicle.

The convoy stopped in place, except for Busch's Saladin and the other vehicles, which carried 175 troops. The reconnaissance element pulled away from the halted convoy and sped toward the pass.

Hermano Busch could not hear them over the roar of his engine, but he could see them: seven tiny specks winging in from the east. They were coming in fast—out of the sun. He squinted against the brightness as the specks became larger, taking the form of silver messengers of death. Tiny flames flickered from their wings.

The converted T-6 trainers screamed over the reconnaissance element, ignored it, and swooped upon the convoy. Its .30-caliber bullets ripped through the canvas tops of the trucks, shredding metal and the human cargo inside. Seconds later, six vintage American-made F3D jets swished in and descended upon the stunned column. Busch watched in transfixed horror as oblong canisters tumbled from the bellies of the jets. They impacted in front of the lead truck and seemed to rebound along the entire length of the convoy, transforming themselves into gigantic lengths of yellow-blue flame.

Helpless tears of rage coursed down the major's cheeks as his command was consumed first by machine-gun fire, then napalm, and now by rockets, as the aircraft banked for their next approach.

"Major!" urged his executive officer. "There is nothing we can do! We must get to the hills and save what's left of the column!"

The remnant of the relief convoy lurched ahead and sped toward the pass as the planes from Hato Mayor completed their grisly task.

Hidden in the bushes along the hillsides which flanked the road, the ambush force of the rapid-reaction force lay in anxious anticipation as they waited to finish the mission of annihilation.

Angel and Raúl lay in a shallow depression just behind the edge of the bluff. It was 3:30 in the afternoon. A slight cooling breeze from the northeast was blowing off the small river. To their left, lined up in three ranks, were a thousand guerrillas of Dr. Salazar's Socialist Christian Action Army. They were lightly armed with the weapons which they had used in the initial assault on Colonia Gardún. Emplaced along the bluff were five light machine guns and the heavy .50-caliber which was used to shatter the piranha tank—an act which signaled the beginning of the revolution. With this force, Salazar hoped to capture the Casa del Swastika.

Puerter, Eli, Jean Trucdeau, and Patty Benson joined the Caros. It was clear that the "foreign advisers" were not welcome in this battle, the glorious, cataclysmic battle to save the fatherland.

"This is a side of the good professor we hadn't noticed before, eh, Raúl?" commented Angel.

"Yeah, his Napoleonic side. What's the old saying? Power corrupts men?"

"And absolute power corrupts men absolutely," added Eli.

"I think we're getting a glimpse of Salazar's future presidential style," he added as he watched the swaggering guerrilla chieftain strut among his men, offering words of final encouragement before the assault.

"He told me in no uncertain words to butt out when I suggested a night infiltration with demolition teams to reduce part of the complex to rubble so our blokes could get in and clean them out," said Nick.

"Yes, the advisory phase is clearly over," sighed Raúl, "and we're gonna watch this egomaniac waste it all. Dammit! They're good troops! I brought them from nothing—*nothing*—to a first-class little army, and Salazar's gonna dash them against the walls of that concrete swastika!"

The screech of a police whistle pierced the cool sunny air. It was a splendid afternoon for photography, and Salazar's three unit photographers were positioned to memorialize the coming battle on film. One photographer caught the chieftain in a dramatic pose as the whistle on its lanyard fell from his lips. In one hand he held a pistol, in the other a large swordlike machete. He was wearing crisp, newly starched combat fatigues. The three gleaming gold stars, freshly pinned on his epaulet, were visible indications of his self-awarded rank: General of the Revolutionary Armies.

"Forward, *muchachos!* For God and fatherland!" the ex-professor barked.

A thunderous roar spilled from a thousand throats as the guerrillas leaped from their positions and vaulted over the lip of the bluff. The machine guns sputtered sharply, trying to provide covering fire as they aimed over the heads of the troops, concentrating their fire on the ugly black barrels of the Gardún weapons, which poked out the windows of the fortress.

All three ranks of Salazar's men were now running wildly down the hill below the bluff. Machetes flailing in their hands caught the rays of the sun. Their fists clutched automatic weapons.

There was no response from the Casa del Swastika. The guerrillas were closing the distance rapidly.

Suddenly from among the twisted arms of the concrete

buildings, five armored cars roared into the open and formed a ragged line along the riverbank. Five 37mm cannons were cranked on their turrets and aimed toward the charging mass of men.

Still, they did not fire.

There was no dispersion of Salazar's forces, no running for cover and concealment, in spite of the deadly presence of Von Reinach's machines.

"I . . . I can't believe this!" stammered Raúl in frustration as he watched the screaming guerrillas run toward the mouth of the cannons. "It's . . . it's like everything I've taught them is thrown away: cover, concealment, stealth. It's all being forgotten."

"Like the French Army in the early part of World War I," murmured Trucdeau softly. "Splendid cavalry charges against the entrenched machine guns. As one observer said, it is beautiful, but it is not war. We had to learn the hard way."

"At least you had some manpower in reserve," said Nick. "Perhaps what we're witnessing is some crazy Latin American need for macho . . ."

Nick's statement was shattered by the roar of cannons and the chattering of dozens of machine guns and automatic weapons fire from the fortress. Well-aimed mortar fire from the stone tower fell among Salazar's men, their shrapnel bursts cutting wide, circular swaths of death in the charging ranks.

It was slaughter, as the "foreign advisers" knew it would be. The issue was never in doubt. The entire operation defied all the rules of rational military logic.

The countercult commandos watched with a mixture of horror, awe, and despair. Raúl hung his head and wept.

Hundreds of guerrillas had been killed or wounded, caught in the open in the murderous fire. Many stood their ground, firing their puny weapons toward the armored cars. One of them actually made it to one of the vehicles and was frantically slashing at its oversize tire with his machete until he was cut down.

"Back to the bluff! Back to the bluff, *muchachos*! Bugler, blow retreat!" screamed the *comandante*.

A young guerrilla blew a series of sharp, ragged notes from

the old battered brass bugle, which hung around his neck by a rope. The notes pierced the sound of gunfire, and the guerrillas turned and fled. They scrambled up the hill, clutching the branches of the low scrub, pulling themselves to safety. Many left their weapons behind.

The bullets of the Gardunians followed the retreating guerrillas, plowing into their backs. Dozens fell and slid down the hill, leaving bloody trails.

"Grenade launchers! Bring those damned launchers over here!" yelled Nick. "All of them!"

Eighteen commandos from Nick's assault force reported with the launchers.

"Spread yourselves along the bluff. Use smoke, purple or red, if you've got it! Lay down a screen between Salazar's men and the armored cars and the fortress!"

Within minutes a thick purplish-red pall of smoke obscured the vision of the Gardunian gunners. The bleeding, stumbling survivors staggered over the edge of the bluff, exhausted and dispirited, into the shallow depression. The screams and moans of the dying and wounded echoed from the hillside, filling thc cordite-saturated afternoon air.

The smoke cleared and revealed the corpse-strewn hillside. Here and there a hand moved or a leg twitched. Every movement was followed by a burst of machine-gun fire from the fortress as the wounded were dispposed of by the gunners of the Holy Garduna.

Inside the jutting stone tower overlooking the battlefield, Von Reinach was jubilant. He had every reason to be, as he looked out at the blood-drenched scene before him. "What supreme idiocy!" he smirked. "So typical of their *Untermensch* mentality. They impulsively threw away their victory when it was within their grasp."

"And the news from the capital is good too, nephew!" said the Hermano Mayor. "The Fourth Infantry Regiment is ready to march into the city and declare martial law when Colonel Ramírez is assured that the guerrillas will not succeed. And what more proof will he need than this?" The old man swept his hand toward the corpse-littered hill.

"Any news of the relief column yet?" Von Reinach snapped at the radio operator.

"None, brother Von Reinach. Evidently they are maintaining radio silence."

"A wise decision," mumbled the Garduna leader, his thoughts elsewhere. His pale blue eyes scanned the bluffs. Somewhere beyond the bluffs, still in the colony perhaps, was Susan. How he ached for her! She would be in their marriage bed now if that damned Von Ziegazar . . . ! But that was behind him now. Had he, alone, discovered her genetic "irregularities" after their marriage, he would have overlooked them. He was certain he could have done that, so deep was his love for this beautiful *chivato*. Perhaps he would have even destroyed the evidence. I'll never know, he pondered.

But all that was past. She had been exposed publicly and he would have had to witness her execution in spite of, and perhaps because of, his feelings for her. Such was the law of the Garduna, and the law was supreme. Everybody must bow to it and submerge their personal feelings in deference to the law.

Carlos swept his binoculars over the battlefield looking for signs of life. To his right he caught the gleam of the sun's rays off something bright. He focused. It was a bugle! From behind a clump of brush in a ravine, which ran from the top of the bluff almost to the fortress, was a hand which clutched a battered brass bugle.

"Gunner! Direct your fire over there," he said, pointing, "toward that reflected light." He focused again. He could see the movement of several more wounded guerrillas.

"Why have we left that little pocket of survivors? Are we saving them for something special? Gun them down!"

"Ah, wait, nephew. Hold your fire, gunner," said the Hermano Mayor.

"What is this, uncle?" asked Von Reinach.

The old man pointed with a gnarled finger. "Just above the wounded on the edge of the bluff are the oil storage bladders. I had the gasoline reserves from the colony stored there, too. I had over a hundred empty bladders filled."

Von Reinach gasped. "The gasoline? Uncle, how could you do such a thing? What possessed you?"

"The gasoline storage area at the colony was so unsightly and it smelled bad. It could be seen from the plaza and I felt that it would be an eyesore during the wedding. So I ordered it moved to the bluff. It was the logical place, and who could have foreseen the attack by Salazar's troops?"

Von Reinach put his hand on the gunner's shoulder as he began to sight along the barrel toward the glint in the ravine.

"No! Forget my order. A stray bullet could set off the gasoline. Let's hope that our enemies don't learn of this." He stared, frowning at the thousands of black vinyl bladders which lined the bluff and loomed over the little pocket of wounded.

Salazar was adamant. "The next assault will ensure the annihilation of the enemy! You will not rob me of victory!" he shouted.

"Benito! Look at the hillside! The cream of your army has been thrown away by your senseless attack."

"Senseless? Senseless, Raúl? No! Those dead are the martyrs of the Revolution! Their blood has sealed our victory! God has demanded that we prove our faith in His guidance of our movement by the shedding of blood. We have done this! Now he will give us victory! He will deliver us if we show more faith!"

Raúl exploded in anger. "You . . . you incompetent egomaniac! When I found you, you couldn't even lace up a pair of combat boots, let alone lead an army! I won't stand here and let you waste your soldiers!"

Raúl started to unsnap his holster, but Salazar anticipated his move. A submachine gun suddenly appeared in his hands. "I will kill all of you if necessary. It would be regrettable, but nobody—*nobody*—will rob me of my hour of destiny!" His eyes were glazed from fatigue and slightly out of focus. Two of his bodyguards ran up, guns pointed at the little knot of foreigners.

"Cover them while I form the ranks. If they attempt to interfere, then kill them!" snarled the guerrilla chieftain.

• • •

Patty Benson had left the little group thirty minutes before. She watched the slaughter from the left side of the guerrilla assembly area with feelings of helpless rage. She lay on her stomach, peering out over the battlefield. Her tears formed dusty little pools as they plopped onto the fine red earth. After the last of Salazar's men struggled up the hill, she put her head in her arms and cried.

She was surprised by the sound of a faint bugle call. It was barely audible, but it *was* a bugle call. She peered through her binoculars and saw the face of the young guerrilla who had blown retreat. Several more wounded were clustered around the youngster.

Again—a faint bugle call. It was weaker now. The notes slurred together; no longer were they crisp or distinct. This time she could hear the cries of the wounded.

She ran up to Salazar, who was pacing back and forth, forming his reluctant troops into four ranks. "Comandante! There's a pocket of wounded about two hundred and fifty meters to our left! They are in a small ravine. A rescue detachment can reach them if you provide covering fire! I'm willing to . . ."

"No!" roared the guerrilla chieftain. "I will not waste ammunition to save those who are consigned to die!"

"Consigned to die!" Patty yelled back at the red-faced *comandante*. "One of them is your bugler! He can't be more than fourteen!"

"Nobody in my army is too young to die!" shrieked Salazar. "Now, get out of my way or you'll join your friends over there!" He pointed a shaking finger at the two guerrillas who covered the foreigners.

Patty shuffled back toward the edge of the bluff, clearly shaken from Salazar's outburst. She looked back at the sullen guerrillas being formed into listless ranks as Salazar raved and exhorted them to superhuman effort.

Then she saw the red cross on the large canvas first-aid pack, which was leaning against a large rock. Alongside was an M-79 grenade launcher and a bandolier of shrapnel and white phosphorous grenades. Deftly she slung the strap of the pack over her shoulder, picked up the launcher and bandolier, and trotted toward the edge of the bluff. She gauged the distance to the wounded. Yes! She could make it, even without covering fire. There must be a reason why the Gardunians hadn't fired at them. She saw the long line of black bladders which lined the bluff and brooded over the wounded.

Of course. They're afraid of puncturing the bladders and wasting their precious supply of new oil from the fields, she thought. She leaped over the lip of the bluff and dashed toward the wounded guerrillas.

Nick saw her and rushed to the edge of the bluff. "Patty! No! Get back here! You'll never make it!"

Salazar's men broke ranks and rushed to the edge, watching as the young blonde raced toward the ravine.

A solitary machine-gun burst was heard from the Casa del Swastika. The hundreds of witnesses along the bluff saw the Benson girl stagger, fall, then wrench herself upward. She continued running while bullets plowed the earth around her, creating little puffs of red dust.

The firing stopped even though she was in a direct field of fire.

"Stop firing!" barked Von Reinach. "She is too close to the gasoline bladders!"

Patty tumbled into the slight depression where the wounded lay. The young bugler's face was wreathed in smiles. "A magnificent sprint, señorita. Are . . . are you hurt?"

She yanked her fatigue blouse out of her shorts and looked at her stomach. Her fingers probed the three bloody holes stitched neatly across her abdomen. Then came the heavy bleeding—in spurts—almost as if an artery had decided to wait to burst until she reached her destination. The guerrillas looked away sorrowfully. They knew that her wounds, like theirs, were fatal.

Patty knew, too, and lay gasping. Blood emerged from her mouth and nose in frothy bright red bubbles. She watched with numb fascination as the blood streamed from her stomach wounds and formed a tiny river which flowed into another but larger river of liquid. She reached over and dipped her fingers in it and sniffed. Oil! Mixed with gasoline.

Her eyes traced the flow of the oil river upward. There were almost a dozen holes from stray bullets in the bladders above. Some were leaking gasoline, some were leaking the tan light Chaco crude oil from the new wells. The natural slope and pitch of the ravine caused the mixture to flow downward and veer to the right toward the concrete complex below.

Patty glanced at the wounded. They were beyond help, as she was. To her left, up on the bluff, she could see the first of Salazar's troops lining up for their final, suicidal assault.

"How many weapons do we have here, amigos?" she asked in short, panting breaths.

The young bugler pulled two automatic rifles and several bandoliers over to her. "This is all we have, señorita," he answered in halting English.

Patty propped herself against a large bush. In a sitting position she faced upward—toward the bladders. She rammed in a fresh magazine and braced the rifle between her legs. She squeezed the trigger and arched the weapon back and forth, pumping round after round into the long line of bladders. One magazine depleted, she inserted another.

"What . . . what is she doing?" stammered Hilda Von Ziegazar.

"Just as I feared!" moaned Von Reinach.

"Gunner! Direct your fire against her!"

"But, Señor Von Reinach, the bladders! At this distance I . . ."

"Silence, you idiot!" He slapped the machine gunner across the top of the head with an empty bandolier. "Do as you are told!"

Nervously the gunner pulled the trigger and watched the puffs of dust dance along the ridge top before the slugs disappeared into the bladders, tearing huge oblong holes in the black vinyl.

"Lower! Lower, you swine! Here—let me!" Von Reinach grabbed the hapless gunner by the collar and spun him off his stool onto the concrete. He aligned the weapon below the stored oil, making adjustments on the sight.

The first burst of fire caught the young bugler in the chest, killing him instantly. The second caught Patty in the arm and entered her back on the right side, puncturing a lung.

She was growing weaker from loss of blood, which now flowed freely in a steady stream, mixing with the ever-increasing river of oil and gasoline. She turned her head slowly to her left and saw the first of Salazar's army scramble over the bluff to start their final assault. With a tremendous effort, she grabbed the grenade launcher and inserted a white phosphorous grenade cartridge into the chamber.

The young countercult commando closed her eyes, braced the butt of the launcher in the hard red earth, and fired. The grenade arched gracefully up toward the brooding line of black vinyl and exploded in a shower of white.

It started slowly: little fires along the long black line. The crude oil caught in little sputtering flickers and then the gasoline exploded with a deafening roar.

To Von Reinach and the Gardunians who watched from the fortress, it looked as if the entire bluff had erupted in a gigantic sheet of oily orange flame.

Patty Benson sat still, the grenade launcher still braced between her bloody legs, as the bladders exploded above her. The flaming liquid began its descent. Streaming slowly at first, it soon became a rushing tidal wave of fiery destruction.

The guerrillas stopped in mid-assault and watched, awestruck, as the flaming avalanche roared toward the girl in the ravine. Their last glimpse of her was when the young American ex-cultist wrenched herself into a standing position and faced the tidal wave of flames with a grenade launcher held high in a final act of defiance. Then she was engulfed.

"Holy Mother of God!" whispered Salazar as the river of flame was channeled by the ravine toward the swastika. He knelt on the hillside and crossed himself. His soldiers followed suit.

The flaming ocean dashed itself against the walls of the Casa del Swastika, breaking through doors and windows and streaming down the paneled corridors, turning the twisted concrete cross into a towering torch.

The fiery liquid was everywhere. It seeped under closed doors, crashed through panes of glass, and set off small but deadly secondary explosions of ammunition as they were ignited throughout the complex.

Two of Von Reinach's men bounded down the stairs of the stone tower, several steps at a time, and lunged for the heavy metal door which separated the armory on the first floor from the adjacent corridor. They were met by a cascading wall of flame which enveloped them, flooding the room and setting fire to the hundreds of wooden crates stored haphazardly on wooden pallets.

From two thousand feet it looked like the visitation of the wrath of God on Sodom and Gomorrah.

Courtney Davenport peered out the Plexiglas window of his C-130. Behind his aircraft were three identical planes, all winging their way to Colonia Gardún to evacuate Susan, the commandos, and the Garden Children who were stranded in the colony.

The first thing which assaulted Davenport's vision as he peered into the shallow valley was the huge concrete swastika, squatting along the riverbank like an obscene gray spider. He had been informed of the battle by Paul Lancaster's radio in Asunción, and knew that the complex below was the temporary refuge of Von Reinach and the remnants of the Holy Garduna.

His aircraft were greeted by an orange sheet of flame which seemed to consume an entire ridge line below. The flames billowed into a pillar of fire, and a flaming river of liquid, like the fiery finger of God, stabbed into the gray swastika.

The planes bounced and yawed wildly as the force of the explosion hit them. The center of the swastika disappeared in a gigantic cloud of flame and smoke.

"Good Lord!" cried Davenport as he stared at the conflagration. "I'm witnessing the revenge of the Almighty! Everybody . . . get over here quickly. See this!"

Andrea and the medical evacuation team stumbled across the aisle of the undulating aircraft and stared incredulously at the devastation below.

"It's like . . . like a scene from the Old Testament, Courtney!" exclaimed Andrea.

"Vengeance is mine, saith the Lord," echoed Davenport.

"Joseph! Susan! It's so good to see you safe and sound!" cried Courtney as he threw his long arms around them.

"I . . . I still can't believe this!" cried Joe Rockland as the last of the C-130s taxied off Colonia Gardún's small runway. "How . . . How did you . . ."

"How did I know what was happening down here, Joseph?" Davenport chuckled. "You can't keep an operation this big a secret, especially in Tulsa."

"Courtney, how's Olivia?" Susan asked.

"I'll let you ask Andrea. Oh, you don't know her. Andrea, come over here and meet Susan Rockland!" shouted Courtney above the roar of the aircraft engines.

The Hungarian psychologist ran across the tarmac, holding her thick honey-blond hair with one hand as the breeze from the jets whipped up a small windstorm.

"Susan Rockland . . . Andrea Macranskia. Andrea is Olivia's deprogrammer and therapist," said Davenport.

Andrea smiled and took Susan's hand.

"So you're the young lady who has turned this part of the world upside down." Andrea laughed huskily.

"Nick and the others have told me so much about you, Andrea, that I feel I know you already," exclaimed Susan. "I guess you'll have your hands full with the Garden Children after you get them back to the States."

Susan's expression became serious. "How's Olivia?"

Andrea smiled reassuringly and patted Susan's elbow. "Olivia is doing very well. She'll be completely recovered in, say, four or five months. There is a great deal of hatred and anger that she still has to deal with, but we can channel that into positive directions, hopefully, until it is dissipated."

Two strong arms suddenly grabbed Andrea from behind.

"Nick!" She fell into his arms, kissing him enthusiastically.

"Andi! You're the last person I expected to see down here!"

"Courtney talked me into it, darling."

"I didn't have to do much persuading." Davenport winked, shaking Nick's hand. "Nick, is that viper Von Reinach dead?"

"I don't see how he could have lived through the explosion at Core Central," answered Nick.

"Well, let's get over to that swastika place and poke around. I want to follow that river a little bit, too, and verify the death of these Garduna people. Susan! Joe! Would you come with me and identify some of these folks?"

"The Casa del Swastika is still burning out of control, but we can check along the river," said Nick.

"Nick, how's Patty?" asked Andrea.

The silence answered Andrea's question.

"Dead?" asked Davenport softly.

Susan nodded through her tears, biting her lower lip.

"Details?" asked Davenport again.

Nick told him the entire story.

Davenport brushed back his mane of silver-gray hair. His face was a mask of grave concern. "It will be hard on Roger. He'll survive. But, damn! This will be hard. I have the feeling that he anticipated this and has already accepted the possibility of her death." The voice of the tall senator trailed off to a near whisper.

"Let's get moving and meet the others," urged Nick. "We have a grisly little task awaiting us down by the river."

The heat from the burning concrete fortress was intense. The timber and plank roofing along the entire complex had caved into the interior of the walls, which added to the conflagration. The raging inferno trapped inside would have to burn itself out—and that could take days.

The little group picked up Salazar and others and walked downriver.

"If any bodies were blown into the river, the piranhas would have gotten them," said Detlefs.

"One of my men claimed to have seen several people jump

from the second floor of the stone tower and run along the roof toward the river just before the explosion," Salazar said.

"Then the bastard might still be alive," shouted Davenport over the roar of the flames nearby.

A few hundred feet downriver the evidence they were seeking began literally to pile up. Around a slight bend, the river was partially dammed by a jumble of logs and brush. A small pond formed behind the natural dam. The grisly evidence was soon discovered as the bodies of the Gardunians were sighted floating in the pond and lined up along the oily shoreline. The piranhas had started their work of destruction, but the heat and suffocation of the flaming liquid in the water killed the little fish.

Susan gasped. There, among the tangled debris, were the half-eaten bodies of the Hermano Mayor and Von Ziegazar. Other bodies were enmeshed in the dam among them. The flesh on the doctor's face was intact—the expression frozen into a contorted mask of pain and surprise. Portions of her skeleton gleamed from her shredded skin.

The little band worked their way around the shore of the corpse-laden pond, poking the barrels of their weapons into the bushes to look for the bodies of other Gardún leaders.

"If I never see this God-forsaken country again, it will be too soon," whispered Angel, mindful of Salazar's presence. "I'm going back with Davenport and lead a dull, unexciting life." He smiled at Susan and squeezed her hand.

They came upon the body of a man half out of the water. His hands were clawing at the muddy bank as he tried to pull himself out. He was immersed in the oil-blackened water from his waist down. The head turned slowly, painfully, as he heard the group approach.

"Von Reinach!" shouted Joe Rockland. "It's Von Reinach! He's alive!"

His electric-blue eyes focused on Susan. The familiar gleam flickered, then flamed as Susan recognized him.

"Carlos!" she cried, kneeling by his side in the ooze. She wiped the blood from his face.

Tears of pity filled her eyes as she looked upon his still handsome features. There were still feelings. Von Reinach sensed it and held out his hand—grasping hers. His breath came in short bloody bubbles. Davenport stared at them in silence.

"I . . . I love you, Susan, but it was the Law of the Garduna. The Law of the Garduna . . . always, the accursed Law. Always the Law." His voice became a whisper and died. His head fell back into the mud, his eyes staring vacantly at Susan.

Susan continued kneeling, her face buried in her hands as she rocked back and forth by the Gardún leader's body. She sobbed loudly.

"Well, I'll be damned!" snorted Angel in disgust. "After all this and she cries over that bastard."

Susan looked up, her face swollen with tears. "Angel. Have your men pull him out of the river and bury him. At least he deserves a Christian burial. Please!" she pleaded.

Angel spun on his heels and angrily walked away. The others, including her father, followed.

"No way, lady. If you still feel anything for that turkey, you can bury him yourself!"

Susan wiped her perspiring forehead, then grabbed the cult leader under the arms and started to pull. He wouldn't budge, his body held fast in the muck. She stood over his upper torso and lifted, breaking the suction, and pulled him toward dry land. It is strange, she thought. He is a large man, but he is so light. She closed her eyes and gave one final tug. The body slid out effortlessly.

Susan's unearthly shriek brought the others back at a dead run. She lay on the bank, unconscious, one arm draped around the shoulder of Von Reinach. The flesh of Von Reinach's body ended abruptly at his pelvis. The gleaming bones of his lower portion contrasted sharply with the oil-blackened mud of the riverbank.

The piranhas had completed only half their task.

Colonia Gardún was abandoned. The spectators who had come by the thousands to witness the wedding had fled to the hills. The Holy Garduna had been destroyed, and Benito Salazar's jubilant soldiers roared toward Asunción in commandeered buses and trucks. Salazar's countrymen, upon learning of his victory, were waiting to proclaim him as the new president of the country.

It was almost dark as the four C-130s, their human cargo crammed on board, roared down the colony's runway and lifted off.

Angel hadn't spoken to Susan since she pulled the Gardún leader's remains from the river. She stared silently and absently out the aircraft's small window as the plane clawed for altitude. It circled the low red bluffs which were now darkening in the rushing dusk. She could barely make out the red tiles on the roofs of the colony's buildings . . . her prison for almost a year.

Suddenly she felt Angel's presence beside her. His arm slipped around her waist and hugged her tenderly. She looked into his handsome, boyish face. His eyes smiled lovingly and somewhat sheepishly into hers. There was no need for apologies. He kissed her softly on the cheek. She leaned her head against his chest and continued to stare out the window.

Colonia Gardún was almost lost from view as Angel and Susan looked to the south. The colony rapidly disappeared beneath the plane's wing. The last glimpse they had of the shallow valley was that of a gigantic flaming swastika which lit up the Chaco sky.

The plane banked away and started to head north toward Tulsa—and home.

EPILOGUE

AUGUST 1995

When Courtney Davenport spoke to his God, it was usually from the Oval Office of the White House and, it was rumored, God usually did the listening.

Elected by a smashing, landslide victory in 1992, President Davenport was turning the cleanness of Tulsa into the cleanness of America.

He had given the electorate just about everything that he had promised in that hectic campaign of 1991–92. Unemployment had plummeted through massive public works programs and the dramatic expansion of the defense industry and the Armed Forces.

The crime statistics had fallen in every category. Crime was no longer a low-risk profession in Courtney Davenport's America.

The key to President Davenport's success was Paraguay. Paraguay, in the summer of 1993, had become the Saudi Arabia of the Western Hemisphere. A shrewd and powerful Benito Salazar had allowed his huge oil fields to glut the world market, destroying the economic power of OPEC. When the tidal wave of Paraguayan oil engulfed the world's economy, a domino effect had occurred. Gasoline prices tumbled and everything else followed suit. By 1991 inflation in the United States was a mere 3 percent.

President Davenport demanded payment for his effective measures. There was a price to pay, and most Americans seemed glad to pay it.

There was an erosion of personal and civil liberties, barely perceptible at first, and directed toward "undesirables." First, what was left of the cults were rooted out and prosecuted, and then came criminal organizations such as the Mafia. The perversion or absence of legality did not disturb most Americans; after all, "they had it coming." Also, these were unusual times which demanded unusual measures. President Davenport restored order out of chaos and put America back on the right track. Through similar means, a journalist recently remarked tongue in cheek, Benito Mussolini made the trains run on time in Italy, sixty years before.

As any loyal American could demonstrate, the proof of President Davenport's effectiveness as a national leader could be seen on any gasoline pump: eighty-three cents a gallon, the result of the American-Paraguayan connection.

Another Benito was making the trains, and everything else, run on time in his country.

President-for-life Benito Salazar stood on the low, long marble structure, the Tomb of the Martyrs, which held the 743 guerrillas slain in the suicidal assault six years before.

The Marshal of the Revolutionary Armies—one of his many titles—was considered by his countrymen as the Savior of the Fatherland, his favorite title. But his closest associates—those who were with him that September day in 1989 at 4:30 in the afternoon—knew that the real savior lay in the magnificent white sarcophagus perched on top of the long marble Tomb of Martyrs.

It was called the Tomb of La Muchacha Héroe, the girl hero. Inside were the charred remains of Patricia Benson, the "foreigner," the teenage countercult commando who made the ultimate sacrifice for Salazar's country. In the city cemetery, several miles from her tomb, were the remains of Roger Benson, her father, who committed suicide within hours after witnessing the massive public ceremony entombing his daughter's body.

The Armed Forces strutted down the Avenue of Martyrs to the lively blare of a large military band. The music was precise, professional, as was everything else in this, the new "Prussia" of the Western Hemisphere. It was another victory parade; one of many conducted in the past few years. The medals and ribbons the troops were wearing were real—awarded for tangible exploits. This parade celebrated the recent conquest of communist "Guevarist" Bolivia and the acquisition of a Pacific port for Paraguay.

Flanking the bemedaled Salazar were his two top generals, the Caro brothers: Raúl Caro, the General of the Army of the Pampas, and Angel Caro, the General of the Army of the Chaco. Raúl had conquered the communist Tupamarist nation of Uruguay several months before. Uruguay was occupied and proclaimed a province of Paraguay. Argentina traded a portion of her territory to Paraguay for a section of Uruguay which she had always coveted, thus giving Paraguay a contiguous land bridge to the Atlantic.

General of the Army of the Chaco Angel Caro beamed with pride as his victorious army thundered by. His lightning blitz had brought him to the gates of La Paz in weeks, instead of the predicted months. A week later, his army was poised on Chilean territory and demanded a corridor to the Pacific.

Brazil glowered at Chile, and Argentina mobilized a division of her best mountain troops in the Andes. The Santiago government swallowed its pride, negotiated a generous oil treaty, and gave Salazar a stretch of nitrate-rich seacoast which had been taken from Bolivia in the 1879 War of the Pacific.

Revolutionary Paraguay stretched from sea to sea, providing a much-needed buffer between the northern and southern tier of nations in South America, and especially Brazil and Argentina, the two regional powers. Chaco oil, whose reserves were estimated to be greater than those of Saudi Arabia and Kuwait combined, fueled the burgeoning industrial might of these two oil-hungry giants. Paraguay, it seemed, had something for everybody.

Susan Caro was bored. She stifled a yawn as she sat stiffly on top of the tomb while her husband reviewed his troops.

Her quiet life as Angel's wife was shattered when Courtney Davenport became president. The Caro brothers were requested to return to Paraguay as military "advisers." They were ready. Three years of civilian life had created a restlessness which threatened the stability of Susan's marriage; besides, the promotion from captain in the U.S. Army Reserves to general in the Paraguayan army was a tremendous inducement.

The DAVROCK Corporation was involved in the transformation of the Chaco on a monumental scale. Even though the "Rock" portion of the company had been bought out—Joe Rockland had split with his partner two years before—the name remained the same.

Paul Lancaster took the salute as the army stomped by. Every soldier, eyes riveted to the right to the reviewing stand, knew who he was. Paul's title was Minister of the Interior and, along with the usual police functions, his job was to provide land, farm implements, and employment to the veterans of Salazar's armies.

And the program Lancaster initiated worked well. His untiring efforts, with DAVROCK and U.S. Government assistance, had transformed the Chaco into a land approaching the Garden of Eden. Massive irrigation projects had created a breadbasket. A new class of small farmers emerged, involved in intensive scientific agriculture. The truck gardens of the Chaco became the envy of South America.

Olivia Lancaster had her role, too, in the power structure of Salazar's government. She was the director of Immigration and National Sacrifice. It was said that the zeal with which this hard-eyed, ruthless American blonde carried out her duties was not restricted to immigration and resettlement, but included "reeducation" as well. There were persistent rumors that Señora Lancaster, known to some as the Bitch of the Chaco, maintained a camp in the northwestern part of the Chaco in a place formerly known as La Cuna. Those who were suspected of "unorthodox" beliefs underwent the unpleasantries of reeducation there.

It was a symbiotic relationship: Paraguay needed the manpower and the United States was saturated with aliens. Under the new Alien Resettlement Act, President Davenport emptied the barrios and Hispanic ghettos of America's major cities and transported them to Paraguay. The alternative was prison.

They came by the hundreds of thousands: alien Hispanics and Puerto Ricans. They filled the regiments of Salazar's army and completed the work of conquest. When Paraguay's borders were finally established, Salazar offered his "volunteers" to such countries as South Africa and assisted in the recapture of Namibia.

The armored formations roared by with the very latest of U.S.-made main battle tanks and armored personnel carriers. Brigadier General Hermano Busch, commander of Paraguay's Trans-Andean Armored Corps, grinned with satisfaction as his tank commanders, dressed in black leather jackets and black berets, saluted him from their turrets. He had come a long way since that day almost six years before when he was captured, bleeding and dazed, after an ambush by Caro's rapid-reaction force. Now the latter-day Rommel had his own, slightly smaller version of an Afrika Korps, which he deployed with great skill from the altiplano of Bolivia to the pampas of Uruguay. His grandfather would be proud—perhaps envious—if he could see him now.

Luigi Palermo's jets screamed low over the armored formations. They were the latest, most sophisticated aircraft which oil money could buy, and Chaco oil bought Vice-General Palermo over a hundred of these expensive new toys, along with dozens of helicopter gunships which clattered after the jets.

Vice-General Ramón Torrejos craned his neck as the jets swooshed by. President Salazar was the third president he had served in his long career as head of the secret police, or *pyngares*. When Salazar's ragged army marched into the Plaza de Independiencia six years ago, he was marked for death; so he did what he did twice before: He offered his skills, knowledge, and records to the incoming president, the records and files on everybody in the country who might be a potential enemy.

Torrejos was retained and promoted, because he knew

where all of the bodies were buried. He was a professional survivor.

In spite of his vow never to return to Colonia Gardún, Angel Caro *did* return with his wife and two children and spent much of his time in the former Gardún colony, renamed Fortín Benson.

It had been an eerie and unsettling experience for Susan when she and her family prowled the ruins of the Casa del Swastika two years before. The ghosts of Carlos and the Holy Garduna seemed to inhabit the buildings. She never did visit the mass graves along the base of the bluff. Somewhere along the bluff, now overgrown with scrub, were the remains of Carlos.

In contrast to the unmarked and neglected graves of the Gardunians, the memorial to La Muchacha Héroe was large and well maintained. A giant statue of Patricia Benson, her hand raised in defiance clutching a grenade launcher, was erected at the very spot where she was last seen alive. She faced the top of the bluff, where the Paraguayan and American flags flew continuously at half mast; where the black vinyl bladders once squatted. At 4:30 every afternoon, a young bugler would blow a series of mournful notes on a battered brass bugle which he would retrieve from the nearby Museum of the Martyrs.

Fortín Benson was the headquarters for Angel's Army of the Chaco. The Casa del Swastika had been rebuilt; its walls were still sturdy. Buildings were added, changing it from the shape of a swastika to that of a square, with a cross in the center.

Fortín Benson soon became a large complex of barracks, runways, helicopter and tank parks, and storage facilities. Farther south, connected by a modern two-lane macadam road, was the Escuela para Comando and the Airborne Parachute Center at Mariscal Estigarribia, also under Angel's command.

Susan, a bored expression on her face, bounced little Valerie, her eight-month-old, on her knee to the music. The other child, a boy of five, stood stiffly at attention in a little uniform patterned after his father's. It was given to him by

President Salazar. She looked at her son and smiled wryly, her eyes reflecting resignation to a future life with a conqueror. She could have done worse, she often mused. For one who didn't even graduate from high school, she occupied an important niche in the social strata of a country that was one of the "comers" on the world stage. She often wondered if her life was any different married to Angel from what it would have been had she married Carlos and been his Queen of the Chaco.

The tidal wave of "cleanness" and order which was sweeping over America was acceptable to most, but not all, of her citizens. There were many who felt that the "temporary" measures enacted by the Davenport government would soon become frozen into the law of the land.

Davenport's unorthodox politics had all but destroyed the two-party system, which had been in a state of disintegration anyway. A coalition of smaller parties and single-issue groups, loosely identified as the Ramrod Right, had coalesced around the Oklahoma senator and swept him into power. The name of Davenport's new organization was the Unity party; Unity above everything else: personal liberty, civil liberties, and individual identity. Everybody and everything must serve the cause of Unity.

It was a tiny beginning, but it *was* a beginning: a rented, patched-up old circus tent in Shreevesport. The tent held five hundred, but there were many more thousands outside. The media coverage was more than adequate and it was impartial. Unity did not control all of the organs of communication . . . yet.

The birth of a new political party and the introduction of a challenger, a new choice in the election of 1996, *was* news, and the national networks jumped at the chance to cover the minuscule convention.

Already, the questions were being asked: why Shreevesport of all places, and why a patched-up old circus tent? It was these very questions which drew the media and gave the convention national coverage. Soon, when the timing was right, there would be leaks to the press, and the story of what happened here—on this very spot thirty-three years before—would be known. It was dirty politics, but the stakes were high; the very existence of the American system of liberty under law was the issue.

The speeches over, Nicolas Portumo took the rostrum and looked over his shoulder, smiling at Andrea, his wife of four years, as she patted the swarthy candidate's hand.

"And now, ladies and gentlemen, charter members of the Sanity party, and people of America. It is my distinct pleasure to present the next president of the United States—the man best qualified and equipped to return this country to the people . . .

"JOSEPH JESSE ROCKLAND!"